RAIN WASHED

Suzanne Cass

S C
STORM CLOUD
PRESS

Rain Washed

Storm Cloud Press, Perth Australia

Copyright © 2023 by Suzanne Cass

Edits by Evermore Editing

Cover by Vikncharlie

All rights reserved.

To all the wild places. May they stay forever wild.

CHAPTER ONE

Lacey glared at the back of the two men standing in line in front of her. They were taking forever to order their coffees. Did these hipster guys always have to order the most complicated drink on the menu? She thought she heard the man with the impeccably trimmed beard asking for a caramel macchiato with half whole milk, half soy milk, topped up, double the froth, and no lid. What was wrong with a simple flat white? Or even a cappuccino?

Her stomach grumbled as she caught sight of the pastries displayed in the glass case to the side. Breakfast had been a long time ago. Her shift had started at eight am this morning and it was now nearing eleven. Maybe she'd get an almond croissant. She should probably get one for Linc too.

The little coffee van was often parked in this side street a block back from the beach in South Burnie, near to a small shopping center and a couple of office buildings. A vintage trailer, decked out in navy blue with cream highlights, they made the best coffee this side of Devonport. The barista, Conner, was getting to know her on sight as she and Linc visited the van whenever their duties allowed.

One of the hipsters glanced back at her and must've seen her dark-blue uniform, because he immediately flinched, then straightened and took a step away. She gave him a pleasant smile that she hoped made it seem like she was completely fine having to stand in line and wait while these buffoons ordered their stupid trendsetting drinks. Why did some people react as if they had just been caught killing the neighbor's cat whenever they saw a police officer? Was it a good thing that her uniform instilled a certain wariness in people? She wasn't sure. They must have a guilty conscience, she decided.

Out of the corner of her eye she spied a group of young boys on scooters hanging around near the curb a few feet away. They were looking at her with something akin to awe. *Shit, not again.* She turned her head, pretending not to notice them. But it was too late.

One of the boys—the leader of the little gang—broke away from the group and came toward her. "Hey, aren't you the lady who jumped out of that car that went over the cliff?" His eyes were big and round. She sucked in a breath and tried not to roll her eyes, but the boy continued, "You're like a superhero. Like Batman. Or Spider-Man."

She sighed. Her death-defying leap had turned her into a small-town celebrity, much to her mortification. She just wished people would find something else to catch their interest. It'd been over six months since Gabriel DuPont had tried to kill her by driving her Kombi van over the cliff—with her inside it. And now all she wanted was to put that episode behind her and get on with life. But the faint scars still crisscrossing her body made it impossible to forget entirely. As did the constant questions from well-meaning citizens.

"How did you do it? Like, weren't you scared and stuff?" the boy continued.

"Yeah. Weren't you scared?" Another kid came closer, as if emboldened by his mate's questions. The rest of the crew remained on the curb, but were all staring at her with interest.

And now the hipsters had turned to look at her, speculation in the curve of their finely groomed mustaches. She turned to face the group of youths, plastering on her best grin and silently gritting her teeth. She'd told the story so many times at least she had it down pat and was now able to keep her face impassive, not giving away how memories of sailing over that cliff still haunted her at night. If it wasn't for Nico and his strong arms wrapped around her in their bed, she might still be an emotional wreck. But his love, along with some intensive counseling, had helped her overcome the worst of it.

She opened her mouth to speak and was interrupted by a shout from a little way down the road.

"Lacey, we got a call." Linc stood beside their police cruiser, waving an arm urgently in the air.

"Coming." Lacey gave the coffee van one last longing look before jogging over to where the cruiser was parked. "Sorry, boys. I'll tell you about it another time," she said as she shot past them.

Her partner, Senior Constable Lincoln Jackson frowned as she slid into the passenger seat beside him, clearly as bummed as she was to be missing out on their morning coffee and croissant.

"What's up?" she asked.

"Someone has called in a suspected body. They were hiking along Emu River and found something in the water. We're the closest unit," Linc said in his now-familiar American accent. He liked to tell her it was a midwestern drawl, not like those southerners, whose vowels were so relaxed it took them five minutes just to say hello.

Linc Jackson was Senior Constable Tyrell Jackson's nephew. He'd been lured over to Tasmania to take part in an active officer exchange from his hometown of Detroit in Michigan by Tyrell, who was nearing completion of his own stint in that same program. Interns in the program usually worked in the force for a while—Linc had been on active duty for nearly nine years already—and were often in line for a promotion. It was a way to compare and share policing styles, leadership, and training in other countries.

Tyrell had waxed lyrical to his nephew so much over the past two years that Linc had finally come to see what all the fuss was about, arriving in Tasmania around the same time as Lacey restarted her career with the Burnie police. Both Linc and Tyrell were part of a growing group of African-American recruits enlisting in the force in Detroit. Linc had never told her openly, but she understood intrinsically how hard it must be for him to deal with the levels of racial tension and inequality people of color encountered over there and she respected him for being part of the change in community perspectives.

She admired Linc, but she also liked him as a person. He was easygoing and down-to-earth, and she was glad she'd been partnered with him. Yes, he was a bit of a charmer, good-looking, with a white, toothy smile that contrasted starkly against his dark skin, and extremely broad shoulders that had all the girls' heads turning. But once she'd made it clear she was madly in love with Nico and she would never be interested in him in that way, he'd become a great friend and an even better partner. Solid, dependable and with high moral standards. He could be a typical outgoing Yank who liked to joke around and annoy the shit out of her, but he could also be deadly serious when the situation called for it. This morning, he had his serious face on.

"Where are we headed?" Lacey asked, putting her professional mask back on. A suspected body was a serious thing. The most serious thing she'd had to contend with so far in her six months on the job. The most serious thing since she'd watched poor Rania Samaan die even as she tried to resuscitate her with CPR a little over seven months ago. She shook her head and pushed that memory back into its box. This might be Lacey's first proper trial since starting active duty again. She hoped she was up to it. Hoped she was up to confronting a dead body again. Hoped she didn't collapse in a heap at the sight.

"Platypus Reserve." Linc cast her a sideways glance, the frown on his face letting her know that he understood how hard this might be for her. Lacey gritted her teeth. She was determined that she didn't need his concern. Determined to show everyone that she could do this. She was a good cop and she could handle everything this job threw at her. She just had to keep telling herself that.

"Platypus Reserve, huh?" She plugged it into the GPS on the dash monitor and watched as a large green area showed up on the screen. "It's less than ten minutes away," she informed Linc, who was maneuvering the cruiser with skill through the suburban traffic of South Burnie, lights and sirens blasting to warn vehicles to get out of the way. Lacey was still getting to know this town and the surrounding area. There were so many gorgeous places with endearing names. Like Platypus Reserve and Emu River. It was a shame such a delightful sounding place was now marred by death. Or worse, murder.

Before long, they'd left suburbia behind, and the cruiser was winding its way up an asphalt road, tall trees crowding in on all sides. "Take this turnoff." She directed Linc to take the road to the BBQ picnic area. They passed between two large trees painted blue, marking the entrance, and then the road took them down again into a valley where the Emu River had cut a path through the black earth millions of years ago.

Freshly mowed grass, green and lush, curved away from the road, soon replaced by thick bushland the farther down the road they traveled. Winding the window down, Lacey took a few seconds to acknowledge the country around them. Tasmania was an endless source of beautiful, natural wonders that could be found around almost every corner, and this place was no different. The reserve was an oasis on this warm day. Birdsong filled the air. Moss covered tree trunks lurked in the cooler shadows. And between glimpses of the river through the trees, she could see large tree ferns lining the edge of the river, their emerald-green fronds dipping into the water like a ballerina pointing her dainty toes.

"Do you think you can see platypus in this river?" Lacey asked, reading the sign at the edge of the road as they sped by.

"I guess so." Linc shrugged, more intent on getting to the crime scene than thinking about the surrounding beauty.

She should take a leaf out of his book; this wasn't a nature-appreciation field trip. Winding her window up, she focussed on the job ahead. The dirt road opened up into a large cleared area, with a parking lot down one end and what looked to be an amenities block and some tables and benches set up near a couple of free-to-use barbecues. A perfect spot for a family picnic. Three cars were in the lot, parked at right angles, and a young couple stood waiting beside one. Lacey silently catalogued the cars. If one belonged to the people who'd called in the body, then it meant there were other people still in the reserve somewhere. The guy had his arm firmly clasped around the woman, almost as if without his support she might fall to the ground. The woman's face was deathly pale and streaked with tears, eyes red rimmed and so big they almost swallowed her dainty face.

Linc was out of the cruiser almost before he'd pulled on the handbrake. "Are you the ones who made the call?" he asked, striding toward them.

Lacey scurried to catch up, keeping one hand on her duty

belt to stop it flopping around. A new belt had been ordered in for her, but head office were taking their sweet time dispatching it out to the rural precinct of Burnie. So for now, she had to put up with one that was a size too big for her and slung so low on her hips she looked more like one of those olden-day western gunslingers. Sometimes she cursed all the paraphernalia she needed to wear as an active police officer. It was heavy and unwieldy, especially the dark-blue vest slung over her collared shirt, but it was there to keep her safe and she knew she'd get used to it again sooner or later.

"Yes, sir," the man replied, visibly shaking, but trying to pull himself together. "We were just walking the river trail when Penny saw something floating in the water. We thought it was an old jacket or some sort of clothing someone had thrown in the water. Until we got closer." The young man blanched, a grimace of abhorrence pulling his lips down. "And then we saw her face," he finished in a whisper.

"Oh, God, it was horrible," Penny broke in, looking from her boyfriend's face, to Linc, and then finally settling on Lacey. "I thought I was going to be sick." She stared at Lacey with large, fear-filled eyes. "Henry poked her with a stick and that's when it...she...rolled over in the water and we saw it was a woman. Her skin was all white and blubbery like a ghost. It was... I've never seen anything like it." Penny doubled over to lean her hands on her knees, and Lacey thought she might actually follow through on her threat to vomit.

Now she was closer, she could see the couple were really young, perhaps late teens. Shock was etched clearly in both their features, and Lacey felt a moment's compassion. Nobody wanted to find a dead body, if that was indeed what they'd found. The grisly sight would likely stay with them for a long time to come, and she hoped it didn't affect them permanently.

"It's okay." Henry soothed his girlfriend, rubbing comforting circles on her back. "The cops are here now. Everything is going to be fine."

Lacey silently wished that were true. If there really was a body in the river, it meant there was a possible killer lurking out there somewhere.

Penny finally straightened, although it was with a noticeable effort. She was pretty, long blonde hair pulled back in a ponytail, wearing a pink T-shirt and very brief shorts with a pair of hiking boots. The couple had obviously been about to embark on a day walking the trails around the reserve. But now their plans were ruined.

"Yes, we'll go and check it out," Linc replied, his features a mask of cool competence. "Where did you see the body?"

The couple nodded in unison "Over there." The young man pointed in the direction of the river. "By the lookout platform that juts over the river." He couldn't hide his trembling voice as he tucked his girlfriend tighter under his arm.

"Another unit is on the way," Linc said, keeping his voice low and calm, as if talking to a pair of skittish animals. "Wait here until they arrive," he directed the young couple. He didn't add that he needed to preserve the crime scene—if that was what it was—and they didn't want anyone else traipsing around the area destroying evidence if it could be helped.

"Yes, sir," Henry replied.

Lacey knew that Constable Karl Hickey and First Class Constable Tag Gorman had been dispatched as backup and to help cordon off the area, keeping out any unwary tourists and to keep an eye out for anything suspicious until Lacey and Linc could confirm—or deny—the presence of a body. She'd worked with both officers already and they knew what they were doing when it came to preserving a crime scene.

She'd first met both officers when they'd been assigned to

guard her after she'd been attacked at Nico's house, directly after Rania's murder. Gorman and Hickey were reliable and steadfast, like the rest of the officers at Burnie station. Lacey was learning that trusting your fellow teammates was essential if you were to get the job done properly.

"Did you see anyone else while you were walking?" Lacey asked as Linc took a few steps toward the trail that disappeared into the tall grass, deep shadows from the overhanging branches making it seen a little eerie.

"No." They both shook their heads in unison.

Linc cast her a knowing look over his shoulder. That was good news. Hopefully, the people who owned the other two cars parked in the lot had passed on by the body without seeing it, and were now well out of the way of the crime scene. They would still have to be rounded up and interviewed, however.

"Stay behind me, Shorty," Linc demanded as he stalked warily into the shadows.

Lacey bit back a retort. Both at the nickname, which she hated—just because she was shorter than him, really?—and because Linc still saw her as a rookie cop. He saw it as his role to keep her under his wing. She couldn't count the number of times she reminded him that she'd already spent over a year on the force as a junior constable back in Melbourne and she was nobody's *rookie*. But it didn't help that as part of the terms negotiated by Chief Inspector Shadbolt for her return to the force, that she be put under another six-month probation—which was due to end in two weeks' time—and because of that, Linc treated her like she was a newbie who needed his guidance. Which she didn't. It irked her that Shadbolt had put this stipulation on her, but she understood why he'd done it. He needed to make sure she was still fit for duty after suffering severe PTSD from a traumatic incident she'd witnessed in her previous posting in

Melbourne. Linc was also aware of her past trauma, and he was merely trying to shield her from what was to come. It didn't cool her irritation with him, however. But she did as she was told, following in his wake, eyes searching the surrounding bush for anything out of place.

Linc went straight toward the boardwalk that curved along the edge of the river, his booted feet thumping along the wooden treads. At a bend in the river, the boardwalk veered out, so they were suspended above the water, giving them a good view of the pretty waterway in both directions.

"There." Linc leaned over the railing and pointed at what looked to be a pile of floating rags. As Lacey looked closer, she could make out the shape of a submerged human figure beneath the clothing, face down and arms splayed out like a starfish. A large stick floated next to her, probably dropped by Henry in his shock at his find. Her stomach surged at the sight, but she gritted her teeth and forced herself not to look away. She was a cop now. This was part of her job. A grisly, sad, and distressing part. But a part nonetheless.

"Call it in," Linc directed, his face a mask of steely resolution. "I'll retrieve the body."

She opened her mouth to protest; she was more than capable of wading into that dark, forbidding water if that's what it took. But one look at his face told her not to argue, so she nodded and pressed the button on the police radio resting in her shoulder holster. Hickey and Gorman were already on their way, but Lacey asked for more backup to secure the scene, as well as a homicide team from Devonport, and the local forensics guys to attend the scene. As she talked into her radio, she watched Linc unstrap his duty belt, take off his police vest, boots and socks, snap on a pair of latex gloves, and wade into the river. At least the water looked clean, but she knew it must be cold. He was up to his waist by the time he reached the body, and he gingerly took hold of the fabric of her sweater and towed her toward the riverbank. Tugging the body onto dry land, Linc emerged with water running off his clothes.

"Holy frack, that water is freezing," he declared, standing dripping next to the body. As she looked at him, still in her dry uniform, a tiny part of her was glad she had a big, burly, testosterone-fueled partner who was prepared to do the physical side of the job. Not that she would ever tell him that. And yet another part of her was amused that this strapping partner of hers refused to swear. He never took God's name in vain either. Said his grandma would wash his mouth out if she ever heard him blaspheme. It was kinda cute.

Being extra careful where she stepped, she bent her knees and got down on her haunches to get a better look at the body.

"Poor woman," she muttered under her breath. She wasn't a pretty sight. Penny had been right in her description. Her face was pallid and wrinkled, like a ghost who'd escaped from the depths of a watery grave. "She must've been in the water for a while," Lacey mused. "A few days at least." Lacey knew a body usually sank quite quickly at first, then floated to the surface again later, once the putrefaction gases filled the cavities and brought it up.

"Hmm." Linc bent down next to her. "Whoever did this must've known the body would be found, eventually. This is a public reserve, lots of people use these walking trails every day. They were either incredibly sloppy, or they wanted us to find her." Linc was right on the money, and Lacey lifted her head to look around. Everything was peaceful and idyllic. The birds were still singing in the trees; they didn't care that a human had lost her life here. The grass still swayed in the warm, gentle breeze and the bees still buzzed. It was only her who was freaked out. Why would someone choose this place to dump a body?

"It's good that your detective is due home today," Linc said. "We're going to need him on this case." He sat down and began pulling on his boots underneath his soaking wet pants. Poor guy was going to have to wear damp trousers all day now.

"You think it's definitely murder?" Lacey queried, ignoring Linc's referral to Nico as *her detective*. They never made it obvious they were a couple when they were at work. Lacey intentionally kept any public displays of affection at the precinct to zero, not wanting to rub it in her colleagues' faces that she was dating the lead homicide detective. Not wanting them to think she took any liberties just because she and Nico were together. He was a detective, and she was just a junior cop on the beat, so they were almost never partnered with each other. But people always talked. And they made their own judgments. People could be spiteful and unkind at times, and she knew she was the topic of some of the gossip around the lunchroom table. But she knew Linc didn't hold any grudges against her dating Nico. He was a fair-minded guy, and he got on well with Nico. They'd become squash partners of late, playing a weekly round of heated tournaments, much to Nico's delight. He'd missed playing squash after his friend Gabriel DuPont had become a convicted murderer and was now spending the rest of his life behind bars.

Her heart gave an involuntary jump at the thought of Nico. She couldn't wait to see him again. Anticipation had been fizzing in her veins ever since she'd awoken this morning. He'd been away on the mainland for the past week. Had taken personal leave to see his mother in Canberra. As well as follow up some leads regarding his father. But Nico was keeping the fact that his supposedly dead father may have faked his own death on the down-low. No one at work, except his boss, Shadbolt, knew anything about this surprising turn in Nico's life. Including Linc. So she kept her face impassive as she waited for him to answer.

"Yep. I'm pretty sure. Look." He pointed and Lacey saw what he meant. There were ligature marks around her neck and wrists. "She's been tied up and possibly strangled," he added.

Lacey's mind went immediately to the board set up in the second meeting room at the station. To the images pinned in a row, of the faces of three women, all victims of horrific murders. A suspected serial killer was on the loose somewhere on the northwest coast of Tasmania, and Nico was liaising with the cops from Hobart to try and help solve the case. Could this be the work of the serial killer? The other three women had all been involved in the sex worker industry. Cause of death had also been strangulation. Was this woman a prostitute? Perhaps Linc was wrong, and the marks on the dead woman's neck were from something else altogether. But a shiver went down Lacey's spine at the eerie similarities.

She caught Linc's eye, and they both knew without speaking that they were thinking the same thing.

A shout echoed through the trees from the direction of the parking lot and Linc stood, buckling on his duty belt as he narrowed his eyes in that direction. "Looks like Hickey and Gorman are here. I'll go and organize them to cordon off this area. Are you right to stay with the body?" That look of concern was back on his face. "I know this might be hard for you, and I—"

"Of course," she interrupted him. "I'm fine. I'll guard the scene, you go and make sure everything else is secure." And surprisingly, she was fine. The first surge of nausea when she'd spotted the body had subsided to a dull feeling of... perhaps emptiness was the best way to describe it. This was nothing like Rania's death, filled with blood and desperation.

This crime scene was completely different. Lacey was able to look at this woman with a somewhat detached interest. She felt sorry for this person and wanted to find the killer who'd cut her life short. But she wasn't about to become an emotional wreck at the sight, as distressing as it was.

CHAPTER TWO

Nico strode through the gravel parking lot toward the cruiser Lacey was leaning against, waiting for him. She stood straighter as she spotted him, a smile forming on her gorgeous lips and he couldn't help but smile back. It'd been a whole week since he'd seen her in person; the longest they'd ever been apart. Of course, they'd stayed in touch via video calls, but it wasn't the same. A whole week since he'd been able to feel that soft skin, kiss those perfect lips. He pulled her into a swift embrace, not caring if anybody saw them and ignoring their no fraternization while at work rule, needing to feel her in his arms.

"I missed you," he said, breathing in the clean scent of her hair as he kissed the top of her head. He couldn't help himself; he dropped his lips to hers, just to taste that sweetness that was all Lacey.

"I missed you too," she said, breaking their kiss and looking up, her amber eyes filling with a soft affection, a lingering heat hovering beneath that love. A look that was for him alone. But all too soon, their tender moment was broken as a loud cough came from the other side of the cruiser. Shit, he'd forgotten about Linc. Lacey's partner was a good guy, and Nico couldn't have hoped for a better partner for her in her first months back on the job. Linc must've been waiting with Lacey until Nico had finished interviewing the young couple who found the body. He was still here with her, even though both their shifts had ended two hours ago.

"Afternoon, Linc," he said a little gruffly, letting Lacey go and taking a step back. Lacey flicked Nico a gaze, her amber gaze bright and thoughtful. But there was no censure there. They'd both agreed to keep it strictly professional while they were on the job. Nico had broken that rule, but he just had to touch her, ever so briefly, to put his heart at ease. And she clearly felt the same way, because she laid a hand on his arm, almost as if checking he was really there in the flesh at last.

"Helluva thing to come home to," Linc replied and Nico silently agreed. Who would've thought he'd be called out to a homicide the second he touched down in Devonport? It'd certainly been the last thing on his mind. The only thing he'd been wondering while the plane landed was how soon he could get Lacey alone, preferably in their bed. Now he needed to force his mind away from Lacey and back into work mode.

"You were the first unit on the scene? You pulled the body out of the water?" He directed the question at both of them, but it was Linc who answered.

"Yes, sir."

"What's your take on our suspected homicide?" Nico asked. He valued Linc's knowledge and policing skills. He'd seen a lot of things over his nine years on the job in Michigan, including at least a dozen other murders. Nico had read his file as soon as he'd joined the Burnie station; it always paid to know your team's strengths and weaknesses. And Nico was sticking to that story, even though Shadbolt had raised an eyebrow when Nico had requested Linc's personnel file. His scrutiny had nothing to do with the fact Linc was to be partnered with Lacey. Nothing at all.

"I think the woman may have been murdered elsewhere and dumped in the river," Linc replied.

Nico nodded, pursing his lips. He'd come to a similar conclusion, but he wanted to hear it from Linc and Lacey. "Why?"

"Because there's no sign of a struggle nearby," Lacey chipped in. "And this place is too open, too well populated, especially at this time of the year. Someone would've seen something. Plus, there're ligature marks on her wrists, as if she'd been tied up. If it was a spontaneous crime, of passion or coincidence, and she'd been murdered here, why bother to bind her wrists?"

"I think you might be right," Nico conceded. "I'll wait for the forensics report on the crime scene, but I think we need to look for a separate murder scene."

"Have we identified the victim yet?" Linc asked.

"Nothing found on the body. No wallet, purse or phone," Nico confirmed. "Dr. Lagos, the local forensic pathologist, corroborated that she's around twenty-two to twenty-five years old, Caucasian, medium height and build. I've already got Sally-Ann scanning the missing person's lists, along with any wanted lists and other useful databases."

There were a few seconds of silence before Lacey asked the question they were all thinking. "Could this be connected to the serial killer?"

"Too soon to tell." Nico shrugged and had to quell the urge to take off his jacket. It was unseasonably warm for this early in summer, and the humidity down by the river made the air hot and dense. He knew as soon as he'd seen the age of the girl and the ligature marks that this case would be compared to the other three still-unsolved murders. He suppressed a shudder. If this was the work of the serial killer, then this community was no longer safe. There was a dangerous wolf somewhere in town, hiding beneath sheep's clothing.

Much the same as Gabriel had done. His friend had pulled the wool over everyone's eyes. An upstanding member of society, a well-respected doctor who was supposed to save lives. Not take them. But it turned out Gabriel had been living a double life. Hiding the fact he was gay behind the many and varied affairs he had with as many eligible women as he could date. It turned out Gabe had been well and truly screwed up as a child. His mother had manipulated him into an incestuous relationship when he was in his early teens and it'd severely fucked him up mentally, leaving him unable to let his true personality show. Gabe was so desperate to hide the fact he was gay from the world, he'd resorted to murder to keep his sexual preferences under wraps. Poor Rania had been murdered because she'd seen Gabe with another man, and then Lacey had become his next victim when she also pieced it together. The ex-doctor would now spend the rest of his life behind bars, but Nico felt little sense of satisfaction at catching this particular killer.

"I'd better get back to it," Nico said. "The ME is just about finished with the body, and the forensics team are waiting to get in and process the site, so I need to oversee that." He met Lacey's gaze. "Sorry." His mouth twisted in a small grimace of regret. "I'll be late home tonight."

"I already figured that," she said with a smile. Then, as Linc ducked his head to slide into the driver's seat, she moved closer and whispered in his ear, "But I'll wait up for you. No matter what time you come home, I'll be awake. Naked. In bed." She tilted her head to the side seductively and lowered her eyelashes, and a shot of heat went straight to his groin. Shit. Now he was going to think of nothing else but how quickly he could get this thing wrapped up for the evening and race home to her. Even after six months together, their sex life had only become more interesting, more intense. She was a distraction that he probably didn't need right now.

But he couldn't begrudge her that flirty little wink. He just needed to corral his libido back into a box for the coming few hours so he could think straight until the time came when he could let loose with her.

He watched the police cruiser drive away, leaving a trail of dust in its wake. Then he drew a deep breath and turned on his heel, heading back into the organized chaos of a murder crime scene.

* * *

Nico rolled his head sideways on the pillow to check the time on the digital clock beside the bed. Two-thirty-nine am. He smiled to himself and decided it was worth every second of lost sleep.

"Maybe I need to go away more often, if that's the way you show how much you miss me." His breath still hitched in his lungs and his chest was slick with sweat from the recent exertion.

"Don't you dare." Lacey slapped him lightly on the shoulder. "I need you here. With me. All the time. And so does Smudge," she added soberly.

It was true; his loyal dog had been over the moon when he'd greeted him at the door earlier tonight. Almost turning himself inside out with wriggling delight, even breaking the rules by jumping up and licking his face. He was pleased that the border collie cross had taken immediately to Lacey on the very first day they'd met, and had been her loyal companion ever since, because it put Nico's mind a little more at ease as he'd lain in his bed on the mainland thinking of her every night he was away; that she had Smudge to keep her safe and give her much-needed companionship. He suspected Smudge had been allowed to sleep beside the bed while he'd been away, rather than in his designated spot on his mat by the fire, but that was okay. The loyalty of a dog was a special thing, and his little black-and-white mutt had seen him through a lot of good and bad times, and it was nice to know that Smudge now shared his love equally between his two most special humans. It was always a pleasure to come home to his faithful dog, but it was a revelation to land in the arms of his hot, eager woman. A new experience for him, but one he could definitely get used to.

Lacey snuggled in closer to Nico's side and he luxuriated in the feel of her naked skin on his as they lay without even a sheet to cover them. The window was open to let in a waft of cooler night air. Early-December was technically summer, but here in northern Tasmania, it was often cooler than on the mainland. Not this week, however. Temperatures had soared to almost thirty degrees Celsius. Hopefully not a sign of a hotter-than-normal summer to come.

"I know it's late, and we both need some sleep, but I'd love to hear how it went in Lorne. Did you manage to talk to the Normandys?" she asked, pushing locks of blonde hair away from her sweaty face so she could look up at him. When he'd first arrived home, they'd both been too caught up in each other's body to discuss anything else but the language of love. Nico had pushed everything about the dead woman found in the river this afternoon, as well as the reasons for his trip to the mainland, to the back of his mind. But it was only a matter of time before they intruded on their peaceful bubble once more. Lacey had chosen the topic of his missing father to pursue first, and he was fine with that; he had a lot to tell her.

"Yes, I did." Nico pummeled the pillow and propped himself up slightly, and Lacey followed, resting her head on his shoulder, settling in to hear his news. Nico had been keeping Lacey updated on how his search had been going while he'd been away, but because of early flight times and her shift yesterday, he hadn't been able to talk to her for nearly two days. A lot had happened in that time.

"I met with Marco and Priscilla at their place for dinner

two nights ago," he said. Lacey tensed beside him, but kept quiet, waiting for him to go on. "They showed me the original photo they took. The one they told my mother about." He hesitated, not wanting to say the words out loud. That it was definitely his father in that photo. It was still too raw, his feelings a labyrinth of emotions too knotted to untangle.

Six months ago, he'd engaged a private investigator, Patrick McTernan, to look into the supposed sighting of his father. McTernan had already interviewed the Normandys and sent him a digital copy of the photo. But Nico had needed to hold it in his own hands to believe it was real.

"Marco seemed completely genuine about his recollection of meeting my fa— Serge." He couldn't bring himself to call that man his father. He might have the man's blood running through his veins, much to his disgust, but Serge had never been a real father to Nico. "I believed him," he finally said. Nico had wanted to look into Marco's eyes to ascertain the truth. His job as a police detective entailed reading the small signs that someone was fabricating a lie and he knew doing it face-to-face would give him the answers he needed. A small part of him had still hoped Marco might've got it wrong. Or falsified the image as some sort of sick joke. Neither was the case.

"So even without the results from the forensic pathologist, you think it's highly likely your father is actually alive?" Lacey asked quietly.

The private detective had said the very same words in the email he'd sent to Nico five months ago. But Nico didn't want to believe it. So, he'd paid McTernan, thanked him for his thoroughness, and tried to push the whole thing to the back of his mind. But the combined forces of his mother and less aggressive, but equally compelling, Lacey, had convinced him he couldn't let this problem lie unsolved. He'd finally agreed to start his own investigation, and had convinced Shadbolt to give him a week's unpaid leave to take care of this business once and for all. Except his trip had opened more doors and asked more questions than it'd answered.

"I got the results from the DNA test this morning," Nico said with a grunt.

Lacey sat bolt upright. "You did? That was quick."

"Yes. Drummond pushed it through for me. I think he wanted to know if they'd buried the wrong man as much as I did." Mike Drummond was now the chief forensic pathologist in Canberra. He'd taken over when Dr. John Stillman—the man who'd originally examined Serge's body —had retired three years ago. Drummond was young and proactive, and just as keen as Nico to make sure his predecessor hadn't made a terrible mistake.

Nico had requested his father's coronial files from the Chief Magistrate in charge of the ACT Coroner's Court a few months ago. They'd substantiated that the body found in the burnt-out-wreck was assumed beyond doubt to be that of Serge Favreau, and so no DNA test was applied. The body had been so badly burned in the ensuing fire that it was unrecognizable, but the coroner on the case could've requested dental records, or even looked for X-ray or other medical records that might identify him. Back then, DNA testing was expensive, and the coroner found no reason to think it might not have been Serge in that car. So, an inquest into Serge's death had never been held. It'd been deemed accidental death by incineration.

Armed with this information, Nico had gone ahead with proceedings to exhume his father's body, giving the reason that new intelligence had come to light that suggested Serge Favreau might still be alive. The request had to go through the coronial courts and it'd taken up until last week to finally get the go-ahead to dig up the grave.

"And?" Lacey queried when he still hesitated.

"It's not him," Nico replied, releasing his breath on a gust of air. "The body found in the car is now considered unidentified, which means Serge must be alive."

"Oh, God." Lacey encircled him with her arms, pulling him in tight. He buried his face in her neck, drawing in her warmth and comfort. When he'd received the phone call this morning, right before he'd boarded the plane, his mind had gone numb. Even though he'd been expecting the news after talking to the Normandys, it still struck him with the weight of a thousand tons of cement. How could his father still be alive? How could he have faked his own death? They were two questions he found impossible to answer.

"I haven't told Mum yet," he mumbled into her hair.

"Your poor mum. Your poor brother and sister. How do you think they'll take the news?"

"Probably much the same as me. We discussed it at length while we were waiting for the body to be exhumed." Nico had stayed at his mother's house in Canberra for a few days while they waited for the last small details to be finalized and the local police chief to organize a day and time for a couple of officers to attend the grave site. Nico was happy to see his mother, Catarina, hadn't lost any of her renowned poise and style because of this unwanted stress in her life. She was still smartly dressed in one of the pantsuits she loved to wear, her blonde hair done up in a loose chignon. There were a few more grays showing through, but on the whole, his mother hadn't let this news change her at all.

The man his mother had been dating for the past five years, Andy Katsulis, was there by her side, supporting her with his solid presence, but not interfering in the Favreau family business. It was heartening to see how good they were together. He never talked down to Catarina; instead, lifting her up with his positive air and unruffled demeanor. Andy was dependable, generous, and charming. The exact opposite of Serge Favreau.

His younger sister, Gaëlle, also lived in Canberra; she'd chosen to live close by their mother. And his older brother, Brice, had driven down for the night from Sydney to be there when the coffin was pulled from the earth. It was good to catch up with them all, even if it was under strained circumstances. Having the family united under one roof didn't happen nearly often enough, and it rankled that it was because of their no-good father they were drawn together. It was a pity Lacey couldn't be there with him to meet everyone in person but she hadn't been able to get any extended leave after only a few months on the job. Everyone had talked to her via a video link on his computer, however. Afterward, his mother had been over the moon to hear he'd finally found *the one*. He'd held up his hands and told her to slow down, that he and Lacey had only known each other for six months. But he couldn't object to her enthusiasm, as it gave her something else to focus on in those few awful days of waiting. Then watching the coffin rise from out of the crumbling earth. And somewhere deep inside, he knew Catarina was right. Lacey was *the one*.

"She's a lot more philosophical about it now," he said. After his mother's almost hysterical reaction six months ago at hearing that her dead husband wasn't really dead, she'd calmed down as the news slowly sank in. Nico guessed it had a lot to do with Gaëlle's calming influence. "My sister keeps telling Mum that if Serge went to such lengths to fake his own death and leave his family to grieve for him without any feelings of remorse, then he clearly never planned on coming back."

"It's good she has your sister near," Lacey murmured.

"Yes," he agreed, feeling a small stab of guilt that he couldn't be there as well in her time of need. But he'd chosen to move to Tasmania to pursue his career and he couldn't regret that now. Catarina had confided in them all that her main fear was Serge would somehow want to reclaim his family. Start back up where he'd left off. Catarina was adamant that could never happen. She had a good life now, with a good man, and she would rather die than take her husband back. Nico understood where she was coming from, as Serge had been a bully and a bastard to them all. Using words to cut his wife to the bone, often beating his sons if they didn't conform to his standards. They were all better off without Serge in their lives. Nico was thankful that Gaëlle was able to convince Catarina if Serge had stayed away for this long—fifteen years—there was no reason he'd want to come home now. And if he did do the unthinkable, then she, Nico, and Brice were prepared to protect her. To tell him to go back to whatever hole he'd crawled out of and never come out again.

"And now this Drummond guy has the unenviable task of trying to identify whoever it was they really buried in that grave," Lacey said in a low voice.

"Yes. I don't envy him," Nico replied, wondering not for the first time who had taken the place of his father. Had Serge killed an innocent man to continue his lie? Drummond had already requested the case be reopened, and police would now be going through the lists of missing persons from around the same time, as well as looking into other unsolved crimes or similar cases of people dying in fiery car crashes from fifteen years ago to see if they could find a link.

"No, but I think you have an equally hard job. This can't be easy for you. What are you going to do with this news?" she asked, rubbing soothing circles on his chest with the palm of her hand. "I know you've had a while to digest the idea that he might still be alive. But it must still come as a shock to hear it's actually true. That your father did indeed fake his own death and then left his family without a word to cope by themselves. It's a cruel thing to do to anyone. I know if it were me in your situation, I'd be an emotional wreck." She tilted her head up so she could look directly into his eyes. "I want you to know that I'm here for you. Anything you need. If you need to talk about it. Yell about it. Hide under the covers for days. I'll understand. Well, I know you wouldn't hide under the covers, because you don't hide from anything. But you know what I mean," she qualified.

"Yes, I do." He smiled softly. "And thank you." Even though he knew Lacey would be there for him, it was nice to hear the words said aloud. She was correct; his mind had been a swirling cesspool of dark thoughts all morning. One thing had been for certain, he'd be throwing all his resources into finding information on a man called Reginald Smith, the false name his father had adopted. Wouldn't rest until he found him. But upon his return to Tasmania, the discovery of a dead body in a reserve had replaced his anger and resentment with something more urgent and concrete to focus on. He wouldn't give up looking for his father. But for now, it'd have to go on the back burner.

He pulled Lacey in closer, needing to feel her lithe body next to his. Her soft skin was a soothing balm on his soul, as always. Lacey was the one who showed compassion. She felt everything so deeply, while he was always more cool and logical. He loved that she was so sensitive; it made her good at her job, because she had empathy for the victims, and didn't just treat them as one more case to be solved. It was also the reason she was good for him. She was able to draw him out of that protective outer shell he kept around himself, forced him to make sense of feelings he often wanted to bury deep. She kept him from becoming bitter, like the hardened cop they often portrayed in those crime books she loved to read.

From the very first moment he'd met Lacey, offering her a place to park her broken-down Kombi van, he'd known she was an intriguing woman. One with definite goals and ideals. A determined woman, who could also protect herself using her well-honed judo skills. Her sharp mind sometimes saw things that even he missed. She was his equal in every way that mattered. Some men might be scared away by a strong woman, but not him. He liked the idea that Lacey didn't need him; she didn't need any man. She could cope perfectly well on her own. But she wanted *him*. Wanted him in her life and in her bed. And that was the exciting part. He loved the fact they could talk over ideas, discuss cases and crime scenes, spar over who was right and who was wrong, then afterward, they could stand side by side preparing dinner together, or make love until the wee hours of the morning and be genuinely in unison. A perfect partnership. It was something he'd never encountered before. In the beginning, that'd scared him, and he'd almost lost her when she decided to return to Melbourne. But he knew he couldn't live without Lacey in his life, and he was glad every day that he'd jumped on that ferry to stop her.

He took her chin between his thumb and forefinger and tipped her head back so he could stare into her eyes. "I love you," he said.

"I love you too." She looked at him with such open adoration and trust. Right in that moment, he knew she was the most beautiful woman within a thousand miles. No, that was wrong. Anywhere. Ever. She was the most beautiful woman in the world.

His mother had definitely been right. She was *the one*.

Suddenly, he knew he wanted to marry Lacey. Wanted to build a forever life with her. Hell, even have kids with her.

At the thought of marriage, an image of another woman entered his mind.

Marietta.

She was the reason he was gun-shy whenever the word wedding was brought up.

Lacey still didn't know about Marietta.

His ex-wife had been ten years older than him and for a while had totally bewitched him. At least he'd come to his senses and divorced her less than five months after they'd spoken their vows. No one outside his family knew of his quick, failed marriage.

If he was going to ask Lacey to marry him, either soon or sometime in the future, he needed to come clean about Marietta. But not tonight. Tonight, he needed the balm of Lacey's lovemaking to soothe his tortured mind.

CHAPTER THREE

Lacey breathed in the early morning air and rubbed the sleep from her eyes. Even though they'd had a late night, Lacey had decided not to sleep in because she'd been waiting to get started on her new project for weeks and she actually had a little time to herself this morning. Stepping into the large shed, she switched on the light. Parked up next to Nico's Jeep was the new love of her life. A blue-and-white Kombi van, with the registration plate DOTTI44. Smudge gave the van a cursory sniff before disappearing back outside, clearly not as enthusiastic. She could hear the flock of geese honking at something down in the orchard, but they didn't sound distressed, so Lacey guessed it was perhaps another egg being laid and so she made a mental note to check it out later.

Lacey had found the van online, and she and Nico had driven down to Hobart to meet the seller and check her out only a few weeks ago. Dotti 2.0 was perfect. Still in roadworthy condition, but in need of a lot of TLC. And Lacey was dying to get her hands on the cute little van and put her personal stamp on her, smarten up the interior, and add a few little touches that'd make her a perfect little home away from home. But first she needed to decide whether to keep the current exterior colors or change them, and then line up a spray painter to do the job. She wasn't about to fool herself that she could do a professional paint job on her own. There were lots of other things that needed sprucing up—new chrome on the bumper and all her VW bits, new glass in the split windscreens.

Dave had already checked Dotti out from head to toe and declared that while she was roadworthy and the engine ran okay, there were some vital things that needed attending to. A new exhaust system was in order, as were new shock absorbers all around. Dave was due to start work on Dotti next weekend, and Lacey was excited.

She still mourned her first Kombi van. Gabriel had turned her into a pile of scrap metal when he'd driven her over a cliff. But she tried not to think about it, because that brought up dark, disturbing memories she'd rather remained hidden.

She was so deep in thought, that when a noise came from behind, Lacey spun around on her heel, hands instinctively raised to protect herself, ready to fight for her life.

Nico stood in the doorway, one hand raised in surrender, the other hand wrapped around his motorcycle helmet, and she quickly dropped her stance.

"Sorry," she apologized, letting her gaze linger on Nico, who was wearing his leather motorcycle jacket over jeans. Mmm, that jacket suited him, highlighted his height and broad shoulders, and gave him an untamed edge that was decidedly alluring. Trust her to always want a bit of bad boy in her man. But who didn't like a bit of bad boy, really?

"I made that noise on purpose," he said. "I know better than to surprise you from behind." He came up and laid an arm across her shoulders, dropping a kiss on her cheek. Lacey winced but acknowledged the truth of his statement, remembering back to the first time she'd met Nico and how she'd used her judo skills to throw him over her shoulder onto the ground.

She wouldn't admit it, but she was always a little on edge now. After Gabriel had attacked her, then abducted her and tried to kill her, she was extra vigilant. Nico seemed to understand it, even though he never commented directly on her heightened sense of awareness.

"Contemplating what's next for the new Dotti?" he asked. Smudge strolled in and sat at Nico's feet, as if contemplating the van too.

"Yes, I thought I'd spend the morning pulling out those old cupboards the last owner had built in. They're a bit dated, and I have lots of ideas of how to make the interior work so much better. And I'd like to construct a comfortable couch along the rear, like my old Dotti. Remember?"

"How could I forget? That couch was where I first fell in love with you."

"Don't be silly," she said, punching him lightly in the shoulder.

"I'm dead serious." He leaned in and took her mouth in a kiss that was decidedly possessive, sending a buzz of electricity through her. She turned and wrapped her arms around his neck, running her fingers up so they tangled in his long hair that he'd pulled back into a man bun. She loved that man bun. It made him look so sexy. Made her want to go up and kiss his strong neck, down to his equally strong shoulders. And she loved that he could still put butterflies in her stomach with one touch of his lips. Those wondrous feelings of excitement and raw need from their first few weeks together had never subsided. If anything, they'd become stronger; he'd become more irresistible. She dipped her tongue between his teeth, deepening their kiss.

Last night had been good, but it hadn't been nearly enough to overcome a week of missing him. A week of celibacy where she pined for his body beside her. Who knew she would miss having sex that much? Before she met Nico, she'd gone nearly a year without sex and hadn't thought much of it. But having sampled Nico's seductive ways, she now couldn't seem to get enough of his body. Those muscular thighs, ridged abs that went all the way down to that line of hair, biceps that bulged exactly right as he held his weight off her while he hovered above her on the bed…

She sighed and wrapped her arms tighter around his neck. She was going to drive herself crazy if she didn't stop.

When they finally broke apart, it took her a few seconds to remember where they were.

"What time does your shift start today?" he asked, a husky note in his voice hinting at the residual lust their kiss evoked.

"Midday," she said, disentangling her fingers from his hair and reluctantly letting him go. Most police shifts were eight hours, usually starting at eight in the morning or four in the afternoon, with reduced staff rostered on for the night shift of midnight to eight. But there was also some overlap shifts, to make sure the station was well-staffed during the busiest afternoon and evening hours. Hence her midday start. Lacey was due to go on night shift in a few weeks' time, so she was making the most of her daytime shifts. That was the hardest time for her, when she and Nico often passed like ships in the night, him returning from a late night at work just as she was leaving to go start her shift.

"I'll see you at the station then," he said, touching her face one last time before heading toward his motorcycle, parked in front of his Jeep. He'd graciously given over half of his shed to house Dotti until she was fully restored.

Settling himself onto his bike, he pulled on his helmet and lifted the visor. "You want to come for a ride on my motorcycle soon? Maybe we could go this weekend." He sent her a cheeky grin that made the scar on his face dance. He'd received the scar as a child and now, so many years later, people could easily mistake it for a dimple. She loved that scar, it was part of him that made him imperfectly perfect. And now she had scars as well. To remind her of her near-death experience. To remind her how lucky she was.

That cheeky grin made her suddenly imagine herself sitting on the tiny booster seat with her arms wrapped around his middle, leaning into his strong body as they flew around yet another sharp corner, her thighs gripping his lean hips. Lacey enjoyed riding behind him, liked the speed and the rush of adrenaline.

"Yes, please," she replied on a gush of outward breath. As long as he could spare the time this weekend. With a new homicide to solve, Nico was going to be busy. But she kept the thought to herself.

As she watched Nico rumble down the driveway, her mind turned to the dead girl they'd found yesterday. That poor girl deserved Nico's full attention, she decided. She needed her killer to be found so she could finally rest in peace. Lacey had always been cognizant of Nico's dedication to his job. It was one of the many things she loved about him. His drive and determination; his need to solve the case, sometimes putting it above all other things. He was a damn good detective, and she'd known going into this relationship that she'd have to share him with his job, perhaps even give him up completely at times, because what he did was important.

But she also loved being back in the police force. She was slowly regaining the strength of character she'd thought she'd lost forever after witnessing Cindi's death. She'd never lost her independence; that wasn't her problem. It was one of the reasons she'd enjoyed her travels around Tasmania in Dotti 1.0, because she had always loved her own company, was strong enough to endure being alone. But her mental health had suffered in other ways, and she'd been afflicted with nightmares and a severe lack of faith in her abilities. It wasn't until she'd found Nico and been forced to stop traveling, forced to take a good hard look at herself and receive some much-needed counseling, that she put a name to her problem. PTSD. But she was getting on top of her inner demons slowly, bit by bit every day. And being a cop was helping her win back her old sense of purpose. Whenever she found the lost dementia patient who'd wandered away from their care facility, caught the thief who'd robbed the liquor store, took the drunk teenager home to their worried parents late at night, and generally helped the community function for the greater good, she felt better. Like she was growing, healing.

In some ways, being part of the force made her and Nico's relationship even stronger. He was now free to discuss most things with her about cases he was working on. Because Burnie was a rural station with a small team compared to larger metropolitan stations, she was sometimes assigned to work with him directly. She loved how they seemed to think in parallel. Like their minds were in perfect sync. But also, being a rural station, the rates of true homicides were also less. Nico was sometimes seconded to other smaller precincts to help with a case if they had no detective in residence. There'd been a death in custody and two domestic disputes that ended in the husband being charged with manslaughter in Burnie over the past six months. But they'd all been cut-and-dried cases, with solid witnesses and no doubt who the killer was. There hadn't been a murder case without a clear POI before or since Rania's murder.

But she also found that Nico had become a little overprotective. Well, not *become* overprotective, because he'd always been solicitous when it came to her safety right from the start. They'd had a long talk about it right before Lacey had started back on the beat, and she reiterated that she could take care of herself and he couldn't always be looking out for her. She had a strong partner who she trusted implicitly; she had her police training—including a weapon—and it was part of her job to put herself in harm's way if the situation called for it. Nico had agreed in principle, but she knew he still kept tabs on her through Linc and other officers in the team. If she was ever late home from a shift, he would worry. And if she was ever assigned to a case where the felon had become violent, he would be on the phone making sure she was all right. She got the fact that he fretted about her, her job was dangerous, but he needed to let her do her job without freaking out, and without interfering. Because if he was freaked out, his worry wormed its way into her psyche, and then it ate away at her confidence. Which wouldn't do. She needed to be one hundred percent sure she was capable of doing this job.

Lacey leaned down and patted Smudge's black-and-white head. He turned warm, brown eyes up to hers and she smiled. Smudge never judged. Just gave out unconditional love. She sighed. Perhaps it was time to have another heart-to-heart with Nico. Let him know he had to back off a little with his need to safeguard her. This was the only real point of contention they had as a couple, and she didn't want to fight with him.

Now wasn't the best time to be bringing her grievance up, anyway. Not with Nico's undead father on his mind. Poor Nico. She tried to imagine how she would feel if her own father had died while she was young and then found out he'd faked his own death. It was a mystery that needed solving. But she wondered exactly what Nico might discover about his father and about himself if he did indeed solve it.

Dotti was calling to her, and her time with the van was limited before she was due at work, so she needed to put disagreements out of her head and get her hands dirty. "Come on, Smudge. You can give me a hand." She led the way to the back of the shed where a small workbench was set up with an array of tools on display. Smudge gave a short bark as if to say, *Yes, I would love to help.*

* * *

It was the sound of swarming flies that first attracted Lacey's attention. A low electrical buzz that got louder as she got closer to the water's edge. There were plenty of the annoying insects around this afternoon, she could attest to that as she constantly waved them away from her sweaty face. For a single disloyal second, she wanted to curse Nico for his harebrained idea that the rest of the river and the larger natural pools near where the woman's body had been found yesterday needed to be searched. What she was looking for exactly, she didn't know, but her brief when she'd arrived at work this afternoon had been simple. Go back to the crime scene and search upstream from where the body was found. Search the surrounding trails and waterways, looking for… something, anything that might be suspicious.

Linc thought perhaps Nico was sending them all out on one of his famous hunches and they would find nothing because it was all a wild goose chase. But Lacey knew better. Nico was just being thorough. She would probably have done the same thing. The reserve had been closed to the public since yesterday, so if there were any clues to be found, hopefully they hadn't been disturbed further by many feet tracking the trails. Hickey and Gorman had already searched the section of the trail from the parking lot to Ferndale Lookout this morning, and now she and Linc were searching from the lookout a few miles farther up the river. There were numerous trails winding through the reserve, the longest was nearly six miles and made a loop back to the parking lot via a forest road. Nico and a constable he'd managed to acquire from another case were searching the section along the road themselves, as Shadbolt had no other manpower to spare for a search that he declared was based on no clear evidence.

Lacey was ahead of Linc, he'd stopped a little way back where the trail forked to kneel down and poke at something in the base of a large tree, while she'd continued on down toward a big expanse of open water she'd glimpsed through the trees.

The buzzing sound urged her on, and she suddenly got a sick feeling in her stomach.

It was only early summer, so there was still plenty of water in the river. By next March, the river banks would be much lower, the water only flowing sluggishly. The trail led her to a small clearing, with a sloping earthen bank covered in leaf litter where people could enter the water if they wanted to swim. Ferns and sedge grasses lined the edge of the water, and to the left of the clearing, a dead log, felled long ago, protruded a few feet out into the river, making a superb jumping-off spot to dive into the deep pool of water.

The swarm of flies were massing near the giant dead tree trunk. But Lacey didn't need the insects to tell her what she was about to find. The smell got worse with every step she took toward the log. She desperately hoped she was going to find some dead native animal. A poor little pademelon that'd slipped into the river while taking a drink and drowned, perhaps. The alternative was too grizzly to contemplate.

But as she stepped up onto the log and peered over the edge, her hope was destroyed by the sight before her.

The woman was half buried in the sticky mud at the lake's edge. The rest of her body floated like a clump of dead leaves, her arm caught in a clump of sedges at the water's edge. Her face was gnawed in places, as if some hungry creature had snacked on it. Shifting position to get a better look at the woman's face, Lacey saw that one eye was missing. She shied away from the sight, but knew she'd be haunted by nightmares for a long time to come about rotting faces and fathomless holes for eyes regardless.

"Oh, shit," she said, standing up and backing away from the body. "Linc," she called out to her partner. "Get down here. I've found something." Lacey grimaced and resisted the urge to block her nose. Oh, God, the smell. This body was much further along in decomposition than the first one. Had this woman been murdered too?

What were the odds of finding two bodies so close together in the space of two days?

Surely, this had to be related to the first body they'd found.

Why wasn't Linc coming? She turned to look back up the slope of the bank, tilting her head to listen for his footsteps. "Linc?" she called again, louder this time. "Whatever you're doing, you have to get down here. I found another body." Where was he? Had he found something and gone back down the track and was now out of earshot? No. Linc wouldn't do that. Not without telling her. They had a good partnership, and excellent communication was a big part of that.

It was then she realized how deathly quiet the forest had become. The birds had stopped singing, and the leaves hung on the trees in complete stillness, as if holding their breath. Listening. Waiting for something.

Lacey's hand went instinctively to her gun. Something was wrong.

"Linc," she called again, but this time she scanned the area with increased awareness, suddenly alert to any small noise or movement. Nothing. She tried to raise Linc on her two-way radio. There was no reply.

Shit. She was going to have to backtrack and see if she could find him. Which meant leaving the body here, unguarded. Climbing warily up the slope, Lacey peered through the trees, trying to make out where he might've got to. Even as she walked, she pushed the button on her police radio again. It was time to request backup. Nico was the first to answer.

"I've found another body," she reported. "About a mile on from the lookout up the trail. I'm at a bend in the river, there's a large swimming hole here."

"Shit, really?" Nico sounded flabbergasted, but she didn't have time for him to catch up.

"Can you please hurry," she said, sounding a lot calmer than she felt, using her judo training to breathe in deep through her belly, out slowly through her nose. She needed to stay composed; she wouldn't be able to think clearly if she didn't. "Linc is also…missing."

"What do you mean missing?" Nico demanded.

"I don't know. He stopped a little way back up the trail and nows he's not answering my calls."

"Right." She had to hand it to Nico; it hadn't taken him long to process the situation. "It'll take us fifteen or twenty minutes to get to you. Stay put," he demanded and she could hear him puffing as he ran to get to her location.

"Negative. I'm going to look for him."

"Stay where you are," Nico commanded. "We're on our way."

Lacey didn't answer. She didn't want to disobey a direct order. And she really didn't want to piss Nico off by defying him. This was why working in the same precinct as your lover sometimes got tricky. But something was wrong, and she needed to find Linc.

She'd been walking as she spoke into her radio, and she'd made it back to the main trail. The air in the forest was sticky with humidity now she was away from the cooling waters of the river, and a trickle of sweat ran down her spine. She cursed her heavy police vest, which made it even hotter in this closed-in forest. She also knew her fluro-yellow vest would stand out amongst the dull greens and browns of the forest. Making her an easy target. If she took it off, her dark-blue uniform would blend much more easily into the shadows. But that was strictly forbidden while out on a search. She swiveled her head from side to side, checking out the trail in both directions. Nothing stirred. Even the insects had grown quiet, apart from that swarm of flies down by the body. The dry leaf litter crackled beneath her boots as she retraced her steps toward the fork in the trail where she'd last seen Linc.

Resting her hand on her gun, she stepped warily, narrowing her eyes against the bright sunlight as it speared through the canopy overheard, casting strange shadows and randomly blinding her when she least expected it.

What was that? A dark lump on the path ahead, near the top of a small rise. Then she caught a hint of bright yellow.

"Linc?" She began to jog up the slope, eyes fixed on the shape. His black boots appeared first, his body stretched out limply on the forest floor.

"Oh, no." The words escaped her on a whisper. She was on her knees beside him in an instant. "Linc, wake up. What happened?" She touched him lightly on the shoulder, but dare not roll him over in case of spinal injuries. Linc remained still and unresponsive, and when she laid a hand on his forehead, his dark skin was clammy and cold. He lay on his side, right where she'd left him poking at something on the ground at the base of a tree. Without moving him, she checked him over for injury, patting him all over and checking her hands for signs of blood. Nothing. But when she moved to his head, dark red stained the ground beneath his cheek, and when she gently parted the hair at the back of his head, she could see a nasty gash. While it was bleeding profusely, she knew it wasn't enough blood loss to cause a problem—head wounds always bled more than they should. Except for the head wound, she could see no other injury, and she sat on the ground beside Linc with a grunt. A head wound could mean anything from a mild concussion to bleeding on the brain, and Lacey had no way of knowing how life-threatening his injury was. That she couldn't rouse him didn't bode well, however.

Slowly, as her shock cleared, she remembered the number one rule of first aid. Always make sure your surroundings were safe before you approached the patient. Damn, she'd got that one wrong. She'd raced up to Linc with no thought for herself. Lifting her head, she studied the forest, checking the trail in both directions. It was empty. But it was hard to see far into the scrubby forest encircling her and Linc. Large tree ferns competed with fallen logs and a myriad of small saplings. A hundred places for someone to hide.

The only sound was the rasp of her own breath in her chest. She counted to ten and took two deep breaths, while keeping her eyes trained on the forest, swinging her head from side to side.

Something flashed in her peripheral vision. Movement. She stared at the spot between two trees, waiting. Was someone there? The same person who'd hit Linc from behind and left him for dead? She drew her gun, keeping it pointed toward the ground but out in front where it'd be obvious to anyone watching. This wasn't the time to second-guess herself. Someone was out there. Possibly the perp who killed these two women. And physically assaulted a police officer. She wasn't about to be their next victim.

Suddenly, her police radio crackled to life. "We're seven minutes away." Relief flooded through her at the sound of Nico's voice.

"Linc has been hurt," she replied, never taking her eyes from the spot between the trees. "Someone hit him over the head, and he's unconscious. We need an ambulance."

"Shit, Lacey," Nico swore and she could hear him running even harder. "I'm coming, stay where you are."

She had no intention of moving. She wasn't about to leave Linc unprotected. As she hunkered down over his body, gun still drawn and at the ready, she wondered at the gall of someone who'd attack a cop in broad daylight. Had Linc actually found something? A clue perhaps? And if so, had the murderer tried to kill him in an effort to get it back?

"Please, Linc, be okay," she pleaded under her breath, taking the time to check his pulse, which was still strong. The firm beat of his heart beneath her fingertips gave her some relief. Linc was tough, a hard man to kill. But a lump still formed in her throat at the thought that he might've died. That he might still die if an ambulance didn't come soon.

It seemed to take forever, but she finally heard the pounding of boots on the dusty earth along the trail. "Up here," she directed. Then Nico was standing defensively above her as she knelt over Linc's body, his fierce gaze assessing the area until he was sure they were safe.

Not caring that the other officer could see, he pulled her up into his arms and squeezed her so tight she had to fight for breath. "Fuck. You scared me," he whispered. It was only a second or two before he had himself under control again.

"Are you okay?" he barked, the detective-in-charge once more.

"Yes. I'm not hurt. But Linc—"

"The paramedics are on their way. Where's the dead woman?" he asked.

Lacey was taken aback. Nico seemed more concerned about a body than her flesh-and-blood partner who was lying helpless and wounded on the ground.

"Down at the water hole." She pointed back down the trail, to where the smaller pathway forked to the right. "She's caught in some weeds at the edge of the water behind the big log. Just follow the flies," she added.

"Can you get down there and guard the scene?" Nico

commanded the other officer. Lacey recognized Constable Lawson. She was acquainted with her female colleague, but they'd never been partnered together, or even worked on the same team, and so she didn't know her well.

"Yes, sir." The officer turned and followed the direction of Lacey's outstretched hand.

Nico watched Constable Lawson jog down the path, then turned back to her. "Sorry, but it's imperative the body not be disturbed. If someone else is in the area, they might have come to move the body or tamper with it in some way, and we can't have that." He was still using that brisk, commanding tone. The professional one he used when he was in charge of a team. She tried to tell herself it didn't matter. Nico was on the job, and he wasn't letting anything get in the way of that. Including, it seemed, her. Or her partner.

He dropped to his knees beside Linc, and his face finally softened. "Where is he hurt?" Lacey glowered at Nico for a second. She understood where he was coming from. The crime scene was his first priority. And perhaps he was correct. If they lost a vital clue because of something she had or hadn't done, they may never catch the killer. Perhaps she shouldn't have left the body unprotected. But that was where she and Nico differed, because a living, breathing victim was always more important in her eyes.

But at least he was now turning his attention to Linc. "It looks like someone hit him from behind. Maybe with a rock. I don't know. But it's bad." Lacey couldn't stop the slight tremble in her voice.

"It'll be okay," Nico soothed. "Linc's tough. We'll get him to hospital, and he'll be fine." Lacey was glad to have the concerned, compassionate Nico back. The one she could relate to.

CHAPTER FOUR

Nico gritted his teeth and told himself to concentrate for the hundredth time that afternoon. He was supposed to be studying the crime scene, inspecting the body still floating in the water below him. But his mind refused to cooperate, drifting off at random intervals to Lacey. Where was she? What was she doing now? The last he'd seen, she'd jumped in the back of the ambulance to be with Linc, who was still unconscious.

He understood Lacey was annoyed with him, and he could guess why. He rewound back to their conversation right before she left.

"Where are you going?" he'd asked a little confused as she'd turned to climb into the ambulance. He'd wanted Lacey to stay here with him. "I need to debrief you," Nico had said.

"And you can do that when I get back to the station. Once I know Linc is going to be okay. Something you don't seem to be that worried about." She'd glared at him then, amber eyes sparking with flecks of gold, her mouth set in a hard line. That's when he understood she was mad at him. He probably should've seen it earlier, but he'd been so damn worried about her. When he'd heard her voice on the radio, urgent and shaken, saying that Linc had been hurt and she thought the perp might still be in the area, adrenaline had spiked through him as a rush of pure fear took over. Lacey could be in danger. All he was worried about was getting to her as fast as he could, and Lawson had struggled to keep up with him. Nothing else mattered. It was only once he was sure Lacey was safe and his crime scene secure, that he'd turned his attention to Linc. He wasn't very proud of his reaction, but at the time, it was all he'd been capable of.

Lacey was deeply compassionate; it was one of the special traits he loved about her. Of course she was more worried about Linc's welfare than anything else. She wouldn't be Lacey if she wasn't. But as she turned her back on him and sat next to Linc, her hand on his shoulder, a flicker of jealousy had spiked in his gut. Rationally, he knew there wasn't anything going on between them. Lacey was in love with him, and he trusted her implicitly.

He needed to get this irrational fear out of his system. It was making him second-guess himself. Driving him slowly and quietly insane. Lacey was a police officer, her job required she be put into dangerous situations sometimes. The logical side of him understood that. He just needed to get the message through to his heart, but it didn't seem to want to listen.

Who knew love could be this complicated, turning him into a bowl of emotional mush? Nico needed to be strong, needed to be rid of all distractions so he could do his job properly. He had to find a way to make this work. To reconcile his love for Lacey, along with his need to protect her at any cost. And balance that with doing a good job. Somehow he needed to learn to separate his love life from his professional life. Back when he and Lacey had first started living together, Nico had thought it'd be easy. But if anything it was getting harder and harder to see Lacey off to work every day and not worry about her constantly.

"Forensics just arrived," Lawson called from her position fifty feet away, where she waited at the trail junction, breaking Nico out of his reverie.

"Right." Nico just had time to compose himself before the team from Devonport walked single file down the trail. Harry McCormick was head of the Forensic Science Service of Tasmania, a group of civilian scientists who leant their expertise to a lot of Tasmanian police precincts. Burnie—along with many other smaller police stations—didn't have the resources to employ their own team, so they outsourced to a couple of reliable companies. Nico had gotten to know Harry well over the past few years and he greeted him with a warm handshake.

"Wow, you guys are keeping us busy," Harry commented. Then he introduced Nico to his two assistants, neither of whom Nico had met before. A petite brunette with glasses, and a tall, gangly guy with a spotty face who looked no older than a teenager. Nico hoped they knew their stuff. Harry wouldn't have brought them otherwise, he surmised.

"What a mess." Harry grimaced as he snapped on a pair of latex gloves and leaned in to study the body.

"Yes," Nico agreed. This second body had been here much longer than the first and had been compromised by local fauna. "I'm hoping you can tell me what animal made the teeth marks in her face. My bet is that a family of Tasmanian Devils had a good feed." Nico stood back to make room for Harry and his assistants.

"Can't give you a definite until I get her back to the lab." That was Harry's catch phrase. He never gave away anything until he was one hundred percent certain. "Is this body related to the one you found yesterday?" Harry queried.

"We don't know yet, but it seems likely," Nico acknowledged. "Both found so close together. Both females of a similar age. Both with ligature marks around their neck and wrists. No ID or anything that can identify this victim on the body either." Nico ticked the pertinent points off on his fingers. The one niggling difference was that this victim looked to be of Asian descent, while the first was definitely Caucasian. "I'm still waiting to hear back from Dr. Lagos about the cause of death on the first one," Nico admitted. The local forensic pathologist carried out all the autopsies for Burnie and surrounding areas, and Nico hoped and prayed that the doctor had no other murdered bodies on his list of this week; otherwise, it could take days or weeks to get the results he needed.

* * *

Nico stared at the evidence board stuck to the wall. He'd commandeered the same meeting room he'd used to solve Rania's murder from which to run his operations for this new crime. It was large enough to house four or five desks, had a big whiteboard at one end where he could set up his evidence board, or murder map as they liked to call it, and large expanses of wall where they could pin up other photos of the crime scene, maps, or any other reference material they might need. A junior officer was setting up a couple of computers and a printer on the rear desk, but otherwise, the room was empty. They really needed a dedicated room—or better yet, a suite of offices—that could be used specifically to run his investigations from. Until now, Shadbolt had refused Nico's request for an exclusive area assigned to his use, but if this investigation got any bigger, he might well have to admit defeat and stop complaining about his budget.

Nico dragged a hand through his hair. It was after five in the evening and he'd just returned to the station after leaving the crime scene. Dr. Lagos had retrieved the body, and it was now on its way to the local morgue for autopsy. Harry and his forensics team were still at the site, but Nico had decided he'd seen enough and wanted to return to HQ because he had a lot on his mind.

There was still no word from Lacey, and Nico jiggled his phone in the palm of his hand, wondering if he should contact her. If there was anything to update him on about Linc's condition, surely she would have messaged him by now. Lacey had said she'd come back to the station and give him her account of what'd happened later. But Nico had no clear idea of when that might be. She was still technically on shift till eight tonight, but no one at the station would begrudge the fact she wanted to be by her partner's side. He fretted over his decision for a few more moments, and then finally tapped out a message, asking if she had any news on Linc.

There was no reply, and Nico began to pace in front of the whiteboard. Should he go to the hospital and see for himself? Linc was made of tough stuff, but if he died... Nico didn't even want to entertain the idea. Lacey would be a complete mess if that happened. As would Tyrell. The senior constable had taken great delight and all the credit when his nephew had requested an internship in Burnie. And knowing Tyrell, he'd probably be taking all the blame for Linc now ending up in hospital. He made a decision, if he still hadn't heard from her in half an hour, he'd drive over to the hospital.

But for now, he had a murder to solve. Well, two murders. A second dead body, found only a day after the first. It was almost unheard of, especially in Burnie. Nico considered the photos of the two dead women he'd pinned to the board. Like he'd said to Harry, there were a lot of striking similarities about the girls, including the fact the girls were around the same age. But also some differences. The first girl was clearly blonde and of Caucasian descent. But this new girl had long dark hair and was perhaps Chinese, if he had to guess. The different ethnicity had him stumped. And without any form of ID found on the girls, this case was proving tougher to solve by the minute.

Of course, the specter of the possible serial killer had raised its head as soon as the first girl was found. But his female victims of choice seemed to be slightly older, and they'd all worked in the sex industry. These two new victims looked too wholesome to be mixed up in that trade. But Nico had learned to be cautious before jumping to conclusions. Just because these girls' clothes, hair and makeup were more of your girl-next-door variety, it didn't mean they weren't still prostitutes.

To their knowledge, the serial killer had not struck again. The trail had gone cold since the third victim had been found over near Zeehan. Hobart detectives had flooded into the small town and had gone over the evidence for months. But they'd not been able to uncover anything conclusive. And they were still in the dark about his methods and motivations. A profiler had come up with a vague description of the perp they were looking for but there wasn't a lot to go on. Male, probably not a local, more likely a drifter. Had perhaps killed before, as he seemed experienced with killing, and the crime scenes were always left spotless—the killer careful not to leave anything behind that might give him away. And perhaps this man had a military background, because of the spotless conditions of the crime scene and when the bodies were found they were laid out neatly on their backs, hands folded onto their chests above their hearts. But these two new murders seemed to scream of a lack of finesse, the bodies just dumped in the nearest river. And why were they left where anyone could find them? Unless this killer didn't understand how a dead body behaved once it'd been submerged. Or they wanted the bodies to be found.

As he pondered a possible link to the serial killer, Sally-Ann poked her head around the doorframe. "Oh, good, you're here." His friend came all the way into the room. "I think I might have some information on the dead girl from yesterday."

Nico lifted his head and motioned Sally-Ann over. He needed some good news. An ID on the victim would be a good start.

"A woman came into the station just after lunch wanting to file a missing persons report," Sally-Ann started. "The junior officer at the front desk took down the information, but didn't twig that it could be related to our case, and I only found out about it ten minutes ago when I overhead the junior officer briefing her superior. The woman who filed the missing person report is named Anastasia Kibel, I think that's Russian, and she said her twenty-one-year-old daughter hasn't been seen for at least three days. The daughter's name is Zoya Kibel. Her description fits with our first vic." Sally-Ann looked up, a gleam in her eye.

"Great catch," Nico congratulated. "That'd fit the time frame," he continued thoughtfully. They still didn't have the official autopsy report, but Nico had enough expertise to realize the body hadn't been left for more than two or three days in the water. "Could you take Hickey over and talk to this lady?" Nico would like to do it himself, but he still hadn't heard from Lacey. He trusted Sally-Ann to get it right, she was a great officer with good instincts, and had earned her promotion to senior constable after she'd been instrumental in helping to catch Gabriel. If this missing girl was their victim, it'd really help kick-start the investigation. Normally, he'd send Tyrell and Sally-Ann together, they worked great as a team. But Tyrell was sitting by his nephew's bedside in hospital.

"Sure, boss." Sally-Ann grinned, looking like a bloodhound on the trail.

"Call me when you've finished," Nico instructed. "I'm going to pop over to the hospital and check on our courageous officer."

"Good idea." She sobered. "Tell Tyrell I'm thinking of him. That Linc has all our prayers and wishes for a full recovery."

* * *

Nico found the waiting room just down the hall from the nurses' station. Tyrell and Lacey both sat in plastic chairs, not speaking, staring at the floor. Lacey jumped up when she heard him come in. She let Nico enfold her in his arms, all her previous irritation dissolved, her face awash with worry.

"Linc just came out of surgery," she said, lifting her head to stare at him, then bit her bottom lip. "He had an intracranial hematoma, and they had to drain it. They've put him into an induced coma." Her face was pale, and she felt small and vulnerable in his arms. Nico silently thanked the powers that be that Lacey wasn't also lying in a hospital bed. It could just as easily have been her the perp had chosen to hit with a rock. He didn't think he could handle that.

Tyrell lowered his head into his hands with a groan. "My sister is going to kill me," he muttered, his brown skin appearing to have gone shades paler, his knuckles going almost white as he clenched his hands into fists beneath his cheekbones.

Lacey left Nico's embrace and went over to lay a hand on Tyrell's shoulder. "This is not your fault," she said soothingly. "Linc is a police officer. We all know the risks. This could've happened to him no matter whether he was working in Michigan or here."

"She's still gonna kill me. He got hurt on my watch." Tyrell never lifted his head out of his hands, his voice tight with anguish.

"If anything, I'm the one to blame." Lacey sat down carefully next to Tyrell. "I should've stayed with my partner, not gone off ahead of him." Lacey's mouth tightened in a grimace of guilt.

"All right, enough of the blame game," Nico interceded. He took a seat in the chair on the other side of Tyrell, also laying his hand on his friend's shoulder. "I know this is hard for you to bear right now," he said quietly. "But you've been a cop long enough to know that this job is never predictable. And playing the what-if game never helped to stop a perp committing a crime or bring that same perp to justice. I need you at your best, so we catch whoever did this." They were harsh words, but Tyrell needed to hear them. The last thing Linc needed was his uncle to sink into a cesspool of blame and depression.

"You're right." Tyrell lifted his head and sat back in his chair. "I know you're right." He turned to look at Nico. Not only was Tyrell a good cop, but they'd become steadfast friends over the past two years. "I need to stay strong for Linc. And the best way to do that is to catch the bastard who did this. Have you got any leads? Do we even know if the person who hit Linc is related to the murders?"

Nico shook his head sadly. "I'm afraid we don't have much to go on. There is one thing, however." Lacey sat up taller in her chair and Tyrell turned his sharp gaze on Nico, eyes so dark they were almost black. "You said that Linc had stopped to look at something on the trail while you kept going." Nico looked pointedly at Lacey.

"Yes, but I never saw what it was that caught his eye," she replied.

"Well, when the paramedics lifted Linc off the ground, I found something directly beneath where he'd been lying. Perhaps the perp hit him in an attempt to stop him picking it up, but when Linc fell, he landed directly on top of it."

"What was it?" Tyrell leaned forward on his chair.

"It was a little charm, like one of those you find on a bracelet. It was heart-shaped and on the back were the words *practice makes perfect*." Tyrell and Lacey stared at him in silence, probably not what they'd been expecting to hear.

"What does that mean?" Tyrell finally asked. Nico shrugged. It didn't mean a lot to him. Yet. But it was somewhere to start. A clue they didn't have before.

"A lot of people use that phrase," Lacey said thoughtfully. "Artists. Musicians. Footballers. Athletes. Students. Anybody who wants to become good at something. I guess it can be applied to most careers or even hobbies at some time or another. Hell, we even use it in police training. Especially on the shooting range." She was right. The words could be linked to just about anything or anyone. But Nico wouldn't let himself be discouraged.

"Are you saying that the murderer may have dropped something out there and come back to retrieve it because it might link them to the crime scene? But they were too late, and Linc had already found it?" Tyrell questioned.

"It's just a theory at the moment, but yes, that could be a possibility."

"But a charm from a bracelet would probably belong to a woman, wouldn't you say?" Tyrell was thinking out loud, but at least he was concentrating on the case and not wallowing in self-pity any more. "So why did the killer want it back? Did it belong to one of the victims? Or did it belong to the killer? Was it a keepsake of some sort? And if so, what did it mean to the killer?"

"All very good questions," Nico replied. But none of them had any answers.

CHAPTER FIVE

It was after midnight when Nico finally convinced Lacey to go home with him. They'd sat in the hospital waiting room for hours, Nico never leaving her side, until a harried-looking doctor finally came along and said that Linc was stable, but still in an induced coma in intensive care and he could let one person in for five minutes to see him, preferably next of kin. Tyrell's face had hardened at the news, but of course he had to be the one who went in to see Linc.

Lacey spent another twenty minutes fretting, pacing the small room to and fro, much like Nico did when he was trying to work out a tricky twist in his latest investigation. Tyrell returned at last, his mouth still set in grim lines, but with slightly better news. Like the doctor said, Linc was stable, breathing on his own, and the blood clot had been removed. It was just a wait and see game now, but the doctor was optimistic that Linc would make a full recovery.

"Come home, Lace," Nico had implored. "There's nothing else we can do for him tonight." It was true, but Lacey was still resistant to leaving. It wasn't until Tyrell said that he was going home to catch some shut-eye before he came back early tomorrow that Lacey finally gave in.

The drive home had been unusually quiet, as she was lost

in her own world of recriminations. But as always, Smudge's ecstatic greeting when they let him off his lead was enough to bring the smile back to her face. She got down on her knees and hugged him to her chest, enjoying the soft fur on her skin and the wriggling energy in his body. Then she stood up and breathed in a deep lungful of cool air, with just the hint of salt, reminding herself how lucky she was to live in this gorgeous cottage by the sea with Nico, and the band of tension around her heart eased slightly.

She followed Nico in through the back door and copied his actions by placing her duty belt on a hook in the mudroom and her weapon in the small kitchen safe before locking the door. Nico bustled around, feeding Smudge and turning on the kettle. But she just stood in the middle of the kitchen in a daze, bone weary and unsure what to do next. She should probably have a shower, or at the very least, change out of her uniform, but she couldn't muster the will to walk down the hallway.

Nico answered that question for her, by enfolding her in his arms. She nestled her head against his chest and drew in his strength. They stood this way for many moments, until he murmured into her hair, "Come to bed."

She let him lead her to their bedroom—their bedroom; it still gave her butterflies to think she shared a bed with Nico, shared his home, and his life—where he sat her on the edge of the bed and leant down to unlace her police-issue, sturdy, black boots.

Once they were off, he turned his attention to the buttons on her blouse, undoing them one by one, letting his fingers graze her collarbone as he went. He was so tender, his hands gentle against her skin. He pulled her up to her feet and her trousers were unfastened and discarded on the chair in the corner, leaving her standing in her underwear. White cotton underwear, highly serviceable and extremely comfortable.

Her underwear of choice. Sometimes, she thought she should go out and buy herself a couple of lacy pairs, but Nico always said he liked the simplicity of it, the way the band at the top of her panties sat so snugly over the curve of her hip. He liked to trace that curve with his tongue. At the thought of his tongue on her skin, a slow burn began deep down in her belly. He took her hand and led her to the side of the bed, where he lifted the blanket and waited until she slid under, then tucked her in, stroking her hair as she laid her head on the pillow. She was acquiescent, like a puppet, or a child, giving into his control, letting him take care of her.

He left her side then, and she wanted to call out for him to come back, but in under ten seconds, he'd undressed, flicked out the light and slid into the bed beside her, spooning his body protectively against hers. The shock of his warm skin on hers was a welcome one, and she snuggled back into his chest. They lay together for many long moments, and she exhaled, letting go of some of the anger and fear that'd threatened to overwhelm her over the past few hours.

This, she thought. *This is what love is.* Such a deep connection that Nico knew what she needed even before she did. It wasn't all about the hot sex and the romantic gestures. Sometimes love was about the simple things. Like holding her until her distress evaporated. God, she loved this man.

But then her mind got thinking about the other ways she loved him and circled back to the hot sex. Wiggling her butt into his groin, she gave a secretive smile when she felt his erection growing. He might be trying to give her chaste comfort, but Nico was still a man first and foremost. A virile man, who couldn't hide his desire for her. Which was also a good thing. She didn't want to worry about Linc lying in that hospital bed anymore. Didn't want to think about those poor women who'd lost their lives to some sick, twisted madman. Didn't want to wonder how they were going to catch the criminal. All she wanted was to feel Nico. To get lost in him.

She slid a hand in between their bodies and stroked his erection through the fabric of his boxer shorts. He groaned reflexively as she caressed him, and her stomach twitched at the thought of him deep inside her. Long and hard. Suddenly, she wanted him. Needed him. Turning over so she faced him, she tugged the waistband of his boxers down to give her greater access, and began to stroke with purpose. She loved the contrast of the silken layer of skin over the hard, pulsing eagerness of his cock.

She lifted her lips to his, and he kissed her, his mouth hot and demanding on hers. But all of a sudden, he drew back. "Are you sure?" he queried. "This wasn't what I intended. I just wanted—"

She covered his mouth with hers once more, loving him even more for giving her an out. But she didn't need it. Yes, she was sure. She wanted to revel in the fact they were both alive and healthy and able to make love whenever and however they wanted to.

Without letting go of his mouth, she maneuvered her panties down over her hips with one hand. Then she rolled on top, sitting astride him and levering up so she could look down on him. Enough moonlight filtered through the half-closed curtains for her to make out Nico's features as he lay on his back below her. Longish hair that fell over his forehead, almost reaching down to his shoulders, square jawline with a hint of stubble, full lips, sharp slash of his nose that hooked ever so slightly to the left, the scar on his cheek, and his piercing blue eyes. She couldn't see the color in the dim light, but she knew them off by heart. The way they changed with his mood, sometimes deep and fathomless like the ocean, sometimes bright and clear like the indigo sky right after a sunset. Those deep creases that appeared between his eyes whenever he frowned. The tiny lines around the edges that helped her gauge just when a laugh was about to erupt from deep in his belly.

Tracing the line of his jaw with her finger, she inscribed his face into her memory, wanting always to remember it. His erection thrummed beneath, distracting her from her focus.

One of the best parts about having a long-term relationship was no longer needing to use a condom. She was on the pill now, and they both knew they were safe from disease, and the feel of his naked cock as it slid inside her was one of the best things in the world.

Afterward, they both fell into an exhausted, dreamless sleep.

* * *

Lacey slipped into one of the last remaining chairs at the back of the operations room. She'd made it with seconds to spare before the morning briefing started. Nico glanced up from where he stood in front of the whiteboard, his expression not changing, but she knew he'd seen her come in. She gave him a quick thumbs-up, indicating all was well.

Lacey had just returned from the hospital, where she'd stopped in to visit Linc before her shift started. Tyrell was already there, but he'd just received good news from the doctor, and she could see some of the strain had left his face. If Linc kept improving, they were going to bring him out of the induced coma this afternoon. Lacey had spontaneously hugged Tyrell when he'd told her, not caring that he was a senior officer. After a second's hesitation, Tyrell had accepted the hug, clearly happy to have someone with which to share the news.

Now she knew that Linc was on the mend—he wasn't out of danger yet, but the signs were good—she could begin to concentrate on the task at hand, finding the person who'd done this to him. And finding the murderer who'd taken two innocent girls' lives. They were most likely one and the same person, which would make Lacey's job all that much easier.

Nico cleared his throat at the front of the room and everyone stopped talking, fixing him with attentive gazes. Nico had a big team assembled, especially considering the size of the police station. He must've been given permission to purloin officers from other cases, Shadbolt deciding this double murder was more important than anything else at the moment. Sally-Ann sat near the front shuffling piles of paper. Nico had probably promoted her to his second-in-command while Tyrell was preoccupied watching over Linc. Hickey and Gorman were there, as was the female constable from yesterday, Dawn Lawson, and a few other constables from the station she was less familiar with. But there were two faces she didn't recognize sitting at the front with Sally-Ann.

"Morning, everyone, thank you all for attending. I'll catch you up on what we know so far," Nico cleared his throat before he continued. Lacey knew that was a sign of nervousness—even after nine years in the job, Nico still hated talking to a roomful of people. But to everyone else it would've looked as if he were gathering his thoughts.

"First of all, please welcome Detective Jay Pederson, and Senior Detective Tasmin Saito, who have been seconded from Launceston to give us a hand with the case."

Lacey hid a grimace. Nico wouldn't be happy about having two detectives foisted upon him. But he could be a team player when it was required, and they probably needed as much help as they could get, she conceded. And he was still lead on the case; nothing could take that away from him.

The male detective had darker skin and a deep frown that never seemed to leave his face. She guessed by his looks that he was indigenous and silently congratulated him. It took a lot of courage and determination to become an indigenous police officer, and she could only imagine some of the hardships, racist comments, and lack of respect from other people in his culture that he'd had to endure on his journey to forging his career.

With a name like Saito, Lacey guessed the female detective was perhaps of Japanese descent. Petite to the point of being almost childlike, she had long dark hair pulled back in a severe bun and a smooth complexion that made it hard for Lacey to pinpoint her age. An interesting duo, and she looked forward to watching this pair work together.

"Let me recap the facts as we know them so far." Lacey abandoned her study of the two detectives and tuned back in to what Nico was saying. "Two days ago, the body of a young woman was found by civilian hikers floating in the Emu River near the Platypus Reserve picnic area. We have an approximate time of death of around three days before she was found. We immediately closed off the reserve and searched the area. Yesterday, a second body was found in a swimming hole three miles farther up the river. This body showed more decomposition, and we believe she could've been in the water for up to two weeks. Cause of death is yet to be confirmed on both victims, as we're still waiting for the results of the autopsies, but the likelihood is they died by asphyxiation due to hanging. I hope to have the final results of at least the first body by this afternoon. But it's looking more and more likely that both young women were drugged to make them compliant, then tied up and transported to the place they were killed."

None of this information was new to Lacey; she'd been involved in both discoveries. She hoped Nico might have some new details to share.

"One of our officers was attacked at the second crime scene. He's still in intensive care, but we're hopeful of a full recovery." There were a few unhappy murmurs at this. Nico stopped talking and looked up to meet Lacey's gaze. "We think he was attacked because he found something on the ground and stopped to pick it up." Nico gestured to Sally-Ann, and she leapt up and handed out a document to everyone with an image of the bracelet charm found beneath Linc's body.

"We think the criminal dropped this clue and was desperate to get it back. I believe this charm is linked to the two murders. And I'm hoping it is a vital clue that might help us all solve this case."

"It could also be a red herring." Lacey craned her neck to see who had spoken. Detective Pederson was drumming his fingers on the tabletop. "A mere coincidence, nothing more." Pederson kept his face impassive. Hmm, he was already challenging Nico's assumptions. Which was a good thing in relation to keeping everyone open to all ideas, but she hoped it wouldn't put Nico offside.

Nico studied the man for a second, before admitting, "You're correct. This could be mere coincidence." Lacey let out a quiet gust of air. Nico wasn't taking this as a direct challenge. Yet. "The person who hit Senior Constable Jackson over the head could well be a random stranger. Someone who has a particular hatred for cops. Not the killer trying to stop us from discovering a vital clue. And the fact we found the charm directly underneath his body doesn't mean it's related to the crime either. That charm could've been dropped days, weeks, or months ago." Nico let his words hang in the air. Now that he said it like that, Lacey even began to doubt her own opinions on the subject. But she knew his hunch was right. She knew that charm was a critical clue in this crime, even if other people didn't want to believe it.

Some people might put Nico down for always following his famous hunches. But that gut instinct was usually based on hard facts, the way he put puzzle pieces together and saw the full picture that other people couldn't see, rather than just individual pieces most other officers worked with.

"But it's more logical if the charm is a clue and the killer came back to retrieve it. A random attack just doesn't make sense," Hickey piped up from his seat just in front of Lacey. "Why would the killer put themselves in that position otherwise? Why come back to the crime scene and risk being caught? And why take the chance of attacking a policeman in broad daylight?" Hickey questioned. "If it wasn't to retrieve something that could identify them?"

"Killers are sometimes known to return to the scene of their crimes," Pederson swiveled so he could turn his deadpan stare at Hickey. "For all manner of reasons. Voyeurism. To relive the crime. To get off on the power of taking someone's life. To watch the police do their thing." Pederson shrugged and returned to face the front, and Lacey decided then that Pederson was not going to make many friends at the station with an attitude like that. Saito, on the other hand, sat and watched everything with bright, almost birdlike attentiveness, but kept her mouth shut.

"Moving on," Nico said, pointing to the picture of the first girl they'd found. "We finally have some good news. We have identified one of the victims." Lacey sat up taller at Nico's words. They hadn't discussed much about the case last night after they got home, but Lacey was sure Nico would've told her if he had a positive ID. So the verification must've only come in this morning. "She is Zoya Kibel, a twenty-one-year-old local woman. Her mother reported her missing yesterday and came in this morning to positively ID her body." Nico wrote her name beneath the photo of the body, then added another photo of a pretty young woman who was very much alive, smiling for the camera.

Lacey's heart went out to the mother. What a horrific thing to have to do. But then her cop brain kicked in and she started turning this new information over in her mind. An ID was powerful, because now they had somewhere to start.

This also added more humanity to their search. They now had an actual name and a previous life to put to this nameless body.

Nico continued, "As far as we know, Zoya had no enemies. She lived alone in a one-bedroom flat on the outskirts of Burnie. Her mother told us that she only moved out a few months ago. She'd been working as a gymnastics coach over at the Somerset Gymnastics Club for the past year and a half and decided she'd enough money saved up to become independent. I believe the father died in a car accident around five years ago, and there are no other siblings. The mother is distraught, as you can well imagine, and cannot comprehend why anyone would want to kill her daughter."

Lacey digested this news thoughtfully. From the outside, it looked as if Zoya had a perfectly normal life. A young woman just starting out on her journey. Such a shame. She wondered if this young lady was related to the second body. Or were they complete strangers, merely victims of the same crazed killer? So many threads to untangle.

"Hickey, can you take Lawson and search the victim's flat?" Nico asked, and Lacey snapped her attention back to the room.

"Yes, sir." Hickey sat straighter in his chair, obviously pleased with being given such an important task. Lacey wondered at Nico's reasoning in splitting Hickey and Gorman up, as they usually worked together. He must have his reasons. She also wondered what stories they might uncover in their search of the young girl's things. It always seemed like such an invasion of privacy. But without it, the police had no hope of piecing together a victim's life.

"Good," Nico replied, then his gaze flicked to Hickey's normal partner. "Gorman, I'd like you and Senior Constable Smith to concentrate on getting as much detail on the charm as you can. See if anyone in Burnie sells anything like it, that sort of thing." Gorman looked a little downcast by the task. He'd probably much rather be out on the street. "Sally-Ann is one of the best when it comes to the small details," Nico went on. "You could learn a lot from her. And every little piece of the puzzle is equally important." It was true; Sally-Ann was one of Nico's best assets when it came to targeted research on a case. She was a whizz at finding little details that others missed. Perhaps Nico could see some similar traits in Gorman and hoped to train him up to be equally astute.

Nico switched his attention to the front of the room. "The mother has agreed to an interview, she's desperate for us to catch whoever did this. Pederson and Saito, I'd like you to take this one, if you don't mind." Nico zeroed in on the two detectives. Saito nodded and quickly began to gather her notes. Pederson's somber demeanor didn't change, but Lacey thought she caught the flicker of gratification in his eyes.

Saito asked, "Anything in particular you want us to concentrate on?"

Nico considered the woman's question. Lacey wished it'd been Pederson who'd asked, it might lessen the tension that seemed to be pulsating between him and Nico. But he just frowned at the murder board, as if committing Zoya's face to memory, and ignored Nico.

"Ask about the bracelet charm, of course," Nico said. If it belonged to Zoya, then they could finally admit it to evidence as a solid clue. "We also need to get a feel for Zoya's life. Who her friends were. What she did for fun. Dig into her past if you can. See if there's anything there that might raise a red flag." Nico followed Pederson's gaze and also considered the new photo of Zoya. "We need to look at the mother's life as well. Does she have any enemies? Could this murder have been something to do with someone wanting to get at the mother, and they used the daughter as a scapegoat or a form of punishment? With a second, seemingly unrelated body, I don't think this is much of a possibility, but we still need to ask."

"Sure," Saito said, and they stood as one, waiting for the briefing to be over. A low buzz of chatter filled the room as the rest of the officers prepared to receive their allocated tasks.

"Carmichael, you're with me." It took Lacey a second to comprehend that Nico meant her. He rarely ever called her by her last name, but having these two detectives in the room, he was obviously putting on his most professional front. "We're going to check out Zoya's place of work, see what her colleagues have to say." A thrum of excitement went through Lacey. Not only was she getting to partner with Nico, which was unusual and she'd jump at the chance to work alongside him, but they might well find something of value at this gymnastics club. But then a sliver of doubt tempered her delight when she wondered what other ulterior motives Nico had for taking her as his partner.

"Yes, sir," she replied, hiding her grin. She could see Sally-Ann was also hiding a smirk as they all got ready to file out of the operations room.

"Thanks, everyone," Nico called over the increasing hum of conversation. "We'll have another briefing same time tomorrow morning."

CHAPTER SIX

Somerset Gymnastics Club was housed in a modern building, all sharp angles and glass faces. There was money here, Nico mused. Most gymnastics clubs he knew of—he had to admit, his knowledge was limited, he'd been more into soccer back in the day—occupied in some dingy old building, bequeathed by the city council decades ago, with no money or work going into the infrastructure as it slowly fell to pieces.

"Nice place," Nico commented as they strolled through the front door. Faced with an empty desk and a large reception area filled with plastic chairs, Nico rang the bell on the desk. While he waited, he perused the framed certificates on the wall behind reception, most of them stating the qualifications of the various coaches. One particular frame caught his eye, holding center stage in the middle and larger than the rest. It was a silver medal of some kind. Actually, it looked remarkably like an Olympic medal. He leaned in closer to get a better look.

Lacey was looking at the certificates as well, but then she turned and said, "You didn't assign me to be your partner just so you could keep an eye on me, did you?" Lacey's question caught him off guard. He should be used to it by now; he could always count on Lacey to ask the hard questions. She'd obviously been stewing on the idea all the way over in the police cruiser, as the air inside the cab had been tense. At least he now knew what was bugging her.

"No," he replied patiently.

"Are you sure?" She narrowed her gorgeous hazel eyes and fixed him with *the look*. *The look* was meant to make his stomach feel jittery, letting him know that she was onto him. He'd always been aware their road would be paved with pitfalls when Lacey decided to take a job in his police station. But he'd encouraged her anyway, knowing they were strong enough together to manage whatever troubles came their way. But he never dreamed it'd be the subtleties that'd catch him out. The way she could tell if he was spinning a white lie, or not telling her the complete truth. Everyone told white lies now and then, it was the grease that helped him avoid conflict or soothe someone's ruffled feathers. But with Lacey, he always had to tell the truth.

"Yes," he replied equally as patiently. He wanted to reach out to tuck a stray strand of blonde hair that'd escaped her ponytail behind her ear, but knew better than to attempt to touch her. While they were in work mode, and while Lacey was in this mood, she wouldn't appreciate it. "You don't have a partner at the moment, and I needed someone to accompany me." Which was kind of true. He could have done this on his own, but this was a good learning process for Lacey; she was still on probation after all. "I could reassign you to help Gorman with the research, if you like?"

"No, I'd much rather be here, thank you," she finally replied, but that sharp edge never left her eyes. She was way too clever for her own good sometimes. No way in hell was he going to admit there was even a small grain of truth in her question. Ever since Linc had been hit over the head, Nico found himself unaccountably worried about Lacey.

"I don't think anyone heard the bell," Lacey said,

effectively ending the conversation. He hoped that'd be the last of it. Lacey wasn't one to hold a grudge, and she also understood there needed to be separation between her and Nico at work. She'd never undermine his status as detective sergeant in public. In private, it was a different matter. But he had to hand it to her, most of the time she did a good job of leaving work stuff at work and not bringing their disagreements home.

She turned to the rear of the large atrium, where they could hear rhythmic thumping, punctuated by a voice raised in command. "Shall we?" she asked.

"Lead the way," he replied gallantly, following her to the door. When they walked through, they found themselves in one of the largest gymnasiums Nico had ever seen. This cavernous room increased his belief this gymnastics club must have a rich benefactor. Either that, or some highly ranked gymnasts who brought in lots of sponsorship money. It was chock full to the brim with all kinds of gymnastic equipment. From those he recognized, like the three balance beams in the corner, a set of uneven bars, a pommel horse and some spring boards, lots and lots of crash mats, and a large blue area in the center where the gymnasts could perform their routines. To those he didn't, such as the spiderweb of ropes in the corner, and the two complicated contraptions that reminded him of something you might find in the weights room of a gym.

"Wow," Lacey mouthed as she turned a full circle to take in the huge room. "This almost makes me wish I'd taken gymnastics as a child."

Nico spied two figures in the far corner. "Hello," he called out a greeting. A girl of around thirteen was madly practicing with a jump rope while an older lady tapped out a beat with her foot, sometimes shouting a command at the top of her voice. The pair hadn't seemed to have heard him, so he strode down the length of the large space until he was close enough to catch the woman's eye. She raised a hand, and the girl stopped skipping with what Nico thought could only be called genuine relief.

"Can I help you?" The woman couldn't keep the irritation out of her voice as she fixed them with a steely glare. "We're not technically open right now. If you'd like to enroll your child, you can come back at three when Claire will be on the front—"

"I'm Detective Sergeant Favreau, and this is Probationary Constable Carmichael," Nico interrupted, holding up his badge for the woman to see, while Lacey did the same beside him. She might be forgiven for not recognizing Nico as a cop because he was in civilian clothing, but how could she miss the fact Lacey was wearing the Tasmanian Police Department uniform?

She stared at them down her long nose for at least three seconds before she seemed to relent. "Take a break, Lily," the woman said, indicating the girl head to the change rooms on the other side of the room. Lily did so with alacrity, casting a few curious glances over her shoulder as she went.

"My name is Erica Nellenbach. I'm the head coach of the club. What can I do for you?" Erica didn't smile, merely regarded them with cold indifference. She was a tall woman with a large beak of a nose, her hair pulled back in a severe bun.

"We didn't mean to interrupt your lesson," Lacey said, stepping up beside Nico.

"Yes, well, you're lucky I'm here. The place is normally empty at this time of day. Classes don't start until three. But Lily needs some one-on-one attention. And jump rope provides valuable conditioning for a young gymnast," Erica said, as if Nico had asked the question. Which he hadn't. It made him wonder why she offered the information in the first place.

Erica lifted her chin and stared down her nose at them again, and Nico began to understand this was Erica's stock-standard attitude, designed to make everyone feel inferior.

He decided to ignore her aloof disapproval. "We believe a lady by the name of Zoya Kibel worked here, and we'd like to ask you some questions regarding her work ethic and interaction with her colleagues," Nico said, pulling out a notebook from his top pocket and making a show of flipping the pages, but he was really studying her face.

Finally, a flicker of emotion flashed across her features. Was it unease? "What do you mean worked here?" she asked in a clipped voice. There was a slight accent, probably Germanic, Nico concluded.

"We're sorry to inform you that Zoya was found dead two days ago," Nico said, keeping all emotion out of his voice.

Erica's face paled. "Dead? You're kidding, right?" It seemed the woman wasn't made completely out of stone after all. Her hand flew to cover her mouth.

"No, we're not," Lacey interceded, her face a mask of concern.

"Oh, *scheisse*," the woman muttered under her breath. But Nico caught the German swearword. He didn't think a woman like this was easily rattled, and this news seemed to have come as a great shock. "I wondered why she didn't turn up to work yesterday. I had to get Janine in at short notice to cover her class. She's usually very committed to her job. I just thought..." Erica didn't finish her sentence. "How did she die? When?" she demanded.

"We're not at liberty to share those details at the moment," Nico replied blandly.

"So, it wasn't normal for Zoya not to turn up for work?" Lacey asked, jumping into the breach.

Erica shifted her sneakered feet and pursed her lips. "No,

she was usually reliable. She was very committed to her group of gymnasts. She taught our junior development squad, aged six to ten. The talented ones who might make it through to the state or national competitions." Erica's face relaxed a little as she talked about the gymnasts. "But it happens more than you think. Coaches call in sick at the last moment, or find another job and leave me in the lurch. When you work with young women who don't take things as seriously as they should, it makes it hard to find good employees." *It's no wonder the other coaches might want to escape a shift or two,* Nico thought. Having to work with this woman would be his own personal nightmare.

He was very good at keeping his thoughts under wraps, however, and so he asked, "You didn't try and contact her? To see why she'd missed work?"

"No, I was too busy," Erica snapped. Then she seemed to relent a little. "If she hadn't turned up today, I was going to call her."

"Right," Nico said vaguely, not impressed with the woman's answer. She clearly cared more about her club than she did about her employees. "And how many days did Zoya work here?"

"Four days. Wednesday, Thursday, Friday, Saturday."

"And she worked her full shift on Saturday?" Nico asked. Erica merely nodded. And Nico did a mental calculation. Zoya's body had been found on Tuesday. If she'd been killed sometime on Saturday night or Sunday, that fitted with the theory she'd been in the water for around three days.

"Thank you," he replied, consulting his notes. "How were her relationships with her work colleagues? Did she get on well with everyone? Were there any disagreements that you know of?"

"Disagreements? Of course not. We are all very civilized here. We all get on perfectly well. Zoya was a good employee and was friends with all the other coaches here." Erica stood up straighter, clearly resenting his implication that everything might not be perfect in this gymnastics paradise. Nico doubted that. There were always minor altercations and personal disagreements in any workplace. But Erica seemed intent on sticking to her dogma.

Nico saw Lacey raise an eyebrow in his peripheral vision, but tried to ignore her skepticism. He was quickly running out of questions and decided to wrap up the interview. He could always ask her to come down to the station if he thought of anything more. The idea that he might inconvenience Erica Nellenbach didn't worry him in the slightest. In fact, his lips twitched with the urge to smile.

Lacey grasped his mood and took over.

"Thank you for your time, Mrs. Nellenbach. We do need to ask one more thing of you, please. We'll need a list of all Zoya's work colleagues, as well as everyone associated with this club. Parents, gymnasts, that sort of thing. Along with contact details for all of them."

"Well, that's preposterous. That list includes hundreds of people, you can't possibly expect me to give that all to you now." Erica was back to glaring down her nose at Nico and Lacey.

"No, just a list of employees and their contact numbers for now would be good," Lacey replied with a tight smile. "The rest you can send over later. Tomorrow would be fine. But this afternoon would be better." The smile was still painted on Lacey's face, but Nico could recognize the effort it cost her to keep it there.

"Fine. Claire can do a list." Erica's mouth was a thin line of disapproval. "As for employees, we have at least twenty on the books at the moment. I have quite a few part-timers. There's Janine, who I just mentioned." She began ticking the names off on her fingers. "Claire who works the front desk.

Then there's—"

"A typed record sent to us as soon as you can, will be fine, thank you," Nico interrupted. "Here's my card. My email is on the back."

Erica's mouth thinned even more, as if asking her to find a list of employees was tantamount to mutiny. She was obviously above that sort of task. Nico wanted to show Erica a picture of the second murder victim to see if she knew of any connection between Zoya and the second body. But her face had been too badly mauled, and so Nico came to the conclusion that he'd gain nothing by freaking the woman out showing her a mutilated face that she most likely wouldn't be able to recognize. A certain perverted part of him wanted to pull out the picture anyway.

"If that's all then, Detective?" Erica fixed her glare on him and he noticed for the first time the ice-blue color of her eyes. She was certainly one cold fish, and he felt sorry for her husband, or children—if she was even married.

"Yes, thank you. You've been very helpful," Lacey replied, even though Erica had just pointedly ignored her. "Don't forget the list of employees," she added cheerily, turning on her heel to head back across the vast gymnasium floor. Nico snapped his notebook shut, thanked the woman for her time, and was one step behind Lacey. Their boots tapped out a noisy tattoo as they walked to the exit, the sound echoing around the high ceiling.

"Shit." Lacey stopped dead in her tracks. "Look, Nico." She was pointing up to a sign that hung above the door. He'd been so focussed on dissecting Erica's words he hadn't been taking in his surroundings.

Practice makes perfect.

Nico felt a shiver course through him as he read the words.

"Jesus," he whistled through his teeth. "Good catch, Lace, I would've missed that."

They both stared up at the sign. It was big enough to fill the wall above the doorway and had a set of stylized figures in various gymnastic poses along the bottom.

"Do you think that's it?" Lacey asked, taking a photo on her phone of the sign. "I know we said that phrase could be used for anything, but this makes a certain kind of sense, don't you think?"

"Totally agree," Nico replied. "Send that photo to evidence, will you?" He watched as Lacey's fingers flew over the buttons on her phone. "But we can't make assumptions, or arrest anybody because of a sign on the wall," he added when Lacey turned to stare suspiciously at the retreating woman's back. He also turned to take another look at Erica, who was striding toward the change rooms as if on a mission. Nico felt sorry for poor Lily, who would most likely have to resume her skipping now they were leaving.

He held his tongue until they exited through the large double doors at the front and were walking back to the cruiser.

"What are your first impressions?" He wanted to know what Lacey had made of the whole interview. Stopping to unlock the car, he glanced at her over the roof and she grimaced at him.

"I didn't like her."

He held in a laugh. Trust Lacey to state the obvious.

"Me either," he replied. "But we shouldn't let the fact that she clearly thinks she's better than the rest of us cloud our judgement," he chided gently. Nico had also taken an immediate dislike to Erica, but he knew from experience just because a person was repellent, it didn't make them a murderer. Opening the door, he slid into the driver's seat.

Lacey did the same on the passenger side and she turned her head to regard him. "I know. But she reminds me of a tennis coach I had when I was young." Lacey closed her hands into fists on her thighs. Nico wondered if she realized how much her body language was giving her feelings away. "My mother loved that woman, but she was the bane of my life. She would keep me on the court for hours in an attempt to correct my serve. I was never good enough." Lacey's eyes took on a glazed appearance, as she became lost in memories. "Much like my own mother. I was never good enough for her either. Which was probably why she loved that tennis coach so much. They were both cut from the same cloth." Lacey's tone took on a bitter edge.

Nico laid his hand on her knee. She hadn't been in contact with either of her parents in the past six months, and he knew it cut her deep that she'd had to break off all communication. But it was the only way Lacey could stay mentally healthy right now. She and her mother had a thorny relationship that hadn't been made any less so after Lacey had been kidnapped and he'd accompanied her back to Melbourne to confront her whole family. Lacey had told them about her PTSD and what'd caused it, and how her family's complete lack of support had made her spiral into the depths of depression. But it was more than that. It was also the way her mother had absolutely no empathy for Lacey; that she actually blamed Lacey, saying she was making it all up and needed to toughen up and get over herself. Lacey's mother, Elora, was the most self-centered person Nico had ever met. She liked to manipulate people—especially Lacey—by using emotional blackmail to get her own way. And the father, Barry, wasn't much better. He enabled Elora's behavior just to keep the peace.

"I feel sorry for the poor kids who have Erica as a coach every day. She probably browbeats them into submission, believing that punishment is its own form of reward. That method may have worked fifty years ago, but not anymore."

Nico silently agreed, gently stroking her knee. Glad that

they were out of the public eye for a second, so he could give into his urge to touch her.

"But it wasn't just her attitude toward the kids that has me riled up," Lacey conceded. "She was just hostile from the first second we walked in. Almost as if she had something to hide. Why is she so reluctant to give us the lists? Is she trying to hinder our investigation?" Lacey asked.

Nico was glad he'd brought Lacey along. It was good that she could see all this without being told. A good learning experience, and she handled it with levelheadedness, not letting the other woman get under her skin.

"I wondered the same thing," Nico agreed. "Let's dig into Erica's past. I want to know more about her. I also want to know more about everyone who works at the club. And where all their money comes from. Something's going on there. Maybe they just have a generous benefactor, and it's all simple and above board," he added. "But it definitely needs more investigation."

"Hmm," Lacey mused. "Maybe Erica is just picky about who she trains. Only takes on rich clients. The ones who can afford to pay higher fees. You saw those awards hanging behind the reception desk?" she asked. When he nodded, she went on. "That looked like a silver medal from the 1984 Los Angeles Olympics." Lacey couldn't quite keep the respect out of her voice. "If it's real, then this woman can probably command higher prices. Parents would be prepared to pay through the nose. It's not every day your child is trained by an Olympic medal winner."

"That's true," Nico conceded.

"Maybe it's some kind of elite training club where only the kids of the rich and famous are allowed to join." Again, Lacey's tone held a dark bitterness. Because she of all people would know what that was like. Her family were ridiculously rich, and as a child, Lacey had been sent to only the finest clubs or institutions for the betterment of her sporting and musical prowess. Lacey had hated every second of it.

There was a complicated tangle of emotions and beliefs all tied up with her family money that Nico had yet to fully explore because she didn't like to talk about it. It seemed Lacey was almost ashamed of her wealth, wanted to leave her affluence behind, and live a simple, grateful life. Because money had never made her happy. Which was one of the reasons she was so eager to move in with him. Share his comfortable little cottage, when she could live in a mansion if she chose to. And he agreed with her. Money didn't buy you happiness.

"Whatever's going on there, I'm sure we'll get to the bottom of it. But for now, we should head back to the station. Pederson and Saito will be back from interviewing Zoya's mother soon." He hoped they had some more insights into the young girl's background. First and foremost, he wanted to know if that charm had belonged to Zoya. "If you could start digging into that gymnastic club when we get back, that'd be great."

Lacey nodded as Nico started the car and eased out onto the main road. "Shadbolt is fronting the media this afternoon to speak about the second body," he told her, his mind already sorting through the raft of information they'd amalgamated. This would send the media into a frenzy. Two bodies in two days. But there wasn't a lot they could share right now, mainly because they had little to go on, apart from the name of the first victim. "We don't have a lot to tell them, which always annoys Shadbolt," Nico went on. Shadbolt hated it when he didn't have the answers, he thought it made him come across as looking incompetent. The media, who always wanted more, and would be the first to call the police out on their lack of progress.

They continued to discuss their thoughts on Erica and her

gymnastics club as Nico skillfully guided the cruiser through the late morning traffic. "Shall we stop at the bakery and grab a sandwich on the way past?" he asked as his stomach rumbled. It was still too early for lunch, but he'd skipped breakfast this morning. The little Burnie Bakery was famous with the locals for their delicious baguette sandwiches. His favorite was beef and mustard and Lacey's was salmon and brie.

"Yes, please." Lacey might not have left the house as early as he did, but they'd missed morning tea, and she was always hungry.

He found a parking spot a few shops along from the bakery, and they both jumped out. As good fortune would have it, there was no one waiting in line at the bakery and Nico greeted Jayden, the young apprentice, with a smile, asking him where he planned to go for his next hiking adventure. Caving, abseiling, mountain-bike riding, endurance runs through the heart of Tasmania, they were all things Jayden, an adrenaline junkie, was keen to do. The young man loved the outdoors and freely admitted he only worked to get money to feed his addiction. Nico was vaguely jealous. He would've loved to have done the same thing when he was younger, but now, he was tied to the job and getting too old to do the daring things that Jayden attempted.

Seeing Jaden always brought back memories of Gabriel though. In some ways, Jayden had been the catalyst who'd started Gabe on his killing spree. Rania had seen Gabe and Jayden kissing behind the bakery one day, and it brought all of Gabe's fears of being outed as a gay man to the surface. While Jayden was openly gay, he'd known that Gabriel was terrified of his secret getting out, but he'd been cleared by the police on any charges of collusion, because he knew nothing about Gabriel's murderous intent.

Nico tried not to let his feelings show as he ordered for

himself and Lacey, adding two strawberry tarts at the last second because they looked so damn good. Lacey touched his arm as if she wanted to say something, so he leaned toward her. But just as she opened her mouth to speak, there was a loud cough from behind.

"Well, look who we have here," a female voice purred.

It took a second for Nico to place the voice. But when he finally did, he spun around so quickly he almost knocked Lacey over.

What the fuck was she doing here?

"Marietta?" He couldn't believe it was her. He'd forgotten how tall she was. Wearing a pair of habitual bright-red high heels, Marietta could look him directly in the eye. Long curls of sleek auburn hair fell down over her shoulders, accentuating her perfectly tailored dove-gray suit jacket and pants. Shit. He fumbled for Lacey's hand, needing to ground himself, needing to let her know that everything was going to be okay.

"If it isn't the delectable Nicolas Favreau. So nice to finally see you again, husband." She put a loud emphasis on the last word.

"What?" Lacey scoffed. Her hand clasped his so tight it almost hurt and he knew she must be wondering who this strange woman was. "Who the hell are you?"

Oh, holy fuck. This wasn't good.

"I'm Marietta Favreau, and he's my husband. We're still married, didn't you know?" She looked directly at Nico, a lazy smile unfurling on her face, making her look exactly like the cat who just got the cream.

CHAPTER SEVEN

"You're married?" The question fell from her lips. They were words that she'd never thought to say. Nico couldn't be married. He would have told her. She would know. They told each other everything. He knew all about her broken family, and she knew all his deep secrets about his father who'd come back from the grave. How could he have kept this from her?

The little bakery seemed to swirl around her, Jayden a blurry figure in the background, watching with wide, curious eyes. She tried to make sense of who this glamorous stranger was, of what she was saying. This couldn't be true. It just couldn't.

"No, I'm not," Nico ground the word out between gritted teeth. He was still holding her hand she realized, and she snatched it away. But her eyes refused to focus on his face. On his familiar, imperfect face that she loved so much. He was denying it was true, but her heart felt like it was being squeezed in a vise.

"Oh, yes you are, lover."

Lacey swung her gaze to the tall woman who towered over her. This spectacular woman, who looked effortlessly stylish and had the body and hair of an Amazon. She was smiling at

Nico. A smile that spoke of intimacy, of shared secrets, of a familiarity a stranger wouldn't have had. And in that moment, she felt utter betrayal. This woman had known Nico, had perhaps even been married to him as she stated. But it wasn't that fact which shattered her heart. It was the fact Nico had never told her.

"No, I'm not," Nico repeated. "We signed the divorce papers eleven years ago." Even as he spoke, he turned to face Lacey, imploring her with his eyes to believe him. She took a step away. Then another.

"No, you didn't," the woman assured him.

"I'll see you back at the station," Lacey said, urging her feet to take her out of the store. Her legs were like jelly and the pavement seemed to roll beneath her feet, as if she could no longer find stable ground. But she had to get out of here. She couldn't breathe. Couldn't think straight.

"Who is that, Nico?" she heard the other woman ask in a sexy, seductive voice. "Is she your current piece of ass? A little work fling on the side?" The woman's voice faded as she strode away, but her words cut like knives.

Then she heard the sound of running behind her, and Nico's arm came around her waist, tugging her into him, forcing her to look up into his indigo eyes. "Lacey, don't go. God, I'm so sorry. I never..." he became lost for words as he stared into her eyes. But she could barely hear him over the crashing cymbals of pain radiating through her body.

"I have no idea what she's doing here. I'm so sorry," he said again. "I should have told you about Marietta. We were only married for a few months until I figured out she was using me to gain citizenship. Then I divorced her. I promise, I divorced her." His eyes were so full of anguish. He was nearly as shocked and hurt by this as she was. Nearly. But nothing could equal her pain right now.

Maybe he had obtained a divorce. But that wasn't the

point. The point was he hadn't told her he'd been married in the first place.

Her mind was still spinning with this news, but one thing she definitely understood was that the middle of the main street of Burnie wasn't the place to have this discussion. It wouldn't do for Burnie's detective sergeant and his constable girlfriend to be airing their dirty laundry in public.

She shrugged him off and straightened her uniform. "I'll see you back at the station," she repeated, keeping her gaze averted, not wanting to see the torture in his eyes. Not wanting him to see the agony in hers. She began the slow climb up the hill to the Burnie Police Station, not glancing back even once.

He didn't follow her.

But by the time she finally reached the main front doors, she was no better off. She couldn't seem to grasp a single thought for more than a second. Her whole life had just been turned upside down. What was she supposed to do now? She needed time to think. Time to process. Work was the last place she wanted to be. She wouldn't be able to concentrate. And wouldn't know what to say to Nico when he finally came to find her. Nico. Oh, what had he done? But even as she tried to put him out of her mind, part of her wondered what he was doing now. Was he telling that woman to get out of town and never come back? Escorting her back to her car and running her out of town? She really, really hoped so.

Making a sudden decision, she jogged up the steps and through the front door. The young officer on front-desk duty buzzed her through, and she strode down the corridor to the small open-plan office she shared with three of her peers. Gorman looked up in surprise from behind his computer, and Lacey belatedly remembered he was researching the small bracelet charm. Sally-Ann was nowhere to be seen, which was probably a blessing, because that woman would've seen straight through Lacey's thin layer of disguise. Hopefully she could pull the wool over Gorman's eyes long enough to make her escape.

"How did it go?" he asked. "Did you—"

"Good," she replied hurriedly. She didn't have time to answer his questions; she needed to be out of there before Nico returned. A little distraction was hopefully all she needed. "We just saw the phrase practice makes perfect on a huge sign inside the Somerset Gymnastic Club. Look that one up, it might help you."

Gorman blinked in slight confusion, before saying, "Wow. Thanks, I'll get onto it."

Lacey was already packing her work laptop into her backpack. "I'm going to sit with Linc," she stated. It wasn't up for debate, she needed somewhere quiet to escape, but she was still on duty, so she couldn't escape completely. "I'm going to do some digging into the gymnastics club while I'm there," she said. She wanted to add that Gorman wasn't to tell Nico where she'd gone, but she couldn't involve him in their personal problems, so instead she said, "Can you tell Nico I'll be back in a few hours?"

"Sure." Gorman looked anything but sure. "Hey, Lacey," he called. But she was already out the door, and practically running down the hallway, not wanting to answer any of Gorman's questions.

She collected her vehicle—well, she'd taken to driving Nico's Jeep, as he rode his motorcycle most days, but maybe it was time she got her own transport—and drove over to the hospital, feeling numb. Her mind was still clogged with endless rounds of the same question. *Why didn't you tell me? Why didn't you tell me?* So by the time she made it up to the intensive care ward, she still had no more clarity on how she felt about this woman and her accusations, or what she was going to say to Nico when she saw him next. She was so numb, she couldn't tell exactly what she was feeling. When Marietta first called Nico her husband, Lacey had felt shock that he'd so easily betrayed her trust. But that feeling had evaporated now. She should probably be angry. Sad. Disappointed. Devastated. But her eyes remained dry, she couldn't seem to conjure up any strong emotions. Just blank numbness.

The nurse in charge couldn't give her any more updates about Linc's condition. All she would say was that a member of his family was in there with him—Lacey assumed it was Tyrell, as Linc's mother wasn't due to fly in from America until later tonight—along with a specialist doctor. It wasn't the hopeful news Lacey had been wanting to hear, but at least he wasn't any worse. She would wait. Hopefully Tyrell would emerge soon with some news.

Taking a seat in one of the low slung chairs in the waiting room, she pulled out her laptop. Opening an Internet browser, her fingers hovered over the keys. She should just type in Somerset Gymnastic Club. Delving into research about the club might help clear her mind of all the other abhorrent thoughts. But she couldn't help herself; she googled the name Marietta Favreau.

And then covered her mouth to stop a groan escaping as images of the woman claiming to be Nico's wife populated the page.

She learned so many things about Marietta over the next forty minutes spent hunched over her laptop. The woman wasn't shy about sharing on social media. Formerly Marietta Domanska—until she took the name Favreau eleven years ago and clearly never changed it back—she was of Polish descent and at forty-two, was a good ten years older than Nico. Images showed a tall, willowy woman, with long auburn hair, and striking features. She was a fashion designer, with her own brand, simply called *Marietta*, with at least three shopfronts that Lacey could find, the main one listed was on a trendy street in Sydney. Lacey couldn't fathom how Nico could've been married to this lady. She seemed so not his type.

Then she found the photo. A photo of Marietta and Nico's wedding. It was from the local Canberra newspaper, and showed the happy couple grinning at the camera, a very young Nico, so handsome in his tuxedo, and Marietta looking all of the sexy seductress in a figure-hugging white dress, with a full veil and a long satin train laid out around their feet.

A spike of pain like pure white heat shot through Lacey's chest.

"Oh, God! Oh, God." She snapped the laptop closed and got to her feet in a rush. Why in hell had she been so stupid as to want to torture herself? She really wished she hadn't seen that photo. Wanted to go back in time and undo the Google search. Because now, she would never rid herself of that image. That blanketing numbness she'd felt ever since she walked away from Nico finally evaporated. Her unfeeling daze morphed into a strong emotion she could finally recognize. Anger. Oh yes, she was angry all right. And also that feeling of betrayal was back.

That snake. How could he do this to her? It was probably lucky that Nico wasn't standing in front of her right now, because she might not be liable for her actions. She wanted to kick something, throw something, pummel something. She began to pace to and fro in front of the row of chairs. The first time she'd met Nico, she used her judo skills to forcibly throw him to the ground. And she wanted to do that to him again right now. She was a black belt in judo, but recently she'd let her training slide as she became busier and busier with her burgeoning career and her life with Nico. Judo had always been a release for her as well as a way to defend herself and give her some much-needed self-confidence. Right now, she craved the physical release of judo practice, the serenity of running through the same drill over and over. Tonight, she would make sure to attend a class. And tomorrow, and the day after. It was a way to funnel this terrible anger; otherwise she would likely let loose on anyone nearby. Especially Nico.

"Lacey?" Tyrell's voice came from down the hallway, and Lacey spun on her heel. Dragging in a deep breath, she calmed herself, pushed all her fury and sense of deception deep down into her stomach. There were other equally important things going on in her life right now, and Linc was one of them. She needed to remember that and not get too lost in her own self-pity.

"How is he?" she asked, walking quickly in Tyrell's direction.

His smile told her everything she needed to know, and she let out a gust of relief even before he spoke the words. "He's awake, Lacey." He gripped her by the shoulders with delight, and she gave him a quick hug in return.

"Oh, thank God," she said.

"They brought him out of the coma a few hours ago. He's awake, and aware of his surroundings, but he's still groggy and disorientated. I've been with him the whole time." Lacey could see the strain of the past few days written clearly on Tyrell's face. But he grabbed her hand, his fingers dark against her light ones. "But the doctors think he's over the worst of it."

"That's fantastic news," she replied, feeling brighter, more able to push her woes aside now that she knew Linc would be okay.

"Do you want to go and see him?"

"I'd love to, but I don't think I'm allowed in." As far as she knew, it was the next of kin only allowed in to intensive care.

"I'll go and talk to the nurse. He's allowed one visitor at a time, and I need to go and call his family and tell them the good news. He should have someone by his side, and I have a feeling he'd like to talk to you."

"Okay, that'd be great." She watched as Tyrell went to the nurses' desk and spoke to the duty nurse, at one stage pointing in Lacey's direction. Finally, the woman seemed to give in and nodded at him wearily. Tyrell wasn't one to take no for an answer. He gave her the thumbs-up and waved her down the hallway.

She quickly packed up her laptop into her backpack and walked the short distance to the double doors at the end of the hall. A bout of nervousness filled her stomach with butterflies and she was suddenly unsure what she should say to Linc. In some ways, she still felt as if she'd let him down. As if it was partly her fault he'd been attacked. She knew better than to say that to his face, because he'd wave off her apology as not warranted. But it didn't make the sick feeling in her gut go away. Straightening her shoulders, she pushed through the doors and immediately saw Linc in the nearest hospital bed. His eyes were closed, his head propped up slightly on two pillows, and she wondered if he was asleep. A nurse hovered beside another man a few beds down the line, and she looked up when Lacey entered.

"I'm Senior Constable Jackson's police partner," she said in a low voice when the nurse approached. "I have permission to be in here."

The dark-haired nurse considered her for a few moments before lifting her chin, then said, "As long as you keep quiet, and don't disturb anyone else."

"I won't," Lacey promised.

"He's still very groggy. He may drift in and out, even while you're talking to him. He needs as much rest as he can get."

"Okay." Lacey pulled the chair next to Linc's bed a little

closer and sat down. At the slight sound of the chair grating on the floor, Linc opened his eyes.

"Hey, partner," she said quietly.

He tried to smile, but it came out a little wonky. "Hey, Shorty," he mumbled in return. He raised his hand off the bedclothes as if searching for something, and she grasped his fingers in hers. His hand was cool to the touch, and she wrapped it in both of hers in an effort to warm him up.

"I'm so glad to see you," she said, and was surprised to feel the prick of tears behind her eyelids. "We were all worried about you." She coughed and sat straighter in her chair. Linc wouldn't appreciate her turning into a blubbering mess in the middle of his hospital ward.

"Nah, I'm a tough nut to crack."

"That you are," she agreed.

"Holy frack, I've got a headache though," he groaned, then seemed to brighten slightly. "I hear they're moving me out of here tonight, into my own room. If I'm a good boy, I might even get to eat some custard. Or Jell-O."

She laughed gently. Linc was a man who loved his steak and potatoes. But she was sure he'd be eating solid food again very soon. He closed his eyes as if the short conversation had exhausted him, and she sat in the silence for many moments, unsure what to do next.

"Have you caught the bastard that did this to me?" His question took her by surprise. Linc opened his eyes, and for a second they were clear and lucid. "I don't remember much," he admitted. "I saw something glinting in the dirt in between the roots of a tree. I bent down to pick it up, and I remember that you kept walking." He stopped talking and took a few deep breaths, as if rallying his strength. "But that's it. I don't remember what it was I saw that made me stop. And I don't remember going down." His brown eyes searched hers. "I was hit over the head, wasn't I? That's what Tyrell told me."

"Yes," Lacey answered slowly, unsure of how much to reveal. Unsure how much he was ready to hear. "And, no, we haven't found the perpetrator yet. But you know I'm not going to rest until we do. And that clue you found on the trail, it was a charm from a bracelet. We think the killer may have dropped it when they were dumping the body. It's definitely a clue, Linc. Your instincts were right."

"Good," he said, then closed his eyes again.

There was so much to tell Linc. He wouldn't even know yet that they'd found a second body. But that'd all come in time. Linc needed to rest and recover right now, it was the most important thing. If he could remember anything else later on, it might help in the investigation, but they shouldn't push him to try and recall anything he wasn't able or willing to do.

His hand relaxed in hers, and she knew he'd fallen asleep.

She still had work to do. Was still involved in a double murder case. Seeing Linc like this made her extra eager to catch the culprit. Easing her hand out of his grasp, she retrieved her laptop and balanced it on her knee. It was time to stop wallowing in her own self-pity and get on with it.

She spent the next twenty minutes researching Erica Nellenbach. And she found some interesting stuff. The silver Olympic medal was genuine. Erica had been a gymnastic star from an early age and was recruited to join the German gymnastic team when she was only twelve. The German team had high hopes for her, and she'd become a celebrity in the gymnastics community as well as with the whole nation. Erica was seventeen when she went to the Los Angeles Olympics and won a silver medal in the individual floor exercise. But then she seemed to disappear from the limelight, as many shooting stars often did. Lacey couldn't find much about the years right after that, but Erica must've moved to Tasmania when she was approximately twenty-five, as her name began to appear in the registry of gymnast coaches around then. The Somerset Gymnastic Club was started ten years ago and had grown in leaps and bounds, moving from an old building on the outskirts of town to the new, modern one three years ago. Without access to Erica's financial records, Lacey couldn't tell for sure, but a lot of children who attended the club came from wealthy families, so it seemed her assumption that the money for the club came from high fees might be correct.

But then things got a whole lot more intriguing. Lacey decided to look up the police databases and was surprised when she found that charges had been filed against Erica less than two years ago. Charges of verbal and emotional abuse of a young girl. The charges hadn't proceeded to trial, as it seemed the matter had been settled out of court. Which meant Erica had most likely paid the family off.

Interesting. It meant Erica had access to large sums of money, these kinds of things usually settled in the hundreds of thousands of dollars. But clearly it was worth it to Erica to keep her reputation clean, so the accusations never came to light.

Suddenly, Tyrell was standing next to her. She'd been so focussed on her computer, she hadn't even heard him come in. "I've made all my calls, and had a bite to eat," he told her quietly as she closed the laptop and gathered her things. "Thanks for sitting with him."

"All good," she replied. "He's been asleep most of the time. But he woke up for a short while. He told me he doesn't remember being hit, and he doesn't remember what he stopped to pick up," she informed him. "I haven't told him about the second body yet. I thought we should wait, there's not a lot he can do about it, anyway."

"No. But you can guarantee he'll be itching to get back on the job," Tyrell said with a frown.

"Probably a lot like his uncle." Lacey smiled at Tyrell and then the nurse shot them a warning glance, so she hurriedly whispered her goodbyes.

The second she stepped out into the hospital hallway, her phone began to buzz in her pocket. She took it out and ducked into the nearest waiting room.

It was Nico. She lifted her eyes to the ceiling and chewed her bottom lip. Should she answer it? She probably owed him that much. Pressing the answer button, she put the phone to her ear.

"Lacey?" So many questions were wrapped up in that single word. The sound of his voice so familiar and dear had her stomach curling in knots.

"Nico," she replied coolly.

"We need to talk. Where are you?"

For a split second, she had a crazy urge to just hang up on him because she didn't know what to say. But that'd solve nothing, and she wasn't a fifteen-year-old girl subject to teenage tantrums anymore. "Yes, we need to talk," she agreed. "But I'm going to judo training tonight. I'll see you after that," she said flatly. Like she'd promised herself earlier, she was going to the dojo and nothing was going to stop her. Nico wouldn't talk her out of it; she wouldn't let him. It'd be to both their benefit if she had a hard training session tonight. She'd be more likely to resist the urge to throw him to the floor that way.

"I don't know what time I'll be home tonight," Nico admitted. He always worked late when he had a big case on.

"I guess I'll see you when I see you, then." She rang off and put the phone back in her pocket. Her shift was nearly over. She'd email her findings to Gorman rather than going back to the station. Call her a chicken, but she wasn't ready to confront Nico in person yet.

CHAPTER EIGHT

Nico let himself quietly in the back door to be greeted by a welcoming Smudge, whose claws made a ticking noise on the kitchen linoleum as he danced around Nico's legs. "Hey, buddy," he whispered. At least someone was pleased to see him. He'd left the station as soon as he possibly could, but it was still after eleven, and he wondered if Lacey would still be awake. The house was dark, only the kitchen light burning bright. A soft orange glow emanated from the living room, and he knew Lacey must've lit the fire at some stage, but it had burnt down to embers now. It was almost too late in the year to need a fire. But after the unseasonably hot run of days, a cold change had swept over the coast tonight, bringing strong winds and drizzle. Tasmanian weather, even in summer, was never predictable.

A plate of food sat on the kitchen countertop covered with a dishcloth. Lacey must've cooked him dinner. What did that signify? Did it mean she'd forgiven him? Or was she just too kindhearted to let him starve? He went over and lifted the cloth. Steak Diane with roast potatoes and steamed veggies. One of his favorites.

Fuck. Had he messed this all up? Had he ruined the only good relationship he'd ever had by keeping this secret? His stomach churned at the idea, and he suddenly wasn't hungry. But just as he was placing the plate in the fridge, a noise alerted him and he turned to see Lacey standing in the doorway leading into the living room, a glass of red wine in her hand.

He stood up straight, plate still in hand.

"You need to eat," she said, looking pointedly at the food. There was no *Hello, how was the rest of your day?"* She just stared at him, making no move to come any farther into the kitchen. She always greeted him with a kiss. Always.

"I'm not hungry."

"Neither was I, but I forced it down anyway."

Coils of guilt furled through his chest at the underlying implication. That she was feeling as shit as he was. It killed him that she'd been sitting there alone in the dark living room, waiting for him to come home.

"Heat it up in the microwave," she suggested. "I've got a bottle open, come and join me in the living room." She turned her back and disappeared, but at least she'd extended the olive branch. And he was going to take it.

Foot tapping on the floor with impatience, he couldn't wait until the microwave dinged and so he retrieved his plate when the food was only tepid. But he needed to talk to Lacey more than he needed hot food.

When he entered the living room, Lacey had turned on the side table lamp and was sitting in the winged chair with her feet tucked up beneath her. Smudge had his nose resting on her knee, as if he could feel her pain.

Nico took a seat on the couch nearest her and rested his plate on his knee. Wordlessly, she handed him a glass full to the brim of red wine. An unfamiliar silence stretched between them.

He understood that he was the one who needed to break the impasse, but he didn't know where to start. He'd already tried to explain back at the bakery, but Lacey hadn't wanted to listen and he couldn't really blame her.

The food was congealing on the plate, so he took a bite of steak while he decided what to tell her, washing it down with a good slug of wine. The truth, of course. It had to be the truth if she was going to believe him. If she was going to forgive him.

"I heard the good news about Linc," he said, taking the easy path, trying to break the ice before he dove into the deep end.

"Yes." She met Nico's eyes for the first time since he'd walked into the room. "He woke up this afternoon, and I even talked to him for a short while." Lacey almost smiled at that.

"I'm really glad he's going to be okay," Nico said around another mouthful of food. "He's a good officer. And I know how much he means to you." He wasn't being sarcastic. Nico understood how close police partners often got. It was more than just a friendship, there was a trust involved, a commitment to have each other's back, no matter what. Lacey had talked openly and honestly about her relationship with Linc, and Nico understood what the other man meant to her, and didn't begrudge their special relationship. There was nothing romantic between them, and Nico was glad she had the opportunity to work with such an honorable, decent cop.

"He was hopefully being moved to a private room tonight, so I'll pop back into the hospital tomorrow before my shift to see him again," Lacey said, but the congenial air seemed to fade as she regarded him once more with her cool gaze, and he knew his short reprieve was over. He needed to tell her everything about his past life.

"Right," he replied, more as a way to give himself time to compose himself. "Ah, where to start?"

But she wasn't about to help him out, she merely kept her

chilly gaze fixed on him, not saying anything, waiting him out.

He coughed and took another drink of wine. He may as well start at the beginning. "I was twenty-one when I met Marietta. In my second year of my police career after graduating the academy in Canberra. We met through a function I attended with my mother. It was a fancy fashion shindig, and my mother needed someone to escort her, so I was happy to oblige." Nico took another mouthful of lukewarm potato, his mind rewinding the years back to that fateful night. "Marietta was the most beautiful woman I'd ever seen," he admitted. "I was blinded by her beauty and her sophistication. I was flattered that she was even interested in me, and…" He hated to admit it, but… "I was thinking with my dick more than my head." Lacey raised her eyebrows at this, but said nothing, so Nico continued, "She asked me on a date and I said yes. At the time I couldn't see how wrong it was. I didn't stop to wonder why a woman ten years my senior was pursuing me; I should've known better. My mother never approved of her."

Lacey gave a wan smile. "You were young and impressionable, I get that," she said, then tipped her chin in his direction to indicate he should keep talking.

"That's exactly right. I just didn't realize it until it was too late. We had a whirlwind romance. It sounds strange to say it, but she swept me off my feet, and before I knew it, I'd proposed to her. My mother told me I was stupid, and it'd never work. What was a hard-working cop going to do with a wife who pursued the highlife and liked to surround herself with luxuries? She moved into my apartment—and perhaps that should've sounded the first warning bell, but I wasn't listening—and we were happy for a while. But the second we got married all my mother's predictions came true. Marietta became demanding and complained I worked too many long hours. She had expensive tastes and was spending all my money. Her fledgling fashion designer brand wasn't doing very well, and she was pumping any spare cash we had into it."

"That doesn't sound one hundred percent fair," Lacey commented, twirling the glass stem between her fingers. "But isn't that what marriage is all about? What's yours is hers and what's hers is yours?"

"Maybe in some marriages," he replied with a grunt. "But I was so blinded by…let's call it lust…that I agreed to sign a prenup signing away any right to half of her fashion brand if we ever divorced. Which was fine by me, at the time."

"Hmm, she sounds like a smart cookie," Lacey mused. "Smart and manipulative."

"Yes, she was both," he agreed. "Anyway, we started arguing all the time, mainly about money. And one night we had a doozy. We were yelling so loud we must've woken the neighbors." Nico cringed as he remembered that night. "I've never seen her so mad. I think I probably used words such as *bitch,* and *cougar,* and *conniving.* And she got so mad she let it slip that she only married me so she could gain permanent residency. It all started to make horrible sense. She tried to take the words back, but it was too late. I was gutted."

Lacey's face creased with concern, and Nico knew he might be finally getting through. "It sounds like a bit of a nightmare," she finally conceded.

"It was," he admitted. "It's a time in my life that I'd rather forget. Looking back on it, there weren't many nice things I could say about Marietta. She was the one who put the idea in my head to do the specialist training. To become a detective. I guess I need to thank her for that. But for everything else…" He wouldn't say the words, but he despised her. No, she deserved a stronger word than despise. Detest. Abhor. Loathe. "I have no good feelings left for her."

"That's very sad," Lacey allowed. "And it goes some way to explaining your behavior today. It's nice to finally have an explanation. So thank you for telling me. But it doesn't change the fact that you kept her secret. You never told me you were married. You have to know that I feel foolish and betrayed. I'm not sure how to cope with all this," she confessed. "And I'm not sure where we go from here."

It wasn't the answer he was hoping for. He understood why she might feel this way, but his reasons for not telling her were valid, he just needed to convince her.

"I never told anyone about the marriage," he blurted, leaning forward in his chair. "The only people who knew were my mother and my two siblings and a couple of people I was close to at work. Nobody in Tasmania knows. I wanted to keep it that way because I was ashamed. Ashamed of the way she used me. Ashamed of the way I couldn't see through my own infatuation to the truth. That she was a conniving snake who only wanted me because I was her ticket to Australian citizenship. That hurt. It really hurt." He sat back quickly, nearly spilling his wine. How else could he convince her? "I was going to tell you. I promise I was." He thought back to yesterday, after they'd made love and how he decided he wanted to marry Lacey. Now he had put that all in jeopardy. Because he couldn't ask her to marry him now. Not with this hanging over their heads. Not now he'd just discovered that he was in fact still married. He closed his eyes, wanting to just disappear.

A warm hand landed on his knee. "I know you were." Lacey's voice was soft and reassuring, and he opened his eyes. "It sounds like a terrible time in your life, and I could see why you would want to forget all about it."

Relief flowed through him, but it was short-lived. Because he knew he needed to tell her the rest. He laid his hand over hers, trying to find the strength to reveal the worst. "I honestly thought we were divorced. I signed the paperwork, and I thought that was the end of it." He drew in a deep breath to fortify himself. "But I should have followed up. I was busy with work, Marietta moved out, and I had no contact with her anymore."

"But?" Lacey questioned, when he let the silence stretch out too long.

"But, Marietta just informed me that she never signed her side of the paperwork. The divorce was never finalized." The words stung like a viper strike to the middle of his chest. "It seems we're still married," he confessed, looking up into Lacey's eyes that were shining golden in the light of the fire, but he could see the confusion written in her gaze. He was definitely going to confirm this was the case, but Marietta had no reason to lie. Not now. "She didn't sign the paperwork, and so her request for citizenship carried on. It can take between three to four years for an application for permanent residency to be approved. And you have to prove you've remained married for that whole time." He hung his head in shame. "Marietta got her citizenship because she didn't sign the divorce papers. She got what she wanted from me anyway, even though I left her. Even though I wanted nothing to do with her little plan." It was so fucking ironic, he could barely believe it. He felt doubly betrayed. She'd used and abused him when he'd married her, and then she'd continued to fuck him over without his knowledge or consent. What a giant clusterfuck of a disaster.

"Maybe bitch was the right word," she mumbled under her breath. "She's certainly a piece of work. And I'm sorry you got caught up in her schemes." Her hand still rested on his knee, but a coolness shrouded her features. "So, what's she doing in Tasmania? Is she after some sort of reconciliation? Does she want to get back together with you?" He could hear the scorn in her voice. But he could also hear the fear and pain. A small part of her was terrified that was the reason Marietta had reappeared.

"God no!" He got to his feet, and began to pace, no longer able to sit still. Smudge moved quickly from his spot by the fire, standing out of the way in the door, his ears and tail drooping at the sound of raised voices. "And you have to believe me, even if she did want me back, there is *absolutely* no way I would have any part of it."

Lacey also got to her feet, standing in front of him so that he halted his pacing. Her slight figure was outlined by the flames behind her, and all he wanted to do was take her into his arms. But as he reached out, she put her hand in the middle of his chest to stop him.

"That's good to hear, Nico. But you haven't told me what she wants yet."

"She's met a man that she wants to marry. Some wealthy bloke from America. And to do that, she needs the divorce to go through properly this time. She's had a lawyer draw up the new papers and brought them down here to make sure I signed them immediately. It was just a coincidence that she ran into us in the bakery. She was on her way to find me at the station." He could feel the outline of her fingers pushing into his breastbone. There was no softness to Lacey tonight, she was all rigid resistance.

"That'd almost be amusing if it wasn't so bloody sad," she replied.

"I'm definitely going to sign them," he told her. "But I needed to talk to you first."

"Maybe you shouldn't sign, just to get some of your own back," she harrumphed. Then she took a step backward, but the imprint of her fingers remained on his body.

"I'm going to sleep in the spare bedroom tonight," she said simply.

His heart felt like it'd turned to ice. Everything had been so perfect. They were perfect together. The perfect couple. And because of his one mistake, it was all going to come tumbling down around him.

"Okay," he acknowledged, though he wanted to stop her. Wanted to drag her to bed with him, even if all they did was lie together, skin on skin, connected and as one.

"Come on, Smudge." Lacey put an affectionate hand on Smudge's head, and he followed her down the hallway. Nico didn't object. All he had was Lacey's best interests at heart. She needed time to think, and he had to give it to her. Lacey needed the dog's company to see her through the night, and he wasn't going to take that away from her either. She was hurting, and for once he couldn't be the one to soothe her.

Because he was the one causing the pain.

CHAPTER NINE

Lacey stared at the interior of Dotti 2.0 but couldn't dredge up the enthusiasm to climb inside. She was supposed to be spending a few precious hours working on her Kombi this morning before her next shift, but her mind wouldn't stop churning. Nico had left early for work on his motorcycle after they'd gone through the motions of eating breakfast but not speaking and hardly making eye contact. She was still no closer to an answer for her dilemma. A wall seemed to have gone up between them and she could see no way past it. Yet.

Her night spent alone in the spare bed had been a terrible experience. She'd hardly slept a wink, and at least three or four times, she had to stop herself from flinging back the bedclothes and marching down the hallway to throw herself into Nico's arms. Even her intense judo training at the dojo last night hadn't helped her to sleep. And her lack of deep sleep allowed the nightmares to come creeping in. More than once, Lacey had sat bolt upright in bed, cold sweat running down her spine as memories of soaring over the cliff in her van sent her heart racing and her arms windmilling as she fell through the air. She missed him. Missed his strong body next to hers. Missed listening to his gentle breathing while he lay sleeping, and the tickle of his stubble on her cheek as she snuggled into his shoulder. And she wondered if he were missing her just as badly.

What should she do with these feelings that wanted to burst out of her, like an alien ripping through her stomach and splattering everything with her suffering? The easy way out was to just forgive Nico. To put aside her feelings of betrayal and move on.

She should be able to empathize with Nico. She of all people should know what it was like to be the one who was being manipulated, being controlled by her own emotions. After having to deal with her mother for thirty-odd years. She should be able to forgive him; it wasn't really his fault that woman was a complete nightmare. But there was one little sticking point that was stopping her.

Why hadn't he told her?

Illogically, it made her wonder what else he was keeping secret from her.

Was there something else he wasn't telling her? Was he perhaps still in love with Marietta? Was there some kind of deep connection he'd had with her that he'd never share with any other woman? It was stupid and irrational, especially in light of all he'd told her about that woman last night. But it still hurt deeply that he hadn't respected her enough to tell her this one thing from his past.

She hated keeping secrets. Hated other people keeping secrets. Her mother was the queen of keeping secrets. Because knowledge was power. If you knew something someone else didn't, then you held power over them. And you could wield that power in all sorts of dangerous ways.

Lacey had been completely open and honest with Nico. Once they had become a couple, she kept nothing from him. And even before that, she'd confided in him about her PTSD, and about her broken family.

"Lacey, dear. Are you in there?" an older woman's voice

drifted in through the roller door. Smudge bounded outside with a welcoming bark. "Hello, my beautiful boy. If you're here, she must be around somewhere." Lacey turned to see Margie marching through the door with Smudge on her heels. "Oh, good. I wasn't sure if you'd be working today."

"My shift doesn't start till twelve," Lacey replied, giving Margie an awkward hug, maneuvering her arms around the big plate Margie was carrying. Her arms were a little stiff from her workout last night, and she winced slightly, but it was a good soreness and she embraced the feeling. "I was trying to get some work done on Dotti." She gave a meaningful sigh, because that now looked unlikely this morning.

"I brought you a plate of my famous rock cakes," Margie said, eyeing the Kombi with a stern eye. She didn't think it was right that a young woman might want to travel around the country alone. She'd never say that in so many words to Lacey's face, but she was worried that Lacey was planning to leave Nico once her van was finished. It was illogical but in her own way it showed how much Margie cared.

"Let's take them inside." Lacey knew this wasn't the only reason for Margie's visit. Much as she adored the older woman, Margie was renowned for being the town gossip. She'd be digging for details on the recent double murder.

"I'd love a cup of tea, dear," Margie replied, a question mark in her raised eyebrows. "Herb is in his shed tinkering with his bicycle, and I'm at a bit of a loose end."

Lacey smiled indulgently and took the plate of rock cakes from Margie's outstretched hands. "I could do with a cuppa myself," she said, silently bidding her morning work on Dotti goodbye.

A few minutes later, they were both seated at the small kitchen table, and Lacey sank her teeth into a rock cake. They were still warm from the oven, and she got a burst of sweetness as she bit into a sultana. Rock cakes were no longer fashionable, but she was glad Margie kept up her grandmother's tradition because they were delicious. She was also glad for the soothing babble of Margie's chatter as she sipped her tea; it helped to remind her that her life wasn't really falling apart, and normality was a good thing.

"What's wrong, luv? You're looking a bit peaky today." Margie pierced her with her knowing gaze over the top of her mug.

"What?" Lacey nearly spat out her tea. She thought she'd been doing a good job of keeping her face free from all her inner turmoil. How had Margie unerringly known something was wrong? As if she were a bloodhound on an emotional trail of discovery. "Nothing's wrong. I'm just a little tired. Overworked, you know."

Margie studied her for a few more seconds. "If you say so, dear. But I can see it in your eyes. You're sad about something. Did you and you Nico have a fight? You don't have to tell me, of course. But sometimes talking something out can help." The older woman's features softened, and she reached out and patted the back of Lacey's hand.

Her touch set off a chord deep inside Lacey. It was the affectionate touch of a grandmother, something Lacey sorely lacked in her life. Margie truly cared about her welfare, and Lacey really wanted to confide in her. She needed another woman's advice. Some maternal guidance. Which she would never get from her own mother. Both her grandparents on her mother's side were long gone—killed in a tragic bus crash while on a tourist trip to Italy. It was supposed to be the trip of a lifetime, to celebrate her grandfather's retirement. Lacey had only been three or four at the time and hardly remembered them. And her grandmother on her father's side, Betty, was in an aged care home suffering from early-onset dementia, and had been afflicted for as long as Lacey could remember. Betty's husband, Frank, had been killed in the Vietnam War, before Lacey was even born. So she had no true grandparents to rely on.

Lacey drew in a deep breath. "You're a hard woman to fool, Margie. You should've been a cop, you know," she said with a forced laugh. "Yes, Nico and I did have a disagreement." Actually, now she thought about it, this was their first really big argument. They'd had quarrels about small things, like whose turn it was to clean the bathroom, and Lacey would snap at him when he continuously tried to backseat drive when she was in charge of the vehicle. But otherwise, they agreed on the big things. And they had no need to quarrel over finances, because Lacey had her trust fund which made her financially independent.

Should she tell Margie what was going on? For a second, she almost blurted it all out. About the tall, dark seductress who'd once been married to Nico. But although Margie was well-meaning, she was also renowned as the town gossip, and the last thing either she or Nico needed was people talking about them behind their backs, discussing Nico's past, and dissecting her reaction to it. So she held her tongue.

Instead, she decided on some misdirection. "But we'll sort it out. We always do. I think it's partly to do with how much we're both on edge after those two bodies were found."

"Oh, yes." Margie's eyes lit up with delight, taking the bait, just as Lacey knew she would. "I watched that sexy Chief Inspector on the news this morning." Lacey nearly choked on her rock cake. She had never thought of Shadbolt as sexy before. She guessed he probably was good looking, if you liked that gruff, solidly built, silver-fox type. But Margie went on before she could comment. "He said they'd identified the first victim. That poor wee girl. But you're still no closer to identifying the second one. Imagine that. Two bodies. I can hardly believe we have another murderer in our midst. Does it mean we have a serial killer?" Her birdlike eyes fixed on Lacey.

"It's too early to tell," Lacey said. She knew when she opened this can of worms that she'd have to be careful about what she said. But it was preferable to having to talk about her private life, because these questions, she knew how to handle. "We need to determine cause of death for both the girls. And try and find any links between the two."

"So you still don't know how they died?" Margie had placed her mug of tea on the table, staring at Lacey intently.

Lacey shook her head. "We're still waiting for the results of the autopsy." These were all details she knew she was free to share. It was only the intimate details of the murders and finding clues about the killer that she had to keep secret.

"Gosh." Margie sighed dramatically. "It makes me think about poor Rania. Takes me back to that day, you know, when I found her. At least it was obvious how she died." Margie gave a small hiccupping sob.

Now it was Lacey's turn to be the one to give out comfort, and she patted Margie's hand. "I know," she said soothingly. "It must be hard for you and Herb. Maybe you shouldn't watch the news if it's going to upset you."

"Oh, no, I'll always watch the news. I think it's important to know what's going on around us." Margie sat up straighter. "We need to stay informed. As a community and as individuals. And we rely on you, our police force to give us the facts we need to stay safe. So, are you going to tell me? Is it a serial killer?"

Lacey sighed and wondered how she was going to escape from the canny older woman's clutches.

* * *

Lacey took her now customary seat at the back of the operations room. Nico had called a surprise second briefing just as she'd walked down the hallway to her office ready to start her shift. She lifted an inquisitive eyebrow in Tyrell's direction, but he merely shrugged and took the seat next to her. Lacey was yet to catch up on what this morning's briefing had revealed. She'd like to know how the interview with Zoya's mother had gone. Had she revealed anything important about her daughter's life? Did they have an updated list of any enemies, friends, and relatives they should be looking at? Or was anything found at Zoya's apartment that might help in the case? She jiggled her foot in agitation, wanting to get this over with so she could get herself up to speed on the case.

She glanced over at Tyrell sitting next to her. It was good to have the senior constable back at work—soon-to-be sergeant if the rumors were to be believed. Linc was doing so much better, so he'd finally left his nephew's bedside, happy to leave him in the hands of his mother, who'd arrived last night, and the capable nurses.

Lacey had made a quick stop at the hospital on the way into town and was surprised and pleased to see Linc sitting up in bed looking for all the world like he was back to his normal charming self. He must be feeling better, because he was even chatting up a nurse as Lacey entered the room. The nurse flushed beetroot red when Lacey coughed to make her presence known and excused herself on the flimsy pretext of suddenly hearing another patient calling her.

Lacey had stood at the end of his hospital bed and beamed at her partner, so happy to see him recovering well.

"How's it going, Shorty?" She'd winced at the nickname, but for once didn't take umbrage.

"Not bad," she'd replied, hoping Linc didn't have the same uncanny ability as Margie to draw out the fact she was actually not doing fine. The worry that she and Nico might be on some severely rocky ground had been eating away at her guts all morning. Even after Margie's visit, she still had no clear answer.

But he'd only asked her about the investigation, moaning that Tyrell wouldn't tell him anything because he was trying to protect him from himself. Linc made a rude sound at that, and Lacey had chewed her bottom lip wondering how much trouble she was going to get in if she accidentally told him something Tyrell deemed unnecessary.

Happily, right on cue, Linc's mother had appeared. A statuesque woman, with a mass of dark hair piled elegantly on top of her head in a large bun, wearing a black dress that hugged her voluptuous figure. She looked nothing like a frazzled mother who'd flown halfway across the world to be at her injured son's bedside that Lacey had been expecting. Linc's mother introduced herself as Syl, shaking Lacey's hand with a strong grip, and telling her that Linc was one lucky man to have her as a police partner. She could see where Linc got his charm from. She'd left the two of them arguing affably about whether he should be chatting up that particular redheaded nurse.

"Sorry," Nico bustled through the door juggling his laptop, Sally-Ann close on his heels, and the buzz of conversation quietened. "I know we already had a meeting this morning, but I just got some news back from autopsy, and I thought you might like to hear this." Nico's gaze settled on Lacey for a short second before he turned to face the whiteboard. It wasn't long enough for her to read his face and decipher exactly what he was thinking. It was normal for him to keep his feelings hidden in their everyday work environment. But this was different. Usually, even when he had his detective face on, she could glean some of what was going on in Nico's head. Not today. The walls were up higher than she'd ever seen. Higher perhaps than even back on the first day they'd met. Which scared her.

Just then, the other two detectives hurried in, and quietly

slid into the two chairs next to Lacey.

Nico acknowledged them with the nod before saying, "Autopsy has come back with cause of death for the first victim, Zoya Kibel." He stopped talking until he had everyone's undivided attention. "Just as we thought, she was hung by the neck until she asphyxiated." The silence was deafening as everyone digested this news. It was crystal clear what the ligature marks around the girl's neck meant. Ligature marks didn't always indicate someone had been strung up; sometimes victims were tied up by the neck, like a dog, to keep them constrained. But it was a suspicion that'd been floating around in all of their minds. It was a horrible way to die, because it often took long minutes for the victim to lose consciousness. Nico held up his hand to forestall any questions. "Dr. Lagos is still working on the second body, and he won't commit to a formal written document yet, but it seems likely the second woman also died the same way."

Almost without realizing it, Lacey leaned forward in her chair. This was the connection they'd been looking for. The link between the two women. The first decent bit of information that could help them solve the crime. And this link also possibly pointed to a serial killer. Although usually you needed up to three bodies before they could be classified as serial murders. It could be as simple as someone with a vendetta against these two girls. Not some crazy criminal out to murder half the female population of Burnie.

Everyone in the room looked at Nico with the same intense gaze, and Lacey knew they were all wondering the same thing. Could these murders be part of the state-wide manhunt that was currently being carried out for a suspected serial killer? Cause of death for all three victims in the other cases were all strangulation. And on the surface, both strangulation and hanging might look similar. But she knew both methods of murder were completely different.

Strangulation was much more intimate; it required physical contact and was often done face-to-face. Lacey hadn't had much to do with the serial killer case. That was Nico's department; he was liaising with detectives from Hobart. But there'd been no more victims over the past six months, and the case had gone cold. Perhaps the serial killer had changed his modus operandi slightly. There were all sorts of reasons why he might do this. She wondered if Nico was going to reference them now.

Nico raised a hand. "I know what you're all thinking, but for now we are going to regard these two murders on their own merits."

"But there could be a connection to the sex-worker killer," Pederson said loudly. "I don't see why we're discarding them as a possible suspect."

"We're not discarding them," Nico replied steadily. "I merely want to profile this killer on these murders alone. If the facts point us in the direction of the so-called serial killer, then we will follow that line of investigation. But I don't want us to get bogged down too early in the investigation into thinking these are one and the same person."

It was a fair point, and now she saw it like that, she agreed with Nico's assessment. Lacey glanced sideways at Pederson to see his reaction. He scowled, but said nothing further. Saito kept her unwavering gaze fixed on Nico, not even acknowledging her partner's discontent.

"There's also one major point of difference between these murders and the other three attributed to the serial killer. Autopsy found both girls had large doses of ketamine in their system. So these girls were drugged before they were killed, as we suspected. Probably to make them easy to move around without having them struggle or call out."

Quiet whispers started up around the room, and Lacey turned to Tyrell to gauge his reaction to Nico's news.

Gorman stood up and spoke above the growing hubbub. "Do we know for sure if our victims were hung somewhere in the reserve and then dumped in the river?"

"I'm hoping that's one of the questions you can help me answer," Nico replied with a hint of relief. "At the moment, we're not sure how the scenarios played out. Were they abducted? There was no sign of a struggle at Zoya's apartment, and no sign of a break-in. Indeed, her handbag and phone and other belongings were found on the kitchen countertop, untouched. And her car was in its usual parking space below the apartment, untouched. So why did she just walk out of her house and not take anything with her? And where did she go? It seems likely the killer injected ketamine to subdue his victims, perhaps taking Zoya unawares as she walked into her house after returning from work. We don't know if the girls were then killed at another location, and brought to the reserve under the cover of darkness. And if so why? We need to go back and re-examine the reserve. Look for anything that might point to the location of the murders. Look for a spot where the murders might've been carried out."

"A hanging tree, you mean," Gorman piped up, then quickly looked abashed when Nico frowned at him. "Sorry, that was in bad taste, I didn't mean it like that. I..."

"Funny you should mention that." Sally-Ann took over the slightly awkward silence that'd descended, also standing up next to Nico and adding her frown to his. "Because even though you made a tactless joke, you're on the right track. I think I may have found some information that could be pertinent to this case."

The whispers died down as everyone focussed on Sally-Ann.

"At first I thought it was just a coincidence. But when Nico told me the cause of death in these new murders, it took on a much more sinister meaning." She paused as she flicked through a pile of papers in her arms. Holding out an A4 picture of another young woman, she passed it to Nico, who stuck it to the whiteboard. "This young lady's name is Tia Brown, and she committed suicide four years ago when she was only seventeen by hanging herself from a tree in Platypus Reserve."

So many questions were fired at Sally-Ann, she hardly knew which one to answer first.

"Are they sure it was suicide?" That one was from Saito.

"Yes. Tia left a suicide note. And it was documented she was suffering from anorexia and depression at the time. But perhaps we now have cause to look deeper into this matter," Nico replied.

"Do we know exactly where her body was found in the reserve?" It was Hickey who asked this one.

"Yes. It's in the documentation. There's an old King Billy Pine in a clearing only a few hundred feet from the parking lot. It's believed she climbed up in the middle of the night, dragging a heavy rope with her, tied it around her neck and jumped from a branch around twenty feet off the ground. A local ranger found her the next morning."

"If this was suicide, why do we think it's connected to these two murders? It was four years ago. That girl was much younger than our victims. If the only link you can find is the fact but she hung herself, then it's pretty flimsy don't you think?" This time, it was Pederson. Lacey was beginning to think of him as the thorn in Nico's side. He certainly liked to argue and to nitpick. Was that a sign of a good detective? Or just proof he never believed what anybody else said. An arrogant pig in other words.

"Maybe." This time, it was Sally-Ann who answered. "But if she'd lived, she would be the same age as Zoya Kibel is now. Zoya had just turned twenty-one."

That caused everyone to pause for a second.

"I'm not sure if this is connected in any way," Nico conceded. "But I am going to investigate further. I'm going to talk to Tia's mother this afternoon. And I'd like Pederson and Saito to go out to the reserve and see if they can find the tree where Tia died. See if you can find any sort of connection between it and where the two bodies were dumped."

"You mean, you want us to determine if the murders were carried out there?" Saito asked, cool as a cucumber.

"That's exactly what I mean. But I also want you to try and see the broader picture. Is that tree significant somehow to where the other bodies were dumped? Or are they three completely random sites? Is this merely coincidence?"

"Might not be able to answer that question," Saito said blandly.

Nico gave her a sour look but chose not to comment. "The rest of you can go back to your allotted tasks, but keep this new information in mind, see if it relates to anything new that you find."

People began to stand and mill around the room. The two out-of-town detectives made a beeline for the door. Lacey stood also, readjusting her duty belt, which always rode up uncomfortably when she sat down.

"Carmichael, you're with me." Lacey startled at the sound of her name. Then screwed up her nose and opened her mouth to argue, but shut it again just as quickly. Nico had cornered her nicely, because she couldn't very well object in front of all their colleagues. Pursing her lips into a thin line she waited at the back of the room until he lifted his chin in her direction, indicating he was ready to go. She fell into step behind him, and they walked without speaking through the maze of corridors and down to the undercover parking lot, where he got into the driver side of the nearest cruiser.

With her fingers resting on the door handle, she drew in a

deep breath. She wasn't ready to be cooped up inside a car with Nico just yet. But she had no choice, and she had to handle this like an adult. A couple more deep breaths and she opened the door, putting on her game face.

"Where does the mother live?" she asked in clipped tones, before she'd even taken her seat, preempting anything he might want to say.

"Not too far away," Nico replied, turning the key in the ignition.

"Well, that was a bloody vague answer," she snapped, in no mood for his games.

"She lives in Romaine, less than ten minutes away," he sighed, then finally turned to look at her. "Just long enough for me to say what I need to say."

She huffed out a breath. So he did have an ulterior motive for bringing her along this afternoon. Effectively holding her captive so she had no choice but to listen to him. Crossing her arms over her chest, she pouted through the windshield. Perhaps she was being childish, but she didn't care to be forced into this situation. Especially when he pulled rank to do it.

"I signed the divorce papers this morning. Marietta is on her way off the island as we speak." Nico cut straight to the chase, speaking in an expressionless tone so that she couldn't even judge how he felt about that.

"Good," she replied. But her reluctant relief was more about Marietta leaving than it was about him signing the papers. "At least that means she's finally out of your life for good."

"She was always out of my life for good, as far as I was concerned, Lacey."

"Hmm."

Silence filled the cab.

"I missed you last night," he finally said. His words stung

like he'd shot a barb right into her heart. She knew she was probably being unreasonable, but she couldn't rid herself of the icy feeling in the pit of her belly every time she thought about Nico being married to that woman, and so she didn't reply. "I'm really not sure how else to make it up to you, Lacey," he added as they pulled into the driveway of a suburban red-brick home. "I've signed the papers and sent Marietta packing. I wish with all my heart this had never happened. I'm a stupid ass for not checking the divorce went through all those years ago and I just want to apologize with all my heart." He turned to look at her, the guarded wall he'd erected back at the station finally coming down enough to let her see his pain. "I'm sorry, Lace. Can you forgive me?" He held up his hands in supplication.

Lacey uncrossed her arms and tipped her head back against the car seat to stare at the ceiling. She hated to see Nico hurting like this, almost as much as she hated the ache in her own heart. But she couldn't bring herself to say the words *I forgive you*, they seemed to stick in her throat.

"I just need some time," she replied, softening her tone. Which was the truth. She needed a little space to sort out her convoluted feelings. She still loved Nico. Desperately. And with her whole heart. So she needed to find a way to wash these feelings of betrayal from under her skin and find new common ground with Nico, so she could tell him how much she loved him once again.

CHAPTER TEN

Nico knocked on the door and took a step back, Lacey right behind him. He hoped Mrs. Brown was home. He also hoped he had his game face on, because the last thing he needed was a member of the public to think he wasn't in full control of his faculties. But the ride over here in the cruiser with Lacey had rattled him. She'd been so cold, so uncommunicative. It was like she'd morphed into a completely different person. At least she'd softened at the very end, telling him she needed more time. More time for what?

He couldn't believe how quickly his love life had gone to shit. He'd thought he and Lacey were rock-solid, that nothing could shake their love for each other. How wrong he'd been.

If she needed time, then that's what he'd give her. But he wasn't sure he'd survive the wait. He was trying his damnedest to understand where Lacey was coming from. Surprisingly, it wasn't Marietta that was Lacey's problem—she wasn't jealous or resentful that he'd been married to someone else—but his own stupidity that was causing the rift. Lacey said she'd felt betrayed he hadn't told her about his marriage sooner. That he'd blindsided her. Truth was important to Lacey, he knew that. He couldn't count the number of times they'd lain in bed together, arms around each other, and both swearing to hold nothing back. He was a believer in telling the truth as well. Nothing was ever gained by keeping secrets. So why had he held this one thing back from Lacey?

He could hardly find a solution to that question himself. It was most likely a vain attempt to protect Lacey from inflicting hurt. As well as protecting himself, as he didn't want to spiral again by opening that can of worms. But he knew he needed to dig deeper than that to find the answer if he was to reassure Lacey. He was ashamed at how easily Marietta had tricked him. He thought he was above those types of men who only thought with their dick and had their heads turned by a beautiful woman. Clearly, that wasn't the case. Marietta's betrayal had set off a domino effect in himself, where he'd started to doubt every decision he'd ever made. It'd taken a long time for him to build up his own self-worth again, and a small part of him never wanted to revisit that terrible time.

Now, because of that weakness, he might've damaged the one thing that meant the world to him. He would just have to build their trust back up, little by little, brick by brick. As long as Lacey stuck around for him to prove himself to her. That was the scariest thing, the thought she might end things, and he tried not to let himself go there. If Lacey decided to leave him... No, she wouldn't do that. They would survive this. Their love was strong enough to survive this. If only she'd let him take her in his arms, then he'd feel like everything would be fine. Let him stroke her hair, kiss her, show her with his body, how much he treasured her, how much—

A rattling sound announced someone was opening the door, and so he corralled his thoughts and held up his badge. "Hello, Mrs. Brown. I'm Detective Sergeant Favreau, and this is Probationary Constable Carmichael, ma'am. Are we able to come in and talk to you for a few moments?" The lady peered through a crack in the door, leaving the security screen door firmly locked and squinted at him for a closer look at his badge.

"If you must," she replied, reluctantly unlocking the security door and opening the main door wider. She was a tall woman, who looked to be in her mid-fifties, dressed in black slacks and a blue sleeveless shirt, her long, dark hair pulled back in a low ponytail. Nico wouldn't call her pretty, but her high cheekbones and piercing dark eyes leant her a severe beauty.

Putting all thoughts of his problems with Lacey out of his mind, he went through the door and turned to the left where the older woman indicated he take a seat in a small but tidy sitting room. Lacey took a seat next to him on the couch, and Mrs. Brown took the single armchair facing them with a resigned look on her face. The furnishings in the room were simple, austere even. A double-seater couch, an armchair, a standard lamp, and a coffee table. No pretty cushions, no warming throw rugs, no knickknacks on the shelves. Nico noted three framed photos on the mantel above a fireplace. All of them were of Tia.

"This is about those two bodies you found in Platypus Reserve, isn't it?" the woman asked, not bothering with niceties. Sandra Brown was a woman who was used to dealing with the police it seemed; she'd clearly had her fair share after her daughter's suicide.

"Yes." Nico replied, deciding not to beat around the bush either. "How perceptive of you, Mrs. Brown."

"I'm not stupid," the woman snapped. "I can draw parallels between two crime scenes as well as the next person." She glared at him as if it were his fault her daughter had killed herself.

"Of course you can," he said, more to give himself time to

think than to pacify her. "So, I guess you already know we're here to ask you some questions about what happened to Tia four years ago."

"When my daughter committed suicide, you mean?" This woman was nothing if not blunt. He flicked a quick look at Lacey sitting beside him, wondering what her take on this grieving mother was. "I'm not sure I can tell you anything new. Those cops couldn't help bring back my daughter then, and you can't bring her back now."

"We're really sorry we have to dredge up all these old memories," Lacey cut in. "Would it be easier if you had someone with you while we talk? Do you have a friend you can call? A family member?" She used a soothing, compassionate tone, one woman speaking directly to another. He applauded her use of sensitivity; it was always one of the reasons he'd thought she'd make a great cop. They hadn't discussed who was going to ask the questions on the way over in the car. But much like the interview with the gymnastics coach, Lacey didn't look for permission to take charge of the interrogation. Who knew, perhaps she might find an angle he hadn't yet considered, so he let her run with it. Just because they were having problems in their private life, it shouldn't affect their work relationship. They could work as a team to find the answers they needed.

"No. I live alone now. With only my memories of Tia to keep me company." Sandra's long fingers tapped impatiently on her knee. Now they were in a well-lit room, Nico could make out the muscular curve of Sandra's bare arms beneath her sleeveless shirt. She clearly worked out regularly to get that sort of definition. Perhaps going to the gym was her way of forgetting for a few hours the torment of losing her daughter.

"And the rest of your family?" Lacey asked with a smile, not to be put off.

"My husband left me for a younger woman six years ago," Sandra said primly. "It was a relief after he left, and I feel no further need for any kind of male companionship."

Nico wondered if she'd always been like this, or was it her daughter's death that'd caused her to shut the rest of the world out? Most people would've offered for them to call her by her first name, but Sandra seemed to prefer the title of Mrs. Brown. Perhaps that was part of distancing herself from society, of keeping a level of dignity. And reproof.

Nico already knew all this about Sandra Brown. Sally-Ann had dug the info up from the notes in Tia's police file. Their intel indicated that Mrs. Brown had divorced her husband well before Tia died and he no longer lived in Burnie. But there was a surviving son, Taj, who still resided in town, and it was interesting that she hadn't mentioned him.

"Okay. Well, if you're sure you don't want us to call anybody? Not even your son perhaps? Then we can continue." Lacey slotted the subtle question nicely into the conversation, almost as if she'd read his mind.

"No, I'm fine. Taj will be at work. I don't want to worry him, he's been through enough already. Carry on with your questions." Nico was a little surprised at her offhand reference of her son. But the way she screwed up her face when she mentioned him made him wonder at their relationship. It almost looked as if she was irritated by Lacey's mention of her son. Either that or she was afraid for him. Wanting to protect him from something.

"Right then. So can you tell me, in your mind, was there ever any doubt that Tia took her own life?" Nico asked. Most people would find this a hard question to answer, but Mrs. Brown took it in her stride.

"No, none at all," Sandra replied flatly. "She was a troubled teenager. She was suffering from anorexia and depression. I took her to see numerous psychiatrists, but none of them made the slightest difference. In the end no one could help her." At this, Sandra seemed to lose a little of her composure. But then she sat up straighter. "I'm sorry to burst your bubble, but Tia really did take her own life. So if you're hoping to perhaps link her with these two murders, then you're sadly mistaken."

Nico had indeed been angling toward that conclusion, but she didn't need to know that. He'd been hoping if there were any doubt at all about Tia's death, maybe—and it was a big maybe—they could reopen Tia's case and start looking into it as a possible homicide. If there was any uncertainty that Tia might not have killed herself, any suspicious circumstances surrounding her death, then it might point to murder instead. It was a flimsy link, but a murder four years prior with a very similar MO could point to the same killer.

After a short silence, Lacey took charge of the questioning again. "Don't you think it's a little strange that these two girls were found so close to where Tia chose to end her life?" she asked, tipping her head slightly on the side, as if the idea had just occurred to her.

"No. At best, I think it's pure coincidence. And at worst, I think it's someone trying to play a trick on you. Try and make you think there's a connection, perhaps put you on the wrong path."

"Right." Nico eyed her with skepticism. "I believe that you regularly visit the tree where Tia died." It was documented that Mrs. Brown had erected a small memorial at the base of the tree a few months after her daughter's death.

"Yes. I leave fresh flowers at least once a week. I was last there on Sunday." Sandra gave a curt nod but wasn't forthcoming with any more information.

"And you didn't notice anything out of the ordinary when you visited?" Nico enquired. It was a long shot, but she might've seen something. If Zoya was killed on Sunday as they suspected, Sandra might've come across the killer and not even realized it.

"No." Mrs. Brown dropped her gaze. "Everything was calm and peaceful. I tend to go right on dusk, after most people have left the reserve. It's quieter then. I saw no one at all, if that's what you're asking."

This line of inquiry seemed like it was a dead end. Nico pretended to study his notes.

"Can you tell us where you think Tia's depression stemmed from?" Lacey spoke into the silence. "What I mean by that, was she struggling at school, was she being bullied?"

"You don't need a reason to have depression," Sandra answered coldly. "It's a medical illness, not an affliction."

"I know that," Lacey began. "But sometimes when things are bad at school it can exacerbate the symptoms. Tia was in her final year, and that can be very stressful. Did Tia have many friends she could rely on? Did she have any hobbies she was interested in to give her something else other than school to distract her?"

"Tia didn't have many friends. And no hobbies either. When her depression became really bad, all her shitty friends deserted her. They were useless." Sandra's lip curled with disgust. "Toward the end, all she wanted to do was sit in her bedroom and not eat, and hide from the world."

It sounded like a very sad existence, and Nico felt sorry for the girl.

Lacey continued, "What about at home? Her relationship with you and her brother. Sometimes—"

"Are you saying she was unhappy at home? Are you implying that I made my daughter unhappy? That I was the reason she killed herself?"

Whoa, this conversation had taken a turn for the worse. Nico held up his hands, "Sorry, Mrs. Brown, my colleague meant to imply no such thing."

"I think you should leave now." Sandra Brown stood and glared down at them, finger pointing toward the door.

Shit. Now they'd done it. He glanced at Lacey, but she just shrugged. They really had no choice but to go. As she towered over them where they sat on the couch, Nico was made aware of the woman's physical presence. She was almost intimidating, with her deep scowl and threatening stance. She was clearly unafraid of the two cops in her living room.

"Thank you for your time, Mrs. Brown," Nico said stiffly as he got to his feet. "If you think of anything else that might be important, please don't hesitate to call me." He handed her his card, and he and Lacey filed out of the room and down the front stairs as the door was summarily slammed behind them.

"Sorry about that. I didn't mean to antagonize her with my question. But I should've realized. She's a very prickly woman," Lacey mused as they walked back to the cruiser.

"Not your fault," Nico replied. "Everyone handles their grief differently. But she certainly seems to have taken Tia's death hard. Shut out the world. Probably holding onto a bucket load of guilt if her reaction was anything to go by."

At least Lacey was talking to him, even if it was about the case, and Nico felt relief flow through him. "Did you notice there were no photos of the son? Not even any photos on the walls." he asked as they both ducked into their respective seats in the vehicle. "Any ideas on why that might be?" he asked.

"Yeah, I did." She bit her bottom lip as she considered his question. "It was almost like a shrine to her daughter. If I were the brother, I'd be a little peeved. I think we should talk to him. Get his perspective on the whole sad saga."

"I agree." Nico pulled out his phone and made a call. "Sally-Ann," he said when she answered. "Can you give me the address of Taj Brown, please? Both work and home. Lacey and I have decided we need to pay him a visit." There was silence in the cab as he waited for her to find the information and tell him she was sending it through to his phone. "Oh, and Sally-Ann," he said, just before she rang off. "Can you do a deep dive into Tia's file? See if anything doesn't ring true. I'm not sure what we're looking for, but the mother seemed very guarded and abrupt. Perhaps look into Tia's past. See if we interviewed any friends or other relatives who might've given their thoughts in an interview. A different perspective. Check on the dad, too. I believe he'd moved out of town by that stage, but I want to confirm his whereabouts. Thanks." He rang off.

"Why do you want to keep looking into this?" Lacey questioned. "Mrs. Brown just assured us this was a suicide. And if it was, then it has no relation to the double murder we're investigating. Do you think there's a chance Tia was actually murdered, and it was made to look like suicide? Are you going to reopen her case?"

"I don't know," he replied. "Just going on gut instinct at the moment. But you have to admit, something felt a little off in there today."

Lacey studied him for a few seconds across the cabin. "Yes," she finally agreed. "But I'm not sure it's enough to dredge up that family's pain all over again."

He grimaced at her words. As usual, Lacey was being the caring one; the considerate one. Worried more about what it might do to the mother if he decided to reopen the case and then found nothing. Perhaps that was the difference between her and him. He'd do whatever it took to get to the bottom of a case. Maybe that was why he made such a good detective. But Nico wasn't sure if it was such an admirable trait or not. He decided not to mention the other question floating around in the back of his mind. Was the mother covering up details because she had something to do with her daughter's death? The idea was ridiculous, especially when he could see the raw pain in her face when she talked about Tia. But still... stranger things had happened.

"Let's go and talk to the brother, then we can make a decision," he said.

"Agreed," she finally replied.

Nico checked the information Sally-Ann had sent to his phone. "Looks like he's a carpenter by trade. Works for a place called Complete Builds, a joinery and cabinetmaking business." He rang the phone number and talked to the receptionist at the kitchen cabinet company. The young woman was hesitant at first to give out the address where Taj was working today, but after Nico explained who he was, she readily complied. Plugging the residential address into the screen in his dashboard, he buckled his seat belt and started the car.

"Let's go see this guy," he grunted.

"Yes, boss," Lacey said with a smile. It was the first time she'd smiled at him all day, and he secretly relished the tingle in his guts. On the strength of that smile, he decided to leave any more discussion about Marietta and previous marriages until later. They had a tentative connection reestablished— admittedly, it was work related—and he didn't want to spoil that.

Taking a turn to the left, he guided the car through the suburban streets of Burnie. This area was full of red-brick houses built back in the sixties and seventies. Solid, dependable, but very middle class. He much preferred his little wooden cottage out on the headland.

On the drive over to Park Grove, a newly established suburb where lots of huge, modern houses were going up everywhere, he asked about how Linc was doing, and she told him about the pile of rock cakes they had waiting for them when they got home, courtesy of a visit from Margie.

Taj Brown looked surprised to see them when they strolled into the brand new house at the end of a lot. But his face quickly shuttered when Nico held up his badge, taking on a resigned countenance. The supervisor gave them a suspicious look, but told Taj to take as long as he needed as he led them out the back into a large, unfinished yard.

"Mum already called me," he said with a snarl. It seemed the son was going to be just as prickly as the mother had been. "Why are you digging around again? Can't you people just leave it alone?" From the file, Nico knew the young man was twenty-four years old, but he looked older somehow. As if he had the weight of the world on his shoulders. His short, cropped hair was the same dirty blond as his sister's had been, and there was a definite likeness in his features to the photos of Tia Nico had seen on the mantelpiece. But unlike Tia's almost angelic smile from the photos, Taj scowled at them from behind lowered eyebrows. Nico could see a barrage of tattoos up his left arm, disappearing into the sleeve of his T-shirt.

"We're just following up on a few things," Nico replied cooly, not surprised that Sandra had forewarned her son. "There are some similarities between your sister's death and these new murders, and we'd like to make sure there's nothing from your sister's case that might be a clue to the killer."

Taj gave a rude grunt. "I can already tell you, there won't be."

"What makes you say that?" Nico queried.

"Because I read the note Tia left behind. She was one screwed up kid. There's no doubt in my mind that she topped herself," Taj replied, kicking the sand with his steel-capped boot.

"I'm sorry. That must've been hard to deal with," Lacey

said, stepping around Nico so she could look Taj in the eye. "Were you guys close?"

"Not really. She was three years younger than me, and I was…focussed on my own shit, I guess. I'd just started my carpentry apprenticeship, and I'd broken up with my long-term girlfriend." His shoulders dropped as he spoke and once again, Nico was shocked by how Lacey's sympathetic approach seemed to break down barriers. Taj was still belligerent, but now it seemed to be aimed inward at himself, rather than at them. "I wish I'd known she was struggling. I could've done something. But Mum just wanted to sweep it under the carpet. If I'd known earlier about those girls tormenting her, I would've told them to piss off."

Nico's radar started to jangle. What had this kid just said? He looked at Lacey expectantly. Had she picked up the same thing?

"What girls," Lacey prompted gently, and Nico gave her a mental high five.

"What?" Taj looked up, his eyes refocussing, and he suddenly looked guilty, as if he'd said too much. "Oh, nothing really. Mum told me about six months before she died, that Tia was being hassled by a group of girls. I don't know if they had anything to do with her suicide, but I'm sure they didn't help her peace of mind," Taj said through gritted teeth.

"Do you know who they were? What their names were?" Lacey prodded him again.

But Taj seemed to have had enough of the interrogation and he stood up straight, the belligerent scowl returning to his face. "Nah, I don't know much. Mum assured me that she'd dealt with it. She never told me the details, just that Tia didn't need to see them bitches anymore, so the problem was solved." He glowered at them for a second. "Can I go back to work now?"

After a quick glance at Nico for confirmation, Lacey stepped out of his way, then said, "Of course."

They were quiet as they walked back through the house and out the front to the cruiser.

It wasn't until they were safely out of earshot back inside the vehicle that Lacey voiced the question that'd been bugging them both.

"Was any of that information about her being bullied in Tia's files?"

"I don't know," Nico acknowledged. "But it's the first thing I'm going to get Sally-Ann to check when we get back to the station." He started the car, and they drove off slowly down the road. If it wasn't in the files, then it made Nico wonder why not. Why would the mother withhold that sort of thing? Especially when Lacey had asked her point-blank if Tia had been bullied at school.

"You don't think the brother had anything to do with Tia's death, do you?"

"Not sure," Nico tapped the steering wheel with his finger as he drove. "Does he know more than he is letting on? Probably? Did he murder her and cover it up to make it look like suicide? Less sure about that one."

"I vote for the first one," Lacey said decisively.

He quirked his mouth up in a half smile. "We'll see" was all he said.

They didn't speak much on the short drive back to the station.

"Thanks, Lacey, I think we made good progress today."

"I'm not sure we're any closer to an answer, however," she chided lightly, stepping out of the vehicle. "Are you coming upstairs?" she asked when he remained sitting in the car.

"In a minute. I just need to make some calls," he lied.

"Fine, I'll see you later." She straightened her uniform and brushed imaginary lint from her breast pocket. He watched as she walked to the stairwell, enjoying the sway of her hips, blonde ponytail bobbing jauntily, and the way her blue shirt nipped in at the waist, and her trousers hugged her taut backside to show her hourglass figure to perfection. His heart did a double-tap as she disappeared through the door.

"This is killing me," he whispered into the silence of the car. "I don't want to lose you. I can't lose you." He put his head into his hands and wondered how on earth he was going to get through the next few days.

CHAPTER ELEVEN

Lacey stepped out of the Jeep with a groan. Maybe she shouldn't have gone to judo training twice in a row. But the physical release felt good, helped her get on top of those emotions that threatened to overwhelm her every time she thought about Nico. After sliding the shed door shut, she moved slowly across the grass toward the back steps. Thank God for the security light Nico had installed on the side of the shed after she'd been attacked earlier this year. It was nice to have the whole area bathed in light to help her navigate her way through the backyard.

Smudge had been barking as she'd come up the driveway, and now he was pulling at his tether beside his kennel, straining to get to her, whining loudly.

"What's up, mate?" she asked as she released him from his rope. He gave her hand a quick lick of welcome, but then ran to the back steps begging to be let in. Strange. Normally he liked to run off and lift his leg a few times on various trees around the property before he came in. The geese were also restless, honking and flapping from their roosting spot in the orchard, for them to be awake at night was again unusual.

She unlocked the back door, and Smudge rushed past her. Flicking on the kitchen light, she went back to the alcove to kick off her sneakers and hang up her duty belt, then went to the small gun safe in the kitchen cabinet and locked away her service weapon. It was a routine she followed every night when she came home from shift. She'd showered at the dojo and changed into comfy leggings and a T-shirt after her judo session, but she still needed to throw her uniform in the wash for tomorrow.

She could hear the tick-tack of Smudge's claws on the wooden floorboards as he trotted through the house. Leaning her hip against the countertop, she wondered if she had the energy to bother cooking food tonight. It was already past ten. At least it was warm enough that she didn't have to light the fire tonight, so that was one less thing to do. Maybe a couple of slices of toast and Vegemite might have to do for dinner; she was too exhausted for much else. But then what would Nico eat? She always made sure there was something for him whenever he was working late on a case. Just because she was mad at him, did that mean she stopped caring for him too? She groaned and went to open the refrigerator to see if there was anything she could whip into an easy dish.

What time would he even be home tonight? They'd made some great breakthroughs today, and he'd probably be following up on all the new information flooding in from the other officers as they reported in. While she was still peering aimlessly into the fridge, Smudge reentered the kitchen and looked up into her face, then gave an uncharacteristic whine.

"What's the matter?" she asked, but suddenly, a prickle went down her spine. Smudge never acted like this. He was agitated, lifting his nose and scenting the air, pacing around the kitchen. Usually he was happy to settle on his rug in front of the fireplace or sit in the doorway and watch her cook.

Closing the refrigerator door quietly, she walked silently on socked feet into the hallway, flicking on every light switch as she went. She stuck her head into the living room.

Everything seemed fine. It was all just as she'd left it. Then she followed Smudge down the hallway, opening the door to the spare bedroom. It was all fine in there too. The main bedroom door was always left open, and she fumbled around on the wall for a few seconds before she found the switch. The room was empty.

The dog was standing at the front door, almost as if he wanted to go out onto the front porch. That's when Lacey noticed the door to the formal dining room was open, the room dark beyond. That door was always closed. Always. It was a habit of Nico's that she couldn't seem to break him out of. The prickling sensation got stronger. She halted in her tracks and glanced over her shoulder. Should she go back and retrieve her gun? But surely Smudge would've alerted her if there was someone hiding in that room waiting to pounce.

Slowly, she inched forward until she could peer into the room. Nothing moved in the semidarkness. No one was in there. But had someone been in here earlier? How else would the door have been open? Nico had set it up as a formal living room when she'd first moved in with him. But she thought it was such a shame, because, apart from the bedroom, this room had the best view out over the ocean and the curve of beach spread out below. And so she'd moved in a few armchairs to create a cozy nook from which to appreciate the vista. With the curtains still open, the windows let in enough light so Lacey could be certain no one was hiding in there.

Smudge gave a low growl, his eyes still fixed on the front door, and the hairs on the back of Lacey's neck stood up. Edging into the front room, she stayed close to the wall, then peered around the edge of the curtain, making sure she was hidden from sight. The front porch was dark and empty, as was the front garden. Her gaze roved over the lawn leading down to where the driveway met the main road. Nothing.

What was Smudge growling at? The half-moon lent the scene an eerie glow, but it gave just enough light she could see no one was on the property. Unless they were hiding behind the shrubs at the base of the steps off the porch. She tried to see around the branches, but it was no use.

Lifting her gaze, she focussed on the road and the view farther down the hill.

Over there.

What was that?

A dark figure stood silhouetted at the edge of the road, halfway down to the beach. A man, by the size and shape of his figure. It was hard to tell in the dim light, but Lacey was certain the man was staring straight back at the house. Right at her. She jumped back behind the curtain, her breath catching in her throat, panic making adrenaline spike through her.

She only faltered for a second before she remembered who and what she was. A police officer, with specialized police training, as well as a black belt in judo. Trained to go after an intruder, not hide behind the curtains. Drawing in a deep, calming breath, she went back into the hallway and unlocked the door. Smudge lunged, wanting to get out, but she grabbed him by the collar. Smudge had known all along there'd been an intruder. He might well want to race after this burglar, but he might get hurt, so she couldn't let him free.

Yanking the door open, she flicked on the outside light and stood on the porch, holding back a barking Smudge. There were no street lights in this little out-of-the-way hamlet, so the only light was from the moon. Let this guy see that he didn't frighten her. She stood tall, staring back at him. What did he want? Who was he? And most importantly, had he actually been inside her house? The figure stared back at her, both of them facing off like statues in the night. She was about to push Smudge back inside and run down the steps to give chase, when the deep rumble of a familiar engine split the night.

A bouncing swath of light from Nico's motorcycle headlamp lit up the road as he came around the corner, and Lacey turned her gaze gratefully toward the sound. His black motorcycle appeared on the road down below, and Lacey felt an absurd sense of relief. She ran down the stairs, Smudge still held tightly in one hand, pointing and waving at Nico, hoping to get his attention.

But when her gaze snapped back to the spot where the man had stood, no one was there. It was dark and empty; the man had disappeared. Melted into the coastal scrubland along the other side of the road. He'd disappeared so quickly, she could almost believe he'd been a figment of her imagination. But she knew that wasn't the case.

Nico stopped his motorcycle at the edge of the driveway and lifted his visor. "What's going on?" he queried. A thunderous look soon replaced his confused squint as Lacey quickly outlined what'd happened. "Stay here," he demanded as he leaped off his motorcycle, leaving it idling. Removing his helmet, he dropped it on the ground and sprinted in the direction she'd pointed. Smudge went mad, barking and leaping, wanting to follow Nico, to protect him. It took all her strength to hang on and try and calm him down.

Nico had taken off into the dark without a second's thought. But if that man had been in their house, been purposefully waiting for one of them to come home... She wasn't sure what it all meant. Why would someone break into their house and not take anything? She'd need to go and double-check, but it seemed like nothing had been stolen. This wasn't your everyday burglary. Were they being stalked? And if so, who was this guy after? Her? Or Nico? Now her fear had transferred from herself onto Nico. He was out there alone with some psycho on the loose.

She needed to call in backup, but her phone was in her handbag hanging on the hook inside. Shit. Shit, shit. Suddenly, a figure materialized at the edge of the road. Lacey knew immediately it was Nico by the shape of his shoulders; the bulk of his leather riding jacket gave him away. There was no sign of anyone else. The man must've got away. *Oh, thank God.* Her shoulders dropped, and she loosed Smudge's collar. The dog took off at top speed, belting down the road until he came to Nico, almost knocking him over in his enthusiasm, then dancing around his master like a demented sprite.

Nico stalked up the hill, stopping right in front of her. He raked his gaze over her, and it was only then she realized she'd run out here ready to chase down a fleeing felon only wearing socks. "Are you sure you're okay?" He took her by the shoulders and stared into her eyes. His fingers were warm and reassuring, and her heart rate began to return to normal.

"Yes, I'm fine," she told him, fighting the ridiculous urge to sink into his chest, and let him hold her. She *was* fine. The intruder was gone—if he had actually been an intruder—and she and Nico were unhurt. So why did she feel so freaked out?

"Good." He let out a relieved gust of air. "You scared me. For a second, I thought you were about to chase that guy into the bush with no shoes on and Smudge as your only protection," he said as he let go of her.

Thinking about it, that was exactly what she'd been about to do. But now he said it like that, it sounded slightly foolish. "And what if I was?" she demanded. "I'm a Tasmanian police constable. I'm perfectly capable of looking after myself. And more than able to bring down a criminal if it's required." They'd had this argument before. Nico was always so damn protective of her. It made her hackles rise, and she felt the urge to stamp her foot like a petulant child. No longer wanting Nico's strong arms around her, she wanted to smack some sense into him instead.

Nico sighed, but clearly decided he wasn't getting anywhere with her tonight on this particular subject, and so changed tactics. "Let's get inside. I'll put the motorcycle away later." He leaned over and switched off his machine, snagged the keys from the ignition, and picked up his helmet from the ground where he'd dumped it.

"Should we call this in?" she asked, preceding him up the front steps. She'd left the front door wide open and all the lights blazing. Smudge bounded through the door, happy that his job had been done. He'd warned her of the intruder and he would've given chase if he'd been allowed. With Nico home, he knew they were all safe and he could get back to his happy doggy life.

"Probably no point." Nico shrugged out of his backpack and jacket and then turned to make sure the front door was securely locked and bolted. "Whoever that was is long gone. Is there any sign of a break-in? Are you even a hundred percent sure they were inside our house?" He was peering into all the open doors as he went down the hallway, but his question had her second-guessing herself. Now that she thought about it, both the front and back doors had been securely locked when she arrived home. Which was one of the reasons she hadn't realized someone had actually been inside the house.

"Yes. That door was definitely closed when I left this morning," she replied, pointing to the dining room. "And Smudge was acting really weird, right from the time I pulled into the driveway." She nodded to herself. "I'm sure he was in here," she declared.

"Is anything missing? Has anything been touched?" Nico was peering into the bedroom, all efficiency and in detective mode once more.

"Nothing obvious," she admitted. "But we should do a check, anyway."

Nico merely grunted and went to hang his jacket and backpack up and secure his weapon. Lacey went into their bedroom and did a slow 360-degree turn in the middle of the room. Everything seemed to be in order. Then something over on the chest of drawers next to the window caught her eye. Before she'd moved in with Nico, his room had been that of a typical bachelor, simple and a little on the sparse side. She'd added plenty of feminine touches over the past six months, including three framed photos of her and Nico, sitting in pride of place on top of their set of drawers. But one thing that she wasn't quite so good at, was dusting. They were both busy people and dusting was low on her priority list. Without touching it, Lacey leaned over to inspect the three photo frames. One of them had been moved. And whoever had moved it hadn't quite put it back in the exact same position, because she could see the mark in the dust where it'd sat before. All of her knickknacks—her grandmother's china figurine, some pretty shells she'd collected from the beach, and a stack of books waiting to be read—remained untouched. A shiver went down her spine. Someone had been in here, snooping around, touching her things. But what were they looking for?

She called Nico into the room and showed him what she'd found. To his credit, he studied the photo frame carefully, and then nodded in agreement. At least he believed her now.

They both took turns checking out every room in the house, Smudge following behind curiously. Nico discovered where the intruder had made his entry. One of the windows into the living room had been jimmied open. The window frames were all made of wood, original from when the cottage was first built. Nico had them restored and repainted, but had decided not to update them to a more modern and more secure metal version, because they would ruin the character of his cottage. It would've been fairly easy for someone to slip a knife under the window ledge and pry the latch loose. Actually, the intruder had done a great job, barely damaging the window, and then shutting it again, to make it less obvious how he entered. Now, there was no doubt someone had broken into their house. Careful not to touch anything, Nico took photos, and then called it in, requesting forensics to come out in the morning and dust for prints. Lacey thought the chance of finding any clues was highly unlikely; this guy seemed like a pro.

He sat heavily at the kitchen table and ran a hand through his hair. She was about to sit too when her stomach rumbled loudly. "How about a mushroom omelette for dinner?" she asked, already pulling the geese eggs out of the fridge.

"Sounds wonderful." Nico gave her a tired smile, and some of the tension left her shoulders. She'd been jumpy and on edge after the intruder in the house, then irritated and exasperated when Nico had pulled his overprotective stunt, all of which had probably led to her snapping at him. But now she could see through his smile to the fatigue underneath. Fatigue and something else. Suffering. Suffering she knew she was responsible for. Nico was already under pressure from this double homicide, and she wasn't making it any easier on him. She'd like to go up and run her thumb over the frown lines on his forehead, ease away the stress. But the undercurrent of unresolved issues stopped her. Issues that were blocking their ability to communicate. Blocking their normally open and effortless camaraderie.

"Is this related to the murders?" she asked the easy question instead.

"No idea," Nico admitted. "Could be just a random dude."

"Last time someone came snooping around our house, it

wasn't random," she reminded him. Last time Nico's good friend Gabriel had attacked her. And if it hadn't been for the geese, he may well have killed her. She should've twigged when she heard the restless geese tonight when she first came home. "And this doesn't feel random. It feels premeditated. And targeted."

"I agree," he replied. "Who knows, maybe forensics will get a fingerprint tomorrow."

They both knew there was little chance of that. If this guy was as much of a pro as she suspected, he would've worn gloves, and possibly a hat and balaclava as well, minimizing any hair or skin particles being left behind.

Lacey kept her thoughts to herself as she bustled around the kitchen preparing their omelettes. Nico got up to feed Smudge, then retook his seat and watched her thoughtfully, but she could tell his mind was elsewhere. Probably on new ways to make the cottage more secure. Thick metal security screens on the windows would spoil the classic colonial look, but Nico would probably go for it anyway, just to make sure she was safe.

Suddenly, his face cleared, and he sat up straighter. "I almost forgot with all this trouble, but we just got an ID on the second body."

"That's great." Lacey gave him an encouraging smile over her shoulder.

"Yeah, dental records came back with a hit late this evening. The lab must've been working overtime on this one." Lacey could imagine. This case was garnering huge media coverage across the whole country. Everyone wanted answers as quickly as possible, and no one wanted the finger pointed at them as being the source of a delay. "She was a woman called Sukey Lui. Seems like she still lived with her parents in town. I sent a unit out to inform the family." Nico grimaced at this, and Lacey's elation at finally getting an ID deflated in the face of another family's grief. "I'll leave the interview until first thing tomorrow morning. Let them digest the news first. They emigrated from China twenty years ago, when she was only one, and I don't think their English is all that good, which might be a stumbling block," Nico stated matter-of-factly. A translator who spoke Mandarin might be hard to get on such short notice, but Lacey hoped they spoke enough English to be able to conduct a conversation, because they needed all the info they could get as quickly as possible.

"It's interesting no one reported her missing. Especially if she was living with the parents. The body has to be at least two weeks old," she said. Thinking about the second girl they'd fished out of the river, Lacey decided that her Chinese heritage was an interesting contrast to the first girl who was of Russian descent. What did these two girls have in common? Lacey placed a plate piled high with sweet-smelling eggs and mushrooms in front of Nico and sprinkled some grated cheese over the top.

"Thanks," he replied, flashing her a grin that almost let her see through to the real Nico. The one who didn't have all his walls up, ready for her to say something else hurtful or have to defend himself yet again. "I'm sure there's some sort of explanation. Hopefully, we can get the full story and find the link between her and Zoya once we talk to the parents." His last few words were mumbled through a mouthful of food.

Lacey prepared her own eggs, then sat down opposite Nico, tucking into her food with gusto. All thoughts of strange intruders and double murders banished to the background as she satisfied her hunger for the next few moments, not at all worried that both she and Nico could eat in the face of everything they'd just discussed. Death and grief had become, if not commonplace, at least something that no longer affected her viscerally.

"There's also been another interesting breakthrough," Nico

finally said after half of his plate of food had disappeared.

"Mmm?" She raised her eyes to look at him with curiosity but didn't stop eating. This almost felt normal. Like they were sitting here as they always did, discussing a case over dinner before they headed to their bedroom to make love. But that was off the cards, she reminded herself, at least for tonight.

"Remember, I sent Hickey and Lawson to search Zoya's flat yesterday?" He watched her nod her reply. "There was a lot of stuff to go through in her flat. Seems like she was quite...messy, shall we say." He gave a grimace and took a slug from the glass of orange juice she'd placed in front of him. "They found another bracelet charm. Exactly the same as the one Linc found at the crime scene the other day." Nico's look was exultant.

When the two detectives had questioned Zoya's mother about the charm, she thought she might've remembered Zoya having something similar, but wasn't exactly sure, and so Hickey had been tasked with keeping a lookout for it. But now they had their answer. It was the same charm someone had been brazen enough to attack Linc for, to stop him taking it as evidence.

"Wow." Lacey made an O with her mouth. "That's big." She stopped eating and put her fork down for a second.

"Yes. At least we can definitely say this charm belonged to Zoya. But we're not so sure who the other one belonged to. Was it Sukey's? Is that why the killer wanted it back? Because it points to a link between the girls? Or is there something else going on here that we don't know about? It's one of the things we need to ask Sukey's parents tomorrow. If she owned a charm like the one we found. And if she did what was the significance of it." Nico scraped the last of his food off his plate and sat back in his chair. "I think we need to go back to the gymnastics club tomorrow too. We need another chat with Erica, as well as all the other coaches. It's too much of a coincidence for that sign to be up on the wall, and now to have found a second charm with exactly the same wording."

"Practice makes perfect," Lacey muttered to herself. The puzzle pieces were slowly coming together. And it seemed the gymnastics venue was at the center. "What about Tia? Are you still considering her death to be involved in this riddle somehow?"

"Not sure," Nico admitted. "We definitely need to find out more about these mysterious girls who bullied her."

"I'm not sure how a pack of bullies, even if they did help to drive a poor girl to commit suicide, could somehow then turn around and become murderers four years later," Lacey said.

"Hmm. I know it's a stretch, but stranger things have happened," he observed.

And she couldn't disagree with him.

She sat back and patted her full stomach. That was better. But now a huge yawn nearly split her face in two. She was exhausted. Nico was staring thoughtfully at her, an unreadable expression on his face. She got up and took the plates over to the dishwasher.

Nico came up behind and she twirled to face him "Thanks, Lace," he said, reaching out to pull her closer by her hips. "For dinner. And for everything. I know I get a little... overprotective. But I was scared as shit tonight. When I think what might've happened if you'd come home earlier and found that guy inside our house..." He leaned his forehead against hers. "All I want is for you to be safe. In my arms."

"I know. But I'm okay. We're both okay." She understood where he was coming from, she would've felt the same if things had been reversed. It was terrifying to think of Nico getting hurt. Unimaginable even, to think of ever having to go through the rest of her life without him. She could feel her heart softening toward him, feel the walls crumbling. Wondered why she was fighting with him. But then an insistent little voice spoke up from somewhere deep in her head. *Nico lied to you. Nico kept his biggest secret from you. He didn't trust you enough to tell you this one thing.*

This one thing that changed everything.

Gently, she lifted her head away from his, so she could look him in the eye.

"I'm sorry, Nico, but I'm still sleeping in the spare bedroom."

He dropped his hands away from her waist and turned away. "As you wish," he replied flatly, and her heart ached. Was she doing the right thing? Punishing him for no good reason? She knew she was intentionally shutting him out. But deep down, she still couldn't find it in herself to forgive him. And if she returned to their bed, she'd be lying to him. And lying to herself.

CHAPTER TWELVE

Nico strode down the hallway toward the operations room. He'd requested this morning's briefing start a little later today so that he had time to interview Sukey's parents. And his chat with the young woman's family had been quite enlightening. He had a lot to pass on to his team this morning. Even though it was Saturday, most people had agreed to come in, even if they weren't rostered on. A murder investigation didn't stop just because it was the weekend.

Sally-Ann was the only one in the room when he entered. She looked up as he stood beside her next to the whiteboard on the wall. "Hey, boss. Lookin' a little worse for wear this morning." She elbowed him in the ribs playfully. Nico didn't mind the over familiarity on Sally-Ann's part; he wasn't one to pull rank or keep strict lines between him and his staff, but he wished she didn't know him quite so well. Because there *were* large dark circles under his eyes but he hoped she didn't perceive his restless night was to do with his problems with Lacey. More to do with Lacey sleeping in another room and not in his arms, rather than the amorous night Sally-Ann was hinting at. He'd missed Lacey so much last night. That made two sleepless nights, and it didn't look like their problem was about to be resolved anytime soon, so he'd better get used to more nights alone in his big bed.

"Yeah," he laughed, hoping it sounded genuine. "Goes with the job, I guess."

"Hmm." Sally-Ann skewered him with her laser-beam gaze.

Shit, she'd seen through him. He pretended to be acutely interested in something on the whiteboard.

"Is there something going on between you and Lacey?" She put her hands on her hips and pursed her lips. "I noticed Lacey acting a little strange yesterday, and I—"

"Morning." Tyrell's cheery greeting stopped Sally-Ann midsentence. Hickey and Gorman followed close on Tyrell's heels, and the room began to fill up. Thank God for small mercies. Sally-Ann meant well, but she was a bit like a mother hen. For a few years before Nico had met Lacey, Sally-Ann was constantly trying to set him up on dates, telling him he needed a good woman in his life. And then when Lacey had come along, she'd taken an immediate liking to her, had been ecstatic for them both when they finally admitted their feelings for each other. Now, Sally-Ann saw it as her own personal achievement that Nico had finally settled down with that good woman she'd always dreamed for him. She'd want to help if she got even a sniff that Lacey and Nico were having problems. And although he was very fond of his colleague, he didn't need her meddling in his life.

"I heard you had some kind of break-in last night?" Tyrell walked between the tables so he could stand in front of Nico. "What's with that?"

Sally-Ann rounded on him. "You what? Why didn't you tell me?"

"Because there's not much to tell," he replied. And because she hadn't given him a chance, what with all her sixth-sensing trouble in paradise between him and Lacey. "Someone jimmied a window open, but no one was hurt, nothing was taken, and no evidence was left for forensics to nail him." Nico gave a sardonic shrug. Forensics had paid his cottage a visit early this morning, but like he and Lacey had feared, the criminal had not left a single clue. Not one fingerprint, not one strand of hair.

Sally-Ann narrowed her eyes at him. "Don't you try to pull the wool over my eyes," she growled. "Is this related to the case?" They all remembered clearly how Lacey had been attacked last time he'd conducted a major investigation. No one wanted the same thing to happen twice. Least of all him.

"I can't see how," he replied.

Sally-Ann held up her hand. "Don't give me that bullshit. I don't believe in coincidence any more than you do. Have you asked Shadbolt to put a car outside your house?"

"No," he replied wearily. "Because I know my request would be denied. As do you," he added pointedly. "There was no threat to life, nothing to indicate a danger to either myself or Lacey. And we're both cops. Capable of looking after ourselves."

Sally-Ann opened her mouth to argue, but Tyrell jumped in to save Nico. They both knew Shadbolt was correct, there was no hard evidence, and they couldn't afford to waste any precious police resources chasing a ghost. "I'll make sure we get a car to cruise by your house as often as we can." He patted Nico on the shoulder. Then he gave his big, trademark smile, white teeth flashing against his brown skin, and Nico was suddenly foolishly grateful to the tall man he called friend. They both knew it wasn't much, but it was better than nothing.

Right at that moment, Lacey walked through the door, followed by Lawson and Saito. Nico vaguely wondered where Pederson was. Tyrell returned to the back of the room to take his seat. Sally-Ann shot him one more heated glance before she too took her seat near the front.

Nico would have to put last night's intruder out of his mind. It did no good brooding on the subject, going over and over the scenario in his head; trying to figure out who the culprit might be would drive him crazy. He and Lacey had agreed that she wouldn't go home alone again in the foreseeable future. And he'd already contacted a local security firm. It was time to have cameras and alarms installed. He wouldn't rest easy until he knew Lacey was protected. It was going to be expensive to get the state of art equipment he wanted. But with their often opposing rosters, and his sometimes long hours, it was impossible for them always to be home together. It was a fact of life that Lacey would sometimes be home alone, and he needed to deal with that fact in the best way he knew how. He was going to use all the mod cons and money at his disposal to keep her safe. Lacey had jokingly asked why he didn't trust his guard geese to protect her anymore. His little flock of geese had done a stellar job of driving off her attacker six months ago, but it was time to get real, and get some high-calibre equipment installed.

Nico lifted his head and cleared his mind. Time to get back into the game and back into solving this case. He tapped his notepad on the tabletop until everyone quietened down.

"Thanks for giving up your weekend," Nico started speaking and the rest of the murmuring died away. Not everyone had come in especially to help solve this case, some, like Lacey, were rostered on today, anyway. But others, like the two detectives and Tyrell had given up their recreation time to get this thing done. "If you've all caught up on your case notes, you'll know we finally identified the second victim late yesterday evening," Nico continued. A few heads nodded in ascent. "Her name is Sukey Lui, and she was a twenty-one-year-old local woman, living and working in Burnie." His gaze snagged on Lacey's for a split second, but he had to drag his eyes away before he drowned in his own recriminations that hovered so close to the surface.

"Earlier this morning I was able to interview Sukey's parents. Naturally, they were still incredibly shaken. English is also their second language, and communication was difficult at times. But their daughter Jia, Sukey's older sister was there to help us translate." He could see Lacey lean forward and focus on him intently out of the corner of his eye; she knew nothing of the detail of his interview this morning, only what he'd told her last night. Her blonde ponytail fell forward over her shoulder and she chewed her bottom lip, something she did when she was deep in thought. And something he also found incredibly sexy. He gritted his teeth and pointed to a picture of Sukey that Sally-Ann had pinned to the whiteboard. "I asked them why they hadn't reported her missing, and they said they thought she was down in Hobart visiting her boyfriend. They don't approve of her boyfriend, and she often leaves without telling them that she's going, sending them a text to let them know where she is after the fact. Dan, the boyfriend, works in an importing business down at the docks, and I get the feeling the Luis don't like him because he may have dodgy connections. Perhaps even involved in a Chinese triad." There were a few raised eyebrows at that comment, and he could see the cogs beginning to whir in some heads. Chinese triads were notoriously powerful and thought nothing of meting out violence and death to get their message across. "They received a text from her on Sunday two and a half weeks ago saying exactly that; she was taking the week off work to see Dan. They had no reason to believe otherwise. As Mr. Lui stated, Sukey is a grown woman, and she did whatever she liked."

Nico stopped to draw breath, and Gorman stuck his hand in the air. Nico nodded in his direction. "Surely two and a half weeks is a long time for someone to visit a boyfriend. Didn't you say she had a job here? Would they give her that much time off?"

"You've hit the nail on the head," Nico replied with satisfaction. "She worked for a shipbuilding company, building catamarans, as the assistant to the CEO. We contacted him at home this morning, and he confirmed that while he'd given Sukey permission to have a week off, he was beginning to wonder why she hadn't returned yet. The CEO tried to contact her numerous times last week, but got no answer."

"And he didn't think to report it?" Gorman looked incredulous.

"No. This might seem a little strange, but from the people I've talked to so far, I'm building a picture of a young woman who liked to get her own way, but was also a little flaky and unreliable. This might not have been the first time she'd been...irresponsible. It seems a little sad, but this may be the reason why the killer got away with their first murder without the body being discovered for so long."

There were a few frowns from his team, but no one said anything more.

"I also learned another important detail." Nico paused for effect, waiting till everyone was looking at him with interest. "When I showed them a picture of the little bracelet charm, they revealed that Sukey had one just like it. The sister even went to Sukey's room to retrieve it, and I can confirm they are the same." He let his gaze settle on Lacey for one second. This was an important detail. And she was the one who'd found the possible connection between the charm and the sign at the gymnastics club. "They said the charm was issued to all girls who'd trained at the Somerset Gymnastics Club for one particular competition. It turns out Sukey attended that gymnastics club from around the age of ten, right through until she turned seventeen." There was a collective intake of breath as Nico made this pronouncement, but the best was yet to come. "When I showed her a picture of Zoya Kibel, the mother confirmed the two knew each other, as they were in the same cohort, and were friends in their teens. She and Zoya were in the same team when they were awarded the bracelet charms." Nico couldn't help the self-satisfied smile that turned the corners of his mouth up. They finally had it. The link between the two dead girls.

"But we've been flashing that girl's picture on the news. How did they not see it? Especially if it's one of their daughter's friends," Tyrell asked, his tone confused.

"Not sure," Nico replied. "They don't watch the news supposedly. They're not big television watchers full stop, if the sister is to be believed. They like to spend their leisure time in the garden—they have a huge vegetable garden—or watching Chinese movies. If they really had no idea what was going on in their town, it'd certainly explain why they didn't start to question their own daughter's whereabouts sooner."

"Yeah," Tyrell said sardonically. "Here we are calling for any information on an unidentified body, and they're spending their time watching Chinese movies and gardening." He gave a snort of derision.

Nico was surprised himself that no one in the family had caught a whiff of the local double murder. But Nico understood not everyone lived the way Tyrell and even most of the people in this room did. It took all kinds, and it was clear the Lui family liked to live a simple life and remain in touch with their culture and their roots. They probably missed their family and lifestyle back in China. He had no clue as to why they'd moved to Tasmania, but they were clearly loathe to leave their customs and traditions behind. Maybe that was why Sukey had rebelled, wanting to live a more modern lifestyle.

"Anyway, it seems the two girls haven't seen each other in years. Not since they had some sort of falling out. They both went in different directions afterward, and Sukey at least, gave up gymnastics around the same time as they quarreled." Nico began to shuffle the papers on the desk in front of him, getting ready to assign various duties, now that he had a plan of attack.

"So, we have two priorities today. The first one is to locate Sukey's car. She clearly set out to drive to Hobart, but was intercepted on the way. Her phone is missing too, and I'm hoping if we find the car, we'll find her missing items in the vehicle. Second is to get back to the gymnastics club straight away. The owner never followed through with our request to send us the contact details for all her staff. So, if she won't play ball, then we'll take the ball to her. They need to answer a whole lot more questions about these girls and their connection to each other and the club." Nico could see Lacey nodding emphatically up the back.

"Wait up a sec, Favreau." Detective Pederson strode into the room. "Sorry I couldn't make it earlier, but I think you're all going to want to hear this." Nico froze and drew in a deep breath, trying not to let his dislike for the other man show on his face. Trying not to let the other man's arrogance and bullheadedness get in the way of his normally good judgement. The man must be a good detective, otherwise he wouldn't be here.

So Nico gritted his teeth and said, "Yes?"

"I just got back from talking to Julio down in IT." Pederson held up something in a plastic evidence bag. "I've had him take a look at Zoya's phone, which was found at her apartment the other day." One of the reasons it'd taken so long to identify Zoya was because none of her personal belongings had been found on the body. Instead, her handbag, containing her purse and mobile phone was found sitting in her apartment, as if she'd just walked out and left them there. Which was confusing and posed more questions than it answered, but at least they had a few things clear in their minds. It looked like Zoya had been abducted from her apartment, but she hadn't been murdered there. And perhaps Sukey had been abducted from her car as she was leaving Burnie. Which meant their theory that the killer had drugged and abducted the girls first, then taken them somewhere else to kill them, was likely correct.

"Turns out Julio is a whiz at hunting down recently deleted text messages." Pederson gave a triumphant little smirk. "And you'll never guess who she was texting?" The detective paused for dramatic effect.

Nico merely waited for Pederson to reveal his little secret.

"Mrs. Erica Nellenbach, that's who." That got everyone's attention, they all swiveled in their chairs to look at him. "And the texts were quite interesting. Zoya doesn't state it explicitly, but she was very angry at Erica for something, and she threatened to go to the cops at least twice." The air in the room went so quiet you could hear a pin drop.

"So you think Zoya was blackmailing Erica?" Nico asked.

"There's a high possibility," Pederson said with a smug smile.

"Any idea what she was blackmailing her about?" Nico asked. This was an interesting development, and he should be more chivalrous and stop wishing it wasn't Pederson who'd found it. They were a team, he had to keep reminding himself of that.

"No," Pederson finally admitted. "And we're not sure why she deleted the texts either. This all happened around six months ago. But then the texts just stopped."

"Perhaps Erica paid her off," Saito said thoughtfully.

"Maybe. But whatever it was, the matter seemed to resolve

itself."

"Right. Thank you. We'll keep that in mind when we do the interviews today," Nico said, mustering half a smile.

"Head's up, everyone," Nico said as the mutter of conversation overtook the room. He still needed to assign tasks.

"Pederson and Saito, I want you with me." This time he meant to round up as many staff at the club as he could and question them all as soon as possible. He wasn't going to take no for an answer from that hoity-toity gym owner today. He was probably going to regret this, but… "Carmichael, you're also with me." She'd been there on the first day he'd interviewed Erica Nellenbach, and she'd been the one to spot the sign above the door. He felt he owed her this, a way to help him dig deeper into this mystery. Lacey gave him a surprised glance, which quickly turned into a frown, but then Tyrell tugged on her arm and distracted her, perhaps filling her in on details about Linc's recovery.

Nico asked Hickey and Gorman to make it a priority to locate Sukey's car, then spent the next five minutes allocating duties for the day to the others in his team, so by the time he turned to follow the two detectives and Lacey out of the door, her frown had disappeared and her hardened cop face had taken over her features again.

CHAPTER THIRTEEN

Nico did a 360-degree turn in the main foyer of the gymnastics club. The place was jam-packed. It turned out that Saturday was the best day to find all the staff together at the club as there was a local competition going on, and the place was teeming with kids, parents, and staff.

Nico waded through the throng, determined to find Erica, Lacey hot on his heels. The other two detectives bringing up the rear as they all ducked through the door into the main arena. The room rang with the sound of voices and movement as hundreds of young gymnasts competed on various pieces of equipment, while parents and the kids who weren't competing sat around the edges on temporary bleachers. Some people looked at them with curiosity, but most ignored them as they weaved their way across the floor past yelling coaches and excited children. The gymnasts must be from different clubs or regions, because they were all wearing contrasting, brightly colored leotards. Some were sparkly purple, others were fire engine red, and they all bounced around like pieces of fluorescent candy.

The look on Erica's face rivaled a thunderous storm cloud when she caught sight of him striding toward her. She was standing on a makeshift stage in the back corner of the cavernous room. Dressed in a dark, tightly fitted suit with a streamlined pencil skirt, she reminded Nico a little of Cruella de Ville, minus the black and white hairstyle. It looked like she was getting ready to hand out ribbons, probably prizes for one of the many competitions that were going on around them.

Nico stopped directly in front of Erica, not letting the fact she was looking down at him from her added height of the stage intimidate him. "Good morning," he said but barreled on before she could reply. "We've come to interview your staff. You promised you'd send us a list with all relevant contact details but that wasn't forthcoming. So we've come to you instead."

Erica glared down her nose at him. "You can see for yourself how busy we are today. I can't spare a single staff member at the moment," she declared.

"You can and you will. Otherwise I will shut this whole club down and drag everyone down to the station to be interviewed one by one." Nico wasn't in the mood to take this woman's attitude today. Two women had died and there was a strong connection to this gymnastics club. She needed to pull her head out of her ass and get helpful, or he might just charge her with obstruction of justice. He also intended to get to the bottom of this texting thing between her and Zoya. She might not know it, but Erica was directly in his line of fire today. "I need somewhere I can interview people. Do you have a meeting room?" he said in clipped tones, having to raise his voice over the hubbub of competition. More than a few people were now looking at them with open curiosity. Erica glanced around, and for the first time, Nico detected a hint of nervousness. Good. He wanted her on edge. To make it clear that he was in charge this time.

Erica stared at him for a full five seconds before she finally grimaced and beckoned a young woman who'd been standing on the corner of the stage over to her. "Claire, can you please show these detectives to the big meeting room?"

"Yes, ma'am." The young woman ducked her head deferentially. She was plainly dressed in jeans and a loose T-shirt, with mousey-brown hair and large glasses that almost swallowed her face. Pederson and Saito had kept their mouths shut for the past five minutes, but Nico could see them taking this all in, documenting it all for future reference.

They followed Claire in single file out of the arena and past the reception desk. Nico had to make sure his jaw didn't drop to the ground as they walked through the joint. This place was huge. Probably the best facility on the whole island. They filed past an array of rooms as they proceeded down the hallway. A fully equipped weights room on the left, a large cafeteria on the right which was full of chattering kids, and a parent viewing room, with an enormous glass window, fitted with one-way glass, for the parents to sit and watch without interfering. Four large offices side by side, one with a big mahogany desk right in the center of the room, which Nico guessed was probably Erica's office.

"In here." Claire gestured to the room at the end of the hallway, which was decked out with a large boardroom-style table at one end and a scattering of smaller desks and chairs at the other.

"This is perfect, thank you." Nico smiled at the young woman, who seemed to be perpetually nervous.

"This is about Zoya, isn't it?" she asked. "I couldn't believe she was dead when I heard it on the television." Her brown eyes filled with tears. "I liked her. Zoya was nice to me. Not like—" Claire stopped speaking as if she'd said too much. Nico was glad at least someone seemed to be missing Zoya.

"Yes, it is," Nico confirmed, as the other three moved past him and spread out on the opposite side of the table. "Your name's Claire, is that right? You're the receptionist here?"

"Yes, sir. What can I do to help?" The petite woman stood taller and swiped at her eyes behind her glasses.

"I was wondering if you could get me a list of all the staff who work here? That'd be a great help."

"Oh, yes. I have a list on my computer. I can print it out for you straight away."

"Thank you." So Erica had been intentionally wasting time when she said she'd have to get the receptionist to compile a list. It already existed, she was just withholding information. "And if you could help bring in each staff member as we need them, that would be most helpful too."

"Certainly," the young woman replied, seemingly invigorated now she'd been given a job to do.

"We might as well divide and conquer," Nico told the others once Claire had left. "Do you and Saito want to do individual interviews? Carmichael and myself will work as a team." It was fair enough. The other two were accomplished detectives, but Lacey was still in training.

Interviewing multiple people together in one room wasn't ideal, but the room was big enough that they could spread themselves far enough apart for their conversations to remain private. Pederson and Saito settled themselves at desks in separate corners, and Lacey took a seat at the end of the boardroom table, watching him with wary eyes. They'd barely talked in the car on the way over, merely discussing aspects of the case, and completely ignoring any mention about the break-in, but that was okay, it meant Nico could keep his head in the game.

Claire bustled in with a piece of paper clutched in her hands and laid it down on the table in front of Nico. "Wow." He sat back in his chair. "That's a lot of people," he said, whistling through his teeth.

"We have a lot of kids go through this club," Claire commented. "And our ratio is one of the best in the country.

Eight kids to one coach. Right from six years old and up." She tucked her hair behind her ear and looked at him proudly. "We also have many specialist coaches. And some who work part time."

"And are they all here today?"

Claire nodded eagerly. "Most of them, yes."

This is going to take us all day, he thought grimly. May as well make a start. He pointed his index finger at the top of the list and asked Claire to bring in the first three people.

A middle-aged man called Mike Baldwin was ushered to their table by Claire five minutes later. He was listed as a senior coach of the under fifteens on beam and floor. The man had neatly trimmed, dark hair, and was fit and trim—he clearly looked after himself—but he was barely taller than Claire. Nico hated to stereotype anybody, but he couldn't help the words *small man syndrome* flashing through his mind.

Nico shook his hand and then watched as Mike seemed to linger just a little too long as he reached over to shake Lacey's as well.

"This is just terrible," he said, pulling out a chair. "I can't believe one of our own has been murdered. She was such a lovely girl. So pretty. And an amazing gymnast and coach," he blustered, looking only at Lacey as he spoke.

"Yes, it's always a tragedy when someone so young dies," Lacey replied seriously. She threw Nico a sideways look, letting him know she wanted to take the lead on this one. Which was fine with him. Her interrogation technique was different to his, but over the past few days, it'd proven to be highly effective.

"We're all devastated," Mike continued, leaning over the desk toward Lacey. Was the guy actually flirting with her? Nico wanted to scoff and tell him not to be such a dirty lecher, but held his tongue. As he watched Lacey question the man and listened to his answers, he formed a snapshot of this guy's personality. And he didn't like it. Not one little bit. If he had the balls to flirt with a police constable—albeit a gorgeous one, by his own admission—then he'd probably also have the presumption to hit on the women he worked with.

At one stage, Lacey asked him outright, "You certainly seemed very fond of Zoya. Were you close? Did you two ever go out on a date?" They were pretty sure from their information gathered so far that Zoya hadn't had a boyfriend or significant other. Her mother was adamant she would've known if Zoya was seeing anyone. She told them Zoya had broken up with her high school sweetheart nearly a year before and hadn't found anyone else since. Nico pretended to look down at his notes, as if the answer didn't interest him, but he listened intently.

"No, but I think she was interested in me," he replied coyly. The man preened, running careful fingers through his hair until he was happy it was just right. "I was planning on asking her out to the fireman's charity ball in a few weeks' time. I was just biding my time until I could find the right moment, you know? But then, she…" He covered his mouth as if he couldn't bring himself to say the word. Nico applauded his clever act, but one glance at Lacey told him she hadn't been taken in by it either. Both of them knew this middle-aged little man wouldn't have stood a chance with young, beautiful Zoya.

"What about this woman?" Nico asked, taking over the questioning as he slid a photo of Sukey Lui across the table. "She was a student here a few years ago." He didn't mention that Sukey was the second dead girl found in the reserve. That info would come out later today in a media conference. But for now, Nico was keeping the details to himself, so as to better gauge Mike's reaction.

"She doesn't look familiar." Mike squinted at the photo.

"She would've attended around four years ago," Lacey prompted. "She and Zoya supposedly trained together. Zoya stayed on here and became a coach, but this lady, Sukey, moved on."

"Ah ha." Mike's face cleared a little. "I only started working here around that same time. I definitely remember Zoya, she was an outstanding gymnast even back then. And of course she went on to become one of our best coaches. But now you mention it, I vaguely remember this other girl." He tapped his finger on the photo, thinking hard. "Yeah, those two hung around together, I think. They were good buddies for a while. Then Sukey left abruptly. Gave up gymnastics altogether, or so I heard. Which was a shame, but these young women often don't have the stamina to stick it out. Not like Zoya." He gave a triumphant smile as if he'd just given them the clue they needed to solve this whole mystery.

After half an hour Lacey closed the interview and they sent Mike on his way. Claire brought in the next candidate, Matilda Cassidy, a specialist aerial coach who helped the kids perfect their body lines in the air. Nico was amazed how much he was learning about gymnastics today. An aerial coach; who would've thought?

Over the next few hours, through a few carefully worded questions put to some of the other coaches, he managed to paint a better picture of Mike Baldwin. No one wanted to come out and say it explicitly, but they hinted that Mike definitely had a crush on Zoya. But then it seemed like he had a crush on half the female coaches in the club. Nico felt a little sickened by the man's creepy vibes. But creepy didn't equate to killer, he had to keep reminding himself.

Claire was a whiz at organizing the staff to come in one at a time, bringing in the next one on the list quickly and without fuss when Nico asked. She even organized sandwiches and coffee for them all at lunchtime without him having to ask, when it was obvious they were going to be here well in to the afternoon.

"Have you ever thought of working for the Tasmanian police?" he'd asked her. "We could do with such a highly dedicated person on our team. We have quite a few civilian jobs in admin and other areas," he added. Claire had blushed and covered her face with her hair, but she walked a little straighter from then on.

The last person Claire brought in to be interviewed was Erica. The woman scowled at them as she sat down. "I want to voice my objection loudly and clearly again to this whole debacle," she said before Nico could even phrase his first question. And he hadn't been lying; Claire would make a great asset to the force, if only he could convince her to leave this unfriendly place.

Erica clearly had the past few hours to stew over the situation and work up a good head of steam. She took her seat slowly, readjusting her skirt until it was exactly to her liking, then looked up and pierced Nico with her chilliest gaze.

"Have you been having fun, *Detective*?" She spat out the last word as if it left a foul taste in her mouth. "With your little investigation? I've had all the parents asking me questions about what's going on. Some have even taken their children home early. Do you know what you've just done to my reputation with this little stunt? You've ruined it, that's what you've done. I'm going to put in a formal complaint to your superior officer. This is not good enough." Erica sat back, her mouth in a thin, impervious line.

Out of the corner of his eye, he saw Lacey stiffen in her chair.

"You do what you need to do," Nico said, adopting his most chilly tone. This woman was unbelievable. "But we're conducting a murder investigation here. And your lack of cooperation and outright hostility aren't helping. It makes me wonder if you're trying to obstruct that murder investigation? Because if you are… Well, we have laws against that. I could arrest you for obstruction of justice."

"What? No, of course not." She sat up a little straighter, her pout losing some of its malevolence.

Nico held back the little self-satisfied smile. Erica was a smart woman, she knew the last thing she needed was for the police to charge her with anything that might bring the spotlight down even more on her and her beloved club.

"Glad to hear it," he replied, placing the plastic evidence bag on the table containing Zoya's mobile phone. Happy that he'd shunted her off track slightly, he decided to go straight for the knockout punch. "We found some interesting texts between you and Zoya on her phone. Can you explain why she was blackmailing you?"

"What?" Erica said again, but this time, all the color drained from her face. "No. That's impossible, she—" Erica shut her mouth with a snap.

"She deleted the texts?" Nico asked with a false sincerity that even he was proud of. "Oh, yes, we know. She tried to hide them. But you should never underestimate the power of our resources, Mrs. Nellenbach."

Erica looked like she might be about to throw up.

"So, would you mind telling us what the text conversation was about?"

Erica shook her head. "No. That was private business, and it's in the past. It had nothing to do with what's going on now."

"I think we should be the judge of that," Lacey said quietly but firmly.

Erica raised her head, her scathing gaze raking over Lacey like she was merely a bug beneath her shoes. "I'm telling you, our personal conversation had nothing to do with her death.

Zoya and I had a minor disagreement, that's all. But we smoothed it over, and she was happy to keep working here. That's all you need to know."

Nico had enough of this woman's holier-than-thou attitude. She wasn't above the police and if she wasn't going to answer their questions, then he wasn't above throwing the book at her. "Fine," he snapped. "Please hand over your phone then, Mrs. Nellenbach."

"You can't have my phone," she screeched. "I need it. This phone is my lifeline. To my club, to my parents, to my students. You don't have the right to take my phone." She held it to her chest and stood up, backing away from them.

"We have every right to seize your phone if we believe it is evidence in a murder."

"Evidence in a murder?" Erica's voice was like nails down a blackboard, loud and screeching. "I did not murder anybody. How dare you insinuate I did." Erica's face went an interesting shade of puce as she continued to back away.

Nico almost wanted her to make a scene. Let all the parents and kids see what sort of woman they were really dealing with. But perhaps they already knew. He smiled and took a step toward the woman. She could do this the easy way or the hard way. Nico was in such a bad mood now he hoped she chose the hard way.

Lacey shot him a worried glance, as she too got to her feet, ready to back Nico up if he needed it. Suddenly, Claire was by Erica's side, her hand on her boss's arm, saying something soothing. He heard snatches of phrases, like, "think how this will look," and "you're the life and soul of this gym, they need you," and "they'll give it back as soon as they can..." Soon, Erica's face lost its puce color and returned to a more normal shade of pink. Nico had to hand it to Claire; she sure knew how to handle her boss. Yet another reason she'd make a great asset to the local constabulary. At last, Claire removed the phone from Erica's fingers and handed it over. Erica turned on her heel and flounced out of the room, and Nico let her go. If there was anything on the phone, Julio would find it. Then he could have another conversation with the gymnastics club owner. But until then, he was happy to let her go.

Pederson and Saito had finished with their last interviewees on their list a few minutes earlier and had been watching Erica implode with silent amusement. After Erica left the room, they all came to sit together at the large table with a collective sigh.

"Can everyone get your notes typed up and compiled into the system?" Nico directed. "Then I'll go through them all tonight and see if I can find any common threads." There was a shitload of information here, and he'd probably be up half the night.

Which might be a good thing. If Lacey wasn't going to share his bed, then he may as well not be in it. He glanced at Lacey, who was facing the other two detectives and didn't look his way. Yep, it seemed like filling his head with work tonight might be a good plan.

CHAPTER FOURTEEN

Nico trudged out to the kitchen on bare feet to start the coffee machine, and Smudge slipped out of the door of the spare bedroom to welcome him. It was just past seven on Sunday morning and there was no sign of Lacey, which meant she must be taking a well-earned lie in. He wished he could do the same, but he'd woken early, and his mind wouldn't stop whirling, so he'd decided to stop fighting it.

Last night, he'd stayed up till well after midnight reading the other detectives' reports on the coach interviews and working other angles on the case. He'd brought his work home with him because the security was yet to be installed and there was no way he was leaving Lacey home alone until he knew more about their mysterious intruder. After a quick, fairly silent dinner together, Lacey had taken herself off to bed, leaving him to work unhindered. Also leaving him with a deeply dissatisfied feeling in his gut. She was polite and professional while they were at work together, but they were still no closer to solving this private issue that was slowly driving them apart. He needed to do something about it, before the rift became irreparable.

Lacey had the day off today. In his position as homicide detective he didn't have any specific rostered days, unlike the enlisted cops. But with a high-profile case such as this one, he pretty much worked seven days a week. As the machine whirred and the smell of ground coffee beans filled the air, an idea came to Nico.

Would she go for it?

He fed Smudge, then let him out into the backyard for a quick run before calling him back inside. If his idea came to fruition, Smudge would be getting a much longer walk soon. Filling two mugs of coffee, he headed for the spare bedroom. He gently tapped on the slightly ajar door with one of the mugs.

"Are you are awake?" he called softly.

"Mmm" came the mumbled reply.

"Can I come in?" It hurt that he even had to ask permission to enter her room, but the rules had changed and he needed to respect that.

There was a slight hesitation before she said, "Okay."

She was nestled deep down into the bedclothes with only the top of her head and her eyes regarding him sleepily. She looked so appealing cocooned in the blanket that he wanted to leap into bed and snuggle beside her. Like he would've done on any other day. Smudge's bed was on the floor, and the dog pushed possessively past his legs and flopped down, watching him with big, brown eyes. Ignoring Smudge's silent appraisal, Nico stepped over the dog and placed the mug of coffee on the bedside table. Then he carefully sat on the edge of the bed. Someone had to break this détente, and he wasn't too proud to be the one to make the first move. Lacey's head came off the pillow as she glanced first at him, then at her coffee.

With a resigned sigh, she struggled to sit up, plumping the pillow behind her back.

"Good morning," he said lightly, having to stop the word *gorgeous* before it fell from his tongue. Because she was always gorgeous at this time of the morning. Sleep tousled and warm; there was a softness to Lacey when she first awoke that was replaced with her everyday armor as soon as she got out of bed. He loved her vulnerability at this time of the day.

"Good morning," she replied, reaching for her coffee and raising one eyebrow in curiosity.

He drew in a deep breath and just went for it. "What if we took a picnic and climbed The Nut today?"

The light of contemplation lit her eyes. "I've wanted to do that ever since I came to Boat Harbour," she admitted.

Of course, he knew that; it was why he suggested it in the first place. A way to tempt her out of the house. Get them both away from their everyday routine and give them a different perspective. Perhaps they might be able to talk this over easier if they were outside, with the wind in their hair, and their lungs burning from some good old-fashioned physical exercise.

The very first picnic they'd ever gone on together had been to Stanley, a tiny coastal hamlet farther west up the coast. The Nut was a local tourist icon in Stanley. A large rock protuberance, the remains of a volcanic plug at the end of a headland jutting out to sea. You could climb to the top or there was a chairlift, but Nico knew Lacey would be up for the challenge of a hike to the summit.

On their first visit, Lacey had driven them up to Stanley to celebrate Dotti being back on the road after her breakdown. That time, Lacey had cooked a delicious lemon slice and dragged him away from work for a few hours while he'd been trying to solve Rania's murder. She'd been trying to decide her next course of action back then. Whether to stay in Boat Harbour or continue her travels around the island. They'd gone home and made love for only the second time, and she'd made the decision to stay a while longer. He had a vague hope its charm might work the same way this time.

"I'll make us a picnic, if you like. And we can take Smudge as well. He'd love a chance to run along the beach." A little blackmail never hurt, he decided as he watched her over the rim of his mug.

"Aren't you working today?"

"Yes, but it's Sunday and I need some time off. I'd like to spend that time with you."

He saw the indecision in her eyes. Her desire to get out into the sunshine and climb The Nut warring with her newfound wariness and the need to keep those high walls firmly set around her heart. He held his breath.

"All right," she finally conceded. "How long have I got to get ready?"

He let out his breath quietly, secretly giving himself a high five. "There's no rush. I have to organize the picnic. And I'd like to do a few hours work first. Why don't we leave around eleven?"

"Sure." She gave a delicate shrug and her tank top slipped down to reveal a bare shoulder. Nico had to close his eyes and look away as the urge to lean in and kiss that soft skin almost overwhelmed him. He had a lot of work to do before Lacey would welcome that kind of advance. But now Lacey had agreed to his plan, Nico felt suddenly energized, his lack of sleep no longer dragging him down. This was good.

"That'll give me time to pop into town and visit Linc. I hear they might release him tomorrow, if everything continues to look good. His mum will stay with him until she's sure he's a hundred percent better," Lacey said with a yawn.

"Great," he said, almost bouncing off the bed. Now he needed to create a picnic to end all picnics. It was often said that the way to a man's heart was through his stomach, but Nico understood it wasn't the food that was the way to a man's heart, but the fact it was cooked with love. He needed to show her how much he still loved her. Preparing her favorite foods might not win her back, but it was a way for him to show how much he cared.

CHAPTER FIFTEEN

Wind whipped through Lacey's hair, and she had to tug it out of her eyes so she could take in the amazing view. Her lungs were still burning from the steep climb to the top, and she rested her hands on her knees for a second to regain her breath. She was glad to see that Nico was also sucking in great gulps of air, as his chest rising and falling with the exertion of their ascent. At least she wasn't the only one suffering. Smudge bounded up to them with a carefree bark, and then sat with his tongue hanging out and a great big smile on his face. His jubilant mood was infectious. There was nothing Smudge loved more than a walk with his two favorite humans.

They'd marched straight past the spot where the chairlift stopped at the top edge closest to the town and followed a path along the top to the opposite side of the large plateau, so they were now overlooking the ocean, with a grassy meadow, punctuated by hillocks of tussocks behind them.

"Wow. I thought I was fit, but this was a challenge," she said, straightening up and doing a small twirl to take in the vast scenery spread out below them. Sometimes, it was easy to forget how beautiful this country was. When you lived on the coast and drove to work everyday through the rolling hills, it was easy to become blasé about it all. Lacey needed this to remind her just how lucky she was to be living in this little slice of paradise. So wild and isolated, brilliant blue sky draping overhead, a salty tang in the air, waves crashing on the rocks a few hundred feet below and the fresh wind taking the sting out of the sun's hot rays. It suddenly hit her how blessed she was to be alive on such a day as this.

"You're not wrong." Nico flashed her a smile and thumped his chest, as if his heart was beating too fast, and she smiled back. It was almost like they were the old Nico and Lacey once more. Back to the happy, in-love couple, sharing their delight of the outdoors on a spectacular summer day. Almost like they were back before the time she'd found out he was a liar. Even if it was a lie of omission.

As soon as that word *liar* popped into her mind, it was as if a gray curtain came down, and everything around her dimmed a little. Bugger. She'd been having such a good time. This had almost been the perfect cure to help lift her spirits. The climb to the top had taken them less than fifteen minutes, but they'd walked along the beach first so they could appreciate the large rock from afar, and so Smudge could have his playtime on the sand. That dog was at his happiest when he was wet, salty, and covered in sand from head to tail.

Lacey stole another surreptitious glance at Nico. He stood beside her, tall and broad shouldered, hands on hips, scanning the horizon with his indigo eyes. Her gaze roamed up his tanned forearms to where his biceps bulged nicely out of the arms of his T-shirt. She knew in intimate detail what lay beneath that T-shirt. The muscles of his chest and pecs, the ridges of his defined abs, the dips and curves of his ribs and then down to the spot near his hips where his washboard stomach sloped down to... Nico turned his head slightly, his gaze following the coastline that wound its way east, and

Lacey caught sight of the large dimple in his cheek, and his scar that she always said made him imperfectly perfect. Every single time she looked at Nico she got a jolt of appreciation. Appreciation for his superb male form. Just looking at him set off a low thrum deep inside her, a delicious warmth spreading through her body, down her arms and up her legs to her belly, where it unraveled as it went lower. At least the desire, that maddening attraction, hadn't been dampened by the gulf that'd opened up between them.

What on earth was she doing? Sometimes it was even hard to remember why she was mad at him. She really did love Nico, with all her heart. So, maybe it was time to put her doubts and misgivings aside. At least for the next few hours she decided to embrace the day. Embrace this opportunity to spend time with Nico, just him and her together, and for once, not let her roiling thoughts damage the time they had to share.

He turned and noticed her staring, giving her a curious glance.

"I'm starving," she said, deflecting any questions. All she wanted was to enjoy this moment. The hard stuff could wait till later. "And I'm dying to know what you've got in that backpack." She peered around his broad back to the large bag he had slung over his shoulders. It looked heavy, stuffed full with goodies. Secrecy had been the name of the game while Nico had been packing the picnic. He'd told her to stay out of the kitchen even after she returned from seeing Linc as he toiled over their food. And he'd also popped out for fifteen minutes, not telling her where he was going, so she was desperate to know what he'd created. The walk and the fresh air had amped up Lacey's appetite, and her stomach rumbled loudly.

Nico laughed and said, "I know, I know. You're always hungry. Let me set it up, then." He lowered the bag to the ground and pulled out a checkered rug, flapping it around in the breeze until he found a relatively flat spot on which to set it down.

Lacey sat eagerly on one corner and placed her water bottle on the other, to stop the rug flying away in the breeze, then watched impatiently as Nico unpacked the food.

First, out came the plates, cutlery, and two wineglasses. Then a potato and egg salad, a homemade hummus dip—she knew it was homemade because there'd been no dip in the fridge this morning—with carrot and cucumber sticks, and a fresh fruit salad for dessert were all placed on the rug. Lacey watched with ever-widening eyes. Nico was a good cook, but he rarely took the time nowadays to create in the kitchen. This was a feast for the eyes and the senses. Nico hadn't forgotten Smudge either. He pulled out a dried pig's ear— Smudge absolutely loved to chew on the sinewy, dehydrated meat, but Lacey found them icky; it reminded her too much of the animal it came from—and handed it to Smudge, who took it gently from Nico's fingers and found a spot to lie down amongst the tussocks and started chewing.

"Would you pour us a drink, please?" He handed her a bottle of chilled chardonnay—how the hell had he kept that cold for the past two hours?

She was so absorbed with pouring the wine that she hardly took note of what was on the plate Nico handed her a minute later. Then she looked down at the sandwich.

"Salmon and brie, with sliced avocado," she said, a little breathless. It was her favorite combination from the little Burnie Bakery in the main street, and he'd faithfully recreated it for her.

"I got the fresh bread from Margie," he admitted.

"I was wondering." There was only a little corner store in Boat Harbour, and they barely catered for the basics, like packaged, sliced white bread. Not like this homemade multigrain stuff, sliced in thick, rustic slabs. Margie was the queen of baking and loved her bread-making machine. Herb often declared that her bread would be the death of him, and the only reason he had to ride thirty miles every day was to work off all those carbs.

Lacey took a bite and let the flavors melt on her tongue. "Oh. My. God. This is amazing," she said, her mouth still full of food. "But what have you got?" She leaned over to see what was in his sandwich.

"Sadly, we were out of sliced beef," he said with a grin. "But luckily salmon and brie is my second favorite combination." Nico always ordered beef and mustard from the bakery, and she loved him a little more, because she knew that salmon *wasn't* his favorite. But he was eating it just for her. They ate in silence for the next few moments, Lacey lost in the sensation of eating her delicious sandwich on top of a hill surrounded by the ocean and the sky and the wind.

Nico coughed, and she tensed as he opened his mouth to speak. "So, I'd like to know your take on all those interviews we did yesterday. We haven't really had a chance to discuss it yet."

"Sure," Lacey said, popping the last bite of sandwich in her mouth, and dusting off her fingers and reaching for the potato salad. "As long as I can eat and talk," she added with a cheeky grin. She was happy for him to direct the topic onto safe matters, like work. They both understood there was an underlying current of things left unsaid that'd need to be aired sooner or later. After all, that was why Nico had brought her here, wasn't it? So they could *talk*. But if Nico wasn't ready to address that issue just yet, she was fine with it too.

"Who am I to stop you?" Nico held his hands in the air in mock surrender. Then he waited patiently as she piled her plate high with salad, dip, and even the fruit salad because she couldn't wait to taste it all, and he followed suit. "What was your impression of the first guy we interviewed?" he asked using his detective voice.

"You mean, Creepy Mike?"

Nico threw his head back and laughed, and Lacey was momentarily entranced by his strong, tanned neck, finding herself wanting to run her tongue down his skin, lick off all that salty sweat, and bury her teeth in the muscles at the side. She stuffed a piece of potato in her mouth instead.

"I'm not sure that's politically correct," Nico declared. "But let's call him Creepy Mike for now."

"How do guys like that even end up coaching in a gymnastics club?" Lacey asked after swallowing the potato. "It should be obvious to everyone what a weasel he is. The way he talked about the other female coaches. Ugh." She screwed up her face at the contemptuous little man. It'd been damn near impossible for her to keep her face impassive as they'd interviewed him. Only her cop training and her desire not to give away that she was onto him, allowed her to keep up her blank stare.

"I agree. But—"

"Yeah, yeah, I know," Lacey replied. "You can't judge a person's ability to commit murder on their repellent personality." Of course, she knew all that, had heard it a million times before. Had it drummed into her throughout her probation. But some people just got under her skin.

"But, I've asked Sally-Ann to take a better look at Mike. Do a background check, see if he rings any alarm bells."

"Oh, right. That's good," Lacey amended. "He didn't seem to really remember Sukey, though," Lacey mused, thinking back to yesterday. It was as if Zoya had always been the apple of his eye, even back then. "Do we think he could be a suspect? He did have an unhealthy infatuation with Zoya. But is that enough of a motive? Did they have some kind of lover's tiff? Or did she reject him and he took it badly?" she asked, picking up a whole strawberry and popping it in her mouth, letting the fruit explode on her tongue with its tart sweetness. "And if he did murder Zoya, how does Sukey fit into the scenario? She was killed first. Which is odd if this was a crime of passion. We know there was a connection with the girls from four years ago. But Sukey's parents seem to think they had a falling out. Did they perhaps maintain that friendship without anyone knowing?" Lacey raised her shoulders in a shrug, battling with the million and one questions she had regarding the triangle of Zoya, Sukey, and Mike.

"It's an interesting puzzle," Nico agreed. He didn't add any of his own insights, and so Lacey assumed she'd already voiced most of his own concerns. He'd pored over the notes all night long, so if he'd come up with anything else, she assumed he would've shared them by now.

"What about the rest of the staff? Any gut reactions to them?" he asked, tipping the bottle of wine in her direction, asking silently if she wanted a refill. She nodded and held up her glass.

"You mean, apart from Erica?" Lacey asked with a semiserious tilt to her mouth. That lady was another piece of work. Nico and Lacey had interviewed six other staff members yesterday, including the very helpful receptionist, Claire. No one else had pinged her radar like Mike and Erica had. That didn't mean they were capable of killing a colleague, but you had to narrow the suspect list down somehow.

"Gorman's already looked deeper into her background," Nico consented. "Apart from the child abuse claims you uncovered—and the text messages we still need to get to the bottom of—it seems she has a clean record. She might be a hard taskmaster and her training techniques might not be everyone's cup of tea, but her gymnasium is supposedly the best around, possibly in the whole state, and most people consider her a pillar in society."

"Hmph," Lacey replied. "She's a bully. And I hate bullies." It was good Nico understood her, so she could talk openly about her thoughts on their suspects like this with him. Her kind of frank opinions would not be as welcome in the station where the rest of the team could hear. "And now we might have found a possible motive for murder. I've gone over and over in my head wondering what Zoya was messaging Erica about," she continued. "You need to get Erica back in and interview her."

"Aye, aye, boss." Nico raised his hand to his brow in a mock salute. Then when she frowned at him, he said, "She's coming in tomorrow morning. And bringing her lawyer," he added. "We'll get to the bottom of those messages. And if she still refuses to answer, I might have grounds to arrest her."

"Good," she replied. "I wouldn't put it past that woman to murder one of her employees and an ex-student because of something they knew about her club. Maybe Zoya was blackmailing her. Maybe both Zoya and Sukey were blackmailing her. Or maybe she was having a secret affair with one of them. Or both of them. Maybe she molested them when they were still children at the club and now they've come forward and threatened to tell all. Hell, maybe—"

"Whoa, tiger." Nico held up his hand. "I know we're doing some speculating here, but let's not get too carried away."

"Right," she said, trying unsuccessfully to keep the scowl at her wayward thoughts of Erica off her face. She lifted her glass to her lips and was surprised to find it empty, but she didn't feel even slightly tipsy. The warm day and the exercise had made her thirsty, that was all. But now she thought about it, perhaps two glasses of wine in the sunshine hadn't been the best combination for clarity of thought. She stood by all her previous theories, however. Maybe she did her best work when she was slightly tipsy.

Nico began to pack away their picnic paraphernalia, scraping off the plates as best he could and covering up what was left of the potato salad.

"Thank you, Nico," she said suddenly. "That was delicious. And this"—she swirled her hand above her head to indicate the surrounding plateau—"was exactly what I needed."

"I'm glad." His gaze softened, and he stopped packing up and reached for her hand. "I think this is what we both needed." His thumb rubbed tiny circles over her knuckles, his touch warm and reassuring. Something in her heart cracked open just a little at what she saw in his eyes. Not begging. Nico would never beg. And not quite beseeching. But there was an appeal there. An appeal to her better senses. An appeal for her to talk to him. To end his pain. She was the only one who could do that for him.

Lacey suddenly knew it was time for that *talk* she'd been putting off. Time to sort this out. For good or for bad. What she said to him right now might make or break them. She sat back on her heels, letting his hand drop, and rested her palms on her knees. Opening her mouth, she suddenly had no idea what to say.

Now wasn't the time to be a coward. She squared her shoulders and took a deep breath, looking him directly in the eye.

"You know how I hate secrets. You know how my mother used secrets to bully me into submission." Lacey felt a stab of guilt when she mentioned her mother. It'd been six long months without contact with either of her parents. But that wasn't the point right now, even if it was the rationale behind her reaction to his betrayal of trust. The point was, Nico had lied to her.

"I get it, Lace. I always have. The truth is very important to you."

"Yes," she replied. And so he should; she'd made it clear enough on many occasions. "I guess it's my one nonnegotiable in this relationship. And I thought we had that. I thought you'd told me everything there was to know about you. So you have to understand how the news about Marietta blindsided me."

Nico grimaced, and she could see she'd hit him straight where it hurt. "You know me. You know how I struggle with...feelings. With commitment. I'm not one to wear my heart on my sleeve," he said.

She could surely attest to that. Sometimes, getting Nico to admit to his feelings was like pulling teeth. Even right back in the beginning, when he'd found her on the ferry just as she'd been about to leave the island forever and he'd known he was going to lose her if he didn't do something drastic, he had to drill down deep into himself and eventually he'd come through, telling her that he loved her in front of everyone on the ferry. That'd been extraordinary, and it still made her heart beat wildly when she thought about how romantic it'd all been. It'd taken an exceptional moment in time to get him to come out of his shell, and she really thought that'd been the catalyst for him; that he'd learned since then it wasn't going to kill him to let her in. That they had something strong and special.

Then Marietta had proven her wrong. Proven that he hadn't really learnt anything all along.

"But it was more than that," Nico continued. "I was ashamed that Marietta tricked me so easily. I felt weak. Her duplicity affected my self-confidence and I didn't want to admit that. Especially to you. I'd worked so hard to put that all behind me. But now I know I was being selfish."

She felt the ball of heavy emotions soften inside her heart at his declaration. He was a proud man, she could see how difficult this would've been for him.

"I never wanted to hurt you. All I can give you now is my undying promise that I will do better. I won't ever keep a secret from you again. Surely what we have together is worth taking another chance. On me. On us." His voice was a deep growl, rough with the strength of his emotion. His eyes locked onto hers in silent communication. A silent plea. He reached up and cupped her cheek with his palm. After a second, she leaned into his touch. Let herself fall. Let herself really feel him. Maybe she'd got it wrong. Maybe he had learnt how to express his feelings. Maybe Marietta was an aberration. Him holding onto details from the past because he knew how much it'd distress her to reveal them. Maybe this was more about his wish not to hurt her. Rather than him being a coward and not expressing himself.

"It's hard for me to describe how you affect me. I feel you under my skin," he said hoarsely. "And I taste you on my tongue. I think about you every waking minute of my life. You accompany every breath I take."

She nodded against his cupped hand, tears forming unbidden in the corner of her eyes.

Wow. Just... Wow. Nico had never been so forthcoming with his feelings for her. Never bared his heart in quite such depth. She tilted her head toward his, until they were resting forehead to forehead, their gazes locked on each other.

"It's the same for me," she agreed. What they had together was real. Raw and real. And she'd be stupid to throw it all away now. Her throat ached with the sweetness of it all. Nico was one in a million. Not like any other man she'd met. He was her night and her day.

"I'm so sorry, Lace. Do you forgive me?" His question was a whisper of breath between them. Lacey forgot that they were kneeling on a rug on the top of a hill with the blue sky stretched overhead, where anyone could see them. All she knew was her and Nico, cloaked in their own little world.

Did she forgive him?

Yes. Because the alternative was unthinkable.

"Yes." She nodded against his forehead.

"Oh, thank God," he moaned, the sound like a wounded animal getting to its feet, surviving against all odds. "I love you so much, Lacey Carmichael. I couldn't... I don't..." He didn't need to finish his sentiment this time; she understood every unsaid word.

His lips trailed over her jaw, then lingered at the edge of her mouth. Then he kissed her so deeply, so sensuously, she thought her bones might just dissolve right there. Her heart flooded with so much love she thought it might burst. This was the right thing to do. The only thing. Nico would still have to continue to build her trust in him, but for now she was so happy to just let that emotion go. Kick that word *betrayal* out of her heart and mind. She could see now he hadn't really betrayed her, he was only trying to save her pain, and it was her own issues that'd blown it all out of proportion. He also hadn't wanted to risk bringing all those feelings of self-loathing up again after Marietta's abominable treatment, which was understandable.

"If I keep kissing you, I'm not going to be able to stop." His breathing was ragged, his chest hitching as he pulled away far enough to look into her eyes.

She knew what he meant. A public hilltop was not the place to reignite their passion. They needed their bedroom. And fast. Nico bundled everything back into the backpack without regard to which way up it went, whistled up Smudge, then they bolted down the hillside as fast as they could, holding hands all the way down.

CHAPTER SIXTEEN

Nico smiled up at the ceiling. Makeup sex was the best. No, scratch that. This particular Sunday afternoon makeup sex after he'd thought he'd nearly lost Lacey was more than *the best*. It'd been mind-blowing. Life-affirming. He felt so light and happy, he could possibly be levitating a few feet off the bed, and the only thing keeping him anchored to this world was her.

Lacey mumbled something incoherent and snuggled deeper in to his shoulder, asleep in their warm afterglow. He let her sleep, but he was too buoyant to close his eyes. He was happy just to lie there all afternoon and soak in this feeling of elation. Everything else could wait. Work could wait. Finding the person who murdered two women could wait. This moment needed to be savored.

Things were back on track between them. He wasn't stupid enough to think that he still didn't have some work to do, some ground to make up. But he was determined to keep his end of the bargain, and he'd show her day by day, hour by hour, that she could trust him implicitly. It was a huge responsibility; to bear the load of someone else's trust. It was one of the reasons he'd been so afraid of commitment.

The other reason had been his fear of baring his own soul.

To allow his happiness to rest in someone else's hands. After Marietta had clawed his heart to pieces and shattered his self-confidence, he'd been wary of ever letting anyone else in again. She'd scarred him for life. Or so he thought. Until he'd met Lacey and she'd turned everything he thought he knew about himself upside down.

He remembered back to the second they'd stumbled through the back door and he'd dropped the backpack on the floor, reaching for Lacey before they even had the door fully closed. He'd needed to tell her without words how much he cherished her. He was better with actions than words. And while words had won her heart earlier, his body was going to seal the promise they'd made. They'd both toed off their walking shoes and then he'd pressed his lips to hers, pushing her up against the kitchen table. She'd responded with equal urgency, her tongue sliding over his, stroking and tugging. She'd smelled like sunshine and a salty breeze, her amber eyes wide and dilated with desire.

Her hands slipped beneath his tee, caressing his back but he wanted—no, needed—skin on skin. Breaking their kiss, he'd grabbed the hem of her T-shirt and she obligingly lifted her arms so he could slide it off in one easy motion, revealing her cotton sports bra. That had to go too, and he'd quickly unsnapped it with one hand, while the other tugged the tie from her ponytail to let her blonde hair cascade over her bare shoulders. He drank in the sight of her, resting her hands against the table, naked to the waist, letting him look his fill of her beautiful breasts.

Not able to keep his hands off her, he'd cupped one breast and then leaned in to taste the other with his mouth. She'd gasped and leaned back onto the table, her fingers tangling in his hair, urging him on. His hand drifted down her belly, fingers undoing the button of her shorts and then slipping inside, down to the core of her. Lacey tipped her head back and groaned as he'd touched her, the sound hitting him right in the middle of the chest. A pulse beat erratically in her neck, and he'd leaned in and tasted her skin, savoring the feel of her blood pumping beneath his lips, as his fingers explored between her legs.

"You. Clothes off," she'd demanded through ragged breaths, and he'd done as she commanded, stripping himself naked in a few seconds.

He'd barely had her shorts and panties down over her ankles before he'd lifted her by the hips up onto the kitchen table. There was no time to make it to the bedroom, and he thanked the powers that be they no longer needed to use a condom. Because he was going to take her here, needing to be inside her before he exploded. He was rock hard. Lifting her buttocks, he'd pulled her closer to the edge and then watched her face as he slipped inside. Watched her face as she closed her eyes and let passion overtake her.

They rocked, locked together at the pelvis as he took her, hard, fast, and deep. Lacey's nails dug into the skin on his back as she moaned in pleasure. He became lost in the aching desire, mindless and vulnerable at the same time. His stomach tightened, and he'd known he was close. Lacey was panting in his ear now, urging him on, increasing their rhythm and he could feel her building toward her own crescendo. She'd tensed in his arms, clenching around him and he thrust a few more times, until, with a great shudder, Lacey cried out his name, and he let himself fall over the edge with her.

Afterward, he'd lifted her off the table and carried her to their bedroom, where they'd made love twice more, taking their time now their craving had been dampened by the quick, dirty, and oh so satisfying first time.

A kiss on his cheek woke him up, and he opened his eyes to see Lacey staring at him, eyes half-lidded with sleep. Wow, he must've fallen asleep after all.

"Your phone is ringing," she said, pointing to the door, and he remembered his phone was still in the back pocket of his shorts.

He had half a mind to ignore it. Glancing at the digital clock on the bedside he saw it was after four. Most of the day was gone already. And what a day it'd been. But he knew he needed to answer the call, it was most likely work, and although he'd put it out of his mind for the past few hours, it was probably time to start thinking like a detective with a double murder case to solve again.

With a groan, he rolled out of bed and then leaned in to kiss Lacey on the forehead before walking buck naked down the hallway toward the kitchen and his discarded clothes. The phone had stopped ringing by the time he'd fished it out of his shorts.

It was the station, just as he'd thought. He'd call them back in a moment. Pulling on his clothes, he went to flick on the coffee machine and then let Smudge out the back door. Poor Smudge had lain on his mat all afternoon, ignored and forgotten. But the dog had had a great walk this morning, so Nico pushed the guilt aside, knowing Smudge had probably slept the whole time, twitching and dreaming about chasing seagulls up the beach.

He was going to need coffee if he was to get back into work mode this afternoon. Turning his phone over, ready to return the work call, he was surprised to see he had two messages from an unknown number. Upon opening them, he saw they were from Sukey's father. Nico had left his card with the family after his interview, urging them to contact him if they thought of anything else that might be relevant to their daughter's death, big or small, night or day. The message said: *We found this photo of Sukey and Zoya in an old photo album. Not sure if this helps. Sorry, we don't know the names of the other two girls in the photo.*

There was an image attached to the message. He clicked on it and then enlarged it, peering intently at the picture. It showed four teenage girls, all of them standing in a line with their arms around each other, wearing gymnast leotards. The photo had clearly been taken at the Somerset Gym as Nico could see the sign up on the wall behind them. *Practice Makes Perfect.* He recognized Zoya on the end, her arm around Sukey, both girls grinning and holding up a trophy between them. Perhaps they'd just won a local competition, but the picture was too grainy to make out what the writing on the trophy said.

Nico peered closer.

"Holy shit," he whispered.

Striding down the hallway, he almost skidded through the door to the bedroom. "Lacey," he called, and she lifted a sleepy head from her pillow. "I need you to look at this photo for me." He didn't give her any more details, just handed her the phone and waited. Lacey blinked a few times, giving a confused frown, but took the phone and narrowed her eyes at the picture. It only took her two seconds to see what he'd seen.

"Is that Tia Brown on the end?" she asked, her face going from sleepy to alert in a single second.

"I wasn't sure," he replied. "But I think you've just confirmed it."

"This means Tia knew Sukey and Zoya. How did we not make that connection earlier?" As she'd sat up in bed to look at the photo more closely, the sheet fell away to reveal her spectacular breasts, and Nico had to force his gaze away so he could focus properly.

"The mother never told us she practiced gymnastics," Nico growled. And he suddenly wondered if that omission had been intentional.

186

Absently, Lacey pulled the sheet up to cover herself as she looked up at him, biting her bottom lip in thought. "Do you think these are the girls her brother mentioned? The ones who were bullying her?"

"God, I love you." He bent down and kissed her soundly on the lips, because that's exactly what he'd been thinking. He went to take his phone from Lacey's grasp, but she pulled it back.

"Wait. Who is this other girl in the photo?"

"I don't know, but I think we need to find out damn fast. Don't you?"

"Yes." She was already scrambling out of bed. But then she must've remembered her clothes were also still lying on the floor in the kitchen, as she grimaced, then marched out the door, leaving Nico to follow behind, surveying her very fine ass as she sashayed down the hallway. He watched her getting dressed without uttering a word. Talk about a distraction. How the hell was he supposed to do any work now, when all he wanted was to toss her back up on that table and go another round or ten with her?

"What's the plan?" she asked as she slipped her T-shirt down her arms and over her head, blocking his view of her enticing body, then tied back her hair in a neat ponytail at the same time.

He held up a finger as he listened to the message from work. It was from Constable Hickey asking him to call back when he had time. It didn't sound urgent, but Nico was already feeling guilty that his team were still diligently working on a Sunday, while he'd been lazing in bed. Admittedly, he'd just restored his relationship with the most important person in the world, so the guilt was easy to push down. But now he had what might just be the most valuable piece to the puzzle in that image of the girls, his mind wouldn't stop whirling.

"I'm going into work," Nico declared. This photo was a big breakthrough, and he knew he wouldn't be able to rest until he'd looked deeper into it.

"I'm coming with you."

He started to argue that this was her rostered day off, but one glance at her beautiful, determined face made him shut his mouth with a click. She was just as invested in this case as he was. He couldn't stop her. And he shouldn't stop her. But there was one thing he needed to do before they got back into work mode.

In two steps, he'd swept her up into his arms, lifting her so her feet were off the ground. "I love you." Their eyes locked and as he stared into her gorgeous, whisky-brown eyes, he knew he'd never been happier than in that particular moment.

"I love you too," she agreed. "I never stopped loving you. Things just got a little...complicated for a while."

Amen to that, he thought, as he kissed her lightly on the lips. The world was the right way around again, and now he was secure in Lacey's devotion, he was able to think clearly about other things.

"I'm going to get changed," he said, placing her gently back on her feet. He probably shouldn't go into the station dressed like he'd just come from a day on the beach. He was lead investigator on this case and had a reputation to uphold.

Lacey, however, shook her head and said, "I'm not technically on duty, so I'll forego the uniform tonight. Which reminds me." She pushed out of his arms. "I need to put a wash on before we go, I've got no clean shirts for work." She rushed to the bedroom and then he heard the machine beep in the laundry as she programmed the wash.

While he waited for Lacey, he phoned Sukey's father to thank him for the image, and to ask if they had any further details they could share. But he drew a blank, the sister told him, after translating her father's words, telling him it was from one of Sukey's photo albums she kept in her room, and they'd never seen the photo before. Perhaps one of the other mothers had taken it, but they weren't sure.

Nico didn't let that little drawback bring him down. He had a clue, now he just needed to follow it up and find out where it led.

They were in his Jeep and on their way into town less than five minutes later.

"Can you please call work for me?" Nico asked, handing Lacey the phone as she sat in the passenger seat. The call went through his Bluetooth connection and Karl Hickey answered after the second ring.

"Hi, boss," he said genially. "I've got some great news. I finally tracked down Sukey Lui's boyfriend."

"You're on speaker, Lacey's in the car with me," Nico warned. "We're on our way into work. We've got something to share as well," he said. "But tell me what you found."

"Hi, Lacey," Hickey sang out. For a big, gruff man, who reminded Nico a little of a bulldog and often growled a greeting at his fellow constables, Karl was always polite and friendly with Lacey. Nico thought he might harbor a secret crush on her, but he couldn't begrudge the man, she *was* gorgeous, after all. "Dan Huang wasn't too hard to track down," Hickey continued. "He works for a company called Drift Merchants, an importer who has a warehouse at Macquarie Docks in Hobart. I asked a couple of officers from down that way to go and pay him a visit."

"How did that go?" Nico prompted.

"Dan confirmed he was Sukey's boyfriend, and when they told him about her death, he seemed genuinely shocked."

"But we released Sukey's name to the media on Friday night. Did he not see that on the news?" Nico questioned. Yet another person who didn't stay up-to-date with current events. What was with all these people?

"Sounds like he was out partying all weekend," Hickey replied with a grunt. "The Hobart officers said they had to practically break his door down before he heard them knocking at his apartment. He dragged himself out of bed to answer the door because he'd only got home a few hours ago." Okay, that might explain it. "So what about the story of Sukey going down to visit him?"

"Dan confirmed that Sukey was supposed to come and stay with him on the weekend of the fourth." Nico decided that fitted the timeline, as it was coming up to three weeks ago. "But she never showed up. He just thought her parents had found out and stopped her from coming."

"And he didn't try and call her? Contact her in any way?"

"I believe he did call a few times, but when there was no answer, he wasn't worried…" Hickey hesitated for a moment. "The guy seemed like a bit of a dick," he admitted. "From his point of view, whatever he and Sukey had going on was strictly casual. No strings attached. Sounds like he's seeing other women when Sukey wasn't in Hobart. And he likes to party hard."

"Hmm. Maybe the parents were right to try and keep their daughter away from the deadbeat boyfriend," Nico mused.

"Yeah, he might be a deadbeat, but he has an alibi for the time frame surrounding Sukey's death. He worked a double shift on the docks that weekend. Says he has multiple witnesses who can confirm," Hickey continued. Autopsy had narrowed Sukey's time of death down as best they could to the weekend two weeks before Zoya was killed.

"What about an alibi for Zoya's death?" Nico asked. It was a long shot, but if the two deaths were connected and he couldn't supply an alibi for last Sunday, then…

"Yeah, same as for Sukey's death. He says he takes the weekend double shifts because they pay more. Seems like he regularly swaps shifts with the other workers so he can get paid more."

"So the guy is either partying all weekend, or working all weekend," Nico growled.

"Seems like it," Hickey replied.

"What about suspected links to a triad?" It'd been Sukey's parents who'd waved this red flag, and Nico wondered how many of their suspicions were based on fact, and how much was on sheer dislike of the guy.

"Still digging into that one. The company he works for imports products from China, clearly. But so do a lot of other companies. And they seem legit from what I can tell so far."

"Keep digging," Nico instructed. "We'll be in the office soon." Nico signed for Lacey to end the call.

They sat in silence for a few moments, the only sound being the tires humming on the road, digesting this new info. "Interesting," Lacey finally said, turning from her perusal of the passing landscape to look at him. "So, who's still on our list of possible suspects?" she asked, holding up her fingers so she could tick them off. "Erica Nellenbach?"

"Yes," he agreed. She was a strong suspect, because she knew both of the victims, and because Zoya had perhaps tried to blackmail her. But that still didn't account for why Erica also killed Sukey, unless the other girl was in on the blackmail too.

"Mike Baldwin?"

"Definitely," he agreed. That man had looked at Lacey in exactly the wrong way. The way that had Nico seeing red. When Lacey had called him Creepy Mike, she hadn't been wrong. There was something off with that guy that warranted a deeper investigation.

"The boyfriend, Dan Huang?" He had been on Nico's list, right at the top, but his alibi seemed solid according to Hickey, although that'd need to be confirmed. "And even if he had something to do with Sukey's death, why on earth would he want to kill Zoya?" Lacey continued.

It was true. They still hadn't uncovered the link between why the two girls were murdered. Unless there were two separate killers. The coincidence seemed way too high to surmise they were killed individually, but showed exactly the same mode of execution and then dumped in the same location. There had to be a link, he was just damned if he could see it.

"I don't know about him," Nico admitted. "Perhaps I need to head down to Hobart and interview him myself." But he wasn't sure what that might achieve. With an inexact time of death for Sukey due to her immersion in the water and attack by wild animals, they needed to try and pin down Dan Huang's movements for a few days before and after the given date just to be sure. It was a good four-hour drive from Hobart to Burnie. It was conceivable that Dan had driven up here, murdered Sukey, and then driven home again, all in the space of one night. Conceivable, but not likely.

"Are we still considering this mysterious serial killer as a suspect?" She posed this question in a soft voice while studying him seriously.

Nico was completely stumped on that one. "I don't know," he admitted. "We can't discount them. Even though the deaths don't really seem to fit his preferred killing style or profile. Neither of these two girls were involved in the sex trade." So far, the serial killer had only taken the lives of women who were well known to prostitute themselves for money. Not high-end escorts either, but the type who sold their bodies on the street. Which perhaps made them an easier target. All three victims of this supposed serial killer had also been drug addicts, using the money they scored from their activities to buy their next hit. Another way to make them easy targets. All the guy had to do was offer them a hit, then wait until they were high to grab them. Neither Sukey nor Zoya ticked any of those boxes.

Lacey nodded sagely, staring out the front windshield and biting her lip.

"And now we have this new information. The photo of the four girls." She hesitated as something seemed to occur to her. "Perhaps our murders are somehow connected to Tia Brown's death?" she mused quietly, almost as if posing the question to herself. He loved the way her mind worked. Loved how good they were at this; batting the facts back and forward between each other, trying to come up with an answer. Not only were their bodies made for each other, but their minds were made for each other too.

"I'm definitely going to bring both Sandra and Taj in tomorrow for a second interview," Nico conferred. "I want to ask Sandra about these girls who were bullying Tia, and why she told Taj she'd taken care of them."

"Me too." Lacey nodded thoughtfully. "It's strange she never once mentioned that Tia was being bullied to us. And it's not listed in the notes from four years ago either. Why would Sandra keep that a secret? It could be the reason Tia committed suicide. If she was being severely bullied by these girls. Perhaps they even coerced her into the suicide. You hear about these people on social media all the time now. Hounding and taunting a victim, telling them the world would be a better place without them. Pushing that person over the edge until they finally can't stand it anymore." Lacey gave a shudder. "And they get away with it because no one is held accountable."

"Yes," he agreed, placing a hand on her thigh, feeling the slight trembling as she clenched her fists in her lap. It made him incandescent with rage too. That these people hid behind the veil of social media anonymity. They even had a name for it. Cyberbullying.

"What about the unidentified girl in the photo? Could she be one of these bullies too?"

"Maybe," he conceded. "I'll get facial rec onto it as soon as we get into the office." But there was one angle that Lacey didn't seem to have considered with all this stuff she was throwing around about bullies and suicides. "Or else she could be another intended victim," he added quietly. If they looked at the other side of the coin, instead of fixating on the fact that Tia had perhaps been bullied by these girls—and that was yet to be proven—this photo could also be seen as a list of targets. And now there was only one of them left alive.

Lacey's eyes went wide at Nico's words. "Oh, shit, I never thought of it that way. But of course. The other three girls are all dead. She could be next."

"Exactly. If the killer is picking those girls off one by one, Tia four years ago, and then Sukey and Zoya now, although I'm not sure why there was such a big gap between the deaths."

"We need to find this fourth girl," Lacey said emphatically, flashing her amber gaze at him, determination in the set of her jaw.

"I intend to," he replied. He was going to switch all his available people-power onto identifying this girl, hopefully tonight. She might be the key to this whole investigation. But was she an intended victim or perhaps the perpetrator? Erica Nellenbach might know who she was if he showed her the photo, but she wasn't scheduled to come in for an interview until tomorrow morning, and he doubted she'd answer his calls tonight.

There were so many unrelated details in this investigation it was starting to give him hives. For example, he wished they could find Sukey's missing car and other personal belongings. Perhaps they might offer some leads as to how Sukey was abducted. And why? But they remained stubbornly unaccounted for. Nico had immediately checked all the chop shops in town to see if it'd been sold to a wrecker for parts, but that was a dead end. He'd even had police divers search in the large pools along the river where the two girls had been found, to no avail. Should he widen that search to other surrounding bodies of water? Without any clear evidence pointing to the fact the car had been dumped in there, it'd probably be a waste of time. Where else could a little Toyota Corolla be hiding?

And yet they'd found Zoya's handbag sitting in the middle of her kitchen countertop and her car sitting in its spot in the parking garage, untouched. No one had tried to hide that; it was almost as if it'd been discarded as of no consequence to the killer. The lack of consistency was infuriating. Nico almost laughed out loud at himself. Yeah, right. Why on earth was he expecting consistency from a murderer?

"It's going to be a long night," he said, and Lacey nodded her acknowledgement. "I'm going to order in Chinese takeaway from down the road once we get to the station," he added. The least he could do was feed everyone if they were going to pull an all-nighter. Because he had a feeling this was going to be exactly that.

"That'd be nice." She covered his hand on her thigh with hers and they drove the rest of the way into Burnie discussing the finer points of the case, their hands remaining connected as one.

He didn't ever plan on letting Lacey Carmichael go.

CHAPTER SEVENTEEN

Lacey woke with a start and took a few seconds to orient herself. Lifting her head off her hands, she blinked a couple of times, letting her eyes adjust to the bright room. She must've fallen asleep at her desk she realized guiltily. A quick glance out the windows told her it was early morning, the weak sunlight playing off the window panes. Nico was still there at his makeshift desk at the front of the room, tapping away at his computer. Tyrell was at a desk to her left, and he looked at her as she raised her head and gave her a crooked smile, rubbing his neck and yawning like a hippo. Another pang of guilt lit up her insides. Everyone else was still hard at work, and she'd fallen asleep.

Lacey remembered she'd been scanning through hundreds of images on Facebook, trying to find a match to the fourth girl in the photo. Looking at the other girls' profiles and then trolling through all their friends and relatives, following links and hunches to see if she could track down the mysterious woman.

"I found her." Sally-Ann was standing in the middle of the operations room, waving a sheet of paper above her head and almost jumping for joy. It must've been Sally-Ann's entry that had woken Lacey.

"I hacked into the Somerset Gymnastics Club website," she admitted. Something that probably technically required a warrant, but Sally-Ann clearly didn't have the time or patience to wait for a judge to issue that. Her hacking skills were world-renowned. Nico often commented that she should've joined the IT department instead of becoming a constable. "It has a parent's and gymnast's portal, where they can go in and look at training schedules, awards, upcoming competitions, and, best of all, a whole album of photos of the kids going back for the past eight years. I found the exact same photo on the website that Sukey's parents gave us. And the best part is, it lists the girls' names as winners of the under fourteen group floor routine for the western highlands district." Sally-Ann couldn't keep the jubilation off her face.

"Great." Nico stood up and beckoned Sally-Ann to the front.

Hickey appeared in the doorway, rubbing his eyes and yawning, his face curious and Lacey suddenly knew she hadn't been the only one to succumb to heavy eyelids. He must've been woken by Sally-Ann's gleeful shouting as well.

"Karl, go and round up everyone you can find. We need to get onto this right away."

"Yes, sir." Hickey shook himself and stood a little straighter.

Nico huddled in close when Sally-Ann approached and showed him the information she'd uncovered. Lacey stood and stretched her arms above her head. She was still wearing her cargo shorts and T-shirt from yesterday, with a cardigan draped over her shoulders to combat the colder-than-necessary air conditioning. She reached up to pat down her hair and decided she must look a sight. But then, as she looked around the room, she noticed others had fared no better. Lawson, who was still in her uniform, now crumpled and creased down the back, had huge dark circles under her pretty brown eyes, her long, dark hair also escaping her ponytail in whips. Pederson was hunkered by a desk in the corner, his normally clean-shaven countenance showing signs of a lot more than a five o'clock shadow. He also had dark rings under his eyes.

Tasmin Saito strode into the room, holding two mugs of coffee, placing one in front of Pederson and then taking the seat next to him. The Asian woman looked annoyingly well-groomed, her clothes spotless and unwrinkled as she quietly surveyed the room. That woman never seemed to have a hair out of place or let anything ruffle her. Lacey would kill for one of those cups of coffee.

More people began to spill into the room and the noise level rose higher as Lacey retook her seat.

Nico held up his hand, and the room immediately became quiet. "Her name is Teresa Thompson," he announced without preamble.

Lacey took in the name, even as she retied her hair into a ponytail and ran her hands over her face.

"We have a home address but very few other details," Nico went on, writing her name and details up on the murder board as he spoke. "I want everyone to throw everything they have at finding out more about this girl," he commanded. "She could be the key to this whole investigation." Nico tapped the pen loudly on the whiteboard, emphasizing the line he'd drawn under Teresa's name. "Sally-Ann and I are going to check out the home address right now."

There were a few crestfallen faces as Nico announced this. Everyone was itching to accompany him. Lacey looked down at herself, still in her civilian clothes and cursed silently. She had a spare uniform in her locker, of course, but it'd take a while for her to go and change and make herself look presentable. Of course, it should be Sally-Ann who went with him, she'd found the girl, after all. She hid her disappointment behind a tired smile as his gaze found hers.

"Saito and Pederson, I want you to go back and talk to both Zoya's and Sukey's parents." He'd swapped his intense gaze to the two detectives seated in the corner. "See if they remember any more about this girl. And what they got up to together. Were they just friends at the club? We've already ascertained they didn't all go to the same school."

Lacey went over what she knew about the three girls in her head. Tia went to that private Anglican school in the outskirts suburb of Wivanhoe, Sukey attended the Burnie's regional public school, and Zoya was at the alternative indie school in a trendy rehabilitated old warehouse in the middle of the main street. It was one of the reasons it'd been so hard to track down the connections between the two murdered girls at first. And the reason no red flags had immediately gone up when they'd heard from Tia's brother that she'd been bullied. Their connection had been through the gymnastics club all along.

"We need to know why three out of the four girls in this photo are now dead," Nico finished.

Pederson nodded his acknowledgement, but Saito sat up straighter. "What about the mother of the girl who hanged herself?" Saito asked in her smooth, no-nonsense tone.

"Leave her to me," Nico said with a serious frown. Saito merely raised one perfectly manicured eyebrow.

Nico ignored her skeptical look and turned his head. "Tyrell," Nico caught the man's eyes. "I have Erica Nellenbach and her lawyer coming in this morning for another interview. Can you handle that one?"

"Yes, sir." Tyrell sat straighter in his chair, a grin tugging at the corner of his mouth, as he seemed to relish the thought of questioning the gymnastics coach.

"We need to know the exact details of what was in those

texts between her and Zoya," Nico said. "You should make it very clear to her and her lawyer that if she doesn't comply, I will put out an arrest warrant in her name for obstruction of justice."

"Yes, boss." Tyrell's white-toothed smile got even bigger.

"And I want to know everything she does about those four girls. How long they were at the gymnastics club, how long they knew each other, that kind of thing."

Tyrell nodded and gathered up his things.

"Everyone else, track down as much info as you can on Teresa Thompson. See if we can figure out what her connection is with the other three girls in that photo. How does a possible friendship and the fact they were teammates when they were fourteen, relate to one of them committing suicide four years ago and then two of them being murdered now?"

There was a flurry of activity as everyone got to their allocated tasks. It looked like she'd be deskbound for at least the next few hours, unless a priority call came in, which probably wasn't a bad thing given how tired she was feeling. She watched Nico gather his things and could hardly believe it'd been barely less than twelve hours ago they'd been cocooned in their bed reigniting their love for each other. Now reality hit like a baseball bat to the side of the head and yesterday felt like a dream.

Nico picked up his pile of papers and began to follow Sally-Ann out of the room, but took a detour through the desks, aiming straight for Lacey. "You okay?" He touched a hand to her cheek, and that brief contact was enough to remind her how much he cared as she fleetingly leaned into his palm. It reminded her how much she loved him in return. It also reminded her of their erotic afternoon in bed yesterday and her mind flooded with images of Nico, of the way he brushed the silky locks of her blonde hair away from her face while he stared deep into her eyes, as his other hand trailed down her stomach to the juncture of her thighs. Or the look on his face as he hovered above her, ready to plunge in deep. She felt the blood rise up her neck at the debauched memories. Nodding, she quickly kissed his cheek, then waved him away, hoping nobody saw those few seconds of intimacy that'd passed between them. Part of her was delighted that he'd taken the time to make sure she was fine before he left. And part of her was feeling a tad uncomfortable that everyone had seen their exchange. Delight won out in the end. He was taking the time to show her how special she was, to reinforce their bond, and he didn't care who saw it.

"I'll see you soon," he promised as he headed toward the doorway, where Sally-Ann stood waiting, and again she nodded her reply, willing the heat to leave her cheeks. When her gaze swept the room, most people had the decency to look preoccupied with whatever they were doing, but Tyrell cast her a mischievous grin, and she groaned silently. Oh yeah, they'd all noticed all right.

Her official shift started at eight this morning, so Lacey took herself off to the locker room to shower and change. At least she'd had the luxury of a few hours' sleep, unlike most others on the team, it seemed. She almost wished Nico had woken her up, but then part of her was glad she'd caught that nap, it might be the only thing that got her through the next eight hours.

With two strong mugs of coffee and a pastry from the break room under her belt, she went back to the operations room to tackle the job of gathering as much intel on Teresa as she could. Ten minutes later, Hickey and Gorman were called out to investigate a break-in over at a car wreckers on the outskirts of town, and that left her and Lawson riding the computers together.

Lacey established that Teresa worked for a wilderness expedition company offering outdoor activities for the adventurous. The website listed Teresa as a guide for all wilderness walks, including the Overland Track. *What an interesting job*, Lacey decided, as she dialed the company number listed on the website, hoping someone would be there to answer the phone at such an early hour. Often the best way to gain credible information was to talk directly to an employer or colleague. She got a recorded message telling her the office didn't open until nine am, but if she liked to leave a message, someone would get back to her ASAP. Lacey asked them to call her back and hung up before going back to the wilderness activities website to see if she could glean any more information.

Less than an hour after Nico had left, he and Sally-Ann blew back into the operations room, a heavy frown marring his handsome features. "No one was home, and there was no car in the garage," he reported when their two pairs of curious eyes rested on him. "None of the neighbors knew where she was either. Actually, they were decidedly unhelpful," he added. "What have you two found out?"

Lacey showed him the information on Teresa's workplace and told him she was hoping for a call back in an hour or so. Lawson had no luck uncovering any police records or misdemeanors, not even a speeding fine. But she got him a make and model of the car Teresa drove as well as the license plate number, and he asked her to put out a trace on the car.

Now what? Lacey glanced over at Nico, but he was standing staring at the whiteboard, tapping his chin with his index finger, Sally-Ann right next to him. Both looked a little stumped and more than a little tired from their all-nighter.

"If you don't need me anymore, boss, I'm going to head home for a few hours and catch up on some sleep," Sally-Ann said, smothering a yawn with her hand.

"Sure thing. You did great Sally-Ann, you deserve a rest," Nico said, draping an arm around her shoulder and giving her a quick hug. Lacey liked that he had an easy camaraderie with most of his staff. Other women might be jealous, but Lacey knew Nico and Sally-Ann had a strong friendship and she was fine with that.

"We could send someone over to the wilderness shopfront. They might not be open yet, or answering the phone, but someone may be there," Lacey suggested. If Teresa had gone to work early, it may answer the question as to why she wasn't at home. Problem was, the main shopfront was in Devonport, over half an hour away. By the time they got there someone may well have called Lacey back.

Nico shook his head and seemed to be considering something. "Why don't you and I pop over and pay Mrs. Sandra Brown another visit while we're waiting for more info on Teresa?" Nico said, looking straight into Lacey's eyes. "You did a good job of picking up on the little things they seemed to have missed the first time around after Tia died. I'd like you to come with me this time as well."

Lacey felt a tingle of pride at his assessment, which she knew had nothing to do with the fact they were a couple and everything to do with her growing aptitude as a junior constable.

But instead of agreeing straight away, she gave him a searching look. Nico was exhausted; she could see it in the pallor of his skin and the way the lines around his mouth stretched tight. She wanted to tell him to go and get a few hours' sleep. He was running on fumes. Nico could lock the door to his office and stretch out on the floor behind his desk. She knew he'd done it before. But then Lacey glanced over at Lawson, who was watching their exchange with curious eyes. It wasn't Lacey's place to tell Nico how to conduct himself at work, and so she had to remove her personal feelings from the equation and trust him to know what he was doing when it came to his professional life.

"Good idea," she said, standing and readjusting her duty belt.

"See if you can track down Teresa's family," Nico said to Lawson as he turned to follow Lacey out the door. "If they live locally, we need to talk to them as well."

"Yes, sir."

Lacey felt a twinge of guilt that poor Lawson got stuck behind the desk to do all the research alone, but Lawson gave a resigned shrug and went back to her computer. In the end, they all had a job to do, and Lacey knew they might grumble about it at times, but the fact-finding and analysis was just as important as the fieldwork, often more so.

She retrieved her service weapon from the firearms cage where it'd remained locked up overnight and followed Nico, who'd already signed out a cruiser. The drive took less than fifteen minutes, but instead of talking work, Lacey took the time to rest her hand on Nico's knee as he drove—police protocol be damned—and let her gaze wander over his familiar face, enjoying their time alone in the car together. They didn't even need to talk; she just used the time to reconnect. She studied his profile as he drove. He'd pulled his shoulder-length hair into a man bun at the nape of his neck, his intense blue eyes fixed on the road, full lips set in a firm line, a three-day growth running over his chin and up his square jaw, his slightly crooked nose that gave him the look of a warrior about to go onto the battlefield.

When Nico pulled the cruiser up to the curb beside Sandra Brown's house, Lacey leaned over and kissed him on the lips. A quick, light kiss, but letting him know without words how much she loved him. How much she loved that they could work together. How glad she was they'd sorted out their problems, that he'd stayed strong and true until she came back to him, even while she struggled with her own foolish internal demons.

Then they both turned to look at the house across the street. The curtains were drawn, and the place was dark, the little brick building looked run-down and a tad forlorn. And sad. Lacey could almost feel the wretched aura of a mother living with the death of her beloved child hanging over the place.

As they stepped out of the car, Lacey's phone rang. Nico indicated that she should take the call. It was a young woman, called Gina, from Wilderness Activities returning her call. Lacey waved Nico over and put the girl on speaker.

Lacey identified herself in her most professional voice and then said, "Thanks for returning my call. I was hoping I could speak to one of your employees, Teresa Thompson."

There was a slight pause on the other end of the line as Gina seemed to absorb her words. "Teresa isn't here right now," she said with a slight wobble in her voice. At least she'd confirmed the woman worked for them, but why did the girl sound worried?

"Do you know when she'll be in?"

"I'm not sure I'm allowed to give out that information," Gina hedged, and Nico rolled his eyes. The last thing they needed was some young girl wary of cooperating. She was obviously afraid of getting in trouble with the boss.

"Yes, you are allowed to give out that information. It's actually required by law," Lacey replied, using a more conciliatory tone. "If anyone tells you anything contrary, you just tell them to phone the Burnie Police Department and we'll set them straight."

"Oh, okay. If you're sure." The woman hesitated a moment longer, then she blurted out, "Teresa is taking a group on a guided tour of the Overland Track. They left yesterday, and they won't be back for a week."

"Oh, shit," Nico mouthed. That wasn't what either of them had been expecting to hear.

"I guess that means she's out of contact?" Lacey asked. She assumed there wasn't much phone reception up in the wilds of Cradle Mountain. "We'd really like to talk to her, sooner rather than later. It's very important."

This time Gina didn't hesitate. "All our guides carry satellite phones," she told them with an air of triumph. "Teresa is required to check in every night once they've made camp. It's a safety protocol, you see."

"Okay." That sounded a little more promising. "Can you send me that number please?"

"I guess so." Gina had gone back to being unsure again. "I'll just check with Jake, the owner, first," she added, and Lacey let out a quiet sigh of frustration. "He's due in to work really soon," Gina said by way of placation.

"Could you please get back to me as soon as you have his answer? This is really important." Lacey sent Nico a dissatisfied look. They could always try and force the issue, but if this Jake was due in soon, they could wait a little while so as not to upset Gina further. If need be, they could go and pay the Wilderness Activities company a visit after they finished with Sandra.

"But just so you know, Teresa only turns the sat phone on for around half an hour in the evening. You won't be able to call her until then. But you can leave a voicemail, if you like."

"Okay, thank you." Another stumbling block. It was almost as if the universe was conspiring against them.

There was a momentary silence on the line, then Gina asked, "Can I ask what all this is about? Is Teresa in trouble or something?" The girl sounded genuinely worried about the other woman.

"We just need to ask her a few questions, that's all." Lacey quoted the words that'd now become rote. It was a stock phrase police used to placate a member of the public, but not for the first time, Lacey wondered if people actually believed they were going to get some juicy gossip straight from the mouth of the local constabulary.

"I'll call you back soon." Gina rang off and Lacey tucked her phone back into the top pocket of her uniform shirt, disgruntled at their lack of progress in getting to talk to Teresa.

"She's gone for a whole week," Lacey repeated in a disgruntled tone.

"I know," Nico agreed. It was always harder to get information from a person when you couldn't see their face. It was one of the reasons she knew Nico liked to conduct as many interviews as possible himself. You could tell things by looking at their body language, little giveaways in their faces they didn't even realize they were making. But a voice over the phone was much harder to get a good read on.

"She's only been gone a day. Could we get her to turn around and come back?" she asked, thinking aloud. Nico was walking across the street, so she followed in his wake.

"Not sure," Nico mused, looking at her over his shoulder. "Not even sure that's warranted yet. Let's see if we can talk to the family first, see if we can get a better read on this woman and her backstory. See if they can give us any more information on this little teenage foursome." He reached the front steps and bounded up them to the small porch where he lifted his hand to knock on the door.

While they waited for an answer, Lacey said, "I know this is just purely speculation at the moment, and is probably stretching the parameters of the case, but..." Lacey stopped to gather her thoughts before going on. "You said it yourself last night. If the killer is targeting all the girls in the photo— even though we have absolutely no proof of that—shouldn't we warn her? Let her know she might be in danger?"

"Yes," Nico agreed. "If it comes to that. But on the other hand, she could also be the killer. And then the last thing we want to do is tip her off that we're onto her."

"Hmm." Lacey frowned.

Nico knocked on the door again, then they both listened for any movement inside. "Doesn't look like she's home," Lacey said. It was only eight thirty, where could Sandra have gone this early in the morning?

"Damn," Nico growled.

He stepped around her and went down the steps and into the driveway, staring at the garage door which was shut tight. There was a gate leading down the side of the garage to the backyard, and Nico poked his head over the gate and stood on tiptoe. Technically, they weren't allowed on the property without an invitation, a warrant, or probable cause that a crime was being committed.

"The garage is empty," Nico reported. "Her car is gone." Lacey remembered back to the other morning when they'd interviewed Sandra. She'd noticed the garage door had been up that day, and a little white Subaru was nestled inside.

"She could've popped to the shops. Or have a doctor's appointment." Lacey ticked off any number of reasons that Sandra Brown wasn't home. But she could see by the look in Nico's eyes that his gut feeling was telling him something was off. And she agreed with him. "Do you think she's avoiding us? She never mentioned she might be going out of town," she said, but Nico didn't seem to be listening. He looked like he might be about to clamber over the side gate instead. Lacey opened her mouth to caution him, but was drowned out by the squeal of tires as a four-wheel drive ute pulled into the driveway.

She stared at Taj Brown through the windshield in the driver's seat, her back against the garage door, while he gaped open-mouthed back at her. Clearly he hadn't seen her until he pulled into the driveway. He'd almost hit her. Why was he in such a hurry?

"What are you doing here?" he demanded as he exited the truck.

"I could ask you the same thing?" Nico was suddenly between her and the young man.

She watched a number of emotions flicker across Taj's face as he stood with his car door ajar staring at these two cops in his mother's driveway. She could almost see the cogs turning in his mind as he tried to decide his next course of action.

"I got a text from my mum," he said finally. "It worried me."

Okay. What did that mean? Lacey kept her mouth shut, as did Nico, knowing that silence was often the best way to put someone off-balance and keep them talking.

"I need to see if she's at home," he said, turning his back on them and making his way to the front door. They could already tell him that she wasn't home, but she followed Nico's lead and shadowed the young man to the door.

"Do you think she's in danger?" Nico asked right before Taj put the key in the door. He turned shocked blue eyes on the detective. "Should I go in first?" Nico clarified, putting his hand on his gun holster. Lacey reached instinctively for her own weapon, resting her hand on the catch of her gun holster, ready to release it in an instant if required.

"Oh, God. No." Taj shook his head with urgency. "There's no one in there holding her at gunpoint, if that's what you mean." Then he hesitated as he seemed to think of something else. "And she's not a danger to me either, if that's what you're thinking." Clearly, Nico was thinking exactly that as he peered suspiciously at the door.

"I think she may have done something...stupid. I need to make sure she's okay," he said finally. Whatever that meant. They watched as Taj opened the security door first.

"Do you mind if we come in?" Nico asked, hand still on his gun holster, eyes still fixed suspiciously on the wooden door as Taj turned the key in the lock and it swung open to reveal a darkened hallway. Taj merely shrugged, which Nico clearly took as an affirmative, because he followed the young man into the house, with Lacey hot on his heels.

"Mum, it's me," Taj called, switching on lights as he worked his way through the house. With all the curtains drawn, every room was dark. There was an eerie silence and Lacey already knew that Taj wouldn't find his mother at home. But he kept calling, opening doors, and hollering for his mother, Nico and Lacey taking a slower perusal of the empty house, until they all finally met in the kitchen at the rear of the house.

"Fuck," Taj swore loudly.

"Do you want to tell us what's going on?" Nico said, standing up to his full height and towering over the young man.

"I don't... Fuck," Taj said again. He rubbed a hand across his face, and she could see the uncertainty in his face. "She said she was going to finish a job. That she would finally have peace of mind, after all these years."

"Do you know what job she was referring to?" Lacey asked, pushing her way in front of Nico. Intimidation wasn't going to work on this young lad, Nico needed to back off and let her talk to the guy.

"No." But there was the light of sudden awareness in his eyes. "Maybe. I mean... Maybe I suspected. But I never really thought... Oh God." He covered his eyes and bent over at the waist as if it was suddenly all too much to bear.

"What do you mean?" Lacey coaxed gently, laying a sympathetic hand on his arm. "What did you suspect?"

"In the shed out the back." He stood and pointed toward a dilapidated wooden shed at the back of the yard. The roof looked to be made of wooden shingles, bowing badly in the middle, and what was left of the red paint was now peeling off in big chunks. Lacey was surprised to see how big the yard actually was. This was one of the older blocks that still allowed plenty of room for backyards when it'd been built.

"Do you want us to go and look in the shed?" Nico clarified.

The kid just nodded.

"With me" was all he said to Lacey. This time she did draw her weapon, as they went out the back door and down the three steps to the slightly overgrown garden. They stalked across the lawn toward the shed hunkered in the corner where the two fences met. Her entire concentration was on that shed. What was in there? What would they find? Was it a trap? Was someone hiding in there? Or would they find Sandra's dead body? She had no idea, but she kept all her wild thoughts to herself and when Nico motioned that he was going to take the front and she should take the flank, she veered to her left where a small door bisected the shed halfway down the wooden slabbed side. She watched Nico approach the double doors at the front carefully, slowly. There was a window up high right beside the door, and she stood on tiptoe and peered inside. It was dim and dusty, with an earthen floor, but she could vaguely make out a large shape filling most of the space. A car perhaps. There was no sign of movement, and so she signaled to Nico. He slid back the bolt, and it made a rusty screeching sound that had them both flinching. Her heart was beating like a jackhammer. But still nothing moved, and so Nico threw back the double doors, at the same time as she reached for the doorknob and yanked. The old wooden door was stuck fast, and she had to give it two good kicks before it came loose and she could finally lever it open, terrified that Nico had gone inside without her.

But there he was, just standing in front of the large, bulky shape, holstering his gun. "It's okay," he told her. "There's no one in here."

She holstered her gun.

"Is it a car?" she asked, as he lifted the corner of the large, blue tarp.

A quick glance through the open doors back at the house told Lacey that it was possible to drive a car straight through the garage, as it wasn't enclosed on this side. What was so dangerous about a car, she wondered? Unless... Perhaps they'd find Sandra's body inside the car?

Nico threw back the tarp, uncovering half the car and filling the small shed with dust. Lacey walked around to the front to stand next to Nico.

That's when she saw it. The license plate number was seared into her memory. They'd all been on the lookout for this car. It was one of the missing pieces of the puzzle.

"Holy shit! Is that Sukey Lui's car?" she asked on a whisper.

"I believe it is," Nico replied in a voice that held as much confusion as her own.

CHAPTER EIGHTEEN

Nico looked out the kitchen window to see Sandra Brown's backyard swarming with police officers. Forensics was going over the car still parked up in the shed, taking fingerprints and documenting everything they found as evidence. Nico had already scrutinized the interior—wearing gloves and being as careful as he could not to disturb anything—and had ascertained there were no obvious signs of blood or of a struggle taking place inside the car. A purse and phone were in the car, and he'd already admitted those to evidence. There were more officers in the house, striding up and down the hallway, opening doors and cupboards, picking through the paperwork in the study, pulling out drawers in the main bedroom. All of them looking for the same thing: a clue as to Sandra Brown's next movements. Something to hint at her mental state. Anything so they could track her down.

Taj Brown sat dejectedly at the kitchen table, watching the organized chaos of the police searching his mother's home, his gaze becoming more mutinous with every cupboard door the officers opened or every piece of furniture they moved. Lacey sat opposite him, ostensibly to support him through this traumatic time, but both she and Nico knew she was acting as his unofficial guard as they waited for his lawyer to arrive. Taj wasn't their main POI, his mother was. But that didn't mean he didn't have important information that might help them crack this case, and he couldn't be allowed to run. Which, judging by the increasingly distrustful glances the boy was sending Nico's way, he could possibly be contemplating. A stupid move with this many cops in the vicinity, but perps under pressure often acted in strange and unpredictable ways. Shame he'd clammed up and refused to tell them anything more after they'd found Sukey's car in his mother's shed.

Nico still couldn't believe they'd found her car. After expending so much time and energy on looking for it, they would never have found it if it wasn't for the sheer chance they'd been here when Taj had arrived upset and agitated enough to let it slip that his mother had sent him a peculiar message hinting that something was hidden in her shed.

Nico had come to the swift conclusion that Sandra Brown was in possession of the car because she'd murdered Sukey Lui. There was no other explanation. Even though his mind had struggled to put two and two together when they'd first lifted the tarp and seen the license plate. Both he and Lacey had stared at each other for a full minute in complete silence, incomprehension written all over their faces.

At first, Lacey had tried to fob it off as some sort of terrible coincidence. "There must be some explanation," she'd said. "Maybe the real killer planted the car here to make her look guilty. They're trying to frame her." Lacey had said with a flash of inspiration. "Or maybe it was Taj who hid it here. Maybe he's the murderer." That was a concept Nico was happy to explore. But his gut told him it wasn't correct. The look on Taj's face when he'd first arrived, just after receiving his mother's message, had been one of pure shock. He'd been completely appalled by his own suspicions at what his mother might've done. But those emotions had faded from his features, to be replaced with a sick kind of inevitability. Like he knew exactly what his mother was capable of. Like he knew he'd not only lost his sister four years ago, but was about to lose his mother as well.

"She can't be the person we're looking for. Surely Sandra isn't a murderer? She's just a grieving mother who lost her only daughter," Lacey had said, continuing her argument.

And Nico had replied, "Exactly. A grieving mother with an axe to grind. If she believes those other girls were responsible for Tia committing suicide, that'd be motive enough for murder, don't you think?"

Lacey had been shocked at Nico's words, like she didn't want to believe him. This was the first time she'd come across a potential female killer, and it was always hard to swallow. The idea that a woman, a mother no less, someone who was supposed to be nurturing and compassionate, was capable of something as coldhearted and heinous as murder.

"Perhaps she decided we were getting too close for comfort and she's done a runner," he'd said, his mind already past the obstacle of whether Sandra was the killer and onto the next question of where she'd gone. Maybe their visit the other day had set off alarm bells in Sandra's head and instead of toughing it out, she'd decided that discretion was the better part of valor and hightailed it out of Burnie. "If Taj hadn't turned up when he did and given away her little secret, we may never have found Sukey's car. Never have put it all together," he said to Lacey thoughtfully.

Nico had already put out an APB in an attempt to stop her leaving the island. But it might be too late. If she'd caught the overnight ferry, she might already be on the mainland. It was also conceivable that she'd driven down to Hobart overnight and caught a flight out of the international airport there. Which meant she could be on her way to just about anywhere in the world by now. If that was the case, they might have a better chance of catching her when she landed at the other end. He already had the guys in Hobart trying to trace her movements, but so far, they'd had no luck. There was one other scenario, but Nico didn't think Sandra would be that stupid.

Right then, his phone rang. It was Sally-Ann at the station, helping Lawson with the legwork in trying to track Sandra; she'd come back into work after he and Lacey had found the car and called in all available officers. "We've had a development," she said, not bothering with any of the normal platitudes. "Sandra Brown's car was found parked up near Cradle Mountain. Not in the main parking lot, but down a dirt track a few miles from the main lodge."

"Shit," Nico swore softly. This was the exact scenario he'd just been trying to convince himself wasn't going to happen.

"Do you think Sandra is going after the last girl on her list?" Sally-Ann asked into the ensuing silence. "Is she going to try and kill Teresa?"

It'd make sense. If Sandra was out to get her retribution for her daughter's suicide, and she'd already killed the other two girls, then Teresa was the last one left before Sandra's vengeance was complete.

"Maybe. Shit," he swore again as he dragged a hand through his hair. Why would she be stupid enough to put herself at the risk of getting caught just to fulfill a vendetta? It wasn't the logical choice. The logical choice would've been for her to get the hell out of Tasmania, before the police apprehended her. But criminals didn't always have a logical thought pattern. If Sandra was mentally disturbed enough to actually murder two of the girls she saw as responsible for her daughter's death, then she was mentally disturbed enough not to care about the consequences of going after the third. As long as she achieved her goal, then perhaps it didn't matter if she spent the rest of her years in jail or not. "Thanks,

Sally-Ann," he said and ended the call.

"What's going on?" asked Lacey; she must be able to see the consternation on his face, even if she couldn't hear the conversation.

Nico glanced at Taj. They needed the boy to talk. Needed him to confirm what Nico already suspected. He took two strides over to the table and loomed over Taj, who remained seated. The kid needed to understand how dire this situation was.

Not bothering to make his words gentle, he said, "We found a photo of four girls. One of them was Tia. They were all in a gymnastics team together back when they were fourteen. Two of the other three girls are now dead. That car we found in your mother's shed belonged to one of the dead girls. Is this the group of girls your mother alluded to? The ones she said were bullying Tia?"

Taj glanced up at Nico, eyes widening with fear as he cringed back in the chair.

"I'm waiting for my lawyer to arrive. I don't have to answer your questions. I know my rights," Taj said in a small voice, running a hand over his short-cropped hair, the tattoos on his arm stark against his pale face.

"You need to answer my question. A girl's life might depend on it." Nico leaned in, ever so menacingly.

Lacey stood and put her hand on Nico's arm in warning. Nico was skating on thin ice and they both knew it. Now that Taj had requested his lawyer, Nico wasn't technically allowed to question him until the guy arrived. Questioning him now might make everything Taj said inadmissible in court, but Nico was prepared to take that risk, if it meant saving a life.

"I think you knew what we'd find in your mother's shed. I think you knew what she was capable of," he growled, leaning in even closer so he could get right in Taj's face. "Your mother's car was found up near Cradle Mountain,"

Nico rushed on, ignoring Lacey's hand. He knew the rules, probably better than she did. Knew what he might be risking. Even so, Nico stared at the boy, letting glimpses of his simmering rage show; if he could intimidate the boy into telling him the truth, it might just be worth it. "The third and last girl in that photo is taking a guided walking tour in that area. I need to know if your mother intends to go after this last girl. Will she try and exact her revenge?"

The kid seemed to crumple in on himself, all the self-righteousness and belligerence now gone. "I don't know," Taj confessed. "I truly didn't know what you'd find in her shed."

Nico backed off slightly. "Maybe not," he finally conceded, his gut telling him the boy was telling the truth. "But you had an inkling, didn't you?"

Taj merely nodded. Then he took a deep breath. "My mother was never the same after Tia's death. Like I said before, she mentioned some girls were bullying Tia, but then she told me she'd take care of it, so I never gave it a second thought. Until you guys turned up and started asking questions, and then some things began to make sense."

Lacey's hand dropped away from Nico's arm as the son continued to talk, a frown forming on her face as she processed what he was saying.

"Other things my mum's said since Tia died all started to make a horrible sense," Taj continued. "She has been acting strange for the past few weeks. She became really cold and distant. Not letting me come around and visit, not returning my calls." Nico almost snorted his contempt. How could the woman possibly become any colder? You could already freeze ice on her ass as far as he was concerned.

"My mother has always liked her privacy, especially after Tia's death, but this was different," Taj said when he saw Nico's look of contempt. "I felt something was wrong. So I came around one night to check on her. It was about two weeks ago, and it was late, I'd been out at a mate's place for a few drinks. I drove past and saw her lights were still on, so I came in. She looked kinda flustered when she saw me at the door. And instead of looking like she was getting ready for bed, she was dressed in sort of outdoor gear. I jokingly asked her if she'd been out hiking in the dark. After a moment, she told me that she'd been to visit Tia's tree. That shut me up, as she knew it would, because she still went sometimes to put flowers by the base of the tree."

"You didn't think it was strange she was out doing this so late at night?" Nico queried.

"Yeah, a little," Taj replied. "But what was I supposed to say? This was two weeks ago. Those girls' murders weren't in the news until a few days ago. I never even suspected until then..." Taj stopped talking and his breath hitched. The tough-guy persona seemed to be slipping until it was replaced by a scared and alone little boy whose mother had just turned into a monster.

Nico's mind was racing. If this had been two weeks ago, Taj could have unwittingly walked in on the same night as Sandra had committed the first murder. "You still haven't answered my question," Nico prompted. "Do you think your mother will go after the last girl?"

Taj's face was a picture of misery. "Yes," he whispered. "Once she starts something, she always finishes it. That mantra was drummed into both me and Tia when we were kids. It's probably the reason she wouldn't let Tia quit gymnastics, even if she was being bullied. Mum never liked to admit defeat."

"Shit." Nico stood tall and gritted his teeth.

"I know Mum used to say that it was her fault Tia killed herself," Taj went on, seemingly lost in his own tortured world of memories. "I always told her not to be stupid. Tia was clearly depressed, and she'd done everything a mother could do to try to pull her out of her funk. But thinking about it now, I bet she blamed herself because she was the one who forced Tia to keep going to gymnastics, even though those girls were so mean to her. So in a way, it *was* kind of her fault."

Nico looked down at Taj, and a sliver of sorrow for the kid skittered through his guts. Now he would have to live with not only the wretchedness of his sister's untimely death, but the shame of knowing his mother was a murderer.

"It would've been Tia's twenty-first birthday today," Taj said in a faraway voice.

"What?" Nico froze.

Taj looked up at him, his eyes clearing a little. "After Tia's death, Mum always celebrated her birthday by spending the day sitting by her tree. I knew this one would be extra hard for her. Turning twenty-one is a big milestone, isn't it?" Taj's mouth twisted in a grimace.

"Yes, it is," Nico replied thoughtfully as more of the puzzle pieces slotted into place. Of course. This could be the final clue to Sandra's motivation for murder. If her daughter never got to see her twenty-first birthday, then she was going to make damn sure the other girls didn't either.

"If this is true, we need to get up there and warn Teresa." Lacey said, breaking into his thoughts. She'd stood quietly beside Nico as the boy recounted his story, but now, her face was animated, urgency in her lovely hazel eyes.

He agreed with her. They needed to get up on that mountain ASAP. It could already be too late. Sandra may have followed the girl onto the Overland Track and already completed her dastardly deed. Although, if Teresa was leading a group of walkers, then Sandra may have a hard time getting the girl alone.

"We need to get back on to Gina at the wilderness company," he barked. "We need as much information as we can get on exactly when Teresa's party left yesterday, their planned route and where they intend to camp tonight." He was already strategizing, organizing logistics in his head, working out how he could get up on that walking trail sooner rather than later. A helicopter could get them where they wanted to go, drop them into the wilderness. But they needed to be careful not to tip off Sandra, so they couldn't get too close. If she knew they were coming, it might force her to kill Teresa before she was ready. And then—

"I want to go with you," Lacey interrupted his thoughts. Instead of pulling out her phone to call Gina like he thought she would, Lacey had squared her shoulders and was staring at him. Looking every inch of the competent police officer that she was in her smart, blue uniform, one thumb tucked into her duty belt which hung low on her hips, a look of defiance in her eyes. Except for the dark smudges under her eyes that reminded him both of them had had little to no sleep in the past twenty-four hours.

"What?" Nico hadn't got as far as deciding who he'd take with him up onto the mountain. "I don't—"

"I need to go with you, Nico. We make a good team together, we know what each other is thinking. That might be important up there in the wilderness." Lacey wasn't pleading, she was demanding and logical, and he couldn't help but admire her boldness at confronting him like this. Lacey could be a headstrong, determined woman. He knew that on a deeply personal level, and it was one of the many things he found attractive in her. But sometimes her stubbornness was also a thorn in his side. Like now, when she decided to flaunt her willfulness at work.

This operation was going to be a grueling, arduous task. Physically demanding; they'd most likely have to run part of the track to catch up to Sandra. Lacey was definitely fit enough to keep up with him, that part wasn't the problem.

But she was still a junior officer, only just finished probation. Was she mentally ready for such an operation? And they were both suffering from lack of sleep, which'd make things harder. It'd also look like he was giving her undue preference if he took her with him. What would the rest of the team say? Their roles didn't usually correlate. He was a homicide detective, and she was a cop on the beat—who had a great partner in Linc. But what she said had a certain kind of logic. They often knew what the other was thinking, sometimes surprising themselves when they both voiced the same idea at the same time. Up until now, Lacey had only been paired up with him less than half a dozen times. But the times they had worked together had been seamless; maybe because they trusted each other with their life. She was a good cop, with good instincts.

And yet… "I can't promise you that," he replied evenly.

"I need to do this for Linc. If Sandra is the killer, then she's the one who hit Linc over the head. Nearly killed him," she added, deadpan.

"Given that reasoning, then won't his uncle, Tyrell, want to come too?" he asked a little sardonically

"I'm assuming there will be more than one unit going out," she replied. "Tyrell definitely deserves to be on that other team." Lacey had clearly thought this through in more detail than he had in such a short time.

He nodded, because that was almost certainly true. A backup team should be dropped at each end of the trail, to make sure Sandra didn't escape overland that way.

"Please, Nico." Lacey moved in closer, her amber eyes suddenly entreating.

Shit. He sucked in a breath. He knew he couldn't say no to her when she looked at him like that. And the worst part was, he did want her with him on this op. At least if she was with him, he wouldn't be worrying about her at home on her own with that mystery intruder still out there on the loose.

Almost as if she could sense his change of heart, she gave a small, hopeful smile.

"I'm not promising anything," he said again, holding up a hand in warning. But he knew it was too late. He'd already made the decision in his own mind. Now he just had to get it past Shadbolt.

CHAPTER NINETEEN

Lacey had never flown in a helicopter before. It was exhilarating, and she soaked up every second of the flight and the amazing scenery unfolding below her, despite the circumstances. A rich fabric of forests, deep ravines, soaring mountain precipices, waterfalls and lakes mesmerized her as she looked down through the window. She already knew Tasmania was a beautiful place but seeing it from above was something else indeed. She tried to find a way she might describe this to Sally-Ann when they got back to the station, because her colleague demanded to know everything; she'd always dreamed of a helicopter flight over the mountains. All those cliché words, like dramatic, diverse, and iconic were actually true, and Lacey couldn't come up with any better description if she tried.

The pilot's voice came through her headset, interrupting her sightseeing and reminding her to stop gawking and get back into work mode. "The spot I'm going to set you down is just up ahead." He pointed toward a bald knoll in the distance. "You guys need to get ready to exit the aircraft as soon as I touch down. I'm not stopping, I'll merely be hovering. The wind is picking up, and I won't be able to hold it still for long."

The pilot's words didn't instill Lacey with a lot of confidence, but when Nico laid his hand on her arm, she nodded that she was ready to go when he gave the word.

They'd been warned by Jake, the wilderness company owner that a change in the weather was forecast. A storm was brewing off the coast, washing away the unseasonably hot spell they'd just endured with an equally unseasonable cold front sweeping in from the northwest. But that was the Tasmania highlands, Jake had cheerfully told them. Expect four seasons in one day up there. Dark clouds were already gathering on the horizon, and the wind had become noticeably stronger, even as they waited at the airfield for the helicopter to pick them up.

Jake had also been kind enough to lend them most of the equipment they'd need to endure the wilderness for at least the next few days, a small backpack stuffed full of gear sitting at her feet. They were traveling light, and moving fast; they were supposed to be tracking down a killer, not playing tourist and stopping to gawk at every new vista. Jake had suggested they take him along as a guide, and Nico had seriously considered it. But then they discovered the helicopter they'd procured to take them up the mountain only had room for three people. Nico, herself, and the pilot. It was the only one capable of performing the delicate and difficult hover-landing on top of the hill rather than on a purpose-made helicopter pad.

She was surprised to learn there were at least five helicopter landing pads along the trail, situated at the main huts where most people overnighted. This not only allowed Parks and Wildlife to deliver services and supplies, but allowed the police rescue units to pull out injured hikers if necessary. There was even a helipad at Lake Windemere, but they weren't going to use that drop-off-point. Nope. They were going to land on some isolated little barren hilltop, where there was no safe, purpose-made landing site. This was the reason they were using such a tiny helicopter, because it was maneuverable and could land just about anywhere. Or so the pilot had told her. Lacey gritted her teeth and pushed down the roiling sensation in her belly. Heights were not her friend. But she would deal with the fear the same way she dealt with most things. By facing it head-on and coming through the other side, hopefully unscathed.

Lacey had learnt a lot about this popular walking trail over the past few hours. The Overland Track was highly regulated, with only sixty walkers allowed on it every day. You had to book months in advance to secure a place. It was a one-way walk, beginning at Ronny Creek at the base of Cradle Mountain and finishing nearly fifty miles away at a place called Lake St Clair. It was possible to do the track in twenty-four hours if someone wanted to. But that was an extreme case, and most people stuck to the seven-day structure. There were also plenty of side-trips walkers could partake in to make the walk even longer and more protracted, usually up the top of a peak so you could get the best views.

Jake had confirmed that Teresa had taken her group through to the first official campsite, Waterfall Valley, and spent last night in the large communal hut there. Today they should be on their way to the next campsite, Lake Windemere, with a side trip to somewhere called Lake Will, where they were going to have lunch. Jake had tried numerous times to try and raise Teresa on the sat phone all morning, but so far, he'd only been able to leave messages. Teresa may turn her phone on when they stopped for lunch, he'd told them. But she may also not bother until her compulsory check-in at six pm tonight. At least they knew Teresa had been alive last night, which meant Sandra hadn't yet caught up to her. Or was biding her time until she found an opportune moment. And they were working on the fact that no news was good news today. If anything had happened to Teresa this morning, a report was bound to have come in from one of the other hikers. But Lacey knew they were working against the clock. The longer Sandra was out there, the more chance she had to get her revenge. They needed to find Teresa and her group soon. By tonight at the latest.

"Get ready, I'm going in," the pilot's disembodied voice sounded in her ears. Lacey's stomach lurched at the thought of jumping out of a helicopter into an unknown wilderness. Nico's blue eyes met hers, his steady gaze calming some of the butterflies in her belly. She nodded that she was ready and grabbed hold of her backpack with one hand and prepared to undo her seat belt with the other. "Don't forget to take off your headset," Nico reminded her, tapping his own headset with a finger, then watched as she stripped it off and placed it on the seat beside her, following suit a few seconds later. The noise of the helicopter was almost unbearable without the headphones, but she watched with more than a little trepidation as the small helicopter got closer and closer to the ground, until the pilot signaled Nico, and he yanked open the side door. The fierce wind threatened to suck her out of the aircraft and she clung on to the handlebar with all her might.

Nico glanced back quickly; then he was leaning out of the helicopter. She saw that the landing skids hovered a few feet off the ground, and she watched him jump onto the rocky terrain, ducking away from the rotor blades, backpack held tightly in one hand. He turned and beckoned her down. Lacey had no time to think, had no choice but to jump out. So she did, bracing for impact, making sure she didn't stumble and fall as she landed. The downdraft made it almost impossible to speak, blowing dirt and debris in the air, and

Lacey covered her eyes. Nico grabbed her and they both hunkered down on the ground, waiting until the helicopter had lifted off again before standing.

"Let's hope nobody spotted us," Nico said gruffly, shouldering the backpack and turning to check his surroundings.

Lacey very much doubted they'd escaped the notice of everyone on the track. A helicopter—even a small one—landing on top of a rocky outcrop was bound to attract attention. The pilot, in consultation with Jake, had chosen this particular spot because it was less than two hours walk from Lake Windemere, and near the turnoff Teresa and her group would've taken to Lake Will for their lunchtime sojourn. It was also away from the main trail, which threaded down into a ravine by the side of a beautiful lake to their left, keeping curious eyes from hopefully seeing what they were up to. Unless someone was standing on top of that pimple-shaped peak over there—in which case they would've seen the whole thing—they'd hopefully remained unobserved. This was a clandestine mission. They were hoping to stay under the radar and away from Sandra Brown's notice until they had her in their sights.

With no clear idea as to where exactly Sandra might be along the trail, another team was traversing from the beginning of the trailhead. Gorman and Tyrell had been chosen for this task, and they'd already started the trek an hour or so earlier. They were to sweep the trail right from the start to make sure she hadn't doubled back, or perhaps wasn't going as fast as everyone expected. While it was clear Sandra wasn't an experienced hiker—she never did much of anything outdoors according to Taj—it seemed she'd kept herself extremely fit by using a personal trainer at a local gym. Nico had commented on how buff she'd looked back when they'd first interviewed her, so they knew she was physically up to the task. Another team, Lawson and Hickey, were on their way via helicopter to the next scheduled overnight stop, Pelion Hut, which had a proper landing pad, to make sure Sandra hadn't somehow got ahead of Teresa and her group and was perhaps planning an ambush. Three teams all intent on finding one woman. Surely they could do this. Each team had a satellite phone in order to stay in touch.

"Lake Windemere is that way." Nico pointed down the slope. "We should be able to join up with the trail if we head straight down," he added. She shouldered her pack and slotted in behind him. His long-legged pace was fast, and she almost had to jog to keep up. Dressed in casual shorts, T-shirt, and hiking boots—courtesy of Jake—Lacey felt a chill breeze ripple over her bare arms as the sun disappeared behind the encroaching cloud bank and was glad of the thick fleece and rain jacket she had tucked in her bag. Glancing at the dark rain clouds, she decided they might well need their wet weather gear sooner rather than later.

A large pimple-shaped peak got steadily closer as they walked. Lacey decided it must be the peak they called Barn Bluff, and they were going to pass right by it on their way to Lake Windemere it seemed. It was the most prominent mountain for as far as Lacey could see, its low, scrubby, scree-filled foothills giving way to soaring rocky outcrops that reached stone fingers to the sky, bare and barren, where nothing grew. The view from up there would be spectacular, Lacey decided.

As they came down off the ridge, Lacey spotted a gray line weaving its way between the trees below them. It was a raised boardwalk marching off into the highland plateau beyond. They'd found the trail. Casting furtive glances below, Lacey could see no one else in either direction. They hurried down the last bit of the slope and their feet landed safely on the wooden walkway. They'd made it to the trail, hopefully undetected.

"Over the first hurdle," Nico announced as his head swiveled exactly the same way Lacey's had.

"Now we just need to find her," Lacey replied. They were taking a bit of a gamble, because if Sandra saw them both, she might recognize them, even in their civilian clothes with caps pulled down low and sunglasses on. But Nico was determined to be the one to capture her. His reputation relied on getting this right. Not that he didn't trust the rest of his team. But like most detectives worth their salt, he thought he was the best man for the job.

Nico increased their pace even more after they hit the boardwalk, an air of tension humming between them. They walked in silence, their crucial task keeping them moving at a brisk pace, the fatigue from lack of sleep fading with the adrenaline needed to keep going. A girl's life may well be on the line, and she and Nico might be the only ones able to save her. At least the raised boardwalks made the hiking easier, as well as saving the fragile vegetation from hordes of trampling feet. Lacey had studied a map of the area while they were waiting for the helicopter, and she knew the turnoff to Lake Will should be coming up soon. It was now after midday, and Jake had assured them Teresa and her group would be heading in that direction, if they weren't already at the lake, lazing around enjoying the scenery.

She was puffing hard by the time they reached the sign to Lake Will, and while Nico stopped to get his bearings, she took the opportunity to take a long drink from her water bottle. She'd also warmed up considerably, and the chilly wind was almost welcome against her hot skin. But the clouds were still gathering on the horizon. Lacey hoped, perhaps in vain, they might capture Sandra and this might be all over and done with before the storm hit. But the pilot had warned them that depending on how ferocious the storm became, a helicopter may not make it back into that terrain until the weather was more favorable. Meaning, they'd be stuck on the Overland Track for at least tonight, and maybe longer.

"What do you think?" Nico stared at the fork in the path. "Shall we follow them in?"

"Jake said they'd stop for lunch by the lake for at least an hour." She glanced at her watch. "It's only half past twelve. They've probably just arrived." She wondered where he was going with his musings.

"But Jake also said they'd come back out this way to continue the trail to Windemere," he said, pursing his lips.

"But what if they don't? Or what if we miss them somehow?" Why was Nico second-guessing himself? Now, of all times?

As they talked it over, Lacey spotted two people farther ahead on the trail. "See those people up there?" She pointed to the tiny figures in the distance. The trail ran clear and straight for a good couple of miles from here. "We've been steadily gaining on those two for the last half an hour. But I haven't seen anyone else ahead of them. I reckon if Teresa hadn't turned off, we'd be able to see their group up ahead." Jake assured them Teresa's crowd would be the biggest on the trail today. There were other groups, mainly in twos or fours booked in to traverse the trail, and another guided tour of eight walkers was due to start tomorrow, but for now, Teresa's bunch would be the biggest and most obvious.

"What if one of us stayed here, at the turnoff, just in case?" Nico pulled his sunglasses down his nose, his blue gaze meeting hers.

"No, Nico." Lacey was adamant, because she knew who the *one of us* would be. It'd be her, and no way was she staying behind. "We need to stick to the plan." She lowered her own sunglasses so she could look him directly in the eye.

She was eternally grateful that Nico had agreed she be the one to accompany him. She knew she'd pushed the boundaries of their relationship by asking. Because she knew he couldn't refuse her anything right now, not while their relationship was still fragile. And she used that weakness to get what she wanted. She'd played on his insecurities. On his innate need to protect her at all costs. That was probably unfair of her, putting him in such a predicament, but her need to accompany him had outweighed any feelings of guilt. She'd been prepared to play her ace, if he hadn't readily agreed—tell him that she felt unsafe alone at home while the mysterious person who'd broken into their house was still at large. Which wasn't strictly true, because she was only mildly worried the man would come back, especially now Nico had more security installed. And there were other options for her to avoid being alone at home; she could go and stay with a friend, or a colleague. But she needed to be with Nico, because this was a dangerous op, and while she trusted him to look after himself, she couldn't stand the idea of not knowing what was going on. He might claim that his overprotective nature was what drove him to keep her safe no matter what, but she also had a vested interest in his safety. She couldn't bear to lose him, and the best way she knew to safeguard him was to be the one protecting his back.

He considered her for a few unnerving seconds, before he finally said, "Yes, you're right. We need to stick together."

Thank God for that. She offered him a swig from her water bottle and they set off down the boardwalk to the left, which soon gave way to a rocky path leading them through the low-growing button grass and heath-like shrubs over the alpine plateau. Soon, the lake became visible, and the trail dipped down through a shallow valley. The low heath gave way to a fringing of taller trees that ringed the lake, myrtle beech trees, mixing with taller snow gums, the forest trees marching off in an olive-green blur to the base of Barn Bluff, which reared up on the opposite side of the lake. The place was absolutely stunning. Pristine and beautiful. Lacey made a pact with herself to come back to this place one day soon. One day when she wasn't on the hunt for an alleged killer. When she could truly appreciate the grandeur.

They made their way beneath the tree canopy until they came to the edge of the lake, where a flat grassy section and some scattered rustic wooden tables announced a designated picnic area. But to their dismay, the area was completely empty. Where were Teresa and her walking group? Had they come to the wrong area? They stopped to regroup and consider their options. Teresa definitely hadn't come past them on their way in, so she and her tour group must be in here somewhere. Nico pulled out a map and spread it on one of the tables.

"Maybe we should split up now," he said. "You go that way around the lake, and I'll go this way." He pointed to the right where a smaller trail wound around the edge of the water, looking as if it might head toward the base of Barn Bluff. Lacey eyed the left-hand path with circumspection. Maybe he was right this time. They must've gone on to find somewhere a little more secluded for lunch. Although this place was completely empty as far as she could see.

Almost the second the thought entered her head, a voice hailed them from behind. "Hello. Are you guys lost?" Lacey nearly jumped out of her skin. She whirled around to see a couple of hikers, a tall man with broad shoulders and a dark-blue T-shirt that did nothing to hide the muscle definition beneath, and a woman with blonde hair tied back from her face and inquisitive blue eyes. How the hell had that couple snuck up on them like that? They'd been so absorbed in the map; they needed to keep their wits about them better than that. She gave herself a mental shake.

"Hi." Nico gave them his best winning smile. "No, we're not lost, but thank you for asking."

"No problem," the man replied, "Just wanted to check." He extended his hand to Nico, saying, "I'm Griff, and this is my wife, Mila."

"Nice to meet you." Nico shook Griff's hand and then looked at Lacey. His hesitation was minute, no one else would've picked it up, but Lacey felt his indecision. "My name is Nico, and this is my girlfriend, Lacey."

She was suddenly glad that she'd talked Nico into letting her come along. At least this was one thing they didn't have to lie about. Their relationship. It made any other story they concocted seem more believable. Lacey shook Griff's hand, then Mila's, which was surprisingly firm. It made Lacey pause and take stock of this couple.

They were older, perhaps in their mid-forties. But they had a look about them. Something about the way they both carried themselves. Lacey recognized it as the same quality that surrounded Nico, and most likely herself, if she cared to think about it. A wariness blended with a military stance, shoulders back as if ready to react at a moment's notice, and a hard gaze, observing everything and everyone in the world around them. These people had to have some kind of military background or served in some kind of law enforcement. She could just tell.

And if she identified this quality in them, could they also see it in herself and Nico? Like perceiving like? She shot Nico a glance from beneath the lowered brim of her cap, wondering if he was thinking the same as her.

"This is such a beautiful place, isn't it?" Mila said on a sigh, turning to face the lake and breaking the tension surrounding them all.

Nico began to fold up the map on the table, so Lacey turned to stare in the same direction as the older woman.

"Yes, it's stunning. I'm so glad I got to see it," she replied. Another thing she could say with absolute truth. It was a special place.

"We met up here on Cradle Mountain almost a year ago," Mila said with a slightly faraway look in her eyes. "We were both caught in a snowstorm last Christmas Eve and had to shelter in Kitchen Hut together."

"Wow," Lacey responded. "That's kind of a cool way to meet."

Griff snorted. "She's being modest. It wasn't just any old snowstorm. If it hadn't been for Mila, I would've died." He slipped a hand around her waist. "She pulled me off a cliff face after I fell and then got me down to the hut in one piece in the middle of one of the biggest blizzards this region has ever seen." He gave Mila such an endearing look, full of such deep affection, Lacey was almost jealous. This couple seemed like they had a special bond, forged it seemed in the pits of adversity on a snowy mountaintop.

"Anyway, we always said we'd come back and walk the Overland Track properly one day. So here we are," Mila added.

"What a lovely story," Lacey said, turning to look at the couple standing beside her. Such a good-looking couple. Fit, strong, healthy, and in the prime of their lives. There was something familiar about them, but she couldn't quite put her finger on it. Then it hit her like a baseball between the eyes. They reminded her of an older version of Nico and herself. Perhaps this would be them in ten years' time. Still so much in love, and hopefully still fighting fit, still doing the thing they loved most—policing—while also living their best lives.

Lacey could feel Nico getting impatient behind her. They really needed to get moving. But something about this couple was compelling her to stay just a few moments more. Suddenly, she decided to ask a question. Nico may not like it, but something about this couple told Lacey she could trust them. Griff and Mila had just come from the direction of Barn Bluff. They might be able to help them narrow down where Teresa had taken her tour group.

"You didn't happen to see a largish group while you were walking in this area, did you?"

Mila shot her a sharp look, but didn't answer straight away.

"It's just that they're friends of ours and we're hoping to catch up to them." Nico added, and she was grateful to him for his quick thinking.

Griff spoke up from Mila's other side. "Yeah, we did. It was a guided tour group. Is that the one you're looking for?"

"Yes," Lacey let out a relieved sigh. "Teresa, the guide, is a friend of ours," she lied easily.

"Oh, right," Mila said, but there was a thoughtfulness in her tone.

"Which way were they headed?" Nico asked, tucking his folded map into his backpack and slinging it over his shoulder.

"Up to the top of Barn Bluff," Griff answered.

Nico shot Lacey a keen look. This wasn't in the plan. Why had Teresa changed things?

"We passed them on the trail in the foothills. We were on our way down," Griff went on, seeming not to notice their exchange. "We set off from Waterfall Hut early this morning, because we'd heard the view from there is spectacular, and we wanted to make sure we saw it with plenty of time to spare," he explained. "But because we blew past Lake Will in an attempt to get to the top early, Mila wanted to come back this way and spend an hour having lunch by the lake."

"Oh," Lacey replied. "It's just that we arranged to meet them here for lunch." It wasn't hard to sound confused. Because she was confused. Jake had assured them that Teresa didn't usually veer from the plan unless it was prearranged beforehand.

Griff shrugged. "The guide, Teresa, said they were going to have lunch up there because one of the hikers, Simon I think, was desperate to see the view. Then they were going to follow the trail down to Lake Windemere. She was hoping to get to the next hut before this weather came in."

"So you can get to Lake Windemere straight from Barn Bluff?" Nico asked. They should probably know this, and Nico was showing his lack of knowledge by asking the question. But this was important, because it meant the group might not be coming back this way after all.

"Yes, you can." Mila had removed her backpack—much larger than the ones she and Nico were carrying—and placed it on the table. But Lacey didn't miss the look Mila shot Griff as she eased her shoulders and turned around.

"Shit," Nico swore. "We'd better get going if we're going to catch them. Thanks for your help."

He was already three strides away, turning to see if Lacey was following him, when Griff said, "You might want to keep your eyes open for the other lady we saw up there. She looked a bit lost."

"What?" Nico stopped so sharply, Lacey nearly ran into the back of him. "What woman?"

Griff's eyes narrowed slightly. "She was in the trees a few hundred yards off the trail. It was Mila who saw her, I missed her completely. We thought she was with the group and they might've left her behind, so she was cutting cross country to catch up. We called out to her, to tell her which way they went. But she completely ignored us." Griff shrugged his impressive shoulders. "She was so far away, there wasn't a lot we could do. And people often go off track up here." This time instead of shrugging, he studied both Lacey and Nico carefully.

Could this woman possibly be Sandra? The coincidence was too much for it not to be, Lacey decided.

Lacey stared at Nico, trying to communicate without words. What should they do? Try and find the woman? Or just careen up the track as fast as they could.

"What's going on?" Griff asked suddenly, widening his stance, spreading his legs and adopting an intimidating attitude. "There's something you're not telling us."

"Nothing," Lacey said, at the same time as Nico said, "None of your business, sir."

The two men stood in a sort of Mexican standoff for immeasurable moments eyeballing each other. Shit. What should she do?

In the end, it was Mila who ended the deadlock. "Let me introduce myself formally," she said, stepping in between the two men. "Sergeant Camila Whiteaker. I work for the elite police drug task force at Waverley Station in Sydney. Sorry I'm not currently carrying any identification, but you're welcome to call my superintendent if you'd like to confirm."

Lacey took a surprised step backward.

"And I'm Griffin Porter, ex-SAS and consultant to the NSW Police Force," Griff said, his gaze never leaving Nico's.

So, she'd been right in her assessment of them after all.

"I'm wondering if we can be of service to...whatever you've got going on here," Griff continued.

"If you need any help, we're both highly qualified," Mila added when Nico continued to hesitate. Lacey wondered what he would do. Of course, she'd play along with whatever move he chose to make. It wasn't her place to make these kinds of decisions. But something shouted at her that they could trust these people.

Nico removed his cap and ran an agitated hand through his hair, tugging strands loose from his man bun. Finally, he said, "Are we that obvious?"

"Probably not to a civilian," Mila said, not unkindly. "But to us, yes." She lifted one eyebrow as if it was a no-brainer. "That weapon you have hidden under your shirt is a dead giveaway," she added.

Wow, Lacey was impressed by their powers of observation. She knew Nico was carrying, but she thought he'd done a good job at keeping it well hidden from everyone else. Her own service weapon was tucked away in an easy-to-reach side pocket of her backpack. It'd give away her undercover persona in a second if she wore it around her waist like she normally did.

"It couldn't hurt to have backup," Lacey said softly. "They may have just confirmed Sandra is hot on Teresa's heels. And now Teresa's changed her plans, we really don't know what we're up against." Lacey glanced toward Barn Bluff, staring at the soaring rocky peaks and long drop-offs.

"I need to call this in," Nico said eventually.

"Can you do it while we're walking?" Lacey asked, a sense of urgency filling her when she thought about how far ahead Sandra and Teresa were now. If Griff and Mila had passed them in the foothills as they were coming down, then the group must surely be at the top by now. She squinted her eyes and tried to see if there were any visible figures at the peak. But it was too hard to tell.

"Here." Griff passed her a pair of binoculars he must've had stashed in the top of his backpack.

Before she even had a chance to use them, Nico said, "Let's go." He pointed toward the edge of the clearing and the forest beyond. "Would you mind following us while I confirm a few things with HQ?" he asked the couple over his shoulder. "I'm sure you appreciate I can't reveal too many details, but yes, your help would be appreciated."

"Sure thing," Mila seemed to answer for the both of them, stashing her backpack under the table, Griff following suit, and then all four of them began to stride along the boardwalk, which was only wide enough for one person now, two planks running parallel, leading to the pimple-shaped monolith. Soon, they were all jogging in single file, with one objective on all of their minds.

CHAPTER TWENTY

Nico's lungs were burning, but he kept pushing forward, forcing one leg in front of the other, up the steep slope. He was going as fast as was humanly possible; they had to get to the top before it was too late. Griff and Mila had no trouble keeping up with his pace, and they'd already climbed this mountain once today. Lacey seemed to have no trouble either, with her long legs taking each step easily on the rocky path. To top it all off, a light rain was starting to fall. It looked as if the weather also had a mind of its own and was coming in faster and harder than anyone predicted. Even though it was only an hour past midday, the sky was dark and heavy with clouds making it appear much later. The wind had also increased, whipping the leaves into a frenzy as they'd passed through the last of the forest. Now they were on the barren scree slopes where practically nothing grew, they were being buffeted by the wind from all angles; it was hard to keep his footing as they hopped from rock to rock.

He looked up toward the soaring rocky outcrops above. It was still a long way up. Then he turned his gaze to the vista spread out below. He could imagine on a clear day this would be spectacular. But now, with the low clouds and rain, it was hard to tell where the plateau rose up to become a mountain as it was all draped in a layer of misty clouds. Lake Will was still visible below and it looked bigger from up here.

The rain started to come down in heavy sheets now, blowing into their faces by the wind. But they had no time to stop to put on their rain jackets. Every second was precious. There'd been no sign of either the group of hikers or Sandra. Was Sandra still staying off the trail in an attempt to keep herself hidden? If she was, did that reduce her speed, or would she perhaps find a faster way up the mountain?

Just then, he thought he heard a voice from farther up the path. He lifted his head and squinted into the rain. The trail curved around a large outcrop of tall spires, disappearing into a ravine before leading the climber higher, past the skirts of the mountain. There, in the mist, he caught movement. Nico reached under his shirt and touched his service revolver, ready to draw it at a second's notice. A figure careened down the path at breakneck speed, rain jacket flapping out like a sail behind them, backpack bouncing on their shoulders as they took each jolting step.

"Nico," Lacey called out a warning.

"I see them," he replied, waving her and the older couple behind him, ready to defend them. Although from what threat, he was still unsure. Then another person came around the bend, this one also running, but at a slightly less reckless speed. Nico's already overexerted heart began to beat even faster as he watched the first person approach.

It was a man, and as he got closer, Nico could see he was young, perhaps in his early twenties. His face was contorted with fear and effort as he strove to keep his feet underneath him on the rocky path. These men were running away from something. But what?

Two more people came around the bend, jogging fast, but not running flat out like the first guy. Logic said that these people were most likely part of Teresa's hiking group. But if they were, where were the other two? And where was Teresa? Was she bringing up the rear?

Nico began to wave, to get the man's attention.

"Help!" the guy shouted when he finally saw Nico and the others. "Help us."

"What's the matter?" Nico held up his hands to grab the man, who practically cannonballed into him, almost knocking him into Lacey. But she put a steadying hand on Nico's shoulder and peered around the side of his arm, desperate to hear what this guy had to say. The man's wet hair was plastered to his face, and he had to push it out of his eyes, which were wild with alarm.

"There's a woman up there with a gun. She took our guide hostage, and she threatened to shoot all of us." The man was gasping so hard Nico could hardly make out what he was saying.

"Slow down," he encouraged.

"No, you don't understand," the other man yelped. "She's a lunatic. She told us all to sit down on a flat rock and then she started to tie us up. Told us that if we sat nice and still and behaved ourselves, no one would get hurt. But I didn't believe her. I was sure she was going to shoot us all." He stopped to drag in more deep breaths. Griff and Mila had come closer, straining to hear what this man was saying.

"It's okay, we're police, we're here to help," Nico said, using his most calming tone.

"You are?" The young man stopped puffing and his brown eyes went wide. Nico guessed that looking at things from this panicked guy's point of view, this was probably the most fortuitous thing that could've happened.

The second man appeared beside the first, breathless. "Have you told them, Simon? Do they have a sat phone? We need to contact the police straight away," he said frantically, looking as if he were going to keep running until he came to the nearest police station if he had to.

"They are the police, Jans. Can you believe it?" the man called Simon said with more than a little awe.

"What? How? Are you sure?" The second man eyed Nico and his companions with suspicion.

Nico intervened, trying to get things back on track. "Tell me what happened up there," he asked. "Where is this woman now? And what has she done with her hostage?"

"I'm not sure," Simon answered with a touch of shame. "While the crazy woman was tying Shawn up, I decided no way in hell was she getting her paws on me, so I took off like a jackrabbit."

In other words, the man was a coward. He'd run away and left the others to deal with the situation. Nico tried not to lift the corner of his lip, telling himself these people were civilians. Not trained to deal with violence or danger. Simon had acted like most normal people would. He unclenched his fists and turned to Jans. "Then what happened?" he growled.

"When I saw Simon run, I went for it as well," Jans admitted. "We were farthest from the lady with the gun. She didn't even seem to notice when Simon left, she was too busy tying up Shawn. There was a large pile of rocks right near us, so we ducked behind them. I don't think it was until Tania and Lily took off after us, that she even really knew what was happening, and by then it was too late. She didn't even bother to shoot at us."

No, because she had what she'd come for. She had Teresa, and that was all that mattered in Sandra's eyes. Nico held in a curse.

"So there're still two more people tied up somewhere on this mountain?" he asked through gritted teeth.

"Yeah, I reckon they're still up there," Jans replied.

"That's why we were flying down the track. Going to find someone to help. Teresa was the only one with a satellite phone and she was out of reach. And we don't have any reception out here," Simon added by means of justifying their actions.

"You did a great job," Lacey interjected. She must be able to see Nico's growing frustration and decided it was time to step in. "I think Mila should escort these four back down to Lake Will, don't you?" Lacey asked, but it wasn't really a question. He had to give her credit for thinking on her feet, while his mind was occupied farther up the mountain, wondering if they were going to find Teresa dead or alive up there. "They can wait for the backup to arrive in the picnic area." It made sense. Get the civilians to safety, so they could keep moving. Nico had already called Shadbolt on his sat phone to update him on their situation and ask for more backup. Gorman and Tyrell were still at least a five or six-hour hike away, so two more constables were going to be airlifted into Lake Will—if the helicopter was able to fly in this bad weather, that was. Now they knew where Sandra was, and that she had Teresa, there was no need for secrecy anymore. But the chopper would be an hour away at the very least. And Nico wasn't waiting that long. He was going to the top now.

"Yes, great idea." He gave Lacey a brief smile of gratitude. "Griff, would you follow us up and we'll see if we can locate the other two walkers?" His mind finally kicked into gear just as two females came skidding down the track toward them. If —no, when—they found the other two hikers, Griff could bring them safely down the track, leaving himself and Lacey to continue after Sandra.

"Help us," one of the girls called in a panicked voice, and Nico felt another surge of anger that these two young men hadn't taken the time to make sure the others were fine before they hared off down the mountain.

Lacey stepped forward to meet them, holding up her

hands to stop their headlong rush.

"It's okay, Lily, these guys are cops. They're going to help us," Simon said from behind Lacey.

"Great," the other one replied snarkily. "At least there are some people on this mountain prepared to help us. I can't believe you just left us like that, Simon."

"Now hold on a second, I was—" Simon began to say.

"Enough," Nico interrupted. "You can argue about this later. If you'll follow Mila, she'll make sure you remain safe, while we go up and rescue the rest of your crew."

"Yes, you have to help Teresa. That woman with the gun pumped her full of some kind of drug. She was just lying on the rocks when we left," Lily said.

"Thank you. That's great information," Nico replied, but his heart dropped into his stomach. God, he hoped Teresa wasn't already dead. What sort of cocktail of drugs had been in that syringe? Was she still using her drug of choice, the anesthetic ketamine, to subdue Teresa? An unconscious victim wasn't good. It'd make it that much harder to find her and then rescue her and get her off the mountain.

Mila calmed the four hikers and then corralled them into a group and began to chivvy them down the track, while Lacey took off her backpack and removed her service weapon from the side compartment, tucking it into the waistband of her shorts. A look passed between them. She was ready for whatever they might find up there.

"Stay well behind us," Nico said to Griff as they moved forward. The other man had no weapon, and Nico had no way to know the level of his skills. The last thing he needed was another victim on his hands. Then he led the way, going as fast as he dared up the track in the rain that was now coming down in sideways sheets. He had to shield his face with his hand to be able to see properly.

As they approached the bend in the trail, Nico slowed their

pace and drew out his weapon. Just before Mila took them away, Simon had told Nico where to find the other two hikers. He said they were on a large flat rock around three hundred feet around the bend. It'd be obvious if they were still there; it was as if the crazy woman had wanted to make it easy for them to be found. Which was interesting, because it meant that Sandra wasn't a bloodthirsty killer, and she wasn't too bothered about covering her tracks. Otherwise, she could've just killed them all, or hidden them away so it took police hours or days to find them.

Which was both good and bad. Good, because it made Nico's job easier. Bad because if Sandra wasn't taking any pains to hide her deeds, then it meant she didn't care about the consequences of her actions. Which pointed to the fact Sandra was going to kill Teresa on this mountain. And perhaps take her own life as well. The one ace they had up their sleeves was that Sandra didn't know they were coming. Hopefully, he still had surprise on his side. If she didn't know she was being followed, she wouldn't feel under pressure to rush things. Vaguely, he wondered what she had planned for Teresa. The other two girls had been killed in an almost ritualistic way. Sandra had made sure their cause of death was hanging by the neck, using ketamine to make them easy to handle, to mimic her own daughter's terrible death. But Sandra had the luxury of time and planning to get those murders right. This was rushed because she knew she was running out of time. She'd already drugged Teresa, just as she'd drugged the other two. But Nico didn't think there were any tall trees on top of Barn Bluff where Sandra could string the girl up. So what sort of improvisation would Sandra come up with? It'd have to be something that appeased her terrible need to make this girl die in the same way her daughter had, so Sandra could finally get her retribution.

Sure enough, as they cautiously rounded the bend Nico caught sight of two figures atop a rocky outcrop around halfway up the track that wound upward from the ravine. Nico glanced behind to see that Lacey also had her gun drawn but pointed to the ground in front of her, walking in a half crouch, ready for anything. Griff was doing a great job of keeping far enough back so Nico didn't need to worry about his safety if Sandra started firing wildly at them. He was clearly well trained and took orders well.

Sandra and Teresa were nowhere to be seen. But just because they weren't visible, didn't mean Sandra wasn't lying in wait for them, so he proceeded with extreme caution. Stalking slowly up the path, he kept low and his eyes peeled on the surrounding rocky slopes, cautious of an ambush, or a sniper attack. The pelting rain made it hard to see clearly, and it turned the scrub and rocks into blurry outlines, only half visible. It also made the track slippery and treacherous, with small puddles of water already forming in the dips and hollows.

When they were finally close enough to the pair tied up on the rocks, Nico held up his hands. "It's okay, we're the police. We're here to help," he said in a low tone, almost whispering in case Sandra was still within earshot. A man and a woman sat side by side on a large flat rock, huddled together against the rain and the wind. The man, Shawn, if Simon was to be believed, had caught sight of them at first, and his eyes had gone wide, but that's when Nico saw both of their mouths had been taped shut. They wouldn't be able to answer his call, but Nico wanted to reassure them regardless. The man nodded slowly to show he understood, but the woman stared at them as if she could barely comprehend what was happening.

He knew Lacey was keeping a lookout from behind and so he took a few steps closer to the couple. "Do you know if the woman with the gun is still in the area?" Nico asked, enunciating each word carefully. The man shook his head emphatically, then gestured with his chin farther up the track. "She took the guide and kept going up the track?" Nico asked.

This time, both people nodded forcefully. Nico glanced upward. If Sandra was carrying Teresa up this trail, then she was doing a mighty good job, and must be a lot stronger than even he had believed. He was almost in admiration of her strength and determination. But a dose of ketamine could also be reversed at any time. It might leave a victim groggy and awkward but able to move.

Deciding the couple wouldn't lie to him, he motioned to Lacey to cover him; then he clambered up the rock and removed both of their gags, before untying the man's hands.

"Thank God you're here," Shawn said. "We thought we were goners. We didn't know what that woman wanted."

Nico grunted as he untied Shawn's feet, then went to work on the woman. Griff came silently up behind Nico and helped Shawn to his feet. The guy was a little wobbly, probably from lack of circulation, and Griff took him by the arm to steady him. Both the hikers seemed to be well-dressed for the weather, which was a small blessing, wearing rain jackets and beanies against the cold, driving rain. The freezing air was biting at Nico's bare arms and he could see Lacey had goose bumps on her skin too. They'd make sure to put on their jackets before proceeding. There was no point if they succumbed to the elements before they even caught up with Sandra.

"Thank you. Oh, thank you," the woman said, rubbing her wrists after he untied her arms. "Did you find the others? Simon and Jans, and the two girls? Are they okay?"

"Yes, they're all safe. I've got an officer escorting them down to the lake right now," Nico replied. He was heartened by the woman's concern. She was more worried about their welfare than it seemed they were about hers. But he had to stop comparing those others to himself. *It is normal to want to save yourself*, he reminded himself. He and Lacey and the other sworn officers around him were abnormal, prepared to throw themselves into danger to save someone else.

"My name is Griffin Porter, I'll take you down the hill to meet up with your other companions," Griff said by way of introduction. Nico shot him a grateful glance as he helped the woman to her feet. "You're safe now. No need to worry. These two officers will have everything in hand very soon."

"You have to help Teresa," Shawn said, his voice taking on a touch of panic. "That woman drugged her with something. And then when the others took off down the hill, she got this really mean look on her face, and for a few seconds, I thought she was going to shoot us because she was so mad. But then she gave Teresa another jab of something. But when she didn't wake up fast enough, she just picked up Teresa in a fireman's carry, you know slung her over her shoulder, and kept climbing the track."

"That's what we're here for," Nico replied. "To help Teresa and make sure you're safe."

"What does she want with Teresa? What's going on?" the girl asked, but Griff was already leading them both away, a hand on each of their elbows. He was a good man. Solid and professional. Nico was suddenly glad of their chance meeting.

"Put your rain jacket on," he commanded Lacey, while tugging his own out of his backpack. "We need to be on top of our game, and getting cold and wet will only make us sluggish and not thinking properly." He shrugged into his and found immediate relief from the icy bite of the rain against his skin. Lacey did the same without comment, repositioning her weapon in the back of her shorts, and they both strung their backpacks on their shoulders. He was almost tempted to leave the packs here; the less weight on their shoulders, the quicker they could climb. But they might need the contents of these bags if things went south.

They jogged up the path in silence, concentrating on what was ahead. Nico felt a moment's respect that Sandra was capable of not only climbing this hill, but doing it while encumbered with the weight of the girl slung over her shoulder. All the photos he'd seen of Teresa showed her as a petite woman of around five feet tall, but still. If Sandra had administered an antidote, she was probably forcing Teresa to walk by now, but the poor woman would be disorientated and slower than normal.

Panting heavily, Nico reached the top of the bluff ten minutes later. It'd been a hard climb, clambering up rocky steps cut into the side of the hill, and even navigating a short ladder to ascend one section. But Lacey was right behind him; he couldn't fault her physical fitness.

Nico crouched behind a patch of shrubs and surveyed the plateau wreathed in mist spread out before him. It was eerie, with the swirling rain and rising wind that threatened to push him back down the trail. Neither Sandra nor Teresa were anywhere to be seen. It was a large space, with lots of places to hide behind rocky tors and patches of tall grasses, or deep depressions and crevasses scattered throughout the landscape. Over to the left, the land sloped away and Nico couldn't tell how far it might be to the edge of the plateau. They might have to split up if they were to find the girl and Sandra sooner rather than later. Before Sandra had time to carry out her plan—whatever that might be. There weren't a lot of places for Sandra to take Teresa, they were surrounded by cliff faces.

It suddenly occurred to him that this setting might be triggering for Lacey. The last time she'd been near a cliff face, she was trapped in a van and sent to her death, plunging over the edge. Throughout the whole intense planning of this mission, he'd never once envisaged this kind of scenario. Which was perhaps naïve of him. But Lacey had also never said a word, even on the steep climb up here, knowing what she'd find at the top.

He looked back to where Lacey was crouched behind him, eyes also scanning the stormy scenery. "Are you going to be okay?"

A sudden illogical fear overcame Nico and he remembered back to the day when Linc had been hurt and Nico had almost driven himself crazy in his rush to get to Lacey to make sure she was safe. Back then, he knew he needed to get this irrational fear out of his system, because it was making him second-guess himself; somehow, he needed to learn to separate his love life from his professional life. His fear for her now was still strong, his need to protect her at any cost still screaming inside his head. But this situation, where he needed her as much as she needed him if they were to rescue an innocent woman, was showing him that maybe he couldn't separate love from work. Instead, he needed to find a balance. Lacey could look after herself. Logically he knew that, he just needed to let her get on with the job and trust her to do it.

"Yes, I'm fine," she replied crisply, keeping her gaze trained on the flat, wet tableland beyond. She wouldn't look him in the eye.

Swiveling on his heels, he stood up from his crouch and tipped her chin up with his thumb so that she followed him up and swung her amber gaze around to meet his. "It's me you're talking to. Don't bullshit me," he said, calling her bluff. "As your commanding officer, I need to know you're going to be able to handle this." He watched her face for any telltale giveaways before continuing in a gentler tone. "But as your partner and lover, I also don't want you to do this if you think it will endanger your mental state." He was tempering his fear for her, couching it in terms they both understood and zeroing in on the core of the problem. Trusting her to face her demons alone was one thing, but she needed to be sure she could do this.

She began to pull away from him, but he trapped her face between his thumb and forefinger. "I love you, Lacey. You mean more to me than anything else in this world."

"More than even the chance to save a girl's life?" Lacey asked, disbelief clouding her eyes.

"If it came to that, then yes, more than that." He watched her eyes to gauge her reaction to his admission. "You know I'd do just about anything to save that poor girl. But your safety means more to me than my career, or my reputation, or catching the bad guy." How could he explain just how important she was to him? If he thought this mission was going to wreck Lacey's still-fragile mental stability, he'd even be prepared to tie her up and hide her behind the nearest rock to keep her unharmed and face her wrath later if need be. Nico was more than prepared to take down Sandra on his own, if he had to.

"Wow." She stared up at him, ignoring the rain that trickled down her face.

He watched her warily, half expecting annoyance or displeasure on her part; she'd made it abundantly clear on more than a few occasions that she didn't appreciate him trying to wrap her in cotton wool.

Instead of an explosion, however, she merely stood on tiptoe and gave him a kiss in the rain, her lips warm and reassuring against his. "I'm not going to lie," she replied when she dropped back onto her heels. "I'm not happy about being up here. But I'm also a trained professional with a job to do. I came here to catch a murderer and save her intended victim, and I'll do everything in my power to see that happen. The psych has given me lots of coping tools, but I'm hoping I won't need them. What I do need is your trust," she said, narrowing her eyes. "I need you to trust me to do my job."

Touché. She had him on that one. And he did trust her. Implicitly.

"I do," he replied simply.

"Well then, shall we do this?" She shouldered her backpack a little higher and took a determined step backward. God, he was so in love with this amazing woman.

"I think we need to split up." He didn't like it, but they were racing against time, with a lot of space to cover, and this storm was going to make their job harder.

"I agree."

"I'll go to the right." He pointed to the side of the plateau where it sloped down, hiding the landscape beyond. He had no idea if Sandra had chosen that direction but something told him that if she wanted to find another way off the bluff, then it might be her best bet. She might not realize he and Lacey were following her yet, but she also wouldn't be stupid enough to retrace her steps when she knew most of the hikers had fled down the hill. "Remember, she's armed and most likely desperate. Don't underestimate her."

"I'll take the left." Lacey smiled wanly. "And I'll be careful," she countered. Then she turned her hazel eyes on him. "Stay safe, Nico. I *need* you to come back to me." He saw the flash of torment in her face and knew she was just as worried about his safety as he was about hers. He'd been so focussed on his own need to protect her he hadn't even considered she might be feeling the same. It made him all the more determined to get this over and done with so he could spend the night cocooned in her arms, and soothe away all her fears. Both of their fears.

Before he could come up with a suitable reply, Lacey had melted into the tall shrubbery around the perimeter of the plateau. He took a leaf out of his stubborn, valiant woman's book and crept toward a pile of square boulders close by.

Mind now focussed on his job, he used the rocks as cover, while he mapped out his next move. Slowly and stealthily, he traversed the edge, flitting between the low ground cover and using craggy outcroppings to remain hidden, trying to stay on higher ground where possible. The wind was so loud, howling around the peak, that he wouldn't be able to hear anyone if they were to sneak up on him. But then the reverse would be true as well, leaving him free to make more noise than he might otherwise have considered wise.

What was Sandra planning to do with Teresa? The other two murders had ritual and methodical planning involved. The manner of death—hanging by the neck—was clearly important to her. But this chase into the wilderness was spontaneous, and Sandra must be working on the fly. Perhaps she'd had some scheme plotted out to take care of Teresa once she returned from the hike, but as the police had begun closing in, maybe she'd decided this was her last chance to get to her last victim before it was too late.

There were no large trees up here, so how would she follow through with her murderous ceremony? She could just push her off the cliff. The fall would surely kill Teresa. But that idea didn't sit right with Nico. It was too easy and didn't track with Sandra's psychopathic need for revenge. They were at least fifteen minutes behind Sandra, she could've done a lot of things up on the plateau in that time. Perhaps she was going to take her down the other side of the bluff to where the forest carpeted the foothills to find a suitable tree down there. If she had left the plateau, then their search up here was a wasted effort and they should be concentrating on trying to pinpoint her below. But if she'd descended again, which way would she have gone? Maybe he should be focussing his search on the cliff edge so he could see both down into the lowlands as well as up here on the heights. The heavy rain and eddying winds would make it almost impossible to spot her from this high vantage point. Was this an unfeasible mission? Was Sandra going to get away with murder yet again? He was so engrossed on trying to decide on his best option, he barely recognized that he was now standing in the open.

There was a scuffling noise and suddenly, a loud crack broke the air, and he was knocked sideways. Pain flared through his abdomen, taking his breath away. He groaned aloud and stumbled, falling to his knees onto the hard stone. Fuck, he'd just been shot. On reflex, he reached for his gun in the holster beneath his jacket, but a shout stopped him.

"Don't move, or I'll end you," Sandra warned.

He almost laughed, she sounded like a cheesy biker from a B-grade TV show. But the pain in his side told him how real this was. He froze, hand stalled in the air as Sandra stepped out from behind a stand of scraggly heath. Shit, he'd just done the very thing he warned Lacey not to do. He'd underestimated Sandra, not believing that she'd really shoot him. Because she was a woman. And women didn't shoot cops. Except this one had.

"I could have killed you if I wanted to, I'm a crack shot. I've been practicing for a long time at the gun range," she said, calm as a cucumber. "But I'm not a cop killer."

Small mercies. The pain in his side was excruciating, and he wondered if he might die anyway.

"Throw your weapon on the ground," she commanded. "Then put your hands in the air."

He only hesitated for a split second before he complied. She'd already shot him once, which showed she knew how to handle a gun. He didn't doubt she'd do it again if he didn't comply. Pain twisted his stomach and ricocheted down his thigh as he moved and he wondered how bad the injury was. He could see blood blooming in a red circle on his shirt just above his hip, but he didn't have time to take a closer look. His gun rattled on the bare rocks as he placed it down in front of him.

"Where is Teresa?" he asked through gritted teeth. What had she done with the girl? Had she stashed her somewhere on this mountain top? Or had she already pushed her over the edge in her final vengeful deed? And where was Lacey? He prayed that she hadn't heard the shot and come running, straight into Sandra's trap.

Calmly, Sandra walked over and retrieved his weapon, putting it into her jacket pocket. She was well-dressed for the weather, Nico noted. Wearing a knee-length jacket over lightweight long pants and sturdy hiking boots as she studied him with shrewd eyes. Her long hair was tucked beneath a black baseball cap, the brim keeping most of the rain out of her eyes. Perhaps this had been the plan all along. Even if this trip had been unscheduled, it seemed Sandra was always well-prepared and well-organized.

Ignoring his question, she said instead, "I found you. Now, let's go and find this lady cop of yours."

"What? No. That's not going to happen." His voice came out as ravaged as one of those storm-ripped clouds above. He wasn't letting this madwoman anywhere near Lacey.

"Yes, it is," Sandra growled and shoved the gun into his injured side so he howled like a wounded dog. "I've done what I needed to do, and now as long as you two don't interfere, my daughter will have her vengeance. Today would've been her twenty-first birthday. This will be my final present to her."

Sandra had confirmed what Taj had told them, and he felt a small stab of sorrow for this poor, broken woman. But then she pushed him in the back with the end of her pistol and he had no choice but to go in the direction she wanted. He hoped and prayed that Lacey was hidden somewhere and she stayed that way. Neither of them spoke as they trudged through the rain, Nico's mind racing, trying to work out a way to overpower his captor while also overriding the agony in his side that threatened to send him to his knees.

"You know I never wanted to hurt that other constable," Sandra said into the silence. "I just needed my daughter's charm back. It's one of the few things I had left of her. But that girl cop of yours foiled my efforts. Which makes me less inclined to like her."

It took a few seconds for Nico to catch up through his pain-fogged brain. Sandra had just confirmed it was her who'd hit Linc. She must've been hiding in the bushes, or perhaps retracing her steps, trying to find the lost item. "You assaulted a police officer," he ground out between gritted teeth. "He's in a coma in hospital." Even though she sounded genuinely remorseful, she didn't deserve to know that Linc had woken up. He wanted her to believe the worst, especially if it put her more on edge. It'd certainly been a key piece of evidence. And now they knew the charm had belonged to Tia.

"I hope he recovers," she replied in a distracted tone. "But if I had to do it again to get Tia's charm back, I would." This was said with a note of finality that made Nico's insides shudder with dismay.

CHAPTER TWENTY-ONE

Lacey crept slowly through the thick underbrush. This was an impossible task. The rain and wind made her assignment to locate a crazy woman, who was most likely doing her best to stay hidden, infuriating. She'd made her way almost to the opposite side of the bluff as she worked from cover to cover with no sign of Sandra or Teresa. Lacey had kept the cliff edge to her left and at least twenty feet away as she slogged her way around. She knew the edge was there, but tried not to think about it too hard. Heights bothered her now. After her nightmare with Gabriel at the lookout, she hadn't ventured close to anything higher than the steps into the police station. Her scars began to itch at the thought of that cliff face so close to where she stood.

When she'd asked to come on this assignment, she'd known that this type of scenario might be on the cards. But she'd also hoped she'd be able to overcome her fears if it did. Nico had asked if she could cope with being up here. And she'd tried to fob him off. But really, she had no idea how she was going to react if she had to go much closer to that edge.

She took another step and tripped over something, falling to her knees with a soft curse. Shit, she was so busy scanning the environment for her perp she wasn't watching where she was going. Glancing back, Lacey located the item that'd been her downfall.

Wait a second.

It was a rope. Taught and stretched across the ground. Her gaze followed the line of the rope to where it was tied to the trunk of the largest tree in the vicinity. The other end disappeared into the shrubs, heading in the direction of the cliff face. What the hell…?

Throwing her backpack to the ground, Lacey traced the line of the rope with her hand, crawling along the rock ledge on her hands and knees. The ground was running with rivulets of water, making the rocks slippery and turning the earth into mud puddles around her. Torrential rain continued to slap her in the face, the cold water running down the neck of her jacket and soaking her T-shirt beneath. It was hard to see even a few feet in front of her, but she kept going, feeling her way with her hands. Then the rope jerked against her palm, and she forgot about her physical discomfort as she concentrated on the tether. It jerked again, as if someone was tugging on the other end. *Holy Shit.* It hit her like a brick to the side of the head. Someone was *tied* to the end. This must be Sandra's version of the hanging tree. She must've thrown Teresa over the cliff. But as Lacey scrabbled the rest of the way to the edge, still on her hands and knees, her breathing became labored and her heart rate skyrocketed. When the edge came into view, Lacey found she could go no closer. Terrifying images of her Kombi van plunging over the cliff assaulted her mind, filling her vision until she could no longer see the low clouds and the wet scrub around her. All she could see were her fingers scrabbling at the door trying to open it, even as the front wheels left the edge. Flying through the air. Then falling. Falling. Into the dark trees. Pain. Incredible pain as the branches tore at her skin. A scream threatened to erupt from her throat, she was struggling to breathe, and she knew she was hyperventilating.

No.

Stop.

She needed to remember she was on top of Barn Bluff. Here to rescue a girl. This wasn't Blackpoint Lookout, and she wasn't locked in a van hurtling over the edge. The counsellor had warned her this might happen. Flashbacks. Set off by heights or similar circumstances. But she didn't have the luxury of time to collapse in a puddle of her own psychological trauma. Someone's life was in her hands. She could break down later. But not now. Deep breaths. Take some deep breaths. Lacey closed her eyes and tried to bury the images; telling herself she wasn't going to fall again. This time, she was in charge of her own destiny.

Forcing one hand in front of the other, she belly-crawled the last few feet toward the edge, stopping to take a few more deep breaths before peering over. She nearly drew backward in shock when she saw a dark head only a few feet below her, the girl's legs were flailing wildly in the air, while beneath her there was nothing but misty clouds, the ground no longer visible.

Teresa was alive.

But the girl scrabbled at the rope around her neck with her hands. A noose. A noose was around her neck. And that noose was so tight, it was all she could do to fight to breathe, dangling out in space with her air fast running out. It was hard to see if there were any handholds or footholds for Teresa to use. But even if there were, the girl was fixated on the rope. Terrified out of her mind. Her body would be screaming for air; it was human instinct to try to pry the rope loose, but with all her weight on the end, it was a fruitless endeavor. She'd no more be able to let go of the noose and turn herself around so she faced the escarpment than she would be able to fly to the moon.

Unless…

She had to try and get through to the girl. If she could give her enough support so she was able to breathe, then maybe…

It took all her mental will, but she leaned out over the edge, seeing the tiny white scars crisscrossing the back of her hand as she reached down. *You can do this. You can do this.*

"Take my hand," Lacey called, lying flat on the rock face, ignoring the water that dribbled off her chin and made a puddle beneath her chest. Gritting her teeth, she grappled behind her with the other hand until she found the trunk of a small but sturdy shrub she could wrap her fingers around.

The girl didn't seem to hear her; she must be so completely terrified, all her focus was on tearing the rope from around her neck. Teresa couldn't look up to see who was above her on the ledge, she probably had no idea Lacey was even here.

"I want to help you. Reach up and take my hand," Lacey called again, much louder this time, reaching down even farther, ignoring the vertigo that threatened to take over. Her fingertips brushed against the girl's hair. Could she grab a handful? Would that even help? It'd hurt like hell, but if Lacey could take even a little of the strain, it might be better than choking to death.

There was a strangled gurgling noise from the girl, like she was trying to scream around the rope blocking her windpipe. *Shit*. What else could Lacey do? She could haul on the rope, but that might increase the pressure around the girl's neck and kill her quicker. And even if she tried to drag her over the edge, it may well put her at such an odd angle, it might break her neck.

"Teresa. I know you're scared. But you need to listen to me," Lacey said slowly and forcefully. She could almost feel the girl's terror coming off her in waves, and the images of her own fall pushed hard at the barrier behind which she'd forced them. No, she could do this. She was trained to do this.

"I'm a cop and I'm here to save you. But I can't help you if you don't give me your hand."

The girl's legs stopped kicking out violently, and she gave another strangled noise. Lacey took it as a sign Teresa had heard her. All of a sudden, as if she'd taken a leap of faith, Teresa threw her arm up and behind her. Lacey snatched it out of the air and moved her grip so she had a good hold on the girl's wrist, feeling around behind her for something she could brace her feet against. Where the hell was Nico? She needed him. With his added strength, they'd be able to pull Teresa up easily. But as it was, it was all Lacey could do to take the entirety of the girl's weight. She was bloody heavy, and Lacey slipped a few inches before she repositioned her feet behind a large rock. Her left hand was holding onto the shrub for dear life and she suddenly wondered if it was strong enough to support the weight of two women. She guessed she was about to find out.

Now that Lacey was supporting Teresa's weight, she could hear the girl's rasping breaths as she tore the rope away from her throat with her free hand enough so that she could breathe. The sound almost brought tears to Lacey's eyes. It was the sound of survival. Raw and unfettered. Now she just had to get the girl up onto the ledge. At the thought that Teresa might have a good chance of survival, the clamoring images of her own near-death experience receded slightly.

"You're good. It's all good. I've got you," Lacey called down loudly. The wind was howling around the crags, and Lacey hoped the girl could hear her over the noise. "Take your time and get your breath back," she encouraged, even though it was the last thing she wanted to say. Her arm felt like it was being pulled out of its socket, the sharp, rocky edge digging into the side of her bicep so hard it was as if a sharp knife was slicing across her skin.

Lacey took her own advice and sucked in a few deep

breaths as well, trying to calm her racing heart.

"How are you going?" she asked after ten seconds of deep breathing. She needed to move soon because she didn't know how long she could keep holding on. And she couldn't let go. It was non-negotiable. She wasn't going to drop this girl.

"Help me," came the hoarse reply. "Don't let me go." She sounded almost hysterical, and Lacey didn't blame her. She was facing out into a great abyss, with nothing but the clasp of Lacey's hand to keep her from hanging by the neck, or a two-hundred foot fall to her death. Even just glancing over the edge gave Lacey a sense of vertigo. But Lacey was in the uncanny position of knowing exactly how scared this poor woman must be, and she needed to help her overcome her fear.

"I'm not going to drop you," Lacey said calmly. "But I need you to help me, because I can't pull you up on my own. Can you move? Do you think we can swivel you around so you can grab a handhold? Or a foothold?"

"I don't know." Teresa's wail came out thin and raspy from her damaged throat and Lacey's heart went out to her. But there was no time for compassion. Her arm wasn't going to last all day. There was no time to even wonder where Nico was. She couldn't count on his help; she'd have to rescue Teresa on her own.

"I'm going to turn you slowly, and you need to grab hold of a rock, anything, that will help support your weight."

"Okay." Teresa's reply was tremulous, but Lacey began to rotate her wrist, swinging Teresa to the left so the girl could bring her free arm around and use it to hold on. Lacey was thinking quickly, even as her shoulder screamed in pain at the extra work involved in turning Teresa and then hanging on as the girl wriggled, striving to find a foothold. If she could hang on long enough, perhaps Teresa could move the rope from around her neck to her waist. At least then if she slipped, or Lacey could no longer hold on, the rope would keep her from falling. But that might not be possible with no slack in the line. It also depended on how Sandra had constructed the noose. Lacey prayed it was the same as the other two girls. In both of those cases, she hadn't constructed a proper hangman's knot, which was designed to tighten around the neck if there was any movement. Sandra had merely made a loop and tied it with three or four square knots so it didn't come loose, and then she'd slipped it over the girls' heads. When Sandra had slung Sukey and Zoya up from the tree, the girls had already been unconscious, so all she was doing was cutting off their air supply until they died of asphyxiation.

Suddenly, some of the tension in her arm eased slightly.

"I've found a small ledge to stand on," Teresa called up, her voice still croaky and being blown away by the wind.

"Good girl. Now see if you can grab a rock or another ledge with your other hand," Lacey coaxed. Teresa was an outdoor guide. She should have basic rock climbing skills, at the very least, as well as being healthy and extremely fit. With that added advantage, Lacey realized they could do this. She could help get this girl off the cliff face.

"I've got my fingers in a crack," Teresa called up a few seconds later, and Lacey felt the strain ease off a little more. She almost wept with relief, as the knife edge of the rock face was no longer threatening to cut her arm off under the shoulder.

"That's great," Lacey called down. "You're doing great." She could still see the top of Teresa's dark head, and finally, the other woman looked up at her, dark eyes wide and full of fear. The whites of her eyes were bloodshot, her lips blue from lack of oxygen, and there were red abrasions on her neck where the rope had cut in, but Lacey could've reached down and kissed her right at that moment. She was alive. The worst part was over, now they just needed her to climb the few feet up to safety.

"Do you think you can climb up from there?"

Teresa considered her question for a few seconds before shaking her head. "I'm not sure. I can't see any handholds farther up, and my legs are like jelly, I don't know if my muscles have enough strength to push me up. It's all I can do to hold my own weight."

Not good. But at least Teresa was lucid and thinking logically, her training clearly kicking in.

"Okay. What about if we move the rope from around your neck? Maybe you could use that as a handhold and I could lift you up using that?" There wouldn't be enough length for Teresa to tie it around her waist, but if she—

"Let go of her, and put your hands up where I can see them." The voice took Lacey completely by surprise and she looked up, squinting into the rain to see where it'd come from. Sandra stood on a rock that jutted out over the cliff edge around thirty feet away. Sandra. She'd completely forgotten about the villain in her attempt at a rescue.

Nico stood next to her.

It took her a few seconds to work out what was going on. Sandra held a gun jammed into Nico's side. She hadn't heard them approach because of the storm. They must've come from somewhere over on the northern side of the bluff.

Lacey froze.

"Let her go, or I'll shoot lover boy." Sandra's face was forbidding, her mouth a dark slash against her pale skin, and her voice pitched so low Lacey almost couldn't hear it. But she could hear the grim determination in her tone. Sandra meant business.

Was that blood on Nico's shirt? Lacey tilted her head trying to make out the dark patch, hidden beneath the fall of his rain jacket, which was unzipped and gaped open at the front. Was Nico hurt? Had he been shot?

She searched his eyes, but it was hard to see clearly through the rain. He seemed to be tilted to the left slightly. And now she looked closer, there was pain in the way he hunched over. Oh God. Sandra had shot him.

"I told you to let her go," Sandra's voice boomed out over the bluff, no longer quiet, but still authoritative. She was a formidable woman, and Lacey felt an ounce of something a little like respect for this lady who let nothing get in her way. Not even two armed cops. She was a daunting opponent.

"Don't listen to her," Nico shouted. "I'm—"

"Shut up. Shut up," Sandra yelled, brandishing the gun in Nico's face. "I told you not to speak. I will shoot you again. And this time I'll shoot to kill." She rammed Nico in the stomach with the butt of her gun and Nico doubled over in pain. But his face remained defiant. Nico wouldn't give up without a fight. And that was the part that scared Lacey the most. He was bound to do something heroic or downright dangerous just to save the victim. And her. And she couldn't let that happen. She couldn't let him die.

A million different scenarios flashed through Lacey's mind. Her gun was still tucked into the waistband of her shorts. But she wasn't going to let go of Teresa, and if she relinquished her hold on the small shrub while she teetered precariously on the edge, she may well end up going over herself. Which left her with no hands free to go for her weapon.

"What's going on?" Teresa called up, and Lacey realized she couldn't see Sandra or Nico from her position. Did that mean that Sandra couldn't see Teresa either? She could obviously tell that Lacey was holding her up by her hand, but maybe she couldn't see that Teresa was now facing the wall, rather than dangling out in free space.

"The woman who tried to kill you is here, and she's got a

gun," Lacey whispered through the side of her mouth, hoping her words were loud enough for Teresa to hear, but not to carry to where Sandra stood.

"I mean it." Sandra lifted the gun and pointed it at Nico's head, releasing the safety catch with a loud click at the same time.

There was no way Lacey was going to let Teresa go. But she also couldn't let Sandra shoot Nico.

Nico.

She couldn't let him die.

What to do? Where was Nico's gun? Did he still have it on him? It seemed unlikely. If Sandra was smart enough to have caught Nico unawares and shoot him, she was smart enough to have taken away his weapon as well.

A certain kind of calm descended over Lacey. It was almost as if she was watching the whole scene play out before her, but was removed from the emotion of it all, an idea forming in her mind.

"I'm going to let you go," Lacey whispered. "Slip the rope over your head once I free your hand and hang on with both hands." She hoped Teresa understood how critical it was for her to obey. Her plan would only work if Teresa did as she was told. If she panicked, or wouldn't let go, they may both die.

"What? No!" Lacey could hear hysteria rising in Teresa's voice. Shit. Lacey pleaded silently with Teresa to understand what she needed her to do. Lacey's eyes were locked on Nico's. Almost imperceptibly, he shook his head, telling her no. He didn't want her to let go of Teresa's hand. Lacey had no idea what Nico might have going on in his head, but if he thought he was going to play the hero, he had another thought coming. She held his gaze, praying he could read her mind, and he didn't do something stupid. Sandra had him standing so close to the edge. If he decided to tackle her, they might both tumble over into the abyss.

"If you don't let go, both of us are going to die," Lacey said as quietly as she could to Teresa, trying not to move her lips as she spoke.

"Look at me," Sandra snapped, and Lacey dragged her gaze away from Nico. "Neither of you cops need to die. Once this slut is dead, I'll happily go with you. I'm resigned to my fate. But my daughter's death needs to be redressed. She needs to rest in peace. There is a price that this girl must pay. She needs to learn that her actions have consequences. Just like the other two."

Sandra's words shocked Lacey, but then perhaps she shouldn't be surprised. Sandra had obviously planned these girls' deaths in exquisite detail as revenge for bullying her daughter. In her twisted mind, everything she'd done had been in vengeance for Tia. But Sandra was also a highly intelligent woman; she'd realize it was fruitless to try to escape from two officers. And it seemed like she didn't want to. Perhaps she thought she might feel vindicated after she completed these three murders. And she didn't really care where she lived out the rest of her life, as long as her daughter rested in peace.

"All right," Lacey called out as loudly as she could. "I'm going to let go, just please don't shoot my partner," she pleaded, hoping her near hysterical tone lulled Sandra into a false sense of security. At the same time as she entreated Sandra, she wriggled her fingers, tugging her hand gently away from Teresa. For a microsecond, Teresa's fingers tightened around hers, but then, mercifully, she let her go. All Teresa had to do was hang on long enough for Lacey to take Sandra out of the equation. Lacey hoped and prayed Teresa had a good grip on those rocks.

Ever so slowly, Lacey raised the hand that'd been holding onto Teresa in the air. At the same time, she loosed her grip on the shrub on her other side. But instead of bringing that hand forward, she carefully reached beneath the hem of her rain jacket, searching for the butt of her pistol.

"Good." Sandra's face brightened, perhaps at the thought that Teresa was now dangling by the neck once more, and she took a step toward the edge to see her victim. Then she narrowed her eyes at Lacey. "And the other one," she snarled, shaking her gun in Nico's face to make Lacey obey.

Lacey's fingers closed over the grip, and she eased it out of her shorts. This had to be done just right. She was still lying flat on the rocks, legs outstretched and feet hooked over a small boulder, one arm held awkwardly in the air. As she drew her gun along the ground, then beneath her chest, she transferred her gaze onto Nico, staring deep into his indigo eyes. He stared back.

Leaving her gun hidden beneath the swell of her breasts, Lacey brought her other hand around and into the air, so she now had both hands in front of her where Sandra could see them.

Sandra was leaning to the side, preparing to catch a glimpse of Teresa to make sure her death was now ensured. Nico frowned, but Lacey jutted her chin ever so slightly toward Sandra to let him know something was coming. For a split second, Sandra took her eyes off Lacey, her gun lowering away from Nico's head as she strove to make sense of what was going on at the end of the rope.

It was the moment Lacey was waiting for. Sudden understanding lit Sandra's eyes as she realized the girl wasn't dying as she hoped, but clinging to life for all she was worth.

It all happened so quickly; Lacey was a little unsure herself how it all came about. Her training took over; all those hours spent at the police gun range, and real-life scenario coaching kicked in. She withdrew her gun, rested her elbows on the ground, squinted through the rain, lined up her shot, and pulled the trigger as Nico ducked away from Sandra. Sandra had swung her weapon up in an arc when she saw Lacey move, but it was too late. Her bullet went wide.

But Lacey's bullet struck its target true. Sandra seemed surprised for a second, then covered her left breast with her free hand and looked down to see the blood running freely down her torso. Lacey's bullet had found its mark and lodged in the older woman's heart.

Nico was still crouched beside her, ready to attack if need be. Lacey kept her gun trained on the woman. She had sixteen more bullets, and she'd use them all if need be.

Sandra's knees gave way, and she crumpled in a heap on the rocky ledge, as if she were a rag doll and all her strings had just been cut.

Nico straightened and approached Sandra cautiously. The weapon had fallen from her hand and landed on the rocks with a clunk. He crouched to retrieve her gun, wincing on the way down, then put his fingers to Sandra's neck. The rain continued to fall, pounding out a rhythm on the wet mountain top as Lacey waited.

Nico stood up and shook his head. Sandra was dead.

For a few moments, Lacey was so full of relief she forgot that she'd just taken a life. It was the first time she'd killed someone. Even though it was in the line of duty, and even though it was to protect the man she loved, she suddenly felt a wave a grief, which quickly turned to nausea.

"What's happening up there?" Teresa's voice was both terrified and confused. "I heard a gunshot." Lacey hadn't forgotten about the woman on the cliff side, but the adrenaline was still coursing so hard around her body she was almost paralyzed.

Lacey let her shaking arms rest on the ground for a few seconds as she replied, "It's all right. You're safe. I'm going to pull you up now."

Hauling herself up to her knees, she tucked the gun back into the waistband of her shorts, then called to Nico, "Are you okay?" He lifted his head from where he was still studying Sandra, and Lacey could see the pain he'd been hiding now clearly showing in his eyes.

He pushed a hand over the wound in his side and grunted, then called out, "I'm coming over to help you. Sandra is dead."

She wanted to tell him to stay where he was. To sit down and stop moving. Stop pumping all that life-giving blood onto the ground. But he was so damned stubborn she knew her demand would be ignored, so she just nodded. Once he was by her side, she'd be able to examine his wound to see how bad it really was.

Lacey shifted her focus to the girl hanging onto the cliff for dear life. She popped her head over the edge and managed to raise a smile. Teresa was clinging to the rocks like a monkey, one hand firmly grabbing the lifeline of the rope, which she'd removed from her neck and was using to anchor herself.

Relief washed over Teresa's face when she saw Lacey. Then Nico was by her side, and together, they both reached down a hand, grasping Teresa and helping her to scramble up over the ledge. Teresa tumbled into their arms and they all collapsed in a heap on the wet rocks.

"Thank you. Oh, thank you," Teresa said over and over as she sat on the ground looking stunned, but Lacey's concern had now turned to her man.

Nico grunted in pain as he lay on the wet ground, not even bothering about the rain. His face was deathly pale and his teeth gritted together in pain. Lacey crawled over to him and pulled open his rain jacket exposing the wound. Nico didn't even try to stop her. She pushed all emotion aside and drew in a deep breath before she examined him. Gritting her teeth she lifted his soaking wet T-shirt and took a look. The bullet had entered the fleshy part just above his hip, and exited out the other side. A through and through. She turned and rummaged through her backpack, pulling out everything inside until she found a spare T-shirt and a long-sleeved sweater.

"I think it'll be okay," she said through trembling lips, folding the T-shirt into a makeshift pad that she pressed against the exit wound. Nico hissed in a painful breath.

"I know," he replied, lifting his head off the ground a few inches so he could look at her. "I've already assessed it. I've lost a bit of blood, but I don't think it hit any major organs," he said in his most annoying know-it-all voice. Lacey wanted to smack him. Or kiss him. Or both. But she did neither; instead she used her other hand to push down on her sweater on the entry wound to stem the flow of blood. He was alive. She just needed to keep him that way.

"I grabbed the sat phone off her." Nico held the phone aloft in one hand.

"Help me with this," Lacey demanded of Teresa, who was sitting a few feet away, her hands wrapped around her sore neck. Lacey felt a fleeting sting of guilt; the poor girl was probably in a lot of pain, but Nico's wound was more urgent. Once she had Teresa applying pressure to both sides of the injury, she took the phone from Nico's cold hand and dialed.

Even as she called for help, she continued to administer first aid, pulling out both of the emergency silver blankets from the kits she and Nico carried in their packs. She wrapped one around Nico, pushing it beneath him to get him off the wet ground, and the other around Teresa's shoulders, hoping to keep them warm and ward off shock. Lacey was also probably in shock, and now the adrenaline was wearing off, she could feel the cold eating into her bones from the constant downpour of chilly rain. But she'd have to cope. She also found some proper surgical padding and bandages and as she gave out the details of their situation and waited for confirmation of a rescue, she fashioned a makeshift dressing by strapping some pads on tight with the bandages. Nico moaned and groaned, then gave a sigh of relief once she let him lie back down. Teresa sat huddled under her emergency blanket a few feet away and Lacey made sure she was doing okay once she'd finished with Nico.

They were sending a rescue chopper to do an airborne extraction, estimated ETA around forty-five minutes. The rescue helicopter could handle these conditions, while the small one that'd dropped them off couldn't. Lacey hoped like hell that was true because she didn't like the idea of stretchering Nico down the steep trail; she was suddenly bone tired. Then she remembered she'd been on the go for over thirty-six hours with very little sleep. Griff was coming back up the bluff to give her a hand, leaving Mila to mind the other hikers. Another chopper would bring Gorman and Tyrell from farther down the trail to help them bring the six hikers back to base.

The rain eased off, and then almost as if a tap had been turned off somewhere in the sky, it stopped. Lacey sat back and tipped her head to the sky, staring at the clouds above which were breaking up, revealing a small patch of blue.

They'd done it. Achieved what they set out to do. They'd stopped Sandra and saved Teresa's life. The outcome wasn't perfect; she would've preferred to bring Sandra back alive to face the justice system, and maybe give some answers as to why she'd decided that murder was the only way to absolve her pain. Nico was injured, but he'd be okay; she felt it in her soul. Maybe a little time in hospital and a few enforced weeks' rest might slow him down a little. God knew he worked too hard most of the time. Time recuperating and processing what they'd just endured might be good.

She drew in a deep breath of rain washed air. Clear and

crisp. Lacey took a moment to really look at her surroundings. The top of Barn Bluff was wet, rain droplets shimmering on every blade of grass and scrubby branch, but it was incredibly beautiful. A sense of peace rolled over her. Her demons had come back to haunt her with a vengeance today, but she'd conquered them and come out the other side if not unscathed, then at least with her pride intact. Now she knew, next time she was faced with this type of situation, she'd do better. Sliding her backside over the wet rocks, she lifted Nico's head into her lap and smoothed his wet hair away from his forehead. Running her fingers over his chin, she followed the shape of his jaw beneath the stubble, stopping to gently trace the scar on his cheek. He smiled tiredly up at her and she leaned down and touched her lips to his. He was going to be okay. They were going to be okay. She stared into the clearing mists, thanking the universe for giving her this man.

CHATPER TWENTY-TWO

Nico sat carefully in the winged chair, easing into the backrest. God, it was good to be home. The past two days spent in hospital had been a nightmare. The worst part was having to just lie there while people trooped in and out of his room. Doctors and nurses, then Tyrell and the other officers coming to check for themselves Nico was really going to be fine, Shadbolt, who came to congratulate him on a job well done, Pederson and Saito, who took his preliminary statement and also congratulated him, if a tad grudgingly. Even Margie and Herb had come to visit, bringing some of Margie's famous rock cakes. Lacey vetted them all at the door, guarding him like a prize Doberman, but she barely had time to speak to him, she was so busy running errands, debriefing the rest of the team, and answering endless questions on his health, so they were never alone for more than five minutes. She'd even fielded the phone calls from his mother and siblings, which was a feat unto itself. But all he'd wanted was to hold her in his arms. That would've been the best medicine of all.

He'd been waiting impatiently to be discharged, just so he could be alone with her; finally, just her and him.

"Here's your pain medication, I'm going to watch while

you take it." Lacey rounded through the living room door, Smudge close on her heels. Smudge had been ecstatic to see him this morning, but clever dog that he was, he must've sensed Nico wasn't himself and hadn't jumped up to lick his face, not even once. His faithful dog came to lay his head on Nico's feet as Lacey placed two pills in a cup and a glass of water on the table next to him, then stood over him, tapping her foot. Lacey had been running around like a headless chicken for the past hour, ever since she'd brought him home. Doing the same thing she'd been doing at the hospital. Keeping so busy and frenetic it almost felt like she was avoiding him.

"I'll take them on one condition," he said, eyeing the pills but not picking them up.

"What?" There was a dangerous edge to Lacey's voice, but he forged on, needing to talk her down off this ledge of feverish activity.

"I want you to sit down and talk to me for five whole minutes."

She narrowed her eyes at him, but then finally relented and perched on the edge of the couch closest to him, still watching him intently. "Right, I'm sitting. Take those pills."

He did as he was told, partly because his side was aching like a bitch and mostly to keep her happy.

Once he'd swallowed his medicine with a big slug of water, he gave her an appreciative smile, hoping to soften her up before he hit her with his unpopular opinion. "You need to take a chill pill and stop acting like a drill sergeant." He knew that her certain type of crazy sprung from her anxiety for his welfare, but he was fine, she just needed to recognize that. What he really needed was for her to sit with him so he could relish her company.

"What? I'm not!" she fired back defensively, her eyes going wide with outrage.

He stared back at her, getting lost in the golden tints around the edges of her iris. It was her eyes. They were the true heart-stealers. They were the first thing that'd truly sucked him in on the very first day they'd met. And they could still make his heart beat erratically, even now.

Reaching out, he took her hand. The movement caused a spasm of pain to shoot through his belly, but he hid it well. "You. I need you. Your presence is better than all the pain meds in the whole wide world," he said, tracing small circles on the back of her hand with his thumb. "Come here." He drew her toward him, tugging her off the couch and patting his knee.

"No, I'll hurt you," she protested.

"I'm willing to take a little pain if I can have you in my arms." He looked directly into her eyes. "Please, Lace."

The past few days had occupied his mind with the practicalities of being injured in hospital and the worry of trying to finalize a murder investigation while handling the fallout of Lacey shooting Sandra, which was still a matter under investigation. It was procedure, but he knew the outcome would be in Lacey's favor; she'd had no other choice, but that didn't mean Nico wasn't a touch worried. So he hadn't had much time to actually process everything that'd happened on top of that bluff. Or process how Lacey was coping with it all. She'd been his rock throughout the past two days. But he needed to delve deeper, to make sure she wasn't faking it.

Lacey sat gingerly on his lap, not leaning any weight on him, then slung an arm around his shoulders, resting her amber gaze on his face. It was the first time she'd looked at him, really looked at him, all day.

"I need to know you're doing okay after everything we went through," he said evenly, while a the same time pulling her closer into his uninjured side. She resisted for a second, before slowly melting into him. She felt so good. It was what his body had been crying out for over the last few days.

"I'm actually doing okay now," she replied, resting her forehead against his temple. "I didn't want to worry you, but I saw Imran yesterday, while they were running all those tests on you."

"That's good," he countered. Imran Malik was the local police psychologist, and he was damned good at what he did. Lacey had visited him regularly after her near-death experience six months ago, and he was glad to see she'd reached out to him again. He left a gap for her to fill, hoping she'd finally tell him the truth.

"You were right," she said at last, her eyes taking on a faraway look. "When you questioned my mental state up there on top of the bluff. I didn't want to admit it. I just wanted to get on with the job." She gave him a wan smile, and he lifted a finger and traced the line of her jaw, cupping the side of her face in his hand. "I think hauling Teresa back up that cliff face was a baptism of fire for me," she went on. "When I first saw the cliff and the rope running over the edge, I didn't think I'd be able to face it, I wanted to turn around and run. But I couldn't just leave her there to die. So I did what I had to do, I fought with the images until I got them under control and then I helped her." She gave a small shrug.

"You make it sound easy, Lace. But don't undersell yourself. You did an amazing thing. You're the strongest person I know." He caressed her cheek with his palm, staring deep into her eyes.

"You sound like Imran," she quipped.

"And he's a very intelligent man," Nico shot back. "But I mean it, Lace. I'm so glad it was you up on top of that mountain with me. I wouldn't have wanted anyone else by my side. I love you so much." He tipped his head and took her lips in a delicious, slow-burning kiss. It set off a deep thrum low in his belly. Just the smell of her, the closeness of her, turned him on something wicked. Even while he was in pain and straight out of the hospital.

"Oh God," he sighed. "I cannot wait until my bloody side heals. Because I want to do things to you. Hot, sweaty, naked things." The thought of getting Lacey into bed had him wanting to pick her up and carry her straight to their room right now. She brought out something urgent and fiery in him. It was pure, primal instinct. The kind that made tomcats howl in alleys. The kind that made him so possessive he wanted to keep her chained to his bed forever. He was hard in seconds as he thought about how much he wanted to make love to her. Gunshot wound be damned, he needed to feel her beside him now. He tensed, wrapped his arms around her tighter and made ready to stand and carry her down the hallway.

"What do you think you're doing?" she snapped. At the same time as his injury strained painfully, and he sucked in a sharp breath. "You'll pull out all your stitches." Lacey moved away, glowering down at him.

He frowned and tried not to pout. There was no way he was letting on that she might be right. "I only wanted—"

"I know what you wanted." She spoke more gently now. "I want it too, Nico. But you just got out of hospital today, give yourself a few more days to heal."

"If you were really gentle with me, perhaps…" He looked up with imploring eyes, not ready to give in completely, his erection still demanding action, despite the pain in his side.

She leaned down and put her hands on his knees, effectively stopping him from getting up. "I know you think you're invincible. But I'm in charge for the next few days. And you'll just have to put up with it." Then she tilted her head to the side and regarded him for a few moments. His gaze followed the movement of her throat as she swallowed. So elegant and vulnerable.

"Well, you know how much I love it when you take charge," he said, teasing but also relenting. He knew when he'd been beaten. But the stretch of her throat beckoned to him, and he couldn't help his mouth tracing soft kisses down to her collarbone.

She sighed and tilted her head slightly to give him better access. "Maybe a kiss now and then might be okay," she said, conceding just a little. Her lips landed on his, gentle at first, but soon with increased urgency, as if she too could hardly wait until he was better. God, this was going to kill him if he had to wait more than a few days.

He couldn't see a life without Lacey in it. And now that Marietta was truly out of the way, it was time. Time to ask Lacey to marry him. Even after everything Marietta had put him through, Lacey's love had cured him of the wounds his ex-wife had inflicted. She'd shown him how true love was supposed to feel between a man and a woman. Equals in everything. Nico had tossed the idea of marrying Lacey around before, and there was no better time than right now. The idea thrilled him. His heart was thumping in his chest at the thought, but it was pounding with joy, not fear or indecision. Because he knew she'd say yes.

Nico's phone trilled on the table next to him, and Lacey broke away, both of them slightly out of breath. It took a second for his brain to catch up.

"Do you want to answer it?" Lacey asked, standing up and straightening her T-shirt, which he'd tugged out of her waistband with needy fingers.

Damn, talk about bad timing. He had half a mind to refuse. To pull her back down into his lap and devour her mouth a little more before he popped the question. But it was probably one of his team, calling about one of the loose ends on the case. And the moment was ruined now anyway. "I guess so," Nico grumbled. Lacey handed him his phone and then bent to clear the table of his empty glass and cold coffee.

Caller ID came up as unknown. Nico held the phone to his ear. "Hello?" If this was some cold caller trying to sell him insurance for his cat, he was going to be mighty pissed.

"You look more like your mother every day. Which I always thought was a shame. I hoped you'd turn out more like me. Perhaps it's a good thing you didn't, though."

Nico's heart stopped beating. That voice. So familiar. So menacing. He was sent spiraling back to a time when he was ten years old, his father glaring at him, eyes as cold as steel, berating Nico for some minor infraction. Nico remembered his feeling of rising anger. But also impotence. A weakness flooded his veins, and he grabbed for the arm of the chair to steady himself.

It was one thing being told your dead father wasn't really dead, but another thing completely to be confronted with the absolute truth of the matter. His father was unquestionably alive. He'd recognize that voice anywhere. Lacey stalled in picking up the mug, seeing that his face had drained of all color.

"Who is it?" she mouthed.

But he had no ability to reply, all his focus was turned inward, on that voice down the other end of the phone. "What do you want?" he managed to croak out of a throat that was suddenly constricted.

His father. He was actually talking to his father. It was more than just surreal. It was almost as if he were in someone else's body.

"I just wanted to congratulate you on finding such a good woman. She's a strong one. And beautiful too. You need to take care of that one." Nico's hackles suddenly rose. Was his father threatening him? Threatening Lacey?

"What do you want?" he repeated, but this time with more authority.

Lacey was staring down at him, the concern turning to fear in her eyes. He stood, suddenly unable to sit still.

"I saw you came home from the hospital today. I hope you recover soon," the voice intoned. A chill ran down Nico's spine. Was his father tracking him? Watching him? Nico went over to the window and stared out into the back garden. Smudge followed him, and got up on his hind legs, putting his paws on the windowsill. A low growl emanated from the dog's throat. Holy fuck. Was his father out there somewhere? Nico's property backed onto a large acreage of native bushland. Could his father be standing in the shadows at the back of his yard, watching him?

Lacey came to stand at Nico's shoulder, also looking out into the yard. It was a bright, summer's day, but Nico felt unexpectedly cold. Chilled to the bone.

Then it was like a blinding light went on in his mind, and everything suddenly made awful sense. It was his father who'd broken into their house the other day. Looking for what, Nico had no idea. Information on his son perhaps. Or information on Lacey? But why? What did he want with them?

Nico put a protective arm around Lacey, and she leaned into his shoulder, perhaps guessing by his side of the conversation who was on the other end of the phone.

"You stay away from me, and you stay away from Lacey. And you stay away from Mum and Brice and Gaëlle too," he ground out between gritted teeth. "No one in this family wants anything to do with you."

His father merely laughed, the sound terrifyingly calculating. "We have some unfinished business, you and I. I'll look forward to meeting you soon. I can't wait to look into my son's face and see what kind of man he's grown up into."

With that, the phone line went dead.

Nico wanted to sprint out to the backyard. Find his father and confront him. But a part of him knew Serge was already gone. He threw the phone onto the couch and pulled Lacey into his arms, needing to hold her tight, a feeling of foreboding tight in his chest, even as she slid warm arms around his waist.

As he held her, a dark thought lurked. Was now really the right time to ask Lacey to marry him? With his father suddenly re-emerging from the murky depths in which he'd been hiding? The phone call had left a feeling of intense disquiet roiling in Nico's guts, telling him that Lacey was in danger. From his own father. How was he going to protect her from that?

CHAPTER TWENTY-THREE

Lacey sat beside Linc in the break room. "Are you sure you should be back at work?" The words slipped out before she could stop them. She was still in carer mode after looking after Nico all week at home, and the habit was hard to kick. But she had to admit, it was damn good to be back at work. She touched the new duty belt buckled neatly around her waist. It fit perfectly, no more gunslinging for her. The belt had finally arrived the day she'd been on top of Barn Bluff, but today was the first day she'd been able to wear it.

"For the tenth time today, yes, I'm fine. The doctor has cleared me for duty. Stop clucking like a mother hen, Shorty." Linc gave his trademark grin, hale and healthy and ready to take on the world again. Which was good; one less thing for her to worry about. Linc had no lasting effects from his blood clot and induced coma except for his memory loss of the actual attack, which the doctor had said was normal. His memories may return over time, but it may also remain a complete blank for the rest of his life.

"And talking about mother hens, the Lord knows I love my mother, but just between you and me, I can't wait until she goes home tomorrow," Linc added with an extra twinkle in his eye. "She's driving me slowly insane with her over-caring. I'm a thirty-year-old man but she seems to think I'm five again. She even tried to spoon feed me the day after I was discharged from hospital." Linc gave a horrified shudder and Lacey laughed out loud.

At least she hadn't been quite that bad with Nico. Had she? Maybe Nico was secretly just as glad she was back to work today. Nico still had another two weeks home rest to endure before he was allowed back on desk duty. Then it'd be more weeks of physical rehab until he could move to active duty. Home rest was like a certain form of torture for Nico. He found it almost impossible to sit still, and a small part of Lacey was worried that she wasn't there to force him to take it easy. But she had a job to do, and he was a grown man who needed to learn to regulate himself and his expectations of how much he was capable of.

"Your mum isn't staying for Christmas then?" It was less than two weeks until Christmas now, and Lacey was surprised she wasn't taking the opportunity to stay and spend it with him.

"Nah. Me and Tyrell have got time off and we're heading back to the States for two weeks vacation. Spending time with the family, you know. They all want to know I'm actually okay. And Mum always runs Christmas Day like a sergeant major. I wouldn't be allowed to miss it. The family flies in from all over the country. It's a big thing. Lots of family drama." Linc grimaced, but she could see the affection he had for his kinsfolk beneath the veneer of suffering through a family get-together.

Lacey nodded, but felt a stab of envy. How nice would it be to have a large family like that? Who squabbled and had their petty grievances, but with an undercurrent of love and closeness. At least Nico's side of the family was fairly normal, if you didn't count the father who'd faked his own death. They had plans to travel to Canberra for five days over the

Christmas break to spend it with his mother, sister, and brother. Thankfully, Nico would be well enough to travel by then. His mother was desperate to see him after he'd been wounded. She'd been determined to fly down to Tasmania to see him in the hospital, but he'd diverted her, telling her he was fine, it was only a flesh wound—which it wasn't—and that she could determine for herself how good he was when he arrived on her doorstep. Lacey was looking forward to officially meeting Nico's family. She'd spoken to them over video link when he'd been there exhuming the body in his father's coffin. Caterina had seemed lovely and welcoming over the video, as had Gaëlle. And Brice had seemed happy to see his younger brother finally settling down.

Her own family was another matter. She still hadn't spoken to her parents, and it'd been over six months since she'd last seen them. Her older brother, Mathew, was in touch regularly and was going to pop over to Burnie for a few days in early January to catch up, much to her mother's disapproval—she'd decided that Lacey was dead to her, and everyone around her should bend to her wishes and not talk to Lacey either. But Matt was stronger than her father and didn't give in to Elora's tantrums and let her run his life. Lacey was looking forward to her brother's visit. Nico had never met her family, even though he'd accompanied her to Melbourne to confront them about the way they treated her regarding her PTSD. He'd stayed in the hotel, as she felt it was something she needed to do alone, but had been there to comfort her when she returned. So, this was Matt's chance to finally meet the love of her life. It was a little scary, but also exciting. Nico meeting even one member of her family made it more serious somehow.

And while Sammy's calls were infrequent, she still kept Lacey up-to-date with her parents' lives. Sammy would probably always be the apple of their mother's eye, and she and Lacey were two very different people, but Lacey hoped they could still keep their communication up, as she loved her sister, despite all their contrasting personalities.

Lacey let out a long sigh.

"You okay?" Linc asked, watching her with concern.

"Yeah. Just got a lot on my mind right now," she replied.

Linc studied her for a few moments, then said, "I know I already said this, but I'm really proud of the way you handled yourself up there on the bluff. It sounds like you did an awesome job. So, you shouldn't be worried about any of that." In a roundabout way, Linc was also referring to the investigation into her shooting Sandra. It'd take weeks for an outcome from the commission, but everyone knew it was warranted; Lacey had no other choice. She already knew that Linc supported her decision to shoot, one hundred percent.

"Thank you." She gave him her best smile, grateful for the way he acknowledged her abilities. Linc seldom handed out praise, so when he gave his approval, she knew she'd definitely earned it.

Lacey had driven Nico to visit Linc while he was recuperating at home last week to make sure he was on the mend and to fill him in on the events up on the bluff. Linc had a special interest in how that'd gone down. Nico told him Sandra had admitted to hitting him over the head to prevent him from picking up the charm. But it hadn't been as much to stop him finding a clue, as it had been to retrieve a sentimental item. That locket had belonged to Tia, and Sandra had been devastated to lose it. But Nico praised Linc's instincts in stopping to pick it up. Without that charm, and the link it formed to the other girls, they may not have broken the case so quickly. Now that Sandra was dead, they'd never know if Sandra was aware the other three girls all had the same charm. There were so many questions they'd never have an answer for. Such as why Sandra had waited four years to take her revenge. Nico was pretty sure Sandra's murder spree had been triggered by the fact it would've been Tia's twenty-first birthday, but they'd never know for sure. Lacey couldn't feel sorrow at the woman's demise, however, even though she knew Nico was frustrated by the lack of information.

Taj was helping them cobble together a little of Sandra's story, but even he was shocked by her level of deception and ultimate depravity. Taj blamed himself for not seeing the depths to which his mother had spiraled to, and he'd probably live with that for the rest of his life, although Lacey had tried to explain that he wasn't responsible for his mother's faults. Lacey gave Taj a few tips from her own life experience, where for so long she'd felt like she'd completely failed to live up to her mother's expectations. But in the end, she knew she'd never change Elora, just as Taj would never have been able to stop Sandra's murderous intent. Sandra may have had an undiagnosed mental illness, for all they knew. But then, the grief of losing her child might've caused its own form of mental illness. Grief affected people in different ways, and perhaps it'd finally caught up with Sandra.

Thinking about Sandra, brought another ruthless woman to mind.

Tyrell had interviewed Erica Nellenbach in those few days when Nico was still in hospital and she'd been as unhelpful as ever. But under duress and after a firm direction from her lawyer, she'd finally revealed the messages between herself and Zoya six months ago had been regarding the charges of verbal and emotional abuse of a young girl in Erica's care two years prior. Much as Lacey had surmised, Zoya had uncovered the details of the abuse and then found out that Erica had paid the family to keep quiet. It seemed Zoya sensed a chink in Erica's armor and had tried her own form of blackmail. But when Erica refused to pay what she was asking, Zoya had approached the family of the abused girl to ask them if they'd be willing to go to the police with the matter. Surprisingly, the family had declined, saying it was better to leave that episode in the past. Zoya knew without the family's backing, it'd be no use taking the case to law enforcement. So the two women settled on a much smaller amount, which was more about Erica keeping her reputation intact than keeping Zoya quiet.

Ever since that time, their work relationship had been frosty, and Erica knew Zoya had started looking for other employment. She said she'd be glad to see the back of the girl. Erica never revealed how much she paid the family of the abused girl, or Zoya, but Lacey surmised it was a large sum, probably in the hundreds of thousands. God that woman was a piece of work.

When Tyrell had pressed her on the matter, Erica also revealed one other small tidbit of information. While she said her memory was sketchy, she agreed she'd been aware Tia was being bullied by the other three girls in her team at the time. She believed it was something to do with Tia being a little overweight. Fat shaming by today's standards. Lacey was both livid and terribly sad when she found out. Physical appearance had nothing to do with aptitude—supposedly, Tia was the best gymnast in the group, and maybe the girls' bullying stemmed from jealousy as much as anything else— nor did it have anything to do with personality or kindness. Something the other three seemed to be sorely lacking. It was probably the reason Tia had become anorexic, trying to comply to a social norm that'd never fit her.

Erica told them that even after the team split and took up individual practices, the girls would sometimes still poke fun at her right up until Tia left the gymnasium at the age of seventeen; a few weeks before she killed herself. This news made Lacey even sadder. Why had the abuse been allowed to go on for so long unchecked? Sandra Brown had blamed the girls for tormenting Tia, but Lacey felt that Sandra probably also felt a lot of guilt at forcing her daughter to continue with the club—probably as a misguided way of facing her fears—instead of letting her make up her own mind. Sandra said she'd taken Tia to see a counsellor, but in the end that wasn't enough, and Lacey silently grieved for the young woman who'd endured so much.

Lacey had also attended Zoya's funeral a few days ago. Her mother was grateful the police had caught her killer, but could hardly believe it was a woman who'd murdered her daughter. Let alone another mother, who should know what such a loss like this would mean to her. Anastasia was lost in her own world of heartbreak and was ill-equipped to understand any of Sandra's motivations, much less condone them. She was angry; her life had been shattered, and Lacey couldn't blame her. Lacey cried at the funeral, as did Dawn, and she thought Tyrell might've had a few unshed tears in his eyes, like many of the other officers who attended as a show of respect and honor.

Sukey's funeral was next week, and that'd probably be just as bad. It was a part of policing Lacey found hard to deal with, maybe because she empathized with the victims and their families a little too much.

"How's Nico doing?" Linc asked, distracting her from her maudlin thoughts.

"He's healing well," she replied. It was true, the doctor was more than happy with Nico's progress. "The stitches came out yesterday," she added on a sigh. Now he'd probably decide he was ready to come back to work and want to overdo it. And that was only the tip of the iceberg where Nico was concerned, because his mental health was on more shaky ground than his physical health.

After that call from his not-so-dead father, Nico had become almost overcome with the need to track Serge down. Nico would pore over his computer for hours every day, researching Reginald Smith, his father's moniker, when he should've been resting. He was sure his father meant them both harm and had become even more protective over Lacey, not allowing her to go anywhere alone, and demanding that she take Smudge, even for a short foray into the backyard.

The phone call had been like a bolt from the blue, lighting a fire of simmering hatred inside Nico. Lacey was a little shocked at the depth of his emotions until he'd finally revealed why he was acting so tense. Although he had no proof, Nico was sure the intruder in their house the other night had been Serge. At first Lacey had been reluctant to believe him, but then she thought back to her feelings on the night of the break-in. Back then, she'd had a gut feeling it hadn't been a random break and enter. It'd felt personal somehow. And the shifting of the photo on top of her dresser had confirmed it in her mind. If it had been Serge, then the photo frame had significance. Serge wanted to see what his son looked like now. And perhaps check out Lacey as well.

But they still had no answer to the biggest question of all. Why? Why was Serge back? And why had he initiated contact with Nico after all these years? It was unsettling and even Smudge could feel the extra tension around their house at the moment. Without any solid answers, they were just going to have to keep living their lives as if nothing had changed, and wait and see.

Lacey mentioned none of this to Linc. It wasn't his problem to bear. Nico had informed the chief inspector; it was a matter of procedure when a detective was possibly being stalked. But no one else need know. Yet.

"The couple who helped us up on the bluff, Griff and Mila, are coming over for dinner tonight," she told him instead. It'd be nice to catch up with them again. They'd opted to continue their hike on the Overland Track after the takedown of Sandra Brown. Pederson and Saito had debriefed them on the edge of Lake Will, and happy that their version of events matched Lacey and Nico's, had thanked them and let them get on with their trek.

"They want to come and see how Nico is doing. And catch up on all the gory details, I guess," she added with a smile. As active officers in the force, Griff and Mila had been more than useful in helping to protect the hikers as well as tracking down Sandra, and Lacey would like to thank them personally for their assistance. It was only fair they hear the full story of Sandra's murder spree from Nico and herself.

They wouldn't get the information from the news, even though the media were falling over themselves to get the tiniest detail surrounding the murders with which to feed the masses. But Shadbolt was only giving them the basics, so the journalists were now hounding the poor grieving families of the murdered girls.

At least Griff and Mila knew to stay away from the media. Teresa, on the other hand, was selling her story to the highest bidder. Which rankled Lacey, but she guessed the girl had been through a lot at the hands of a crazy woman. And while Lacey would never be one to sell out to the press, Teresa stood to make a lot of money. Which wouldn't help her get through the trauma any better, but it might help to pay for counseling if she needed it.

"Nico is cooking a roast lamb," she added with a frown. He'd been adamant he was capable of cooking a simple meal, even though she'd offered to bring home takeaway instead. She let out another sigh. *Let it go.* She needed to stop worrying about him all the time.

And he *was* getting better. She could attest to that. Last night had been the first time she and Nico had made love since he'd been wounded. His stitches had come out that day, and Nico was feeling buoyant. She'd spent the afternoon at her dojo, getting rid of most of her tension by taking it out on her hapless instructor. Her muscles had ached when she got home, but in a good way. Needing a quick shower before dinner, she'd ducked into the bathroom to wash off the sweat. A few moments later, she was surprised to hear the click of the bathroom door as it closed, and then a naked Nico slipped into the shower beside her. For a second, her gaze had caught on the waterproof dressings the doctor applied to the back and front above his hip, but then his lips brushed against hers, giving her just a taste of what was to come, and she forgot about everything but this amazing man and how much she wanted his equally amazing body.

Her back had relaxed under the gentle sweep of his hand. Wet shoulder-length hair dark against the side of his face, Nico's indigo eyes burned with intensity, and she gave into the passion he brought out in her. With soapy hands, she'd explored his body, running her hands across his shoulders, down his back, and over his buttocks to his firm thighs. Fingertips finding the ridges of his chiseled abs, careful to miss the site of his injury, then fluttering down to below his navel and beyond. He was hard for her already, and she gloried in the silken skin of his erection. Nico groaned at her touch, his kiss turning heated and demanding. When he drew back, his eyes were filled with tenderness as he planted a soft kiss on her lips.

The gesture moved her more than any orgasm could. She loved this man with all of her being. Her body ached for him.

Not able to wait even the few seconds it'd take for them to leave the shower and make it to the bedroom, he'd turned her around and took her from behind while the hot water cascaded down their bodies. It'd been fast and fierce, her climax coming quickly, surprising her with its intensity. And

Nico had only been a second behind her, nearly lifting her feet off the ground as he thrust into her with abandon, then collapsing against her back, panting and spent.

Their second round had been much more leisurely. After they'd dried off and slipped between the sheets, Lacey had taken charge, just like she'd teased she would when he'd first come home from the hospital. Pushing him gently down onto the bed, she'd been the conductor, straddling him and making him watch her pleasure herself until she climaxed, driving him crazy with wanting and waiting. Then she played him the same way, loving the way he'd shouted her name as he came. It was the best sign that he was recovering well, and it made her heart light to see him like that. Knowing he was safe and recovering well was the best antidote to her heart. She loved this man so deeply and so perfectly, it was a little scary sometimes.

"Sounds like that man is a keeper," Linc said, standing up and stretching. "He can cook the perfect roast lamb, loves dogs, can solve murder cases at the drop of a hat, and he puts up with you." He added a wink as he gave her a sly smile.

"You might be right," Lacey said, also standing and readjusting her vest, shooting him a cheeky smile. "He does put up with a lot from me. But I'm worth it." She loved the way Linc was such a joker. It was good to have their easy banter going again. It was great to have Linc back by her side. Her life was pretty much perfect. She had a great partner to help her through her days at work, and a near perfect man to love her through the nights at home.

"Well, maybe you should make it permanent then. You should ask him to marry you, before some other woman snaps him up," he said, pulling his sunglasses down from on top his head and settling them on his nose. He reminded her a little of the guy from the seventies show, *CHiPs*, Erik Estrada, with that handsome smile, in his aviator sunglasses, and cocky swagger.

"Maybe I will," she declared, slipping her own sunglasses on and staring at him over the rims.

"Shall we head out then?" Linc said, turning to exit the room. "I've been craving one of our barista mate's coffees all week."

"Let's grab one for the road," Lacey agreed. She hadn't been back to the little coffee van beside the road since Linc's accident. They could both enjoy the good stuff together.

But as she followed him down the hallway, she replayed their conversation in her mind. Her reply to his quip about asking Nico to marry her had been a reflex, but a small part of her recognized a grain of honesty in her retort. Getting married wasn't something she thought a lot about. It also wasn't something they'd really discussed yet either, and she certainly hadn't been waiting for Nico to ask. The episode with Marietta had brought the concept of marriage to the forefront, and not in a good way. But she also knew she loved Nico deeply and wanted to spend the rest of her life with him.

Perhaps she *would* ask Nico to marry her. She was a strong, modern woman, and times were changing. It was no longer tradition for a woman to wait for the man to get down on one knee.

Lacey gave a secret smile as she kept up with Linc's fast pace down the stairs. Yes. It was a good idea.

Did you love reading Rain Washed?
Would you like to read a FREE and EXCLUSIVE Novella
revealing Mila and Griff's story?

https://dl.bookfunnel.com/6tgezpymng

Or you can stay in touch via my website
www.suzannecass.com
Or
Facebook: www.facebook.com/suzannecassauthor/
Instagram: www.instagram.com/suzanne.cass/
Pintrest: www.pinterest.com.au/suzanne_cass/

Also by Suzanne Cass
NEW

Dark Tides Series
Mystery and Romance collide.
Into the Rain
Rain Washed
The Clearing Rain

Stormcloud Station Series
(A Stargazer Spinoff Series)
Small Town Romantic Suspense
Clear Skies
Starlit Skies
Crystal Skies
Dawn Skies
Tangled Skies
Outback Skies

Stargazer Ranch Romance Series
Small Town Romantic Suspense
Combustion: Prequel Novella
Wildfire
Firelight
Snowbound: A Christmas Novella
Snowfall
Cloudburst
Silverstorm

Island Bound Series
Mystery Romance (on an Island)
Books can be read as stand-alone
Bound by Truth
Bound by Silence
Bound by the Stars

Colors of the Earth Series

Small Town Romantic Suspense

Books can be read as stand-alone

Shadows in the Dust

Shadows in Deep Blue

Shadows of Red Earth

Romantic Suspense

Single Title

Island Redemption

Glass Clouds

Chasing Bullets

Love in the Mountains Novella Series

Small Town Short Romance

Novellas can be read as stand-alone

Rain on a Tin Roof

Lost and Found

Rescue his Heart

Please Leave a Review

The greatest gift you could ever give an author is to leave a review. You will be helping other people to discover this book and making a difference to me as an Independently Published Author. If you liked this book and want other people to read it to, please leave a review.

About the Author

Suzanne Cass is an Australian author who loves to write romantic stories with the added spice of suspense, mystery, or crime.

She's always had a fascination with the tough resilience of people who live in our amazing red-dirt outback. When not writing about the characters that inhabit her head, Suzanne can be found roaming the Perth beaches with her border collie or drinking copious amounts of tea while contemplating the next garden project for her hapless husband to help create.

Her debut novel, Island Redemption, won the Romance Writers of Australia Emerald Award in 2016. Suzanne was also a finalist in the 2019 Romance Writers of Australia Romantic Suspense RUBY award.

Visit her website www.suzannecass.com or subscribe to her newsletter via: www.suzannecass.com/contact

Acknowledgements

Continuing Lacey's and Nico's love story was a no-brainer. Their journey had only just started in book 1 with so much more left to tell. (Just wait until you see what I put them through in book 3) And because Tasmania is such a beautiful place to write about I loved revisiting the small hamlet of Boat Harbour Beach. The Overland Track features near the end of this book, and this hiking trail is on my bucket list of things I need to do. I have visited Cradle Mountain, and the place is lodged in my soul, calling me back. It's a perfect place to send Lacey and Nico to hunt down the killer, through the wild and unforgiving country.

When I finally decided who the murderer was going to be, it was quite a revelation to me. This is my first book with a female killer, and I knew her journey needed to be torturous and gut-wrenching to make her believable. My heart goes out to all those mother's who've lost children in any circumstance. It is something most people never recover from, and I thought long and hard about using this as her motivation. I'm sorry if this is triggering for some readers.

There is a team of people who I couldn't do this without, beta readers (big thanks to Rebecca, my best typo hunter ever) and my ARC team, who are essential to an Indie Author like me, for their wonderful reviews.

Big thanks to my editor, Nicole at Evermore Editing for keeping my commas in check and my sentence structure so well structured!!!!!

To Gary who is my greatest cheerleader, and my two sons who are such amazing young men.

And to you, the readers, it sounds so trite, but thank you for reading my books. I wish I could reach out and hug you all personally. You are the reason I keep writing.